The PROMISE ROCK SER

D1457608

"*Keeping Promise Rock* probably has a flaw s
falling in love with the characters to notice."

—Rainbow Reviews

"…[*Keeping Promise Rock* is] a book filled with such heart wrenching
emotion that the reader can't stop crying, either tears of sorrow or of
happiness."

—Fallen Angel Reviews Recommended Read

"Amy Lane's *Keeping Promise Rock* is a quintessential m/m romance, a
nearly flawless example of the genre with all its virtues."

—Wilde Oats

"I found *Making Promises* to be quite charming … well-written and
absorbing."

—Book Wenches

"Not only did I love [*Making Promises*], I've officially become addicted to
reading about the easily identifiable and likable characters that continue to be
the focus in this amazing series."

—Night Owl Reviews

"*Living Promises* is a wonderful story about love, hope, faith and dealing with
the cards dealt to you."

—The Romance Studio

"[*Living Promises*] is another fantastic story from Amy Lane."

—MM Good Book Reviews

"*Living Promises* is painful and beautiful and so real."

—Blackraven's Reviews Recommended Read

http://www.dreamspinnerpress.com

By AMY LANE

Published by DREAMSPINNER PRESS
http://www.dreamspinnerpress.com

By AMY LANE

Published by DREAMSPINNER PRESS
http://www.dreamspinnerpress.com

Forever Promised

Amy Lane

Dreamspinner Press

Published by
Dreamspinner Press
5032 Capital Circle SW
Ste 2, PMB# 279
Tallahassee, FL 32305-7886
USA
http://www.dreamspinnerpress.com/

Forever Promised

Cover Art by Paul Richmond
http://www.paulrichmondstudio.com

Cover content is being used for illustrative purposes only
and any person depicted on the cover is a model.

ISBN: 978-1-62380-858-7
Digital ISBN: 978-1-62380-859-4

Printed in the United States of America
First Edition
June 2013

In a million years I did not expect people to love Deacon and Crick so much. Ever. And the fact that they took Shane, Mikhail, Collin, Jeff, Benny, Parry, Jon, Amy, and Martin into their hearts was just amazing. So, along with Mate (who is still along for the ride!), I would like to thank the people who love my people. I know you all have your favorites. When I wrote this book, I couldn't just say goodbye to Deacon and Crick—I had to say goodbye to *everybody*, so for anyone who has fallen in love with The Pulpit and the gang at Levee Oaks, this book is for you.

Chapter 1

Benny: Life with Girl Cooties

WHEN Bernice Angela Coats was three years old, her older half brother, Carrick James Francis, cut church one day and never went again for the rest of his life.

No, that lucky fucker got to spend *his* weekends at The Pulpit, a horse ranch run by Deacon Winters and his father, Parrish, and if Crick's new best friends hadn't spent their time taking Benny and her sisters out to the park or the movies as they got older, she might have hated Crick for that.

What she did instead was fall in love with Deacon.

Benny was a smart girl—she couldn't possibly hate Crick. Crick made her dinner and did her laundry and put Crystal and Missy to sleep after they came along. When Benny was six, Crystal was three, and Missy was one, both the littler kids had some sort of explosive diarrhea, which meant their mother must have cooked. Anyway, Bob (as Benny called her father in her thoughts, because that's what Crick called him) got home and both the kids were crying and dinner was burning on the stove and Crick had Missy on his hip and she'd just crapped all over them both while he was turning off the heat on some mac and cheese that was never meant to be.

Bob backhanded Crick as he stood and the water of the boiling pot splashed up and burnt Missy, and Crick had to tend to her and his split lip together.

It wasn't a new thing—Bob hit Crick all the time—but it was, perhaps, the first time it really sank into Benny's head that it wasn't fair. It was the first time any of the *girls* had gotten hurt, and Benny realized a lot of what Crick did for them was take the punishment Bob ordinarily dished out.

As Benny got older and she saw examples of her brother's hair-trigger temper and shotgun mouth, she started to understand they were *all* lucky. Crick had some of the things that made him a lot like Bob, but was spending weekends at The Pulpit, so he had Deacon and Parrish too, so those bad things didn't mix in the right way, and he stayed her big brother.

And that was why, when Crick came out as gay in the middle of a funeral, she didn't begrudge him to Deacon.

Deacon was the one to come collect him off the front lawn. She'd seen them picking Crick's shit up, like it wasn't even a question. She'd seen how Crick had yearned, even then, when she was ten years old. She had a home, still, and Bob wasn't hitting her yet, so she could give Crick to Deacon. She hadn't known, really, what gay meant, or why Bob thought it was so bad, but she knew her brother deserved the kindness in Deacon's eyes more than anyone else she knew.

As time passed, and she had to duck more often because Bob started noticing *she* was the one in charge of the little kids, and all of that shit little kids did—crap, cry, need food—was all on *her* head, she started to dream she would have a Deacon one day, who would come and save her from what her life was when Deacon and Crick and Parrish weren't around.

When Crick signed up for the military and ran away like a filthy coward (okay, maybe she was a little angry at him), she watched helplessly from afar as Deacon fell apart.

When he started haunting the liquor store like the ghost of winos past, her disappointment was acute. She'd woken up pregnant after a night she didn't remember with a kid she hadn't been all that crazy about *before* he'd roofied her, and Deacon was her last best hope. By that point, he had the DTs so bad after just a day she was shocked he didn't lose his lunch right there in front of the liquor store. When he came through for her? Stopped drinking cold turkey? Showed up on her doorstep with his friends, picked her shit off the lawn, and then (and he didn't know she knew this) decked Bob in retaliation for the black eye the fucker had left *her* with?

She'd sensed, even then, that she was going to love Deacon helplessly, like a brother, a mentor, and a hero, for maybe the rest of her life.

He would never know—*never* know—how hard she'd had to work to not *fall* in love with him as well as love him. Her worthless, cowardly shit-for-brains brother obviously had Deacon's entire heart. That didn't stop her from being just a little bit moony over the man after he held her and helped her deliver her baby. Waking up in the middle of the night during those first months to find him rocking Parry Angel in his arms made her stomach all fluttery, but she was *so* not going to go there.

That didn't mean that etched in her memory, forever and ever, she didn't hold a picture of Deacon, his boy-pretty face relaxed and sweet, his hazel-green eyes closed, lying on his back on the old plaid couch with Parry, wearing a pink onesie, tucked on his chest, both of them fast asleep. Deacon was that guy, the guy who would get up with a baby and who would give the baby's mother a room of her own and an education and safety when she couldn't really remember having any of those things after Crick left.

When Andrew Carpenter showed up on their doorstep with the dubious claim that her worthless brother actually saved his life, Benny was willing to look beyond *that* obvious falsehood and see that Andrew was a fine young man. (Deacon bought it, and only Benny's deep and abiding love for him kept him from losing serious esteem points in her eyes.) Drew was more than fine, in fact. Drew was stalwart—he stayed at The Pulpit even when all Deacon had to pay him was room and board. He didn't fuss if he was suddenly babysitting instead of horse breaking, and he never, not once, asked her who Parry Angel's father was. When he *did* learn who the guy was, he clocked him in the jaw, but that wasn't the point. The point was that when his slow white smile broadened his dark face, the way he looked at Benny let her know that smile was just for her.

It made her stomach flutter and her palms sweat. It made her feel like she had a wasp waist and a size-D rack instead of her plain, thin body with the flat chest; and long, flowing, perfectly styled blonde hair instead of flyaway mouse-brown hair that needed to be cut to her shoulders or it would get all splitty.

From the time she was sixteen, when Drew started working at The Pulpit, to the time she turned eighteen, right about the time of her misguided attempt to leave Levee Oaks to go to school, Drew's smile seemed to grow deeper and more electric, and more and more *just for her.*

Benny started to love it that way.

When she returned from school, frightened (terrified!) because Deacon's health was piss-poor and *everybody* in the family was afraid for him, Drew had been the guy to greet her. She'd kissed him in front of everybody, in spite of the fact that as far as *she* remembered, she hadn't kissed *anybody* that way, and if her body didn't remember the entire pregnancy and birth thing she endured with Parry Angel, she'd flat-out swear she was still a virgin.

It didn't matter.

She was scared for Deacon and missing her daughter, but Drew was *there*, and he was solid and kind and stalwart and funny in a sly way that sort of snuck up on you when you weren't paying attention—she liked that!—and Benny decided that if a man as young as Deacon, who wasn't even thirty, could get so sick so fast, she didn't have any room for dithering about or dillydallying.

Besides. She'd been dying to kiss Drew for two years.

He kissed… beautifully. He opened his mouth and let her tongue in, and he was warm and dark and safe. His big hands were easy on her skinny little hips and he pulled her in against his wide chest and she knew she was home. When the family—Deacon's entire little assembled family—stood on the porch and applauded, she flipped them all off not because she was mad, but because she wanted them to know this moment was for her and it was for Drew, and as much as everyone had seen it coming and wanted it, she'd *made* it come, and she wanted it more.

Of course, then she went inside and saw Deacon, white-faced, his jaw clenched in pain, so immersed in the misery of congestive heart failure he was barely there for his family.

At that point, Jon, Deacon's best friend since diapers or close enough, took Deacon into his and Crick's room and called an ambulance. Jon was a lawyer, and he might look like a surfer or a Hollywood pool boy, but the truth was Jon was smarter and more ruthless than probably anyone else at The Pulpit, and Benny was one of the few people who didn't forget that.

Jon was made to do things like that. He could tell someone to fuck off, they were being stupid, and not sound mean about it. Benny said those things, but she always sounded mean. Jon just had all that authority around him. It's why his little wife adored him, even though she was a bossy little shit, which is why Amy and Benny got along so very well.

That quality was why, Benny thought on this achingly hot August day about two and a half years after Deacon's heart attack, Jon made such a splendid officiator for the weddings they kept having out at Promise Rock.

Today's victims stood suffering in the heat. Why Jeff and Collin thought August was a good time for a wedding was beyond Benny. But they'd had it early enough in the day to stifle the sadistic heat, and the fashion de rigueur was cargo shorts and Hawaiian shirts for the men and sundresses for the women. Benny thought that must have been Collin's idea, and she didn't mind. Any excuse to buy a new sundress was an opportunity she'd take advantage of, even if she was sweating through the side of it already. But it didn't matter that the wedding was unseasonable, or that it would be so hot by two o'clock that the cake would be melting off its fashionably rustic wooden pedestal. Jeff must have still been lost in the romance of the whole thing, because he was crying such a steady stream of quiet tears that Benny had needed to go up to his elbow a couple of times to switch out his Kleenex.

Jeff was dressed impeccably—natty ecru linen suit, double-breasted, nipped in at the waist, with trousers tight enough to bounce a quarter off his ass. Of course, underneath the jacket he was wearing a pastel T-shirt, *Miami Vice* style, but that just made it better. His angular, bony features with a slightly aquiline nose had been pretty and, well, gayer than a roaring twenties revue. He managed to look like a dandy out of an F. Scott Fitzgerald book as he'd greeted his guests at what amounted to a private swimming hole in the middle of nowhere.

Collin, his intended, looked nothing like him. Collin's hair was long and blond, blow-dried straight and tied in a queue; his jaw was square, and his nose turned up on the end. Collin had been the one who insisted on putting "dress comfortably" in the wedding invitations, and he was wearing khakis, a short-sleeved button-up shirt, pink suspenders, and a matching bow tie. He was (and people gave Jeff shit about this all the time just to make him turn red and duck his head) nearly ten years younger than his soon-to-be husband. It was funny, though—Benny had taken one look at the two of them when she'd gotten back from college and told Drew, "Oh yeah, but you can bet that kid calls all the shots!"

Drew had laughed then, but watching the two of them over the last two and a half years had proved her right. Not that she lived on I-told-you-so or anything, but once Deacon moved her out of her parents' place and helped her get her shit together, she got pretty used to being the one who knew best.

She was also damned proud of serving her family quietly and competently. Those things had become her trademarks in the beginning, when Crick was still in Iraq and it was just her and Deacon, trying to keep Deacon's business afloat. She'd been afraid then and had worked like her place in Deacon's home depended on her usefulness, and although she'd outgrown the fear, mostly, she hadn't outgrown that love of being needed.

So she was surprised when, the third time she dodged behind his elbow to take one Kleenex in a plastic bag and replace it with another, Jeff stopped responding to the vows Jon was reciting, wrapped a playful arm around her head, and grinned.

"Benny, my love, are you angling for the same service when it's your turn?"

Benny grinned at him and reached up (way up—he was tall; she was not!) and tousled his absolutely perfectly cemented hair. "Damned straight, Jeffy. Right after you and Collin bear me up the aisle in my own sedan chair."

That elicited a laugh from the crowd, and Jeff bent down and dropped a teary kiss in her hair. "It's a deal, oh short one. You take good care of us."

She smiled at him, a little watery herself. She'd practically sobbed through Crick and Deacon's wedding three years ago, hadn't been much better through Shane and Mikhail's, and had *barely* held it together through Lucas and Kimmy's. The only reason she'd been able to tough it out through this one was because Jeff was doing all the crying for her, but now that she had to talk and look the happiness straight in the eye, she might not make it.

"Well"—she sniffled—"you guys always take good care of us right back." Her voice broke unapologetically on the last word, and Jeffy crushed her to his chest for a good, solid hug.

After a moment, Jon said, "Now, Benny, until it's your turn, you really don't get to spend all that time up here, you know that, right?"

General laughter echoed from the small crowd of friends and family under the oak trees. They stood by the granite outcropping that marked the swimming hole, and for a moment in the shade, her Uncle Jeffy hugged her and she was happy. Then she felt a hand on her elbow as she stepped out of the circle.

Looking up, she saw Deacon, his small, square-jawed face with those pretty green eyes and brown-blond hair, and he engulfed her in his arms. He smelled so good. She picked his fabric softener and bought his bodywash, but there was more to his smell than that. Deacon had worn a suit, to keep Jon company because Jon *never* wore suits, and she could smell sweat underneath and the ever-present, honest smell of horse, and there was Deacon. For six years that smell had meant comfort and home, and as she lost her nut for happiness in his arms, a part of her was crying because she knew that very soon, that would have to change.

Jon finished speaking and Jeff and Collin exchanged what appeared to be a *very* chaste kiss. Benny knew most of the people there in the shade of the oak trees, even Collin's family, although there were a few friends from Jeff's work that she hadn't met yet, and they all applauded happily. Deacon relaxed his arms around her shoulders, and suddenly Benny's pride and joy ignored her mother and said, "Deacon, I was *so* good, I didn't talk at *all*!" at the same time Benny's beloved said, "Deacon, I'll trade ya!"

Benny was pushed gently into Drew's hug so Deacon could heft Parry Angel into his arms. Her riotously curly brown hair was strung up with ribbons, and even though she was nearing six, she could still squeal like a toddler when he swung her plump little body high in the air.

Benny turned to Drew with a sniffly smile only to see something alien shadowing his eyes.

He reached out with a thumb to wipe a leftover tear, and she felt her eyebrows knit. "What?" she asked.

He grimaced, and it wasn't his comforting bright smile. "Benny, you know I love the guy like a brother, right?" he asked soberly, and she nodded. The rest of the company had moved into the receiving line, and she worried about not being there. Drew backed them up into the shade next to the boulder itself.

"Yeah, so do I," she told him, trying to lighten the moment.

Drew just shook his head. He had wonderful eyes—dark, dark brown, intelligent, soulful. When he blinked, dark lashes, obscenely long, swept over his cheekbones, and when he opened his eyes again, they were both hopeful and fearful at once.

"He's a tough act to follow," Drew said softly. "Have you told him yet?"

Benny gnawed on her lower lip. "That I'm ready to move out of the house on his property and into the other house on his property?" she asked factiously, hoping the facts would obscure what a big step this was.

"If you're ready to move you and Parry into my home. Benny, I love it here, and I'm happy to live here, go to school when you're done, raise a family working in Deacon's business. But I need you in my own home. Is that so much to ask? I want to...." He grimaced again and looked around at where they were. It was a swimming hole, plain and simple, but it was also the family church. The shade from the oak trees kept the August sun from pounding too hotly on the two of them, and the water from the irrigation stream burbled as it rounded the bend. It was a pretty place, carved by necessity in what could be a harsh world, and when they weren't having weddings or summer parties or greeting new babies or making love (at least with her and Drew it had happened here the first time), it was the summer swimming hole and family thinking spot.

Important things happened here, and apparently Drew had decided that it was time for one more.

"Benny, don't you want to get married?" he asked rawly, and Benny blinked and smiled huge, delighted because she thought this conversation was going to get a lot more serious than this.

"To you? Because, well, *duh*!" she laughed. "What do you think, Drew? Two and a half years we've been seeing each other?" Her voice dropped, and she splayed her small hand across his chest, hard with weighty muscle underneath his pink dress shirt. "Do you think I... I mean, my whole family knows about us. Do you think that would happen if I didn't want us to be permanent?"

Drew covered her hand with his larger one, and she resisted the temptation to examine it, as she often did, to contrast the coffee color of the skin on the back with the tender pinkness of the palm and the pads of his fingers. These things fascinated her, and she never made any secret about the fact his skin color delighted her as much as the rest of him. She was unafraid of their difference in race, and unafraid of the skin under his prosthetic leg, and unafraid of the complete contrast in culture between his upbringing in the South and hers in Northern California. About the only thing she *did* fear about her relationship with Drew was that somehow it would take her away from her family.

"I want us to be permanent," he said softly. "But you know that means that you're going to need to move you and Parry out of that house. And someday—not now, but someday, after we're both through school, and when we've had another baby or two—we may have to move away from here. From The Pulpit. From Levee Oaks. From Deacon. And I need to know you're up for that."

Benny swallowed hard and tried not to tear up—she still had that leftover hot feeling behind her eyes from the wedding, she told herself stoutly. It was only natural.

"You mean choose you," she said, knowing that this was where it was leading.

"Over Deacon," Drew affirmed. He glanced furtively up, and Benny looked to where Deacon was holding Parry Angel, and now she had to wipe her face with her hand again.

"Of course I choose you," she whispered painfully, because it wasn't that cut and dried and they both knew it. They *both* owed Deacon so much. Leaving him alone seemed a horrible way of paying him back. "I'll tell him we're moving out tomorrow."

Drew nodded and smiled, and he looked like the weight of the world had fallen from his sturdy shoulders. He pulled her close and rested his forehead against hers, and she smiled into his eyes.

"I really love you," she said softly, thinking that it was true, and her heart felt so swollen in her chest it hurt. "You know that, right?"

"I love you too, Bernice."

"Oh hell, Drew. I'll take it all back if you don't stop calling me that."

He laughed and closed his mouth over hers, and she relaxed into his kiss.

And it might have stayed there. She might not have taken that next step in her thinking, or in what she asked of Drew, or what she wanted to give Deacon, if her stupid brother hadn't had a weak spell with his injured leg and needed to be driven back home. She was going to offer to do it for him, and get her stuff to stay the night at Drew's if that was okay, but she needed to find Deacon first and tell him. Besides, Crick would need help walking across the grounds and the cattle gate to get into the truck, and nobody could do that but Deacon.

She looked around the clearing—it was later in the day, and Collin and Jeff were sitting on a couple of folding chairs, talking to anybody who wanted to talk.

"The flowers?" Jeff asked, gesturing to the assortment of wildflowers in glass decanters that Benny had helped him scavenge from yard sales *everywhere*. "Pinterest, girlfriend! I know, they look totally rustic, like you'd think that'd be easy, but omigod! Tracking them down was a *night*mare, and Benny and I rubbed our fingers raw tying off the little burlap bows!"

"I was not allowed to help," Collin said, pulling his lean lips into a Kewpie doll moue.

"Hel*lo,* you'd get *grease* on them!"

"Because rustic is only cool when it involves dust," Collin said dryly, and Jeff nodded his head in complete seriousness.

"Of course! If the wedding was in your garage, *then* you could have gotten grease on the burlap!"

Everybody wanted to talk, and although Collin mostly sat back quietly and let his new husband tell the stories with flamboyant gestures and razor-lightning quickness, he was good for a snarktastic quip or two. Jeff's job was pausing to let him get those in too, and together they could entertain at their own party like nobody else.

Amy, dressed in a pale-green summer dress, sat at the sandy beach of the creek, holding her youngest by the hands so he could dangle his feet in the water.

"Heya, Jon-Jon," she murmured, and the baby—a tow-headed, brown-eyed version of his blue-eyed father—giggled. His little baby three-piece suit (his father's idea of a joke, since Jon only wore a suit to officiate at weddings, even when he was in court) lay neatly folded in the diaper bag over Amy's shoulder, and the royal crowned King of Promise Rock was wearing a diaper and a smile.

Lila Lisa, Amy and Jon's little girl, crouched with Parry Angel; they were looking to see if any minnows flitted in the sandy part of the shore. The little girls wore matching lavender sundresses, because that's why you *had* girls, so you could put them in frilly things that made them smile. Of course, the skirts of both dresses were now tucked, wadded, and otherwise fixed firmly between their legs so they didn't get the hems wet, but since Lila was so short, her bottom was dragging in the water anyway.

Benny stopped for a moment to bend down and kiss Parry on her curly little head, and then turned to Amy—pretty, dark-haired, dark-eyed Amy, the only girl Benny knew who was tinier than Benny herself—and smiled. "Have you seen Deacon?"

To her surprise, Amy looked troubled and a little sad. "Yeah. I think he and Jon are off talking on the man's side of the rock."

Benny snickered. "There's a man's side of the rock?"

Amy had a piquant little face and adorable little chipmunk cheeks, but she could manage a look of total disgust if it suited her. "Yeah, the other side of the rock, the side without shade. It's where they go to talk when they're pretty sure the rest of us plebeians with tits don't want to sweat and won't follow them over."

"Is that what we are?" Kimmy asked, walking over to the creek. She was looking at the children wistfully, and Amy smiled at her and hefted Jon-Jon up so Kimmy could grab him and blow tummy bubbles. Kimmy was a beautiful woman in her thirties, with brown hair that hung unbound to her waist, in spite of the heat, and a serene oval-shaped face with brown eyes exactly like her twin brother's. She blew the tummy bubbles and Jon-Jon giggled loudly.

"Kimmy!"

"Heya, Puppy. Have you had any cake yet?"

Jon-Jon's eyes got big and round. "Cake?"

"Kimmy, you snot!" Amy complained. "You know he wears it more than eats it!"

"That's all right," Kimmy said warmly. "I'll wash him off when we're done." She hefted the toddler over to the table, and Amy stood up from the bank, keeping a careful eye on the two girls.

"Are you going to hang around, Benny?" she asked.

Benny looked over to where Crick sat, looking embarrassed. He tried, while she was watching, to stand up completely, but his leg gave out, and he gritted his teeth. He'd been putting a lot of stress on his leg and his arm, trying to get ready for this event, and he'd overdone it. Pretty much the only person he'd let help him when he was like this was Deacon.

"Crick needs to go home," Benny said quietly. "He's going to need Deacon's help to get in the truck."

Amy looked up and frowned. "God—I *knew* he shouldn't have been helping load chairs yesterday! He said he was fine, but—"

Benny shrugged. "He's stubborn," she said, because it was true. But it was also true he pushed himself, like he *hadn't* almost gotten himself blown halfway to hell, and he didn't like people to know he wasn't just as fit as anyone else. But then, part of that was Crick's reluctance to give up even one iota of the job of taking care of Deacon.

"I'll go find Deacon," Benny decided, because hey! How bad could a conversation with Jon be?

"Hey, Benny—" Amy called behind her, but Benny was already halfway to the tree, and Lila picked that moment to fall into the surprisingly cold water and shriek loud enough to break the plastic glasses for the sparkling cider. Amy didn't try to get her attention again, and Benny didn't look back.

She rounded the corner of Promise Rock quietly, expecting to have to wait until the boys were done talking to get Deacon's attention, and what she heard in Deacon's voice made her pause.

"Damn, Jon! That's a hell of an opportunity!"

Jon's reply, when it came, was rough and shaky, and she stayed quiet in the shade of the oak tree while Deacon and Jon stood facing the sun, their backs to the rock and to her. "It would mean leaving you."

"Yeah, well, that would suck," Deacon said, clapping Jon on the shoulder. Jon made a strangled laugh sound, and Deacon settled back against the rock again.

"I love it here!" Jon protested, and his voice sounded weak to Benny, and probably weak to Deacon as well. "My family loves it here. We grew up here, and my kids love it here—"

"Jon, let's get one thing straight. *Nobody* loves Levee Oaks that much, not even the founding fathers, whoever the hell they might have been. You love *us*. Now, when I was going to uproot this place four years ago, you were going to move with me, so I know you can do this—"

"Okay, so this place sucks, but *Deacon*—!"

"Jon, do you realize what you've been asked to do?"

"Yeah—wear a fucking suit!"

"No! You've been asked to go to Washington and work for a *cause*! Do you *get* that? All this bullshit Crick and me, and Shane and Mickey and all those kids in Promise House, have been through—hell, Jeff and Collin's medicine and treatment—*all* of that bullshit, *all* of that difficulty, has been given the stamp of approval by the powers that fucking be. You got asked to go change all that, Jon! *Jesus*, do you know how huge that is!"

Benny clapped her hand over her mouth, because for once in her life, she needed to keep it shut. Oh hell. Hell, this was enormous. *Jon*? Jon was Deacon's *rock*. Crick was passionate, wound up, and high maintenance—Jon was Deacon's one chance at sanity, and he was *going*?

"I know," Jon said quietly. "I do. And Amy would love to help, and that's big too, because as much as she loves the kids, she didn't get her law degree for nothing either. And we got hired on as a team—I mean, who *does* that? And it's a chance to… I don't know…."

"Change history? Make your mark? Do something important with your life?"

"I thought I *was* doing that by practicing here!"

Deacon laughed a little and ran his hand through his thick dark-blond hair. "Yeah, well, as great as it's been having our own pet lawyer in our pockets, Jon, you really were made for more. I mean, how do you think you got noticed in the first place?"

"You sent my name in to that website," Jon said flatly, and Benny had to try hard not to cackle hysterically when Deacon shrugged.

"It was Crick's idea. They were asking for community members who'd made a difference. That's you, big guy—can't fight it!"

"Jesus, Deacon did you have any idea—"

"That you'd get enough attention to get put in that magazine? No. That the lobbyists in DC would want to come sweep you away? Not a fucking clue. But Jon…." Deacon took two steps out and turned back around, and Benny looked hungrily at his face for some clue as to how he really felt about this. Anybody who loved Deacon knew what he said, even the inflection of his voice, was not a real barometer. Deacon was a master at putting the things he wanted on hold for the people he loved.

But his eyes….

Benny had learned to look at the way his eyes crinkled in the corners, or the skin tightened over his cheekbones, to know what he was really thinking.

The night her stupid brother called him to say he'd cheated while in the service, Deacon's eyes had been wide and earnest when he told Benny he'd be okay. But the crinkles in the corners of his green eyes had been bunched together, like his jaw was clenched too tight to let them get as wide as they *should* be.

They looked just like that now.

"You and Amy were always meant for bigger things than me or this town anyway," Deacon said gruffly. "I'll miss you—God, we'll *all* miss you. But telling you not to go because we'd miss you is pure selfishness."

"And God forbid you be selfish, right, Deacon?" Jon said bitterly, and Deacon swallowed.

"You know, asshole, me and Crick managed to keep together for two years of writing actual letters and tweets. We got two face-to-face chats on satellite phone in two years, and we did just fine. We've got Skype and we've got texting and I'm pretty damned sure I'm not going to wither and die because you left me behind."

Jon shook his head bitterly. "Yeah, Deacon, I remember 'just fine'. Remember the DTs? 'Cause I do, and if I *ever* have to even *know* that you took a drink again, I will come back here and beat you dead."

Deacon rolled his eyes. "Jon, you know damned well that pacemaker or not, if I ever had to do that again, no one would have to beat me to see me dead."

Jon took a swing at him.

Benny might have cried out if it had landed, but Deacon was quick, and he'd been taking *very* good care of his body since his heart attack. He dodged sideways, grabbed Jon's arm, and pulled, and Jon's forward momentum brought him straight into Deacon's arms.

Jon struggled for a moment and then gave it up and returned the hug full force. "We'll miss you," he muttered.

"God, I hope so," Deacon said back, and he'd turned enough for Benny to see his face over Jon's shoulder.

Drew found her ten minutes later, huddled in the little hidden spot where the sun and shade met. Deacon and Jon had gone round the other side, back to the reception, and Benny was pretty sure he was giving Crick a ride home.

Which was good, because she hadn't been able to stop crying, and she wouldn't have wanted to confess to Deacon why.

"Benny?" Drew asked, crouching down by where she was dragging the hem of her new dress in the dust. "What's wrong, baby?"

Benny wiped her eyes with her palm, boy style, and wanted to swear because her carefully applied makeup was now smeared all over her eyes and it stung like a sonuvabitch.

Drew was prepared, though—he pulled out a little package of tissues and handed them over, and she spent a few moments getting the mascara off her cheeks while she pulled herself together.

"Drew?" she said tentatively, hating that she was going to ask him this but not able to change it.

"Yeah?"

"We need to give him something," she whispered. "Something that he can keep. Something that will make his family always here."

Drew's questioning look was hard to face. "I have no idea what you're talking about, Bernice."

It took her a while to explain it to him, and when she was done, it took a week to make it right between them. But in the end, he saw that she was right, that it was a perfect solution. In the end, even Drew saw that if they wanted to leave Deacon, it would sit right with both of them if they promised him forever first.

Chapter 2

Deacon: The Cosmic Smell of Horse

CONTRARY to popular belief, Deacon's father had *not* been perfect.

It was easy to idolize him *now*, because he was dead and, well, because compared to Crick's stepfather, Parrish really *was* a goddamned saint.

But Parrish had been a silent, moody fucker when it suited him, and although it was easy for Deacon to blame his mother for drinking herself to death, Deacon knew living with Parrish—especially in the early days of The Pulpit, when the hours were longer than the day—that could not have been easy. So as much as Crick gave him grief about being an uncommunicative asshole sometimes, Deacon was pretty sure he'd already beat his father in total words uttered in a lifetime.

But that didn't mean talking about his feelings was just going to happen overnight.

So when he and Jon returned to the wedding reception, he was well aware that he wasn't just going to announce Jon's move to the world—not right now. He needed a few minutes. *Jon* needed a few minutes. Deacon could tell by the way Jon walked over to his wife and wrapped his arms around her waist and rested his chin on her shoulder, even in the stifling heat, that Jon needed time.

Good. Deacon would just as soon pretend that entire conversation had not happened for a while.

Instead, he laughed at Jeff's favorite PT client, Margie, a newly thin middle-aged woman who gave Jeff grief about being the Marquis de Sade of physical therapy at the same time she fetched Collin another piece of cake. He said a few words to Martin, the little brother of Jeff's late boyfriend, and asked him if he was ready to help out with the garage. Martin had laughed and shrugged, but Deacon had seen it—the cagey, defiant youngster of nearly three years ago had grown into a thoughtful young man. He'd be fine, and Deacon was glad—Collin and Jeff had more family, and that was almost always a blessing.

After the pleasantries (blissfully short), he helped Drew and Patrick put away chairs. He was not too out of it to notice that Drew was sullen and uncommunicative himself, and although it was a rare mood on his friend and fellow horse-sufferer, it suited his own mood perfectly.

It was Patrick who said something.

"Damn, Deacon—when your daddy was like this, at least he only tormented the horses! Why aren't you bitching to Crick and getting whatever this is off your chest!"

Deacon was forced to laugh. He couldn't remember when Patrick had first started working for his father, but he'd been glad that Parrish's best friend and confidant hadn't dropped completely out of his life. Maybe he should take a lesson from that—Patrick still stayed in touch and made it to the important stuff even though he'd moved a few hours away. There wasn't any reason to suspect Jon wouldn't.

He looked around then, thinking he could actually talk to Crick without losing his composure and pouting now, and realized he was gone.

It took three people before he got to the kid from Promise House who told him that Shane and Mikhail had taken him home, and that he'd needed help. Deacon's funk abruptly returned, especially when he realized he was going to have to take the kids and the chairs back to their respective places.

He stopped yearning for Crick's company by then, and felt his father's gift of uncommunicative bastard slip in place once again. He longed for the silence and the nonverbal company of the horses.

Eventually he got there.

First he had to fix Crick a snack, pausing for a moment to see the lines of pain etched in Crick's face, the way he closed his eyes in the quiet of the house like he trusted, and the way he managed a smile for Deacon even though he obviously felt like shit.

Deacon owed him. Owed him for sticking with him through all the times Deacon *didn't* want to talk, owed him for loving Deacon when Deacon had to admit he wasn't the easiest person to live with. Owed him for smiling all the times he hurt, and owed him for making Deacon laugh all the times Deacon had assumed he would rather chew off his own arm.

Deacon could spend some of this stupid sadness on the damned horses.

Benny had to come get him, and it seemed to be the day for people trying to hide shitty moods, but he let her keep hers to herself.

Sitting in the barn, remembering Crick in there as a kid, remembering the things they'd done in there as adults (those things that made his face heat and had him adjusting his pants) and the way Crick had always loved the horses even though he hadn't been the best rider or even the best person to put in a pen with a skittish, ornery animal, Deacon was able to get some of his peace back.

Jon would leave, Crick would stay. Deacon could suffer any number of losses, any number of people leaving and coming, any shifts of time and family and friends, as long as Crick would stay.

Crick loved him. It was always enough.

Chapter 3

Mikhail: Upon Being Put Out

MIKHAIL eyed Martin with deep suspicion, especially since the boy had *obviously* not heard a word he'd said two and a half years earlier, and had eaten enough to grow to the size of a house. Any boy who grew *that* big was obviously a person not to be trusted.

"You understand, this is a very special vehicle," he said sharply.

Martin, to his credit, eyed the giant purple Chevy van with the freehand pink lettering without batting a thick black eyelash.

"I understand," he said, and his voice was soft and low, but Mikhail still scowled.

"You understand that this is a special vehicle, or you understand how to work on such a thing?" he demanded. "The other boy—"

"Collin?" Martin asked, confused, and Mikhail waved his hand.

"Pfft—yes, he is still a boy. You are all children. I am surrounded by children, and disrespectful ones at that, or that boy would not have gone off and on a holiday when my car chose to break down."

Martin thrust out a pink-chocolate lip and turned big soulful eyes on Mikhail without the slightest twinge of impatience. Martin had been able to make it out for the wedding, and he'd been a mechanic in a garage down south during his entire junior year of high school. Although he was technically an adult, this was the summer before his final year of high school, and he'd come out to attend the wedding and watch Collin and Jeff's house and Collin's business. The two of them were spending a week in Manhattan, seeing plays and museums and generally boring Collin to death (or so Mikhail assumed).

It appeared that Martin had earned enough self-possession in the years to not succumb to Mikhail's little temper tantrum about his beloved Purple Brick. "They're on their *honeymoon,*" Martin emphasized, "and Collin wouldn't have left me in charge if he didn't trust me."

Collin, in fact, had told Mikhail that this boy was planning to come to California *permanently* once he'd graduated, where he would live in Collin's old flat above his mother's garage and assist Collin and Joshua with the business. Next June, he would be a high school graduate as well as an adult, and right now, he was practicing for the job. Mikhail had trouble believing that—the boy had been the next best thing to a delinquent when he'd first arrived at Levee Oaks, and he had certainly hated Jeff's queer ass with everything inside him. But still, Mikhail was walking, irritated proof that people could indeed change.

"This van is very special," he conceded. "When I brought it home, my cop took one look at it and called everybody we know to come out and fix it. It took them four days."

Martin's eyes got a little wider, and he looked under the hood of the van again. "You got off lucky, little man. If you'd brought that thing to me in any worse condition than it's already in, I would have gotten Collin's gun out of the safe and shot it dead."

Mikhail grunted and narrowed his eyes. "You say that, but you? You do not have the guts. It takes a Russian to make a mercy killing, but only on a good day. I have no mercy in me. You'd better fix it, or the damned thing is going to haunt you like whatever small city you ate for breakfast."

Martin grinned. "I frickin' missed you, you grumpy Russian bastard." He straightened up and wiped his hands with one of the cloths he and Collin seemed to sprout from their pockets. "Do you have a ride, or do I have to send you into the garage to make Joshua's life a living hell?" Joshua was Collin's other "employee," who had started working in Collin's garage mostly for the challenge.

Mikhail pulled a corner of his mouth up in a sneer so he didn't have to smile. "No. My cop is coming to pick me up after he is done grocery shopping." Costco. They had ten lost children at Promise House now, as well as four other employees, and those kids each ate more in a day than Mikhail *and* Kimmy ate in a month. The dance circuit for the fairs didn't start up again until late August, so Mikhail's only workout was the one he did each morning in the little studio Shane had made out of their spare room now that Kimmy had moved out. Mikhail had always been aware of his own vanity, but he'd never realized how well it had served him until he'd been faced with eating Pizza Bites for lunch and pizza Hot Pockets for dinner, when he was taking his turn supervising at Promise House. He would *not* get fat for his cop!

Martin shook his head. "You know, someday, you will have to tell me why you call him your 'cop'"—and Mikhail frowned.

"Because he was on the police force when we met. What a stupid question!"

Martin frowned, obviously thinking hard. Mikhail knew his brother had been killed in the service—had *chosen* to be killed when he'd discovered he was HIV positive in a DADT corp. It had taken Jeff almost six years to get over Kevin, and part of that had been making peace with Kevin's little brother. Of course Martin knew all about the ins and outs of strong men in a homophobic world.

"How'd that go over?" he asked carefully, and Mikhail looked at him with distaste.

"He was hurt a lot," he said after a painful moment. "Why is it you ask?"

Martin sighed. "Because Jon's going to Washington to fight the good fight for you guys. I keep thinking I want to help like that—make the world a better place for people I…." He stopped and grimaced. Eighteen and mature, yes, but saying you loved a bunch of gay men when you were not gay, well, that was a stretch for eighteen at all. "My uncles here," he finished, looking wryly at Mikhail. "I tell my family about my uncles here in California, and they start asking if I'm gay."

"What do you say?" Mikhail asked, curious.

Martin shrugged, and his smile was fierce and grim. Mikhail had not seen many black people before he'd moved to America as a teenager. He figured if he'd seen that smile when he'd been fifteen, he'd have run the other way.

"Last time, I said yes, then I leveled the guy," Martin said with satisfaction. His face fell a little. "Not the way to pick up women in the South, though."

Mikhail grimaced, feeling for him. Eighteen and not able to fuck? That *was* a crying shame! "Well, is a good thing you moved out here. From what I understand, the women here are much more promiscuous. You will not be a virgin for long."

Martin straightened up so fast he knocked his head on the edge of the hood and yelped. "Jesus, little man! I'm not a… a… a… you know!"

Mikhail lifted a shoulder. "If you weren't one, you'd be able to say it. Besides. Virginity is not a crime. Unlike being gay in some countries, it is actually considered a virtue." Mikhail nodded sincerely. "You can use it as a selling point when you see a woman who may or may not be worthy of you."

"May not be worthy...?"

The boy did not look stupid. Mikhail sighed. "Well, you are obviously a boy of great worth. If you can fix my van, you are your own weight in gold." Mikhail looked up again at his tastelessly imposing height. "And that is saying something. Who's that?"

Martin didn't even look behind him. "That is who I wanted to talk to you about. Is she going through the trash cans?"

"Yes. There is not much trash... oh, good for her. She has found french fries." It was appalling. She was a pretty thing, probably taller than he was, with skin not quite as dark as Martin's. Her hair was coarse and black and brushed back into a soiled terrycloth band, and her face was a strong oval, with a small broadened nose and dramatically almond-shaped brown eyes. So a potpourri of genetics, one Mikhail had become accustomed to in Northern California. And in order to be like his beloved cop, he had learned to look beyond skin color and even gender, and to look to the more important things. Like the fact she was wearing two shirts, a sweatshirt, and a pair of jeans on this interminably hot summer day, and the fact she was scrounging in the trash for food.

"Martin?" he said, wondering how feral she was. He and Shane had set the children at Promise House on the daunting task of catching the stray cats in the surrounding property so they could take them to the spay and neuter clinic and effectively cut down on the population. Would this cat scratch his hand and bite? Would she bolt? Or was she sufficiently tame enough to be lured to safety with a little bit of food?

"Yeah?" Martin said, looking at the girl and nodding like he knew what was coming.

"Would you like a sandwich? You look faint and frail to me."

Martin snickered. "Yeah, Mikhail, my blood sugar, it's gettin' real low."

Mikhail scowled at him. "Someday," he said with gravity, "you will get fat, and I will enjoy that moment more than you can possibly fathom. Pastrami, with pickles, sauce, and cream cheese, am I right?"

"Seriously? You remember all of that?"

"Pfft!" Mikhail waved him off as he trotted across the small parking lot that was used for Collin's Car Repair toward the even *smaller* lot, which housed Collin's mother's diner. "You virgins—once you get that out of your system, you have some room in your brains for thinking."

"Geez!" Martin whined behind him. "Dammit, Mikhail, do you have to say that so loud!" Martin's voice dropped as Mikhail got closer to the diner, which meant he was smarter than Mikhail had first thought, because the pretty, feral creature crouched behind the diner eating someone else's french fries may *not* have heard him.

Mikhail ignored her on the way in, but he did smile at Collin's sister, Joanna, who actually *had* a job working somewhere Mikhail did not know but who came in to help her mother when she could. Her daughter, Kelsey, was sitting at a table, coloring in an activity book, and Mikhail smiled at her too.

"Mom!" Kelsey said, her voice a little awestruck. "It's Teacher Mikhail!"

Joanna smiled at her. "Yeah, Kelse—you remember? We saw him at the wedding?"

Kelsey had a round little face and blonde flyaway hair, and her chubby cheeks bunched up in her smile. "I remember! You wore a *suit* and it was *hot*!"

Mikhail nodded. "Yes, indeed it was. Made *my* wedding in February look downright sensible." He looked up at Joanna behind the counter, and she smiled back. Her dark hair—very unlike her brother's—was pulled back in a practical ponytail, and she looked hot and disheveled here in the little diner.

"I do hate to put you out," Mikhail started sincerely, "but if you please, might I have three"—wait, Shane might want one—"no, four sandwiches?"

She smiled gaily as though this were not a job for her but rather a break from her regular job, and took his order, talking the entire time.

"So, I saw you at the wedding—you and Shane are looking well! And it was so nice of the kids from Promise House to come out and help. They seem like a well-behaved bunch, don't they?" He would have told her they were only well behaved because they'd all been wearing swimsuits underneath their nice clothes and they'd been promised a chance to go swimming once the chairs and tables had been put up, but she was on a roll. "Anyway, it was lovely to see you all. Collin texted me this morning to say they'd seen *Wicked* last night and, well, he was bored silly, but they were going out on the Circle Line to see the Statue of Liberty and then to a comedy club tonight. Have you heard from them?"

She actually paused there, and Mikhail jerked, surprised to find a response was needed. "Yes. Jeff said he enjoyed *Wicked* very much, and if Collin falls asleep during another show, he will wake up with no eyebrows."

Joanna stopped then, in the middle of slicing open a roll, and looked at him carefully to see if he was joking or not.

Mikhail shrugged. "I have no idea if he's serious or not. You would have to ask Jeff."

Joanna giggled. "You know, I've been watching them for two years, and I knew they were perfect for each other, but until right now, I had no idea how much. So, I know your order, Shane's order, and Martin's order—who's this last sandwich for?"

Mikhail shrugged again. "I have no idea, but she's been living off of your discarded french fries, so I'm thinking she will not care if those little green pepper things are on it or not."

Joanna dropped the roll in her hand. "She's been *what?*"

Mikhail pulled up his lip. "Living off your garbage," he said distinctly. "And hopefully she will still be there when you're done, so if you could possibly hurry…."

Joanna's hands flew, and she put on the basics—mayonnaise, mustard, meat, and cheese—then wrapped it quickly and shoved it into Mikhail's hands. He nodded thanks, grabbed a milk from the cooler, and said, "Excellent. I'll be back to pay you and to get the rest in a few moments."

He figured walking out the back door would just cause the girl to bolt, so he went out the front door and then, delicately, on dancer's feet, walked quietly back to the trash cans.

The girl had her back to him and was scavenging through the second can, but it was full—apparently from the day before—if the stench was anything to judge by.

"I would not eat that if I were you," Mikhail said, wrinkling his nose. "It will make you sick."

The girl jerked and the lid of the big plastic can that she'd been holding over her head fell down on it instead. She pulled herself out from under it, whirled around, and groaned.

"Aw, fuck! Now you made me go and get more of that shit on…." She shut up when Mikhail thrust the sandwich in front of her face, and she took it by instinct.

"Eat," he said, but the command was unnecessary. She was digging into the wrapping and ripping off hunks of sandwich, then shoving them into her mouth with unnecessary force. He watched it catch up to her, and when it looked like she was going to have trouble swallowing, he took off the cap and handed her the small plastic container of milk. She took the milk like she'd taken the sandwich: instinctively, with no question that she'd drink it.

When she was around three-quarters done with the sandwich, she took a deep, shuddering breath and wrapped the remains up and shoved them in her pocket.

"Thanks," she said, her voiced muffled since she was using her tongue to clean her teeth at the same time. She took a final swig of the milk, and her voice was much clearer. "Do I need to give you a blow job for that?"

Mikhail shuddered. "The horror! No. Not necessary. I do have one request, though."

She eyed him up and down, the whites of her eyes dramatic against her dark skin. "I'm not bending over for a sandwich," she said dubiously, and he rolled his eyes.

"Americans! Even the whores are spoiled! No, nothing like that. Here." He dug in his pocket and produced one of the business cards he and Shane had gotten used to carrying around. "You see that road?" he asked, and she looked to where the small road on which the diner and the garage sat, and then beyond, to the larger road that intersected it.

"It's hard to miss," she said. "It's the main road through, like, three towns."

Mikhail nodded. It was true. Levee Oaks turned into farmland and then turned into airport land and then turned into some other small rural suburb he frequently forgot. "Exactly. You follow that road for a mile, and you will come to a place by the levee, with a wrought iron sign that says 'Promise House'. Go in. We have a spare room with a clean bed, a shower, and three meals a day. And snacks." Shane insisted the children needed snacks. Mikhail thought he was spoiling them, but then, Mikhail stayed out of most management decisions altogether.

The girl curled her lip in suspicion. "You're not going to try to sell me on Jesus, are you? 'Cause I'm thinkin' if God was such hot shit, I wouldn't be about to hurl old fries."

"I buy you a sandwich and you repay me with insults!" Mikhail snapped. "The only god at Promise House is the man who runs it, but he's my god, and you are not allowed to worship him!"

The girl held up her hands placatingly. "Okay, okay, okay! I won't move in on your man, I hear you!" Her attitude slipped for a moment. "Clean sheets?" she said wistfully. "A shower? No God'n'Jesus bullshit?"

"None," Mikhail told her, still sulking. "All we ask of you is that you learn a trade—that *doesn't*," he added hastily, "involve offering sex to strangers!"

The girl nodded thoughtfully. "About how far down that road?" she asked, and Mikhail repressed a smile. (Of course, Mikhail rarely smiled unless he was talking to Shane, so that wasn't hard.)

"About a mile. You may start walking now, if you like, or you may wait for my husband to get here. I'm going that direction anyway."

The girl narrowed her eyes. "Naw. I'm gonna check it out first. I wanna make sure I don't end up on a mat in front of some sort of machine, making cheap T-shirts for pennies an hour."

"You know," he said, after digesting that for a moment, "I need to pick up the rest of my sandwiches. You do what you feel you must. If you would like a ride, Shane will be by in a big black GTO that sounds very loud. You'll see him parked there by my van, you see?"

He pointed across the parking lot and her eyebrows rose. "The Purple Brick," she read, surprised, and then looked down at him. Yes, yes, like all of the impertinent children, she was taller than he was. "If that wasn't so loud, I'd say it was a serial killer van."

Mikhail shrugged. "It runs. Mostly. I shall see you later, if you have any sense at all." And with that, he turned into the deli to go pay Collin's sister.

Later, as he rode next to Shane, munching on his chicken and avocado on dry wheat toast, he tried to explain the situation.

"It is like one of the cats," he said after swallowing. Mayonnaise, he thought wistfully. Shane's sandwich had mayonnaise on it. Perhaps, when his dancing days were done, Mikhail too could have such an indulgence.

"Like Katy Perry or Justin Bieber?"

Mikhail scowled. Letting the children in on naming feral cats had been a mistake. "No, like Sweetie."

Shane nodded thoughtfully. He'd lost a little weight in this last year, mostly because he worked so hard on Promise House he forgot to eat. Mikhail made him—in fact, Shane's sandwich was laden with cream cheese and pastrami and sauce, just so Mikhail could feel that solidity underneath his palms again when they were lying side by side in their bed.

"Sweetie. Okay, I hear you."

Sweetie was a plain, fluffy tortoiseshell cat with a light bone structure and sniffing whiskers that seemed to vibrate about forty-five times a second. She'd been a flea-ridden, worm-infested, lice-bitten three-pound disaster when they'd first captured her, and although she was much healthier now, she had topped out at a slender five pounds. She ran away from most people, but sometimes, if you held your fingers out and made the appropriate sounds, she would allow the occasional person (mostly Mikhail) to smooth her whiskers back and rub her between the eyes.

Sometimes.

"You can't put Sweetie in a car and tell her where to go," Shane said after another moment, and Mikhail smiled.

"No."

"First she'd scratch you until you bled to death. Then she'd jump out the window."

Mikhail nodded. "Is true."

"So did you get a name out of her?"

Mikhail grimaced. Details! "No."

"Well then, we'll probably call her Sweetie." Shane risked a quick look at Mikhail to grin, his brown eyes crinkling in the corners while he did so. He turned his attention immediately to the road, but Mikhail had that smile to warm him. Why did a man need mayonnaise on his sandwich when he had that smile? It was a smile to fill the soul.

When they pulled into the driveway at Promise House, the GTO filled with groceries and flats of soda and gallons of milk, Mikhail saw Kimmy out on the porch, talking to his feral kitten.

Her name turned out to be LeLauna Saunders, but it didn't matter. Shane, Mikhail, and eventually Kimmy and all of the runaways at Promise House referred to the girl as Sweetie.

Chapter 4

Collin: Someone Else's Kid

COLLIN stood next to Deacon in the hundred-degree heat of the late-August afternoon, looked at the group of little kids running across the raggedly green field of the schoolyard, and scowled.

"Really?" he asked rhetorically, and Deacon snapped his mouth shut.

"Yup."

"You're going to let him get away with that?"

"Give me a sec, I'm trying not to beat his face in."

That, coming from the ever-calm Deacon Winters, was enough to make Collin shut up and give him some space. What came out of Deacon's mouth next was not what Collin expected, and it was an obvious attempt on Deacon's part to still his rising rage.

"Did you really let him drag you to see *Wicked*?"

Collin winced. Had everybody heard this story? "It was my idea."

"You were trying to please him?"

"Well, yeah. It was our honeymoon."

"Honeymoons mean you go into a quiet room and fuck like lemmings. The play is overkill."

Oh, thank God. Everyone had been treating him like he, Collin Waters and Collin Waters alone, had been trying to kill romance by stepping on it while wearing giant steel-toed, waffle-stomping work boots.

"I'm sayin'!" Collin whined, because that's *exactly* what he and Jeff had been doing the night before he'd fallen asleep during the play!

"Oh fuck," Deacon said quietly, pulling his attention back to the soccer field and the puzzled little kids running around on it. "That's it. That's the line. Hold me back."

And then he abruptly strode onto the field and grabbed Parry Angel as she ran up to him.

"Hey, what are you doing?" yelled the coach. Allan Ness was one of those guys who'd been brawny in high school and was running toward a bit of "extra" muscle now. Collin remembered him from high school, actually—he'd been a few years older, in Crick's class. He'd been one of the benchwarmers on the football team, and one of the kids most likely to rub it in to the kids who weren't on the team that he was way more special by virtue of his mighty man muscles and his personality sphincter.

"Did you really just tell them to elbow the other little kids on the field?" Deacon asked as Parry Angel looked at the coach with a scowl.

Collin had heard the guy do it, and he *still* couldn't believe that's what he'd heard.

"That's the way to get the little losers to win!" the guy said with one of those stupid "these bozos are missing the point!" expressions that made Collin want to slap him, because a punch had too much class.

"Yeah. Well, my kid's not playing on a team that does that," Deacon said decisively. "Parry, darlin', ready to go get ice cream?" Parry smiled in relief, and Deacon put her down. "Go get your water bottle, darling. We're out of here." Collin had watched her little round face get scrunchier and scrunchier as practice had progressed, and he hadn't blamed her. The coach had been screaming and shrill, and Parry wasn't the only kid running around in the spotty grass looking confused. Yeah, sure, the kids got to U12 and they could play a little rough—rubbing was racing, right? But at Parry's age? Under eight? No. You didn't tell little kids to beat up on each other. Collin's mother would have yanked him off the field too.

So when the coach sneered, "Yeah, Deacon Winters, the whole town'll know which kid's being raised by faggots, won't they?" Collin was shocked enough to let his mouth hang open, but Deacon, apparently, was a little more levelheaded.

He smiled easily, tipped his hat, and said, "You come to my land and say that to me when we're not in front of a bunch of children who shouldn't hear that word, and you see who's weak and who's just stupid."

He went to turn around and take Parry Angel's hand, and the coach tried to blindside him.

But Coach Ness really *had* gotten out of shape since high school, and Deacon spent his entire life breaking horses. For a man who'd had a heart attack before he was thirty, Deacon was in some fantastic physical condition.

He ducked instinctively and returned with a sharp and effective punch to the nose. He scooped Parry into his arms and strode off the field as the coach's knees buckled. Collin trotted in Deacon's wake, smirking as Parry said, "But *Deacon*, you're not supposed to hit people!"

Deacon grunted. Given what Collin knew about some of Deacon's history, the grunt carried a whole lot he hoped Parry Angel might never learn. "You don't get to hit first, Angel, but self-defense is perfectly acceptable— even to your mother, I'm sure."

Collin snickered and looked behind them to see what sort of chaos rode Deacon's jet trail. Ness was sputtering blood and struggling to sit up, calling to Deacon that he couldn't do that, and the other parents were grabbing their *own* children by the hands and... uh-oh. Wait a minute.

"Hey, Deacon!" Collin called, running to keep up. "Deacon, they're trying to get your attention!"

Deacon's full mouth lifted in the corner with incredulity. "Well so does a torch and pitchfork mob, Collin, but you don't see me stopping for one of *those*, do you?"

"No, seriously! Deacon, they've got their kids with them—I don't think it's like that!"

Deacon eyeballed him suspiciously and then turned around to look. Sure enough, the parents—lots of women in tank tops and walking shorts and men in cargo shorts and T-shirts, all between Deacon and Collin's age—were gathering their children and their fold-up chairs and blankets and dragging them inelegantly toward Deacon as he walked off the practice field toward the car. A few of them were waving and calling his name.

Deacon's eyes opened wide and if Collin didn't know better, he'd say Deacon Winters, the family patriarch and center of any storm weathered at The Pulpit, was terrified.

The first woman of the group drew near, panting and out of breath. "Wait... up... a... sec...," she breathed and then looked behind her. Her son was galloping up quickly, and her older son was running toward them in a flurry of schoolbooks and dropped papers, because apparently he'd been doing his homework while his little brother was practicing. "Jason!" she screamed. "You dropped your math!" and the kid turned around like a capering puppy and hustled back to fetch it.

"Whew!" she said, smoothing her hair back. "I thought you were just going to take off!"

"Well, uhm, yeah," Deacon said, looking to Collin as though being sought out in a crowd was completely bizarre.

Collin shrugged back. Well, you couldn't always pick your social situation, could you?

"That was the plan. What can I do for you...."

"I'm Megan, Tyler's mother," she said. She smiled at him, warm and genuine. She was a tall woman, taller than Deacon, with blonde hair pulled back in a ponytail and posture that didn't give an inch, although she had a few to spare. "And I can't believe we let that situation go on for so long. Parry's mother—Benny? Is that right?—anyway, she's been distracted a little. I'm not sure she saw how bad it was. But, uhm, anyway. So, do you want to coach?"

Deacon's jaw dropped, and Collin looked at him, curious. It couldn't have been *that* out of the realm of possibility, could it?

But then Collin vaguely remembered the gossip that had circulated through his mom's diner when Deacon had come out during a trial for assaulting an officer, and thought that maybe, well, for Deacon, it was like a slingshot into the sun.

"I beg your pardon?" He still had his eyes wide open, like a possum in the headlights, and Collin almost smacked him to ask him what was wrong.

"Yes," Megan said as Collin blinked and looked at Deacon again. "You're very good with her. We all saw you practicing while we were waiting for Coach Douchecanoe"—Collin choked on a smirk—"to get here. I'm already team mom—I've got no problem helping you with all the administrative stuff. We just need someone on the field who can deal with other people's kids and not want to use them for highway piñatas."

She was so earnest, with big blue eyes and a sort of long-faced prettiness, that when she said things like that, Collin just wanted to fall to the ground and kick his heels in the dust laughing. He couldn't *wait* to tell Jeff about this woman. Jeffy would probably come out to watch the games just to talk to her, because Jeff liked people who could crack him the fuck up.

"I'll be assistant coach," he said quickly. Martin was going back down south for his final year in high school, and, well, Collin and Jeff missed him already. Collin had discovered he *liked* kids, liked his sisters' kids, liked the kids at The Pulpit, liked the kids at Promise House—just generally liked spending time with young people. Jeffy wasn't half-bad at it either. They were neither of them looking to adopt, but still…. "I still play rec-league soccer," Collin said, and Deacon nodded because the guys had been out to a few of his games (much to his embarrassment—Jeffy's pom-poms were adorable and overkill at the same time). "I'd love to help out!" He smiled brightly, and he half expected Deacon to scowl back.

He was unprepared for the look of half-panicked naked gratitude.

"Thanks," Deacon mumbled. "'Preciate it. So, how do we get rid of Coach Douchecanoe for good?" he asked Megan, and she grimaced.

"Leave that to me. My husband's on the board—he coaches Jason's team. I kept telling him that this guy was nucking futz—now they'll *have* to listen!" She grinned happily then. "So, did I hear you tell Parry that you're taking her for ice cream? Because Tyler and Jason would *love* some! And we could talk about details, and—where are you going?"

Deacon opened his mouth and closed it, and Collin had to admit, he was admiring the big guy's discomfiture. Collin wouldn't have expected him to be so utterly undone by a soccer mom and her—Collin did a rough count—six compatriots in mutiny.

"My mother's diner," Collin said decisively. "Mom's treat, as long as it's small. Right over there by the—"

"The garage!" Megan practically sang. "You don't know me, because my husband brings the minivan in, but he *loves* you guys. I didn't know that was your mother running Natalie's. That's awesome! Hey, do you think she could sponsor, because if we could get a sponsor, I wouldn't have to make the banner by hand, and that would be a*maz*ing, because *nobody* makes you get an art degree before you start popping the little goobers out, and suddenly you're responsible for making eight felt fire bunnies, whatever that is—whose kid thought up fire bunnies?" she asked the lady next to her, and the woman—who was much wider than Megan and not as tall—grimaced.

"Mine. Sorry 'bout that, Meggie. I have no idea where she got it."

"Yeah, well, if we could get a sponsor, we could have the damned thing made up and then…."

Collin wasn't sure how the woman did it. Apparently she had a day job and a phone tree and an inexhaustible supply of energy and a mouth that wouldn't quit. It didn't matter how she did it, though—it was done. By the time his mom (who was thrilled, go figure!) had dished up small sundaes for the kids and slightly larger sundaes for the *very* appreciative grownups, they had it nailed. Collin and Megan had talked uniforms, banners, team pictures, sponsorship, and favors (gift bags from his mom—he had no idea she even *had* such things!), and he and Deacon had a tentative schedule and an *amazing* to-do list of classes, rules, meeting places, practices, regulations, first-aid requirements, and games that they had to memorize.

It wasn't until all the parents and kids had cleared out of the diner and Deacon had thrown away all of the ice cream containers that Collin looked at the stack of papers Megan had given him and thunked his head softly on the Formica table.

"Oh. My. God. Why are we doing this again?"

Deacon gave Parry Angel a clean washrag and told her to wipe down all of the tables, which she did with enthusiasm. "But hurry, Angel. I know you like helping, but it's seven thirty on a school night. I think Uncle Crick was making beans tonight, so you're going to want to get home and have dinner now that you've had dessert."

"Beans!"

Collin had tasted Crick's baked beans—the girl was right to be excited.

"I said, why are we doing this again?" Collin didn't really need an answer, but living with Jeff made him realize he too had a hidden drama queen who sometimes needed her dues.

Deacon just curled his lip in disgust. "I have no idea why we're doing this," he said, and it sounded like he meant it. "I don't even know why you were *there*! Remember, you showed up on the field and were going to tell me why before Coach Dou—uhm, Ness opened his giant fu—uh, nky trap?"

Collin smacked his forehead with the palm of his hand. "Oh yeah! Okay, I forgot to tell you that Jeffy and Crick were going to dissect, uhm, debrief, uhm, dish about the honeymoon, and then Crick said that, oh crap!"

Deacon's phone buzzed in his pocket, and he glowered at Collin.

"He said we weren't supposed to go for ice cream after practice, didn't he?" Deacon asked grimly, and Collin smiled with all his teeth.

"Here, Angel," he said, taking the cloth from Parry's unresisting hands. "Let Uncle Collin clean this up super quick for us so we don't make Crick any more pis—uhm, irritated than he already is."

Parry looked at him with those big bluebell eyes. "That's a good idea," she said solemnly. "Uncle Crick gets pissed off when people get home late for dinner."

Collin stared at her for a minute, and Deacon shut his eyes, apparently just as the phone picked up.

"Yeah," Deacon said, like Crick could read his mind. "We're coming. No, Collin didn't relay the message—he was too busy signing us up for coaching duty. Why? Because that other guy was a douchecanoe. Yeah, I don't care if she hears me, you already taught her 'pissed off', douchecanoe is an improvement. Where'd I get that? The team mom. You don't have a corner on the swearing market, Carrick James, and neither does your sister. Yeah, we're coming home. Dinner? Well, sort of. Does ice cream count? No, I'm not being facetious, it was an honest question, dammit!" He listened for a moment and let out a grumpy sigh. "Okay, so beans for them and rabbit pellets for me. I understand. I'm being punished."

Crick let out an indignant squawk on the other end of the line and Deacon just chuckled and hung up the phone.

Collin shook his head. "Wow, Deacon, you can be a real asshole sometimes!"

Deacon flushed and shrugged. "It's cute listening to him get all riled up. Sometimes he needs to remember he was a hell-raiser too. It's good for him."

Collin grinned widely and eyeballed the distance over the counter before aiming and shooting to pop the rag into the hamper by the sink.

"Thanks, Mom!" he called. She'd already gone back to the little accounting room to count up the drawer and the safe while they'd been finishing up their ice cream.

"You're welcome, sweetie!" she called. "Tell me how much I need to donate so they get their banner and their party, 'kay?"

"We're going in halvesies!" he told her and then ushered Deacon and Parry out of there before his mother could protest. He was actually tickled by the idea they'd both be in the team photo. After his severely misspent youth, it seemed like the height of legitimacy to end up on the wall in a picture with a bunch of little kids he could teach his bad habits to.

They got outside, and Deacon grinned at Parry Angel. "So, Collin drove the Camaro, Angel. Do you want to ride in the back with him or in the extended cab with me?"

Parry Angel grinned, eschewing Collin's pride and joy, the recently repainted red-and-black vintage Camaro with the tricked-out engine that featured the chrome-plated intake manifold system on the *outside* of the hood, in favor of the battered family pickup truck with the car seat firmly belted in the back.

"Sorry, Uncle Collin!" she called winsomely, and Collin laughed and tapped her nose with a finger that was only now, after almost two weeks off, starting to lose some of the ever-present grease.

"No worries, Angel. I'll see you at home." It figured. Nobody, not even fun Uncle Collin, was going to get between that child and her Deek-Deek. Yeah, she called him Deacon *now*, but Collin could still remember when she was three and she called him Deek-Deek, and everybody thought it was *adorable*. Nobody was going to let either Parry *or* Deacon live that down.

As Collin followed Deacon to The Pulpit, he reflected that it had been a very, very quick two and a half years. Of course, he would have married Jeffy two years ago, after their painful courtship and Deacon's heart attack and Shane and Mikhail's wedding, but life just seemed to happen, and since they'd been together and living it that way, a wedding didn't seem to be all that important.

It wasn't until Shane's sister, Kimmy, had celebrated her wedding—on a much smaller scale than her brother, actually—and Collin had watched Jeff sobbing through it that he realized they were long past due.

Well, why not? Collin had been ready to marry him before their first kiss. By the time Shane and Mikhail had stood on a miserably wet February day and said funny, singular vows of their own, he'd already started writing vows of his own. It was just that things—wonderful, exciting things, like sharing lives and living with Jeffy's cats and giving the kids at Promise House job training and making love on stifling Saturdays when the joys of air conditioning and sex were both free and decadent—*those* things had gotten in the way.

They were wonderful things. Collin wouldn't trade a moment of them. But traveling in New York, dressed to the nines as they padded around Manhattan and saw plays in Times Square and wandered around the Metropolitan Museum of Art, he had felt such a quiet claiming in the words. "I'm waiting for my husband." "I'm here with my husband." "Oh yeah, my husband made me get tickets months ago." When Collin had been in high school, he'd gotten the snot beaten out of him for wearing a rainbow goalie jersey to a soccer game, all in the name of gay pride. Over the past few weeks, he'd discovered nothing exceeded the pride of living a quiet, productive life on his own terms with the person he loved the most.

And part of that belonging and pride was being a part of The Pulpit. Collin had started out as an outsider, and he had to admit it, he'd been mildly resentful. They'd all been so tight, a group of circled wagons against what had been a hostile environment, dry of tolerance or even simple humanity. Collin had wondered, in those first days, what he'd have to do to squeeze his own wagon into the circle. As it turned out, loving Jeffy had given him a pass. He was in, and so was his family, and as the family at The Pulpit had expanded and his own family had merged into that Calistoga circle, the human desert of Levee Oaks had seemed a little less dry and hostile and a little more inhabitable.

And now Deacon Winters, Levee Oaks' most famous gay resident, had been asked to coach soccer. (Yeah, sure, Crick was a war hero, but in a town like this, having the old valedictorian/football hero/golden boy lit up a far bigger halo than a guy everybody had known was gay in the first place.)

It made the rebel in Collin a little bit proud.

So Collin was riding high when he pulled into the gravel drive of The Pulpit and parked along the wide, flat space of hardpan with the other cars. Judging by the vehicles, Collin could see Shane and Mikhail were there, as was Jeffy, and he was a little relieved. Small. Benny and Drew would be eating, but that was still short a whack of people who could have kept this from being a quiet, easy night he and Jeff could walk away from early.

Excellent.

Deacon had pulled out behind him and gotten stopped at the light, but Collin swung up the long porch and into the front room with the ease of long familiarity. The family was gathered around the big battered wooden table in the kitchen, and Collin didn't think twice before he called to them.

"Hello, hello! Doesn't anybody want to come greet the new assistant coach of the Levee Oaks Bunny Fires?"

He was greeted by a wall of tense, blank faces, and then Jeffy turned toward him and wrinkled his nose. "Jebus, Sparky—have you *ever* learned to read a room?"

"Well, yeah," Collin said, feeling acutely uncomfortable without even knowing why. "But usually I'm not blindsided by this much angst. What in the hell happened when I volunteered Deacon to coach?"

Crick stood up and started moving restlessly around the kitchen, his movements hitching a little like they tended to do at the end of the day. When Deacon had first come out, Collin used to secretly wonder what Deacon— easily the most amazing-looking man Collin had ever met—had seen in gangly, plainly pretty Crick Francis. In the past two and a half years, Collin had seen the town's most famous hell-raiser devote his life to keeping Deacon Winters alive and their family functioning even if it was just by a tart word that made the recipient think twice about saying anything different. He didn't wonder anymore, but sometimes he did get uncomfortable watching them look at each other. That was dangerous love right there, and Collin had spent his first eighteen years courting danger with almost more perseverance than he'd courted Jeff, so he should know.

"So," he said slowly, feeling his way through the high-wire atmosphere, "what in the holy mother of fuck did I miss?"

Benny looked up from the table, which should have surprised him because usually everyone's favorite little mommy was busy moving and didn't *sit* at the table, but there she was. Her small heart-shaped face was pale, and her ordinarily full lips were pinched and almost white. Her eyes—Crick's shape, but wide and blue instead of brown—were shiny, like she'd been fighting tears for a very long time. She was holding onto Drew's hand so tightly, Drew's fingertips had lost all circulation, judging by the white of the finger pads, and Collin was suddenly very, very worried.

"Benny?" Collin said gently. "What is it?"

"It's nothing," she snapped, glaring at Crick. "My stupid brother made a big deal out of something, and then the whole world walked in for dinner and heard us fighting, and now this entire thing is going to go down in front of the entire free world, and that's fine, because it's a family matter anyway."

"No." Mikhail spoke up decisively, and Collin watched as Shane nodded gravely behind him. Well, they read each other's minds more often than not.

"No?" Benny said, her eyes wide and a smile playing at the corner of her lips.

"No," Mikhail repeated. "We shall leave, and we shall take Parry Angel to Jon and Amy's, and Shane is calling them even as I speak."

"Of course I am," Shane muttered, fumbling for his phone.

"That's news to me," Benny said and Crick spoke up, his voice a lot more tense than Collin had expected.

"It's a good idea. There's school tomorrow, but she can still get in some time with Lila before they have to leave."

Collin felt a small pang of loss, and he was aware that the rest of the family felt it more like a fist through the gut. Deacon's best friend was going away to DC to lobby for gay rights—it was a tremendous opportunity, actually, but it was no secret Deacon was fighting against being crushed by the news.

"That would make things easier," Benny murmured, her relief palpable. "But I hate to chase all of you out—"

"Nonsense." Mikhail shrugged, cutting her off in his abrupt way. He walked forward and kissed her on the cheek. "Just remember tomorrow, when you are calling Jeff to dish, that I thought of it, and call me instead." Mikhail arched a smug blond eyebrow at Jeff, who stuck his tongue out back. "That way I can have the news for once, instead of finding out from *him*!"

Benny reached up her arms and hugged him tight, much to the little Russian's discomfort. "Of course," she said and kissed his cheek. "You get first rights of the phone tree, Mickey, I promise."

Besides Shane, Benny was the only other person on the planet who got to call him Mickey—and that included Shane's sister, who had known him first.

Shane finished his conversation with Jon abruptly and walked forward and hugged Benny too, and then patted Drew's shoulder before following Mikhail out of the house. Jeff and Collin repeated the ritual, and besides feeling a little bit cheated, Collin was also *burning* with curiosity at what could have caused the lead wagon to sit in confab with itself.

He didn't have to look at Jeff (although he *liked* looking at him, because in spite of what could have been an awkward face with a long chin and a slightly hooked nose, Jeff's animation and almost constant snarky smile made him a joy to look at) to know that that same willingness to dish was just vibrating out of his little Jeffy heart.

Collin hugged Benny and kissed her on the cheek, and she said quietly, "You'll be a great assistant coach, Collin. I didn't mean to shit all over your news, but that other guy was a douchecanoe. I'm so glad you and Deacon are taking over."

Collin pulled back then and grinned, because leave it to Benny to think about him and not herself when whatever was going on was obviously huge, and then he followed Jeff out to the car.

Mikhail was in the middle of securing the car seat into the back of the GTO, and Uncle Shane was in the middle of swinging Parry Angel high up in the air. He was probably the only one of them still big enough to make that sort of thing not awkward for Parry, whose sturdy little limbs were getting longer every day. Parry squealed when he put her down to kiss Deacon good-bye, and Deacon waved to all of them before he wandered inside the house. Collin paused in the middle of sliding into his car and locked eyes with Jeff.

Jeff practically ran from his Mini Cooper over to Collin's side, where Collin was greeted with a quick kiss and then what they both *really* wanted.

"Oh holy Jebus, Sparky, you will *never* guess what is going down in there!"

"Oh thank God," Collin breathed. "The curiosity was fucking killing me. Spill!"

Jeff looked up at the house and grimaced. "Here. Give me a ride. You can drop me off at my car tomorrow, or, better yet, drop Martin off. He's home right now and needs to get out of the house so you and I can get loud again. Anyway." Jeff trotted around the car and they both got in. He ran a hand through his gelled dark hair, which was a good sign his agitation was true and not just dramatic, and then gestured frantically for Collin to turn the engine over and get the hell out of there.

"Jesus, Jeff, what's the hurry!" Collin grumbled, and Jeff shook his head and looked behind him as Collin pulled back out of the driveway. "It's not something bad, is it?"

Jeff shook his head. "No—it's going to be a good thing, I think, after they get their shit sorted over there in drama central. But in the meantime...." Jeff shook his head again, but more slowly this time. "Oh, Sparky, Deacon is not going to take this well."

Chapter 5

Deacon: Shit Sorting at Drama Central

"I'M SORRY," Deacon said blankly. "Could you repeat that?"

Deacon was having the *weirdest* day.

Of all the things, he would *not* have predicted that group of parents following him and Collin off the field. He'd been sure the only thing that was going to hunt him down was a restraining order, but holy fuckin' damn. Apparently all those nice people who'd watched him deck that ignorant asshole had thought that shit was *cool*. Deacon wasn't sure he approved of a group of people who would condone that behavior, but seeing as it meant he wasn't going to have to deal with the police (and apparently Ness had been convinced it would be in his best interest not to contact the authorities either), he found himself having to deal with *them*.

They weren't so bad, actually, and thank God Megan and her stalwart companion could do most of the talking. (Of course Collin did his share—it was no wonder he and Jeff made such a great couple. They could keep the entire town fueled with chatter if they tried.) Coaching the soccer team actually sounded *fun*, and it would be a chance to spend more time with Parry.

Deacon was well aware his time with her was running out.

In spite of the way everybody tended to coddle him, he was not deluded into thinking Jon and Amy hadn't needed to move on for quite some time, and he had *always* known Benny and Parry were only his on loan. No. Carrick he'd cling to until his fingers snapped off, but staying in Levee Oaks had been a choice for him, not a lack of options. He was well aware the rest of the world wasn't always going to make that choice.

He planned to enjoy the family he had around him, and make the choices that kept him there for as long as he possibly could be, so he ate lots of greens, and his family kept coming by for dinner anyway, and he was pretty damned content with his life. And, well, now he was apparently a soccer coach, and that could be fun too. If nothing else, watching the little buggers run the hell around the field like mice on meth without a maze? That right there was high entertainment, and half the reason he'd been so excited to take Parry to practice. So in spite of the lingering sadness of having to see Jon off, Deacon was becoming used to the idea that the world might not be out to kill him, skin him, and eat him after all.

Or he had been until he'd walked into his kitchen and seen the nerves riding everybody like a breaker rode a skittish colt.

And now that Benny had blurted out what she had in mind, he knew why.

"Isn't that incest?" he asked, honestly befuddled, and Crick smacked him in the back of the head.

"No, idiot, not if she's having *your* baby."

Deacon flushed (and he'd been flushing all evening in the diner as it was) and scowled up at his beloved, his partner, his husband, and the giant pain in his ass.

"Don't get mad at *me*, Carrick James, it wasn't *my* idea." He swallowed against the sudden tightness in his chest and turned to Benny, who was regarding him with those big blue eyes. Oh hells, those eyes held *way* too much hero worship in them, and he shifted uncomfortably. "Benny, I love that you thought of us this way. I do. But you and Drew, you've got your own life to live. I mean, I know you've been waiting until you graduate this year to get married, but it's long overdue that you move in with him in the cottage and start making a life together."

Deacon caught Drew's irritated glare at Benny and smiled. This might just end normally after all. Then Drew looked up at Deacon, his brown eyes sober and his gaze direct.

"Deacon, this was her idea, but I'm behind it 100 percent. This is something we both really want to give you. We're well aware—"

Deacon stood up suddenly, his chest tight enough to make his vision go dark. "No, you're not," he snapped, looking anywhere but at the two of them. "This isn't a puppy. It's a baby, and you're talking about.... Benny, I was there, remember? Being pregnant isn't a picnic, and walking away from a baby—even when you know it's being loved—that's not something you're wired to do, darlin'. I was *here* when you came home, remember?"

"It'll be different this time," Benny said, but she was wiping her eyes with the palm of her hand as she said it. "Deacon, this won't be *my* baby I'll be leaving. It'll be yours and Crick's, and I'll be leaving it right where it'll belong. With you. Don't tell me you don't want this." She wiped her eyes again, and he wondered when she'd started wearing makeup on a daily basis, because it was smeared all over her eyes like a giant raccoon mask. Her full mouth trembled, though, and so did her pointed little chin, and Deacon looked around the kitchen to find someone, anyone, who would help him haul his way out of this rabbit hole.

What he found was Crick Francis, leaning against their battered, peeling kitchen counter and looking at him seriously from brown eyes that were way too grown-up. His narrow face was pinched in at the corners of his lean mouth, and his back teeth were grinding enough to set the pulse throbbing in his scarred temple. He dragged a long-fingered hand through his black hair and nibbled on his lower lip, such painful hope shining out of this face that Deacon felt his stomach cramp.

"I don't want them to do this for me," Deacon whispered, and he had to whisper because it was a terrible, terrible lie.

"I do," Crick answered back, his jaw pulling back a little to assume that mulish set Deacon was used to.

Deacon took three deep breaths, realized that wasn't going to be enough, and decided he needed to be somewhere he could breathe.

"I'm going to check on the horses," he announced and stalked out of the house. The kitchen, with its cracking tile and battered table, was redolent of beans and pulled pork, and the smells alone were enough to make Deacon feel slightly ill. God. He didn't want to think about it. All the reasons Benny's proposition was a perfect solution to the one thing he'd always really wanted and all the reasons it was a perfectly shitty idea.

The barn was full these days, and he hadn't had to rake horseshit in a long time. Shane's kids from Promise House vied for that position, and Deacon understood that the competition for the work was pretty fierce. The kids completed chores and homework packets and went to their counseling sessions and basically kept their noses clean, all for the rewards of honest hard work. Shane's selection process must have been pretty stringent, Deacon had often thought, because the only kids who ended up mucking out the stalls and currying the horses had been the best kind, the kids who were going to find a place in the world when the world had been pretty damned insistent about kicking them out of it to date.

Deacon made his way back, thinking horses smelled even better when someone else had cleaned up after them, and found the stall at the end with his favorite horse. No, it wasn't Shooting Star, who was an incredible fucker and had tried to kill him on numerous occasions. He'd already sucked up to her delicate haunches enough for this day. Instead, he went to where Crick's horse was, the one Deacon had spent two years combing the trades and horse shows for, hoping that he'd find one that would do.

Crick's original horse, Comet, had been the color of fresh yellow baby shit, and had a swayback, a dish face, and big bony hips and joints. He had been, in fact, the singularly most ugly animal Deacon had ever seen, but that horse… man, that horse had heart.

Having to kill him was one of the most painful moments of Deacon's life, plain and simple, and the idea of Crick not having an animal on Deacon's ranch left a hole Deacon had made it his mission to fill.

The animal had to be big, because Crick himself was tall, and it had to be gentle, because as opinionated as Crick was to the humans around him, he still treated horses with an almost childish awe. It had to be bombproof; it couldn't shy at a breeze or kick because it felt threatened; and it had to be comfortable at the end of the line, because Crick wasn't the best horseman in the world, *especially* not after his wounds, and if he and Deacon went riding, Deacon wanted a horse that would keep up without jockeying for position.

Show points hadn't mattered, and neither had appearance or breeding. Deacon had gone looking for a *gentle* horse, and that's what he'd found in Flower Princess. The horse had been bought for a rather spoiled young woman, who had sold her after two years when she realized that horses didn't always smell fantastic. Although Crick had whined copiously about the name, Flower had indeed been exactly what Deacon was looking for. She was big enough to carry Crick as well as a load of saddlebags, and perfectly content to let Shooting Star or another mare or gelding lead the way. She had accompanied Deacon and Crick across the fields and to Promise Rock on more than one occasion, and every now and then, when Shooting Star was just too much of a bitch for Deacon to want to deal with, he took Flower to help train the more skittish horses, because she was so placid, the nonsense of the younger set just washed right over her.

She was an unremarkable roan, and she'd made just enough points in show to keep her breeding record intact. Deacon bred her anyway, because Even Star, their stud horse, was not only gentle but also pretty as a cover model, and of the two foals Flower'd thrown, one had been a beauty queen who'd fetched top dollar, and the other had been an incredibly ugly sweetheart who had been donated (breaking included) to a local ride-to-walk charity. Deacon figured both babies had been welcome, and he planned to give Flower a break for a year and then breed her again. But right now?

Right now, she was content to be used to teach the kids from Promise House to ride when Crick wasn't riding her, and to get a visit from Deacon almost every night.

She was especially content to get extra carrots when Deacon came around.

She snorted softly and shifted as he walked up to her stall, and he was almost disappointed to see that her mane had been brushed and braided and that her stall was spotless. Yeah, the kids spoiled her too, especially that new girl Mikhail had brought by last week, Sweetie.

"How's Sweetie treating you?" Deacon asked softly, and Flower leaned shamelessly into his scratch behind her jaw, as if to say, *Not bad. Could pet me more.*

Deacon allowed himself to be conned for a moment. "Yeah, them kids, Flower Princess, they just don't know what they're doing, do they? No one knows how to scratch you just the way you deserve. It's shameful, a pure crime, oh yes it is."

"That horse is going to break the damned door if you don't stop scratching her sweet spot," Crick said behind him, and Deacon had to fight not to jump. For an entire five minutes, he'd managed to forget why he was out here.

"Yeah, well…." Deacon swallowed. He didn't have a reply, or any words at all.

Crick approached him warily and stood just close enough behind him that if Deacon wanted to lean back and rest against him, he could.

Deacon mostly preferred to stand.

"Deacon, what's so bad about being offered—"

"A chance to watch your sister risk her life and health for us? Nothing at all, Carrick, because it's not like I haven't spent the last seven years trying to get her all grown up and happy and healthy and ready to go have a life of her own! No, I'd *love* to chain a girl I've thought of as my *daughter* to the ground carrying my baby, because I *am* that much of an asshole!"

Crick grunted. "She seemed to push out the *last* one quick enough," he said and then held up his hands. "Just saying! Women have babies all the time—"

"And women get sick doing it—did I miss something? Were you not *here* when Amy was pregnant the second time? Because the first time was no joke either, remember?"

High blood pressure the first time, and the added fun of gestational diabetes the second time. The worst part was, the gestational diabetes didn't leave. It just hung around and became regular pain-in-the-ass, shorten-your-life diabetes. God. Deacon remembered Jon's voice pitching like a child's when he told Deacon the news over the phone. Deacon had run over to his house—literally—and dragged the guy out on a horse for the first time in months. Deacon didn't have any other good cures. Alcohol was out, and Amy had been sleeping while Benny minded the babies, so a road trip to Vegas wasn't going to happen, not that Jon would have wanted to go. All Deacon had was the horse and the fields and the silence a man could have in his own head while he was riding.

It had seemed to work for Jon like it had worked for Deacon during the worst of Crick's absence and recovery, and Deacon could only be thankful. Jon was the sane one, the organized one, the one who bailed Deacon out of shit when the temper he'd hidden so well during his childhood escaped as an adult. If Deacon could give to Jon anything approaching what Jon had given Deacon in the course of their friendship, Deacon would consider himself a good man.

That's why he'd let Jon go without even a whimper. A friend—a *true* friend—didn't hold a brother back from greatness. It would have been a betrayal, and Deacon didn't know how to do those.

Crick sighed and backed away at the mention of Amy, his bad leg making shuffling sounds through the hay on the floor of the stall. Perversely, Deacon missed having him there, warming the space at his back, but it wasn't like Deacon had been accepting his comfort anyway.

"Benny's built different than Amy—"

"That's a justification," Deacon said, his voice tight. "She's got a man of her own now. If she's going to put her body through that, shouldn't it be for her own babies?"

He smiled a little, thinking of what beautiful babies they would make. Drew's calm steadiness, Benny's passion and compassion—those children would have the clear gaze of the angels, he was sure of it.

"He wants to give us this too."

Deacon breathed in sharply. "Yeah, I know, and seriously, what in the holy mother of hell—" Flower snorted, and he lowered his voice so she wouldn't think he was mad at her. "Why would he do that?" he muttered, mostly to himself. "Why?" Deacon turned to Crick, upset enough to give up the illusion of space he'd created. "He's going after his certificate, did you know that?"

"Animal health technician?" Crick asked, and Deacon nodded.

"He can commute from here. They can live in the cottage if he gets a chance to go for the full veterinary medicine degree. I mean, we can help all we want, but Drew has *plans.* And he plans to be with your sister. And I don't understand why he's going to put all of that off when I think he loves her just... just head over fucking heels, Carrick! He's been looking at her with his heart in his throat since before you got back—"

"She was only sixteen!"

Deacon had a moment of irritated humor. "Yeah, and so were you when you first moved to The Pulpit, and you swear on your life you were in love!"

Crick grunted. It was the same age difference, Crick knew it. "Well," he conceded sulkily, "I wish them luck. But before they go on and live their lives together, they want to give us something—"

"This is not a puppy!" Deacon snapped, not sure why people couldn't see this.

"No, it's not!" Crick snapped back. He dragged his game hand through his hair again and narrowed his wide-set brown eyes. God, his eyelashes hadn't gotten any thinner or any blonder, and Carrick James still seemed like he could see Deacon's soul through Deacon's body when he turned that look on full blast.

So Deacon studied his boots instead.

"Then why—"

"It's not a puppy, Deacon, it's a *baby,* and it's going to have the best parts of me in it, and, God willing, the best parts of you! Please...." Crick took a deep breath and ventured into Deacon's vision, his tore-up jeans and boots first, followed by his knees, and by the time Deacon was forced to raise his chin and look up to avoid gazing at his crotch (which wasn't a bad destination, really), Crick was there, his pretty face anxious and tired and struggling so hard for patience, Deacon wanted to hold him just for that.

The Crick of seven years ago wouldn't have been patient. Not even a little. Especially when he didn't understand.

"Please, Deacon. Can't you even think about it?"

"We could adopt," Deacon said shortly, nodding. "People do it all the time. We could adopt. Shane's got connections, we could fill out paperwork, we could—"

Crick snorted. "Yeah. I know. We could. And don't think I hadn't been planning on all that already!"

Deacon blinked, surprised as all hell. "You had? When—"

"Well, I was planning to bring it up after Jon left." Crick stalked over to hay bales set up between the stalls for the next muckraker. They made convenient benches, and Crick sank down onto the double stack gratefully. He worked a full day's load, but his leg and his arm were never going to be what they used to, and at the end of the day, they got weak. Deacon knew. He'd spent hours over both of them, rubbing, massaging with the heated wand—anything to help work the nerves and flesh that had been decimated just as Crick had been leaving a Middle East war zone to come home.

With a sigh, he hopped up so he was standing on top of the bale Crick was sitting on, and leaning on the triple stack next to it. Crick was tall enough that Deacon only had to lean a little to pull on his arm.

"Here, rest it on my knees," he grunted, and Crick did so with the ease of long practice. Deacon had asked Jeff and he'd given Deacon some pointers. Deacon's favorite was this one move that started at the shoulder and kneaded the heavy muscles up around Crick's neck, and then worked the tension out and down his bicep, to the heavy scars of his forearm, and then down to his twisted hand and the tips of his fingers. He didn't spare Crick the pain, and there was nothing sexual about it, but Deacon liked to close his eyes and imagine. He could see all the stress, all the grown-up shit that knotted Crick's muscles like waxy black thread, and as he worked, he imagined smoothing that out, combing through it with pressure and counterpressure, with the magic softening of touch, and that by the time Deacon got to Crick's hand, the darkness had been all combed through, and there was nothing left but shining, woven promise, which was all Deacon had seen in Crick from the moment they'd met.

Crick let out an unabashed groan by the time Deacon got to his hand, and Deacon raised the twisted fingers to his mouth and touched lips gently, stroking the tightness of his grip out with the other hand.

Crick leaned his head back against the stall, heedless of Mercury, the gigantic American saddlebred who was broken to carry men in armor on his back as part of the Faire circuit Mikhail still traveled when he danced. Mercury made an effort to lip Crick's hair up, but Crick swatted him away gently, and Deacon sweetened the pot by giving him a carrot.

"You know, when you do that, you're just telling him he gets treats for eating my head," Crick grumbled, eyes still closed.

"Which is why I do it," Deacon replied mildly, and Crick opened one eye and scowled.

"We're not done with this conversation, you know!"

And now it was Deacon's turn to scowl as he dropped Crick's hand, hopped off his hay bale, and stalked back to Flower's stall. "You need to tell them no," he said decisively, looking at Flower and trying to pretend like that didn't hurt to say.

"I'll do no such goddamned thing!" Crick didn't stand up, but he did cross his arms in front of him and glower. Deacon would have told him he looked cute, but that would mean no sex that night, because you didn't *say* that to a man who stood six feet five inches and had shoulders like a Clydesdale.

"Look, Carrick," Deacon started, and then added, "no, no, don't get up—"

"The only way you'll let me out-stubborn you is if I loom."

"It didn't work when you outgrew me at sixteen, it's not going to work now."

But this time, when Crick stood behind him, he put his hands on Deacon's shoulders, and Deacon finally took the invite and leaned back.

God, Crick felt good. Deacon had spent his whole life being a self-contained package, doing as many things right as he could, being the best person he could be to help his father keep the ranch running, help Crick grow up to be a man, and then, after Crick grew up too fast for either of their comfort, helping to keep together a family out of spit and sweat and pure need. People looked to him. He'd had one lapse to alcohol, and one into heart disease, and yes, he counted that as a lapse, and he'd sworn as long as his heart kept pumping, he wasn't ever going to let anybody down, ever again.

But it sure did feel good to have Crick behind him, shoring him up when he felt all that self-sufficiency like a steel vault resting on his shoulders. With Crick it was bearable, and for this moment, he succumbed.

Crick lowered his head and nuzzled Deacon's ear, and Deacon smiled and ducked his head, feeling shy, which was something he'd never be able to completely conquer, not even in front of Crick, no matter how many soccer teams he coached.

"Deacon?"

"Hm?"

"How come you don't want my sister to have this baby?"

Deacon stiffened, but Crick pulled him right back into the cradle of his shoulders, chest, groin, and thighs, and Deacon had to fight not to relax completely. There was some shit Crick just didn't need to think about.

"I told you," Deacon muttered, keeping that core of iron rigid in his spine, even when Crick was licking the back of his neck. "She needs to live her own life, raise her baby—"

"You love that baby," Crick reminded him, but Deacon knew that, he was prepared for that spike of pain.

"So do you. But we had our time with her in our house. It's time for them to go be a family. It's only healthy—"

"C'mon, Deacon. You've said this before. That's not your reason, or not"—because he must have felt Deacon stiffen to protest—"your whole reason."

"My whole reason is my own," Deacon said. He made to turn around, to walk away, from the haven of Crick's body, from the comfort he was offering, but Crick held him in place.

"You want to know why I want this baby?" Crick asked conversationally.

Deacon twisted his mouth. "So you can tell people your sister had your husband's baby, and watch them lose their fucking minds?"

Crick chuckled evilly. "Yeah, well there is that, but the more important reason?"

Oh God. Yes. Of course Deacon wanted to know. Seven and a half years ago, they'd made love at Promise Rock for the first time, and Deacon had thought he'd seen everything to see about the boy he'd grown up with. But he'd been wrong—there was a strength and a resolve he'd missed at that moment, and since then, there wasn't a damned thing about Crick that Deacon didn't want to see.

"Thrill me," Deacon muttered, thinking he really was thrilled, and that was damned embarrassing.

"I want to see if he'll have your eyes—"

"It could be a girl."

"—or the shape of your nose—which is unfairly small, you know."

"That's not unfair on a girl."

"Shut up, I'm on a roll. I want to know if he'll have your voice—because you've got this really amazing, unexpectedly deep voice—and be as smart as you, and if he—"

"Or she!"

"You're being a pain in the ass!"

"I'm stating a fifty-fifty chance!" Deacon was laughing now, though, which may or may not have been an improvement.

"Yeah, well, let me finish. I want to know if he *or* she has your ability on a horse or your smile—" Crick started to get choked up, because he was a lot like Benny in that they both wore their hearts on their sleeve. Either way, it was a time to put a stop to this.

"Or my shyness," Deacon interrupted, his voice serious, "or my alcoholism, or my goddamned heart defect. Don't get romantic about my gene pool, Crick, it's more like a pig wallow, and you know it!"

Crick stepped back and gasped like he'd been struck.

"That's *it*!" he screeched, loud enough to make the horses grunt and shift and stamp in their stalls. "*That's* the reason you don't want this baby, isn't it?"

Deacon stepped sideways and kept his vision firmly fixed on Flower Princess. "Go tell Benny no, okay? She didn't seem to want to hear it from me."

"Deacon, turn around, goddammit, and face this like a man!"

Deacon did, and met Crick's furious gaze with his own. He wasn't sure what Crick saw there, although he knew his eyes burned from things he didn't want to say and history he didn't want to rehash, and he knew he was dying, just dying, to unload all his fears, his insecurity, on the love of his life, but he couldn't, because Crick didn't want to hear it and would probably never see it.

Crick took a step back in what seemed to be honest surprise, and then he took two steps forward, and Deacon was suddenly pressed back against the partition between the stalls while Crick held his shoulders and ravaged his mouth.

Oh.

Deacon's surprise gave way to need, just that quickly. He'd needed his friend, his partner, his lover, oh so damned badly, it had cramped his stomach and stopped his words. He'd wanted to lay this down at Crick's feet and let him talk it all better, but talking wasn't Crick's strong point, and now Crick's mouth was over his, rough, invading, taking, and Deacon badly needed him to submit.

And Crick kept kissing, wrapping his arms around Deacon's shoulders, then reaching down, cupping Deacon's ass with his hands. Deacon knotted his hands in Crick's long hair and brought him closer.

Crick moved his hands up to Deacon's shoulders, then to his neck, pinning him in place like his hands alone would keep Deacon from sailing off into space.

Crick's hands stayed, even as Crick pulled away, and their groins were still mashed together, and Deacon wasn't the only one bucking his hips, trying to get closer.

Crick leaned his forehead against Deacon's and caught his wind, his chest crushing Deacon back against the partition with every suspiration.

"I'll tell her we'll think about it," Crick growled and then turned around and started walking away.

"Carrick James—"

"Dinner's in five."

"I don't want dinner, dammit!"

"I knew you wouldn't—that's why I'm sending Benny out with a pity plate. Nobody walks away from my beans!" Crick was moving damned fast for a guy with a game leg, and he was almost at the entrance of the barn by now.

Deacon tried one last sally before he sent in the reserves. "I'll tell her no!" he threatened, and Crick turned back around and shook his head.

"The hell you will!" His face twisted in something *very* like hurt. "Because if you do, you'll have to say to her what you just said to me, and you won't do that, I know you won't do that, because it'll break her heart."

And then he was out of the barn and Deacon was left, wishing the fans were stronger because he was sweating now in his jeans and his T-shirt.

"I was *trying* not to tell him that in the first place," he muttered to Flower, feeling like shit.

Flower munched at the hay in her hayrack and ignored him. Deacon wished the whole rest of the world would just follow her damned example.

BENNY gave him ten minutes.

"He gave me extra pork," Deacon noticed grimly, looking at the plate she'd brought out. Crick's beans were in a little bowl balanced on the top, and the pulled pork sandwich was right next to it, along with a cucumber vinaigrette salad. "He's really serious about this."

Benny threw an old kitchen towel on top of a hay bale and set the plate down, then patted the hay bale next to it. "I put the extra pork on the sandwich," she said tartly, "because I know you skipped lunch, but I didn't want to tell him because he's all fucking moody and shit."

Deacon sighed. "Well, Shorty, you did sort of throw a spoke in our wheels, you know?"

"I know," she said quietly. "Sit down and eat. Don't worry. I won't mention the big scary baby machine problem until you're done."

Deacon straddled the hay bale and picked up the sandwich. God, could Crick cook. He chewed, slowing down enough to savor, and then swallowed and grimaced at her. "Do you think if you and your brother stop cooking for me, I'd learn to cook like this?" he asked.

She rolled her eyes.

"No. You'd live on crackers and soup in a can. That's why we're the ones who cook."

He smiled at her, loving how much she'd grown and how pretty she'd become. God, if he had done one thing right, it had been taking this child in and making a home for her and her baby.

"Yeah, well, if I pass this up for tinned soup, I deserve to starve," he said and tucked in to the food.

Benny talked to him while he was eating, mostly about Parry and soccer, and first grade.

"I feel so bad," Benny said. "We've been promising her that Lila was going to get to go to her school, and now we have to remind her that it's only for a little while." Benny swallowed and looked away, and Deacon tried hard to soldier through his sandwich. "I'm really going to hate to see them go."

"Yeah," Deacon said, deciding the last bite could go to the dog Shane had talked them into adopting. Half cairn terrier and half buffalo, Mumford tended to sleep under the porch for most of the day before busting out around twilight and tearing up the joint. Deacon wiped his mouth with the towel and looked up at Benny, trying to keep the bittersweet out of his smile. "It's a great opportunity, though. You know, I'll miss the holy fuck out of them, but think about it." He relaxed for a moment, because he believed this, and it felt so much better when you were being honest. "He's getting to go out and change the world. He lived some hard times with us here. Don't you wish all the people in government had actually lived some sort of real life?" His mouth twisted. "God, it sure would make the country easier to live in."

Benny nodded. She'd been disgusted when she'd first started to vote—he remembered that. She'd asked questions continuously, "Deacon, this guy's been an administrator for human resources in some sort of management company. What does that do?"

"Bureaucrat," Deacon had said shortly—she'd been studying her ballot information while he'd been polishing the horse's tack. Usually this was a meditative time for him, but that day, it was American Government 101.

"What about 'manager of allocations for publicity'?"

"Corrupt bureaucrat." The oil helped keep the leather supple, but it needed to be wiped from the silver parts. That took a lot of rubbing, and the kids from Promise House didn't always see the need.

"What about 'lobbyist for public work allocations for profitable charities'?"

"Ass-raping bureaucrat who needs to be put down," Deacon said without compromise, and Benny grunted.

"I think he's winning the election."

"Yeah, well color me fucking surprised."

So Benny had grown into politics with Deacon's own prejudices—but also his quiet belief that some good men made the world better for the rest of them. Deacon knew deep in his heart his friend was one of the best men he'd ever met. If anyone could make the world a better place, it was Jon.

And now Benny looked at him bleakly. "Deacon, was there ever a time you wanted to go somewhere besides Levee Oaks?"

Deacon thought about it carefully. "Yeah," he said. This was something he'd never told anyone, not his father, not Jon, not even Crick.

"When?"

He smiled a little. "Shorty, when I was eight, Parrish let me watch the Kentucky Derby on television. We've watched it sometimes, remember?"

"And the Preakness and the Belmont Stakes and...."

He laughed. He didn't watch every horse sporting event, but there were some things even people who had never ridden a horse watched, and those were staples. "Yeah. And they did a spotlight on Kentucky, and why it was called the Bluegrass state, and how their fences weren't made with wire. And they showed pictures, and for a year I would fantasize that I lived in a place where the grass really *was* always greener."

Benny snickered. "Why'd you stop?"

Deacon sighed and stood up. "That's not really a good story," he told her, hating this part of himself.

Benny sighed but stayed seated. "C'mon, Deacon. You can tell me."

Well, why not? He *was* refusing her gift, after all.

"It was the usual," he said shortly, thinking that it never *felt* usual. "Spelling bee at school, there I was, in the fucking lead—won too."

Benny wasn't getting it—but then, he'd managed to overcome most of that bullshit by the time she came around. "Yeah, so...."

"So I finished the bee, ran outside, got sick behind the classroom, spent the next ten minutes coming down from the adrenaline shakes... you know. Was just fucking *me*."

"Oh."

He spared a look up at her. "If I had a desire to do anything else in the world, Shorty—anything, be a lawyer, be a teacher, be a banker—I'd walk to a shrink, dump some Xanax down my throat, and pony up. But the one thing I want to do—*still* the one thing I want to do—doesn't need me to be anyone but me. "

Benny nodded. "But you're coaching soccer," she said, so matter-of-factly that he felt a bitter smile twist his mouth.

"You notice that Collin's coming along for the ride?"

"Yeah, Deacon. But I also noticed you didn't say no. You can meet the challenges you need to. If that's what you're worried about, don't."

Deacon shrugged and picked up the plate. It was warm in the barn, and he was ready to go shower. "It's moot anyway, isn't it, Shorty? I mean, that shit costs money, and horseshit we've got, but money—"

He turned and saw Benny had not followed him as he'd expected, and was instead smiling at him with a sort of evil he'd seen a lot in her brother, but not all that often in her.

"What?" he asked flatly.

"Remember how you had me do your taxes for the last two years?" she asked, her smirk growing wider.

Deacon nodded. "Yeah, you did a good job. We didn't owe anything this year, as I recall... what?" Because that look wasn't going away.

"You got ten grand back."

"What?"

"Ten—"

"Oh my God—"

"Thousand—"

"Are you shitting me?"

"Dollars." And when she finished, her look was implacable and a lot more evil than he'd anticipated.

"Bernice, why would you not tell me a thing like that?" he asked, horrified, and *finally* she had the grace to look embarrassed.

"I didn't think it would work," she said, shrugging. "See, since Promise House is a nonprofit organization, and you pay those kids wages, that's a charity thing. So I declared everything you paid the Promise House kids, and—"

"And the government gave it back?" Deacon wasn't sure whether to be overjoyed or horrified. "But... but that was... I mean, that was legitimate work, I don't—"

Benny shrugged. "Yeah, well, all I know was that they sent us the check, and I was sort of freaked out because, you know. Ten grand, right? Anyway, I went to my accounting professor and double-checked, and he said it was good. So I figured I'd try to make you some money, right, so you're not always dependent on stuff, so I put half in a savings account, and the other half I invested."

Deacon's vision was a little floaty to begin with, and now black leviathans started surfacing in the gray fuzz in front of his eyes. "So you lost it?" he asked, because everyone knew the market had been hamster crap, but Benny shook her head.

"I invested in e-readers," she said matter-of-factly. "They sort of took off. That whole industry is one of the few things that's done well in the past couple of years. The money's doubled."

The leviathans in Deacon's vision threatened to eat his head. He flailed back for a moment and found a hay bale and sat down on it. "That money's yours," he said, his throat dry. "Everything you made with it—"

"It's more than enough," Benny said frankly. "You would have given it to us anyway, so I'm not counting it or arguing, but we've got the money. We could try six, eight times with the money we've got, but I'm telling you, I think we only have to do it once."

Deacon spread his knees and hung his head between them and tried not to look at Benny in betrayal, because she really had been looking out after their best interests.

"You really are just like your brother," he managed. One of the biggest fights he and Crick had ever gotten into had been over almost this exact thing. "God, Benny. You got it all figured out, don't you?"

"Yep," she said perkily. "The only thing I don't know is why you're putting up such a fuss?"

Deacon shook his head and cleared the spots from his vision. "That was a real nice offer," he said firmly, "but I'm going to have to say—"

Benny's next smile was all predatory. "Oh, come on, Deacon. Don't you even want to know if it's possible? Let's just go get the blood test done, you can squirt in a bottle, and we can see if maybe this is possible at all." She batted her lashes, and he glared at her.

"I know you think you're special," he said through half a scowl, "but I *have* said no to you before."

"But you're not going to now," she said, all pretense of flirting gone.

"Why's that?" he asked, thinking he might be able to stand up now.

"Because you know how bad I want this," she said honestly. "And I know how bad you want it too."

Deacon hopped to his feet and shook his head, smiling, because he thought he might have this temptation thing licked. "I want it, Shorty, but it's not your place to give it."

Benny used to dye her hair all these outrageous colors—purple, green, stoplight red. But she hadn't done that in a long time. It was a pretty brown, fine and flyaway, so she cut it layered, making it look like all those sixty directions it went flying were on purpose. She ran her hand through it now and shook her head.

"It's exactly my place," she said, her voice steady. "Who else loves you guys like I do? Who else has the same shape eyes as Crick as well as his stubborn temper? I'm the one person out there who can give you a baby just like Crick—"

Deacon was about to state the obvious, the same way he'd said it to Crick. But when all was said and done, Crick was his, and he trusted Crick with the parts of himself he didn't let anyone else see. He didn't want Benny to see that part, the part that had seen Deacon Parrish Winters at his worst and who loathed the bastard. Crick loved him anyway. He was pretty sure Benny didn't love him quite like that.

"Yeah," he said, feeling trapped. "I squirt in the cup, they count my swimmers. Seriously, what's the harm?"

He didn't like that look of triumph on her face, mostly because he couldn't explain it. But she *did* know him well enough to talk about other things as they left Deacon's place of comfort and walked back up to the house.

Chapter 6

Crick: The Whole of You

CRICK didn't get philosophical much, but when he did, it was about Deacon. He'd thought a lot over the years about his early hero worship of the man he loved, and about the surprisingly strong, if sometimes frail, man who was the whole of the person. Deacon seemed to think it was a big deal, that separation, but about the only thing Crick would have done different in his life (besides not running off to Iraq like a complete fucking moron) would have been to seduce Deacon sooner.

Crick didn't like to think about Deacon—the real Deacon, with the human weaknesses and everything—being alone.

Crick feared—a lot—that he would leave Deacon alone. Not through choice, because the last thing Crick would ever do again willingly would be to leave that man's side, but through the fragility of his own human body, which often gave him a kick in the ass to remind him how close it had come to death, and how some wounds didn't heal.

The day of Jeff's wedding, Crick had been humiliated enough when Shane and Mikhail needed to bring him home because his sister had apparently forgotten him. His arm and leg ached, and he was decent with putting up with pain, but they were actually giving up on him. When he found he was not only in danger of dropping Jeff's specialty-made banana-cream wedding cake all over the thin grass under the oak trees, but also in danger of going pitching down after it, he'd needed help, and he'd gotten as stubborn as Deacon about asking for it.

So yeah, that had been bad, even though Shane, man-mountain that he was, had a way of just wrapping his arm around a person's waist and holding steady so that leaning against him while he helped you into the house didn't feel like a big deal. Crick had no idea that the worst was yet to come.

Deacon arrived a few hours later, tired and subdued, and at first Crick had thought it was because he'd been around all those people, even though they were family. In later years, as their family had expanded, Deacon had gotten better with people in general. Since the heart attack especially, he seemed to have lost some of his fear, which was nice, because Crick got to see him smiling a lot more often when it wasn't just the two of them, but that didn't mean he didn't have his moments. He and Deacon had gone to Parry Angel's first Back To School Night when she'd started kindergarten. They arrived home, and Crick was going on and on about how no one in their right mind should give a five-year-old *homework*, for sweet Christ's sake, and he was *damned* if they were going to make Parry do it if it wasn't going on her mythical "permanent record." He looked up from the bed where he'd been worrying off his boots with one hand to find Deacon had slid down the wall to the floor. His face had gone white, his hands were shaking, and he was apparently in the throes of an anxiety attack that he'd hidden for most of the evening. So, better, yes, but that terror Deacon had always had of groups of strangers was never really going to go away. Deacon was just strong enough never to let it stop him from the things he felt needed doing.

So the night of the wedding, Deacon got home and Crick smiled at him tiredly and asked him what he'd missed. And Deacon shrugged and talked about Jeff's best story, and about how Kimmy had made Shane dance the two-step with her, and how Parry and Lila had both gone into the creek fully clothed, and no one had blamed them, because August? What in the hell had Jeff been thinking? While he spoke, he went quietly about the business of pulling out bread and leftover cold cuts and making Crick a sandwich with avocado and tomato and only the tiniest bit of mayo. There was leftover potato salad, and that was nice too. Deacon brought it into the living room and set up the TV tray. When he was done, he fetched a glass of milk and set it down in front of Crick efficiently, along with the remote. After that, he said, "I'm going to go out and check the horses."

And that had been Crick's first hint that something was wrong.

His second was when Deacon didn't come back for an hour.

Crick fell asleep in front of an empty plate and a rerun of *The Closer*, actually, and when he woke up, he blinked against the long shadows of early evening, feeling a sort of ache and chill of loneliness he was not accustomed to having in his own home. He and Deacon had replaced the couch and recliner, because the old plaid ones were hell on the back and they both had enough physical shit to worry about. The new stuff was navy fabric, and it was soothing *and* comfortable, just the way they liked it. They'd redone the carpeting to fake hardwood and a brown area rug when they did the furniture, and Crick had painted the walls sort of a gentle cream color. It was a nice room—masculine and warm. The cosmetic changes didn't mask the fact that it was the same living room Crick had thought of as home since before he'd come to live at Deacon's. This was the living room where Parrish, Deacon's father, had taught Crick some of his most important lessons, and this was the place Crick and Deacon had met every day and talked quietly in the painful time after Parrish passed away. This room was supposed to be sanctuary. The unexpected sad that permeated it right now could only come from one place.

Crick was struggling to his feet, cursing his damned leg, when Benny and Drew walked in with a rumpled Parry Angel asleep in Benny's arms. Benny, who usually didn't walk so much as she bounded, was quiet because of the baby, and Drew didn't have so much as a hand on the small of her back. She walked through the living room to the back bedroom, not even looking Crick's way, and put Parry down, probably in her party dress and everything since she was back in just a moment. Drew hadn't moved, hadn't acknowledged Crick's presence, hadn't even really seemed to see her go, his attention seemed turned so far inward. Benny returned and looked at the man Crick had supposedly "saved" in Iraq, and said quietly, "I'll put her down. I don't suppose you want to stay and—"

Drew shook his head and cut her off. "I promised to go to Promise House and help unload all the leftovers and get the chairs back to the community center."

Crick groaned to himself, because he'd forgotten to tell Deacon that was their job. Oh, Jesus—just when he thought he was mostly grown up, he went and spaced something like a stupid kid.

Benny nodded and turned away without waiting for a kiss or even looking Drew in the eye.

Drew stopped her with a hand on her shoulder. "I said I'd think about it, Bernice," he said quietly. "I'm just...." His sigh held a whole lot of patience. "I was so damned happy, you know?"

Benny nodded. "So was I," she confessed. "I just...." For the first time, she glanced behind her and saw Crick, who felt uneasy at eavesdropping, in the living room. "It's something I think we should do," she said after a moment. "And don't think for a moment I don't know it's your sacrifice too."

Drew nodded slowly and then bent and kissed her temple. "See you tomorrow," he said softly, and then he lowered his lips almost reluctantly, and they shared a kiss so painfully tender Crick had to look away.

Drew was gone in a moment, his gait so even on the wooden porch Crick could hardly hear the difference made by the prosthetic leg.

Benny sighed and then walked into the darkened living room, turned on a lamp, and then turned on the fan they kept near the window and opened the glass. "It got nice outside," she said absently. "I'm going to turn off the AC and open all the windows."

Crick nodded, thinking that might have been the cold he'd felt in his bones with the long shadows. "Okay." He stood and stretched, pressed the remote button to turn the television off, put the remote down, and picked the plate up with his good hand. "I'm going to go outside and see what's keeping Deacon."

Benny grunted softly. "Yeah," she said. "You do that."

Crick looked at her softly. "Is anything wrong?"

Her face twisted. "No. Yes. Life is all." She sighed, and apparently the melancholy wasn't his imagination, because he saw her eyes glittering in the semidarkness. "I love it here," she said softly. "I mean, I get that I've got to grow up sometime, but I'm really going to hate to leave."

Crick blinked. She and Drew had been talking about her moving into the mother-in-law cottage—he knew that. He thought it was actually probably a long time coming, but he didn't see why that would make his sister cry.

"Go," she muttered. "He's going to want to talk. I'm gonna be pretty fucking useless at it, so you might as well kill two dysfunctional communicators with one painful conversation."

Crick nodded and took one awkward step away from the couch, swearing as his knee wobbled and dropping the unbreakable plate as he opened his hand to catch his weight.

Benny swore too. "Forget it," she sighed, moving around the couch to take the plate and shoo him back. "I'll go get him."

Crick sank down reluctantly, wishing, not for the first time, that his body was as strong as his heart.

When Deacon came in later, Benny had retired quietly already, and if Crick hadn't been so worried about Deacon, he might have asked why. As it was, Deacon had his man face on, the one that said it was all good, and that nothing was wrong, and that if there was so much as a loud noise, Deacon's brittle shell would shatter, and Deacon's sadness would be naked to see.

Crick made a sound, leaning on the end of the couch, and held out his arm. Deacon looked around the living room, and Crick said, "Everyone's asleep. Come here."

Deacon moved cautiously, and Crick had to swallow hard past a dry throat. He hadn't seen that sort of ginger "I'm not sure where to put that" movement from Deacon since Crick had come home from Iraq. Deacon settled in his arms, though, and that was gratifying.

Crick buried his nose in Deacon's hair and smelled sun and sweat and horse.

"Tell me," he said quietly, and Deacon said, "Nothing to tell," at almost the exact same time.

Crick grunted. "I'm feeling really fucking peaceful right now," he said, "so don't make me go nuclear on your ass."

"How's the—"

"Everything hurts, everything's tired, everything fucking aches. It's making me cranky. And you're being the wrong kind of pain in the ass." Crick sighed and laid his head back against the couch. "Please, Deacon. I thought we were past this. I thought you could tell me any—"

"Jon and Amy are leaving before Christmas," Deacon said, and Crick choked on his own glottal of whine.

"Why?" he asked, and Deacon shrugged and settled back a little deeper into Crick's arms. He heard a clicking across the kitchen floor and realized someone must have let Mumford in after his late-afternoon wrestling match with the entire freaking world. The dog, sixty pounds of shaggy red hair with a square head, cropped triangular ears, and a snubbed little snout, made his slow, beleaguered way across the kitchen and into the living room, and then collapsed in his customary place directly under the television. Then he rolled over on his back, closed his eyes, and went to sleep, what was left of his little doggy peter just flapping in the breeze, and he didn't seem to give a shit.

Deacon shook his head, looking at the dog, and a laugh escaped. "God, that animal. I have never seen a complete train wreck so happy in his own skin!"

"He's not a train wreck!" Crick defended, feeling lame. Mumford was some damned good company in the day, when everyone else was out and Crick was keeping house and answering phones. Crick loved his life, loved his role in Deacon's life, but he didn't mind company either, and Parry's hours in school last year had reminded him acutely of how quiet the house got without her and her mother.

"No, no he's not," Deacon soothed.

"So tell me!"

And Deacon did. And he went on and on and on about what an opportunity it was, and how Jon couldn't afford to pass it up, and how their children would grow up with the best schools and in some of the snazziest places, and how Amy could finally use her law degree. Crick let him talk himself out on the subject, actually, because when he was done, and his body was limp in Crick's arms and against his chest, Crick leaned over and whispered in Deacon's ear.

"You got yourself all convinced now?" he asked.

"Convinced about what?"

"That this isn't going to break your heart?"

Deacon took a slow, measured breath that Crick felt down to his own toes. "What kind of friend would I be if I wailed about him moving away?" Deacon asked with dignity.

Crick kissed his ear, and the back of his neck, and his other ear, listening for the tiny hitches of breathing that said this was working.

"Well, you wouldn't be you," Crick conceded, rucking Deacon's dress shirt and T-shirt up from his waist and shoving his hands between the shirt and Deacon's hot skin. Deacon still didn't have a lot of chest hair, but what he had was so damned soft, Crick wished he'd grow more.

"I wouldn't be the person Jon needed," Deacon said firmly, and then he let Crick take him to bed.

CRICK remembered that moment now, as he sat on the couch in his customary place to watch stupid, brain-killing television. Deacon was in his *non*customary place, snuggled back against Crick's chest when normally he sat in the recliner and read something that would put Crick to sleep in a smart minute. That was okay, though. Crick liked it when Deacon let himself be cuddled like this. Anything that put them into proximity this close to bedtime was a definite plus.

Deacon hadn't said much when he'd come back from the barn. He'd washed his plate, sat next to Crick as Crick watched television, and said good night to Benny when she took off to spend the night with Drew.

"What did you two decide?" Crick asked before the door had even shut behind them.

"That I'd squirt in a cup, they could count my swimmers, and we could see if this was even possible," Deacon told him back.

Crick grunted and gathered in his armload of cowboy. "So...."

"Don't get excited," Deacon quashed. "We're doing nothing important. I'm not coming in a turkey baster or anything, we're just seeing if it would work in the first place."

"So you're gonna go to a doctor's office and come in a cup?" Crick asked, the idea of blowing Deacon in a doctor's office holding a certain exhibitionistic appeal that he would not *ever* tell Deacon turned him on.

Deacon chuckled like he wasn't fooled even a little bit. "I doubt it," he said. "When Jon was getting his swimmers counted, he squirted in a cup at home and then just made sure to get it to the doctor's within a certain time. I'm sure that'll be what they do here."

Crick made a little hmmm sound in his throat, clearly disappointed. "Well, I get to help, right?"

There was a shifting at Crick's chest, and Deacon turned his head to look him squarely in the eye. "Would there *ever* be a time when you weren't welcome to help with that?" he asked dryly.

Crick grinned. "God, I hope not." Something loosened in him. Yeah, maybe Deacon would stick to his guns and this baby wouldn't happen. But in the meantime....

"Wanna practice?" Crick asked, his whole body tingling.

Deacon nodded, and before Crick could even move from the couch, Deacon slid to his knees and shoved his hands up Crick's shirt. His mouth, pillowy and hot, suckled tender mouthfuls of the white skin of Crick's tummy, while his tongue tickled the places between. Crick groaned a little and shuddered, finding himself pushed back against the couch with his legs splayed in front of him so Deacon could busy himself at the fly of his jeans.

"Oh God!" Deacon grabbed handfuls of denim at his hips and yanked down, and Crick's cock was suddenly ramped up and full as Deacon slid his mouth over it and sucked, *hard*. "Jesus, *Deacon!*"

Deacon pulled back and laughed at him, a slick circle of spit around his full lips. "There is nobody here in our living room, Crick. We can fuck on the couch if we want!"

He sounded like a little kid, and Crick would have laughed at his enthusiasm if—oh fuck, there he went, taking Crick all the way back into his throat. Deacon's gag reflex was usually hair-trigger, so he must have been *hungry* for Crick, and Crick was... oh God... he was dying... it was....

"Not so fast!" he begged, and Deacon pulled back and licked around his head, then tickled his frenulum and lowered his head sideways and mouthed his balls.

"Fast," Deacon panted, his voice strained just from having Crick's cock in his mouth, Crick guessed. "Fast. First I'm going to make you come, and then I'm going to fuck you, and then you're going to come some more—"

"Oh damn!" Deacon sucked one of Crick's balls into his mouth, licked around it, enjoying the hell out of it while pumping Crick with the other hand. "Oh hell... that's a plan... Jesus, Deacon, stop playing with my balls and suck me, will ya?"

Deacon did, chuckling around Crick's cockhead as he went deep throat again, and Crick's whole body shivered, spasmed, and his vision went black and he came. Deacon pulled away, wiping his mouth with the back of his hand, and grinned up at Crick with such innocent evil that Crick whimpered, wanting more, wanting it suddenly, wanting it *now!*

"You ready for part two?" Deacon asked, and Crick nodded.

"Bed?"

"God, yes. Help me up."

Crick had to take off his boots and his jeans first, or he would have tripped and fallen on his face on the way to the bedroom, and it felt *more* naked being naked in the living room of the nearly empty house than it felt in the shower or even in their bed. But make it to the bedroom they did, Deacon carrying Crick's clothes, which he dumped in a muddle on the floor instead of in the hamper, and then stripped at record speed. He blushed a little and dove for the covers, even though it was still quite warm, both outside and in. After Crick ditched his shirt, he slid in next to him.

And was promptly mauled in the best of ways.

Deacon felt him up everywhere—his shoulders, his chest, his hips. Their mouths met, and Deacon stroked the side of Crick's neck, and for a moment he kept his hand there, his palm resting gently on Crick's pulse, and Crick was comforted, was gentled. Deacon would take care of him. Deacon *did* take care of him, every day. Crick worried about Deacon's health and fussed about the secret, damaged parts only Crick knew, but Deacon, by God, took care of Crick and always would.

Crick rested his game hand on Deacon's hip, and Deacon held still while Crick thrust up against him. Oh *yes*! Something about having the soft skin of Deacon's cock and the hardness inside up against him made this one of the most erotic acts Crick knew.

Deacon moved his hand from Crick's neck and reached down to grab them both together, the almost delirious friction and pressure enough to make Crick bury his face in the hollow of Deacon's neck and shoulders.

"I could totally come just from this," he panted. "If you want to do your thing, do it now!"

Deacon chuckled and nuzzled Crick's ear. "My thing?"

"The thing!" Crick muttered, and now, of all times, he was feeling *shy*. Crick didn't get shy. He hadn't been born with the shyness *gene*. But even after seven years of Deacon knowing his body, the things he felt when they were together *still* made him tremble.

Deacon had a dash of predator in him when they were in bed. "The thing?" he asked, still holding their cocks together, still thrusting his hips. "The thing where I lick you and stretch you and fuck you? That thing?" He was whispering into Crick's ear, his lips brushing the sensitive hollow, and Crick wanted to roll over and spread his cheeks, just from the sound of that deep, sweet voice in the whorls of his ear. The grip and slide of Deacon's hand and cock against his own didn't make that need go away.

"Ye-ess!" Crick's voice pitched pleadingly, and Deacon's weight and his hand disappeared, and Crick rolled over and raised his ass, giving his bad arm a stern caution to be steady for this, he had needs. Deacon pressed the flat of his hand against his back gently, and Crick allowed himself to fall, completely vulnerable, ass sticking up in the air, his head on a pillow and his arms around it.

The cool of the damp cloth was not entirely unexpected—they worked hard and got sweaty and it seemed just courtesy to allow yourself to be freshened up—but when what followed was the heat and the wet of Deacon's tongue? Crick shuddered and groaned, glad his body was pretty much stuck in this position until he flopped sideways, because he was shaking with need. Deacon kept licking, kept probing with this tongue, gentling his hand down Crick's flanks, and still, Crick moaned into the pillow.

Suddenly Deacon's hand came down in a light smack across Crick's backside, and Deacon pulled in a mouthful of the flesh of Crick's cheek before releasing it with a pop. "We're alone in the house," he rumbled. "Make as much noise as you want!"

Crick's want-shivers got worse, and he turned his head to the side and started to beg. "C'mon, Deacon, you've played back there en—*nough!*" His voice pitched frantically, because Deacon replaced his tongue with his fingers and started to stretch. Crick whined a little and wiggled his backside and then gave up pride, because with Deacon, what was pride? "Deac-*on,* stop messing around back there and *fuck me!*"

Deacon ignored him and kept licking and wiggling his fingers, and then, oh holy hell, he moved his hand up to stroke Crick's cock again, and Crick just wanted to—

"*Please*, Deacon!" Crick was desperate by now, because he was going to come again, and he needed Deacon inside him *so damned bad.*

He heard a grunt behind him and felt a sudden chill as Deacon sat up and rummaged under the pillow by Crick's head for the lube. It maybe took him ten seconds, but it felt like forever as Crick lay there, exposed and vulnerable, his tender bits cooling in the air.

Deacon's sudden thrusting invasion stopped his breath. For a moment Crick fought him, because it was unexpected and, well, Crick just fought things, but his body seemed to realize this was *exactly* what he needed. He pushed back against Deacon's cock, and a flush of heat washed the want-shivers away. Again, Deacon gentled his flank, his back and his shoulders. Deacon gave a rumbling sigh like this was exactly where he belonged, and Crick wiggled.

"Deacon?"

"Hmm?"

"Ya gonna…?"

"Gonna what?"

Oh hell. Now the irritating man was just playing with him! "Dammit, Deacon! Fuck me *now!*"

Crick could swear Deacon's chuckle actually quivered through his cock, and then Deacon was thrusting in and out so hard he wouldn't have been able to tell. But that was okay. Deacon knew his sweet spot, knew how fast, how hard (*really* hard!) Crick needed, and every thrust stretched Crick to the point of pain while it hit Crick's nerve central. Crick's whole body shook, and he found his cock with his good hand. He was slick and spurting with every pound to his prostate, and Deacon landed a solid *thwack* to Crick's backside and ordered, "Come, dammit, *come!*"

Crick's orgasm swept over him like a herd of horses, and he took full advantage of the empty house, groaning from his gut into the brightly lit bedroom around them. Deacon howled from the same place in his stomach and thrust hard a couple times before stopping and shuddering and pouring himself into Crick.

"Gonna crush you flat, Carrick. That okay?"

With a grunt, Crick shoved his legs back and fell against the sheets, Deacon on top of him, still lodged firmly up Crick's ass. Crick clenched around him, slippery and still hot inside, and tried to keep Deacon there, loving the feeling of having him actually inside of Crick's flesh, merged and pulsing and one.

Deacon kissed Crick's shoulders, his panting breaths hitting the cooling sweat on Crick's back and making him shiver. Crick turned his head, knowing Deacon would take the hint and nuzzle his cheek to find his lips in one of those kisses over the shoulder that were both comforting and infuriating, because they never got deep enough. Deacon broke it off before Crick's neck could give, and nuzzled Crick's ear.

"You can't do that unless the house is empty," he said smugly, and Crick's lips twisted.

"It's a good thing I'm feeling too good to let that piss me off," he said mildly, sighing into the mattress.

Deacon slid out of him and then rolled to the side. Crick shifted so they were face-to-face, without hardly the space of a pillow separating them. Crick lifted his twisted left hand and skimmed his fingertips over Deacon's temple. Deacon captured the hand and kissed it, and Crick's smile untwisted itself.

"It would be worth it," he said simply. "The sex might not be as noisy, but it would be worth it to have a baby."

Deacon's half smile faded, and his green-hazel eyes were sober. "I didn't know you wanted kids."

"I wanted yours," Crick said. He concentrated hard, made his thumb move, brushed it across Deacon's lips. "More now than ever."

Deacon closed his eyes for a moment, and he pulled Crick's thumb into his mouth briefly and then released it. "We'll see," he said vaguely, and Crick sighed again.

"I know you're planning to say no—"

"You do not know—"

"I do! Deacon, look, let me talk one more time, and then I'll drop it and kiss you again, because we're not done with that whole sex thing, okay?"

Deacon's eyes popped open and he smirked. "You know, I *am* getting older—"

"Don't change the subject and don't bullshit me, old man. Just listen."

Deacon sighed and shifted on the bed, propping his head up on his hand and tucking Crick's hand against his chest. "See? Listening."

"Prick much? Okay, moving on. Here's the thing." Crick took a deep breath and felt nerves slither in his stomach, which was absurd because it was something he said every day. "The thing is, I love you."

Deacon's expression softened. "Do you ever think there's a moment when I don't know that?"

Crick nodded, feeling his eyes heat absurdly. "Yes. Yes, I do. I think there's a moment of every day when you doubt it. I think every morning, right before you wake up, you dream of a world where I don't love you, and when you get up and get out of bed, you spend the entire day being Deacon the fucking Great so that world never happens. And I'm a realist. I get I could fuck you into the mattress—"

Deacon cleared his throat and scowled.

"—or vice versa. Either way, we could be fucking like bunnies, stopping long enough to piss and eat, 24/7, and you'd *still* worry that you had somehow missed the Fucking Champion of the World requirements and weren't going to win in that department either. So I can't take that away from you. I get it. I can try every day, but I get that it might not ever happen. But a baby. God, Deacon, a baby. *Your* baby. That baby wouldn't ever have to doubt. We're both a little broken and both a lot fixed, but we could get this baby thing right, I know it. Can't you have faith in that, Deacon? I know you're worried about your physical beating heart, but Benny's got my heart, and it's strong enough for the both of us. Can't you, just once, have a little faith in the things we love in you and believe enough to try to have this baby?"

His voice cracked in the middle, and, oh wonderful, he was tearing up like a weenie in bed.

Deacon didn't say anything, just bent and kissed his cheek tenderly, and then his temple, where the damned tears were trickling down in a salty, irritating stream, and then the tip of his nose, and Crick blew out a noisy breath.

"Oh, hell," he grumbled. "There goes that whole sex for round two, right?"

"Round three," Deacon said softly, his lips curving up gently. "But who's counting."

"Did you even hear what I said?" And God, wouldn't it be terrific now that Crick had just poured his heart out on the love of his life if Deacon's own insecurities didn't shed all that sincerity like a vinyl purse sheds a spilt drink.

Deacon nodded and went for Crick's mouth this time. Crick obliged him by turning his head and parting his lips and allowing the kiss to deepen. Deacon still tasted wonderful, like sex and warmth and Deacon, and none of that had changed, not even a little bit, from their first kiss that summer day after Jon and Amy's wedding, over seven years ago.

Deacon pulled away from the kiss and then scooted up and kissed Crick's temple. "We'll do the blood tests," he said after a moment. "I'll squirt in a cup. We'll get shit checked out. I'm not committing to anything, but I'll think about it. How's that?"

Crick nodded and smiled and wished like anything that he could cup his ruined hand around his lover's cheek. "That's all I can ask," he said hoarsely, and Deacon shook his head.

"When you say shit like that," he murmured, "I know you're missing the point."

Crick shook his head back. "You're the one who's missing shit, Deacon. Now shut up and kiss me again. This time, I'm *really* going to cut loose."

True to his word, this time, when he came, he let loose with a roar that scared the dog into barking circles around the kitchen for a good fifteen minutes. The two of them spent the entire time alternating between calling the damned dog's name and giggling on each other's shoulders, and Crick never doubted that they were stupid happy in love.

Chapter 7

Deacon: Telling Two Friends

"SO," JON said as Deacon and Shane rounded the corner to pick him up for their morning jog.

Deacon didn't even bother to roll his eyes. Instead, he changed the subject. "You'd better keep running when you move to DC, you know that, right?"

Jon held his hand to his heart theatrically. "I'm shocked, *shocked*, that you'd even think I wouldn't."

Deacon and Shane exchanged glances, and Shane's generous mouth curved up into what, for him, was a truly epic smile. "I'm not gonna be the fattest anymore!" he crowed, and he sounded like a little kid.

Deacon laughed, because Shane *was* funny, if you bothered to track back the things he said to their source, and nodded. "You're not the fattest now," he said sincerely. "That honor is going to be Crick's if he keeps eating his own cooking."

"If you ate it, he'd stop having to finish off your plate," Shane replied, and Deacon cringed.

"We're not starting that shit up again," he cautioned. "Jon, are you going to come with us or not?"

Jon was still standing by his porch with his arms crossed, glaring at Deacon like he used to when they were kids and Deacon wanted Jon to take credit for something Deacon had done.

"Please, Jon, please? If you turn in the spelling bee homework, you'll get to be in the bee, and you love it when people clap!"

"I didn't do it, Deacon. It's extra credit. Mrs. Jenkins will never believe I *did anything I didn't have to!"*

"Yes, I'm going to come with you, but only if you promise to spill the beans!"

Shane's thunder roll from Deacon's left shoulder was comforting. They'd been running together for close to three years now, and Shane could always be counted on for support.

"I'm curious too," he said, and Deacon scowled at him. Traitor.

"Who told you?" he asked Jon, mostly playing for time.

Jon sighed and started running to catch up with them, assuming, Deacon gathered, that he would rather have this conversation running than have it while standing in his yard when Deacon and Shane were practically in the middle of the nowhere road. "Oh Jesus, Deacon. Who *didn't* tell me! What matters isn't who told *me*, what matters is who told *my wife!*"

Deacon grunted. Hell. "Benny?"

"She *is* Benny's best friend."

"Don't tell Jeff or Mickey that," Shane said seriously, and the last three years of running really had been good to him, because he wasn't having *nearly* as much trouble keeping up with the conversation as he used to. "They think *they're* the only ones in the ring."

"Pfft!" Jon managed an eye roll that would have done any gay man proud. "Amy's the one with the ovaries, and from what I understand, *those* are the things calling the shots. So?"

Deacon took two steps on the tarmac, gave a slight leap to one of the better-packed spots of dirt on the side of the road, and then leaped again back to the twelve inches of blacktop on the right of the white line. Behind him, he heard Shane and Jon swearing to themselves as they grappled with the holes in the dilapidated country road, while he continued to dodge. He hoped by the time they were done with this stretch, they'd be ready to drop it.

"He's evading us," Jon puffed conversationally to Shane, and Shane grunted.

"I would too."

"What do you want me to say?" Deacon asked, relieved when the road evened out. "That I want a baby? Apparently it's the worst-kept secret in Levee Oaks. That I'm excited about Benny popping one out for me since it's so convenient and all?" He let a little acid drip from his voice then, hoping to shame the whole rest of the world into minding its own business, thank you very much. "No. It's not going to happen. I don't want anybody putting themselves out for me, *especially* not Benny, who is going to love this child and then have to give it up, and that's not fair to ask of her!" With the last word, he forgot to watch where he was going and set his foot down on the edge of the blacktop, where there was a good six-inch gap between the pavement and the dirt. He rolled his ankle, went sprawling sideways, and banged his elbow on a buried piece of granite as he went down. The world stopped spinning and he found himself staring up at a peacefully hot August blue sky, surrounded by tall grass, and wishing he could just stay there and let the rest of this bullshit go away.

Shane and Jon intruded on his vision, though, and he grimaced.

"Did you get all that out of your system?" Jon asked dryly. "Is your rant over? Do you feel justified now?"

"Shut up."

"I was going to ask if he was okay!" Shane said, reproof in his voice.

From his vantage point on the ground, Deacon saw Jon raise his chin and look their earnest friend straight in the eyes.

"Of course he's not okay," Jon said flatly. "He's bleeding and we're going to have to carry him home, and he's probably agonizing in his little soul about all the reasons he doesn't get the thing he wants most in the world."

"I can probably stand on my own," Deacon said thoughtfully, waiting for the dull red throb in his ankle to recede to see how bad it really was. "And don't either of you forget, I *have* the one thing I want most in the world. I have *two* of them. And the fact that I'm lying here in the dust counting my appendages is the reason you don't ask God for too fucking much, do you both understand me? *Fuck!*"

Jon's sigh sounded long-suffering and heavy. "The ankle's killing you, isn't it."

"Shut up." Because he'd just given it a tentative roll, and the dull red throb had gone sharp and black at the edges and his tetchy stomach had threatened to heave. He had rocks digging into his back and some of the grass he was lying on was stained with oil, and he was pretty sure he saw a used condom in the trash over to his right.

"Would you like some help up, Deacon?" Shane asked considerately, and Deacon managed a smile at him.

"I think that's a fucking awesome idea." He raised his nonbleeding arm. "Can you give me a hand—*up!*"

Shane was a big guy. He was almost as tall as Crick, and his shoulders were wide, and he worked steady and long, helping the kids do the jobs around Promise House, things like working on cars and landscaping and working with Deacon at the horse ranch. He ignored Deacon's outstretched arms, squatted down, and thrust one arm under Deacon's knees and the other under his shoulder, and then slowly stood up again, Deacon in his arms like a damsel in distress.

Deacon closed his eyes, surrounded by a big sweaty man who was not his mate but who had just done what probably every alpha male in the history of all species anywhere had always dreamed of doing.

"I hate you just a little," he muttered, and to his relief, Shane grinned.

"Yeah, I know you do. I couldn't do it if you ate like you should."

"I hate you too," Jon said conversationally. "And if my wife never finds out about this, I'd be a happy man." Amy weighed about ninety-five pounds soaking wet and Jon probably couldn't pick her up. Deacon just *bet* Jon would like to keep this sort of strength a secret. It was *embarrassing*.

Shane winked at Jon and then moved gingerly to a place where the ground was even. Deacon was relieved to feel a shake in his muscles, because being carried home like this would probably get his man card revoked forever. "Would you like me to set you down, princess, or should I put you on my back?"

Jon died—disintegrated into laughter, fell into a helpless, giggling heap into the dust—and Deacon eyed him sourly.

"Set me down," he told Shane. "And then let me hobble home while he stays here to get mauled by the next flatbed that passes." It was eight in the morning and they'd seen three cars, but that didn't mean Deacon wasn't hopeful.

Shane set him on his feet carefully, and Deacon gingerly put his foot down and tried to apply a little bit of weight... and went toppling forward until Shane caught him again. Deacon sighed and then leaned against his friend. He looked off into the distance, where Jon's house sat about a half a mile away. He looked behind him and saw Jon hauling himself off the ground with an insufferable smirk on his face, and then about a quarter of a mile behind Jon, he saw....

"Who's that?" he said, squinting.

Jon turned around and shrugged. "Random teenage girl, smoking," he said, then grimaced. "God, Shane, let's go before she starts a fire or something."

"I don't get people who do that," Shane said, bearing much of Deacon's weight as easily as Deacon hefted a bale of hay.

"Smoke?" Jon asked, and Shane shook his head.

"No. Smoke *and* exercise. I mean, doesn't that just confuse the hell out of your lungs?"

"She's a teenage girl," Jon said, drawing along Deacon's other side. "Her whole body's confused."

"You would know this because…," Deacon baited. Deacon had lived with a pregnant fourteen-year old—he didn't doubt it for a moment.

"Dated 'em, known 'em, am doomed to one," Jon said shortly, and Deacon grinned quietly. Jon's answers were worth the question, even if you knew what they were before he said them. "Now move it, Cochise. That girl is gaining on us!"

Deacon grunted and took a giant one-legged hop, trusting Jon and Shane would both support him as he landed. They did, and the three of them made decent time for being a man down, but still, as they neared Jon's house, a stray breeze caught the smell of tobacco, and they heard her footsteps behind them. There was a pause and a crunch of gravel, and Deacon assumed she was grinding out the butt, and then she drew abreast of them.

She was a pretty girl, Deacon thought as she stepped around Jon, although she was already getting bitter creases at her mouth and eyes. She had a gamine little face and thick reddish hair, and eyes that were wide in the middle and narrow on the end in a familiar shape, and even, in the faded blue, an almost familiar color.

"Missy?" he asked, knowing he'd feel stupid if this passing resemblance made him take the wrong guess. But the girl stopped and turned around, squinting at the three of them.

"Deacon?" she asked, her voice half-hopeful, half-hostile. "Deacon Winters?"

Deacon nodded, then grimaced. "How're you doing, sweetheart? Benny and Crick haven't heard from you in ages."

Missy scowled. "Like they cared!"

Wonderful. "Yeah—" Deacon paused while Jon and Shane helped him hop. "—they cared! We send you birthday presents, Christmas presents—hell, a letter a month and random gifts. They've gone in the post. Don't tell me you didn't get that shit!"

There was a quiet moment, and Missy's "I'm a tough bitch" veneer cracked for a moment. "Did you send me a pink Minnie Mouse polo shirt one time?" she asked out of the blue.

Deacon narrowed his eyes. "Yeah. Last year. We went to Disneyland. Benny bought you guys presents. Why?"

Missy let out a little chuffed breath. "Best Christmas gift I ever got. Figures they didn't get it for me." She took three deep breaths and then scowled at him again. "Tell them thank you," she said, half-angry, half-sad.

Deacon blinked. "Thank you? That's all you got? Hell, we're two miles from our house—by the time you get to where you're going, you'll have passed it! Stop in and tell them hi!"

"Why? So they can tell Bob and Melanie where I am?" she sneered.

Deacon and Shane met eyes for a moment. "That's unlikely," Deacon said, standing securely on the one good foot and depending on Shane to hold him up if he went over. "The last time we had anything to say to them, I put Bob in the hospital."

Missy squinted at him for a moment, and Deacon realized that was about five years ago, and she must have been, what? Ten, eleven years old then?

"You... how did you do that?" she asked, and Jon snorted softly.

"Does it matter, sweetheart? Fact is, you can be safe with Crick and Benny if you want."

Missy's shoulders rounded, and while she ignored Jon, the look she sent Deacon was both speculative and hunted. "No," she said ungraciously. "I'm heading for a place by yours, Promise House. Guy running it is supposed to be a total fag pushover, but he'll put you up for a while so's you can find your feet."

Deacon knew his eyes had gone big, and he was torn between asking her why she wasn't living with her folks anymore and defending his friend, the big doofus who had just offered to carry him two miles.

Jon was choking on his tongue when Shane solved the dilemma for both of them. "Yeah, sure. Promise House is down there, take a left at the cross street, a right at the next one, and you'll see the big wrought iron archway. Don't forget to ask for Mickey. He'll be thrilled to help you."

That made Jon shut up right quick, and Deacon too. "Should I tell Crick and your sister where you went?"

Suddenly Missy narrowed her eyes. "Wait a minute. Aren't you a fag too?"

Well, among other things, she didn't have her sister's quick mind. "I married your brother, Missy. What do you think?"

Now it was Missy's turn to get big eyes. "Oh yeah. Hell. God, I'm dumb. You're not going to tell the other guy, are you? 'Cause I *really* want a place to sleep tonight that I don't got to put out to get!"

"Don't say it," Jon muttered, and Deacon looked at him wryly. No, no, of course not. Deacon would be the last person to suggest to her that just because they were supposed to be gay didn't mean they knew each other.

Besides, it would be kind of moot since the guy in charge of Promise House was the one hauling Deacon's bacon through the weeds.

"I wouldn't dream of it," Deacon said quietly back. He looked at her again and for a moment felt a stab of might've's. Before Crick had come home, when Benny was barely sixteen, Deacon had still been trying to take care of Missy and Crystal in Crick's absence. Missy had been ten the spring Crick had come back, and the last Deacon had really seen of her had been when he and Benny had collected them from their house in the middle of the last big flood. Step-Bob hadn't been doing anything useful, and Deacon had a plan, so the girls had gone up east to higher ground, and Deacon, Benny, Jon, and Drew had tried to defend The Pulpit.

When Amy had come back, the girls had gone to stay with their grandma, and who knew how long *that* lasted? Crick and Benny had sent them things religiously, and even though Crick hadn't had much hope, Benny had harbored some faith that Bob and Melanie Coats were such bad parents that at some point one of the girls would spot the package before the grown-ups did. It was a good plan, Deacon had thought then. Now he realized the only flaw in the plan was that it relied on the girls being as smart as their sister.

"Missy, how's Crystal?"

Missy shrugged. "I don't know. She ran off and got married before she finished high school. Some Mex guy. Mom and Bob didn't think much of that, so she ain't been back."

Deacon grimaced. One of Bob's biggest grudges against Crick was that his father had been Hispanic. Well now, wasn't that a nice finger in the face of the old man? But not the sanest way to choose a domestic partner, that was for sure.

"Nice," he said, and not even *he* could tell exactly what he meant by it. "So, uhm, yeah. Follow Shane's directions and ask for Kimmy—"

"I thought he said Mickey?"

"I'm doing you a favor, and when you get there and meet Mikhail, whom you should *never* call Mickey, you will see why." By mutual consent, he, Jon, and Shane all took a giant step forward in hopes of maybe reestablishing their former rhythm.

The girl gaped after him—her mouth opened wide, and looking over his shoulder, Deacon got a view of crooked, uncared-for teeth, and he tried hard not to ponder on a family that could afford her cigarettes but no dental work.

"Is that all you got?" she asked helplessly, her voice trailing off, and Deacon was going to do it, going to take the extra step and offer her the ride once they got to Jon's house, but Shane jumped in front of him, and for a fag pushover, he sounded surprisingly firm.

"You show us you can get to Promise House and work hard, and we'll show you a clean bed and a safe place to stay."

"Work?" the girl said, sounding dumbstruck. "No one said I'd have to work!"

"Don't answer her," Shane muttered as they walked away, although Deacon had hit his ankle then and he was more concerned with not losing his manly nut and making a sound like a wounded moose.

"Why not?" Jon asked for him. "I'd like to answer her right in the—"

"Yeah, I know you would. I've seen this kid—this *kind* of kid. Everybody got hit in her family but her, and when everyone else took off, she realized she needed to get out of there too. She's going to be manipulative and entitled and unpleasant until she figures out that the world doesn't owe her any favors. Once she gets over that, we'll see if she doesn't have a future."

Deacon grunted. "She would have had a better one if her parents had let her stay with us."

Shane sighed. "I bet she would have, but the person she is now isn't going to see it that way."

"God," he said with feeling. "I don't even want to tell Crick and Benny about this. She was sort of a little snot when she was a kid, but *now* she's...." He shook his head.

"Unpleasant," Jon supplied, and they all nodded. Yes. The life she'd been describing hadn't been a picnic, but the person it had created....

"Here," Deacon said, trying for authority. "Let me put some weight on this thing. If I'm going to give Crick news like this, I'm going to do it on my own two fe-*eet! Fuck!*"

Shane had to catch him for real this time, and God, wasn't that embarrassing all over again.

"We can hobble now," Deacon said meekly when they'd all regained their balance.

"Good," Shane said. "Because if you do that again, I *will* carry you through Jon's front door."

BY THE time they got to Jon's house—where Jon ran in and got the car keys—Deacon's ankle had ballooned up to three times its normal size and turned purple. Jon shoved some ibuprofen at Deacon after they got him in the car, and Deacon leaned back against the seat and tried to think of something soothing that would make whatever Crick said to him feel less like a screeching steel violin and more like a lover who had faith that this giant watermelon appendage was no big deal.

Right. If Deacon had wanted an angel with the voice of symphonies, he should have married Amy when he'd had the chance.

"What in the fuck did you do?" Crick asked as Shane carried—yes, carried, damn him!—Deacon through the door.

It was too bad he was pissed, because he was doing laundry today and wearing his old holey basketball shorts and a faded red T-shirt that was falling right off his body. He looked cute and sexy, and when his shorts rode up, you could see his equipment through the thin spot in his underwear, but his shorts were *not* going to ride up when he had his hands on his hips like that.

"I rolled my ankle and alienated your youngest sister," Deacon snapped, out of patience with his day. "Put me on the back of a horse and let's see if I can raze the town!"

Crick came forward and cleared the laundry off the couch so Shane could deposit Deacon there. "Oh hell no. You're staying here until I'm sure you can't damage anyone but yourself. How in the hell did you manage to meet up with Missy?"

"Sheer fucking chance," Jon said sourly, because God forbid Jon ever not be included in something. "He rolled his ankle and we were helping him back to my place when she passed us up."

"Deacon!" Crick exclaimed, giving Jon maybe half an ear. "We're going to have to get this X-rayed—"

"It's not broken," Deacon said stubbornly. It hurt, yes, but he knew the feel of broken bones, and this was not it.

Crick snorted softly. "Like I'd trust your opinion now. And you are *bleeding* on my couch!"

"Oh hell!" Deacon had forgotten about that. Jon had given him a towel, and it had sopped through. "I just need some gauze and some ice and—"

"And a doctor!" Crick snapped, and he turned to Shane apologetically. "I hate to ask you to do this, big guy, but—"

"No worries," Shane said, grinning. "Mickey will like this story."

"You don't have to carry me," Deacon snapped, shooing him off. "You can just help me down the steps—in fact, I think we've got some crutches and some ace bandages and—hey, wait, Crick, you can't leave to take me to the doc. You're in charge of the afternoon water!"

"I'll do the afternoon water," Jon said, "and Shane will help me. Crick, you take Deacon. Deacon, you tell Benny where you're going—hey, see if you can jizz in a cup while you're there. They can count your swimmers and everything—one-stop doc shop, it'll be awesome."

Deacon blinked at his best friend, the man he'd loved like a brother since he was five. "I can't believe I was afraid I'd miss you," he said with feeling, and Jon flashed that white smile and tossed back his surfer-blond hair.

"You will *pine* for me, Deacon Winters. Your soul will shrivel up and die without me. Now get the fuck out of here and go put a bandage on that thing—it's, like, growing as I'm watching it, and it's really grossing me out."

"Yeah," Deacon returned, still fuming, "it would take more than that to put you off your feed."

"Yup!" Jon walked away from them so he could root through the refrigerator. "Crick, since you guys are going, tell me you've got some leftover beans. I need some sustenance before I take care of Deacon's critters. Shane, you're gonna help me, right?"

"You need to help him," Deacon said, loud enough for Jon to hear. "It's been so long since he's been to the stables, I'm not sure he remembers which end of the critter to feed!"

"There's plenty of kids from Promise House here," Shane said mildly. "Lucas is supervising today. We'll just go out and lend a hand. But I can get you to the car, Deacon. Crick can drive up to the ER and put you in a wheelchair—it'll be easier that way."

Deacon looked at Shane appreciatively as he pretty much manhandled Deacon back out the door and down the porch stairs to the car.

"You are damned helpful in a crisis," Deacon told him sincerely. "Jesus, Shane—you're like a superhero."

Shane grinned, as gleeful as a child. "That's what Mickey says about you! Now call us to let us know how you're doing—and don't forget to tell Benny you're going to have that baby!"

Deacon's jaw dropped as Crick said, "Really?" and suddenly Deacon's day got a whole lot more confusing.

"I DON'T know why he said that," Deacon said a few minutes later as Crick drove his little sedan way too damned fast. "We hadn't even really started talking about it when I rolled my ankle."

Crick growled. It was low and intense, like a feral dog. "Nrrrrgrrrrnrrrrr...."

"I'm sorry about the ankle."

"Are we going to have to wrap you in cotton wool?" Crick asked, irritated. "I swear, I thought when I got back from Iraq it would be different, but look at you. Horses are falling on you, stepping on you, throwing you—"

"That was once!" Deacon's pride still stung. Damned SpongeBob Star. Moodiest animal he'd ever had on his ranch, and that included Shooting Star.

"And just when I think, 'Hey! It's a run! He's safe!' you find a whole new way to scare me to death!"

"It's a sprain! People get hurt all the time!"

"No, you get hurt all the time and you just raise the average!"

Deacon thought about that for a minute. "That's not possible," he said doubtfully. "I think you're overreacting."

"No! I'm reacting just fine! You get hurt all the fucking time, and when it's not rolling an ankle or getting pummeled by a giant horse that thinks it's a poodle, it's having a heart attack—"

"That was not my fault!" Deacon snapped. God, two and a half years of good behavior and you'd think the guy would cut him some slack. "And it's not the point!"

"It's *exactly* the point!" Crick snarled, stopping with too much force at a stop sign in the middle of nowhere. Deacon let out a yelp when he tried to brace himself against the floor, and Crick slammed his foot onto the gas pedal while pounding on the steering wheel in frustration. "*Shit!*"

"Carrick, either calm down or pull over to the side," Deacon muttered. It would have been an order, but damn, he was queasy with pain.

"I'll calm down," Crick muttered. "I'll calm down when you agree to this baby thing, *that's* when I'll calm down."

"I don't know that the baby and my damned ankle have anything to do with each other," Deacon said, blinking, because that was some logic that did not track.

"Oh, sure you don't," Crick said bitterly. "That's because when I was in Iraq, you were getting all Zen and shit about what would happen if *I* died. But I came home, and you were all happy! And people depended on you, and you had a *family!* And that whole time, we were all worried about *me*, and the fact is, the gods fucking have it out for you, and what am I going to do if you just up and d… disappear."

Deacon swallowed. "You have the same family I do," he said, and Crick shook his head. "You do—"

"I *know* I do! But I want a little piece of *you*. Do you get that? You've got my sister, and Parry, and any children she and Drew have—I've got bupkes!"

Deacon kept the corners of his mouth from turning up, but it took an effort. "You'll have a useless horse ranch full of overgrown puppies and a shit-ton of debt!" he corrected, and Crick rolled his eyes.

"The debt is manageable, the horses will probably all go tits up without you, and you are, once again, missing the fucking point!"

"Well if someone was trying to stab you in the ass with your own death, you'd be dodging that fucker too!" Deacon snapped, sweating, in pain, and out of patience.

"Oh if *only* your death was stabbing me in the ass. You keep trying to club me over the head with it, Deacon! You want me to calm the fuck down? *Stop getting hurt!*"

"Yeah, but that has nothing to do with—"

"*Or* let's stop this stupid pointless argument and you could just see things my way."

Deacon couldn't help it—*that* made him laugh. It was irritated, savage laughter, but it was laughter. "That is the *worst* way to get what you want in the history of fighting!"

Crick had his mouth open to say something, and then he shut it, took a deep breath, and said, "Yeah. Yeah, that was pretty lame."

Oh no. If Crick was thinking straight and calming down, that meant Deacon was *really* in trouble. "Look," Deacon said, backing down for a moment too. "Maybe we just worry about the ankle, and *then* talk about the baby? Or, you know, even better, run the tests and the blood work, and *then* worry about the baby. I hear what you're saying—or, you know, trying *not* to say. I…." He sighed. It felt so mean, really. So damned petty to remind Crick of all the failings pumping through his blood. Crick thought he was worth something—really, who wanted to shit all over that? "I don't mean to keep worrying you, Crick. I think this all might be easier if you could just… I don't know. Forgive me for the heart attack and take stupid shit like this in stride."

Crick sighed and took a right down Watt, where traffic picked up. "Yeah. You forgave me, I guess. It's only fair."

Deacon laughed a little. "Generous of you," he said dryly, and Crick was too intent on traffic to scowl at him, but Deacon knew his narrowed eyes weren't for the Lexus in front of them.

"Don't say it!"

Say what? That Iraq had been Crick's choice—shit-for-brains though it might have been? And that Deacon had, at no point in his life, elected to inherit a weak heart?

"I wouldn't dream of it." Deacon sighed, and as some of the adrenaline eased out of him, so did some of his defense against the damned ankle. He leaned back and closed his eyes and wished he was on a horse.

IT TURNED out to be a sprain, just like Deacon thought it would be. When he got out of X-ray, Crick was there with a big cold cup of iced tea and a bagel sandwich, since it was lunchtime and Deacon hadn't even had breakfast.

"'Preciate it," Deacon said after a long draught of tea. They were lodged in a corridor, Deacon in a wheelchair, Crick in a waiting room chair, and Deacon was feeling the need for a nap—probably thanks to all the ibuprofen Jon had shoved down his throat.

"You know," Crick said conversationally, "I'm not ever going to get over the worry."

Deacon paused in the middle of a bite of his sandwich, took it anyway, and chewed thoughtfully. He swallowed and said, "Me neither. Do you think, maybe, that's part of the risk of loving someone?"

He was unprepared for Crick's triumphant smile. "Yup!" Crick crowed, throwing back his head to get the brown hair out of his eyes. "Yup! And *that's* what parents have to go through every day."

Deacon leaned his head back and groaned. "I walked right into that one, didn't I?"

Crick took a bite of his own sandwich. "Mm-hm," he said and then swallowed too. "But I'll leave you alone now, since, you know, you're an invalid and everything. But once we get you on crutches, it's on again."

"You mean it's going to get worse than the fight we just had?" he asked with a certain amount of fear. "Because Drew's old apartment is still cleared out—I could always go sleep—"

"Try it, and you'll find a horse shitting on your cot while you sleep," Crick said dangerously. "There is one place you get to lay down at The Pulpit, and it's not the damned barn."

Deacon sighed and looked mournfully at his naked propped ankle. He was still wearing his old running shorts and T-shirt, and so was Crick. Of course, he should have learned years ago the hospital was the last place you got to keep your dignity.

"I would give my left nut," he said, "to have yours and Benny's optimism, do you know that?"

"Family trait," Crick said and took another bite of his sandwich.

"No." Deacon thought about Missy. "No, no, it's not."

"How was my little sister?" Crick asked, and Deacon glared at him.

"God, would you *stop* reading my mind? It's irritating!"

Crick's laugh was evil. "Nope! Won't. Refuse to. I've earned it. It's like one of those magic superpowers. You live through the fear and the anxiety and the oh-hey-he-fucks-like-a-god, and if you do it with your sanity intact? You get to read his mind! You know, like the little gold coin in the video game? So, spill. And don't spare my feelings."

Deacon raised his eyebrows and swallowed his next bite of sandwich. "So you already know she's a flaming twat?"

Crick spit his sandwich out, and Deacon grunted a little, appreciating his discomfiture. Remorse set in almost immediately, of course. It really wasn't in him to speak so badly of people. "I'm sorry, I shouldn't have—"

"No," Crick sighed, "I'm sure that was accurate. She... I mean, she was a burden on everyone, you know? On me, then Benny—didn't give us a lot of time to foster a personality."

Deacon's remorse hit him a little harder. "You were so young, Carrick. It wasn't your fault. I'm sorry. I shouldn't have been... cruel."

"Yeah. You should have been Saint Deacon when you were in pain and dealing with an obnoxious teenager." Crick took another bite and chewed morosely. "Besides. She was a flaming twat when she was eight. She used to tattle on me to Bob—or better yet, break shit and then blame it on me. I mean, I'm sure there's some deep heartbreaking psychological reason for it, but it didn't make it any more of a thrill to live there, you know?"

"God—what a fucking waste," Deacon muttered. "You and Benny— there's so much good in you. I hate to think... man, so many ways to fuck up a kid."

Crick grunted. "And so many ways you wouldn't. See, you keep worrying about *your* gene pool. Benny's got alcoholism too—I don't hear you bitching about *that.* And we both have Melanie.... God, I have no idea what you'd call that. Codependency? Passive-aggressive chromosomal clusterfuck? Doormat syndrome? Whatever—it's not pretty. But I'm betting with you for a father, this baby's got a chance to grow up happy."

"*This* baby?" Deacon argued. He was about done with this sandwich. God, what he'd give for a Quarter Pounder with Cheese and bacon. "You're talking like it's a done deal."

"It is," Crick said, and he sounded like a man who had made up his mind.

"I'm sorry, don't I have something to contribute to this?"

"Yeah, but when I get you naked, you'll do that on your own. I just need to get your head in the right place."

Deacon sighed. "If I promise to listen to this next bit quietly and with an open mind, can we have red meat for dinner?"

"No. That's how people who are a little bit chubby get really overweight. They reward themselves with their addictions. You can't give yourself an ice cream sundae for not eating a Quarter Pounder with Cheese, and you can't give yourself a Quarter Pounder with Cheese for not being a righteous stinking pessimist."

"That's an addiction?" Deacon said, honestly surprised. "I thought it was just a personality defect. And there. You can add another to the list."

Crick's eyes narrowed. "We will eat nothing but soy cake for a week. Or I will beat the smart out of your ass. Make your choice, but if you don't hear me out, it's going to be dire."

Deacon was abruptly tired of the bait and chase. "I'm all ears," he said after a moment. He looked up and down the corridor, but apparently a sprain didn't lend itself to anything that urgent, because no one was coming. Deacon reached out across from him and tapped Crick on the knee. "Please, Carrick. Say what you were going to say. I promise I'll behave."

"Your father, bless him, was not a great planner. You are." Crick waited a moment, probably to see if Deacon was going to be okay with that. Deacon was. Parrish had a vision for The Pulpit, but he hadn't been great at fitting his wife or his son into that. He'd changed after Deacon's mother had died, but still, he'd dropped dead of a heart attack when there *must* have been symptoms. There had been for Deacon. And he'd left The Pulpit in a precarious financial situation, so when things got rough, Deacon had no safety blanket. No. Parrish had been a wonderful father and a good, good man—but he hadn't been a planner.

"That's real," Deacon said levelly. Nothing was going to hurt the memory of Parrish Winters.

"Yeah, it is. And part of the upshot is that you're *always* thinking about the future, and our past has been rough, and I know it. So you're basing your future on what you know of the past. But you're not looking at the *recent* past. Sure, you're looking at two young heart attack victims, you and your dad. But you're *not* looking at all the science we have to deal with that—and it's more than that. You're looking at two alcoholics, you and your mom. But you're not looking at all the things you can give a child that will help that not happen, including some love and support through things like grief and some warning about how bad it can get. You're looking at this baby being raised by one parent—you or me—but you're not looking at the fact that I haven't done anything stupid in over five years, and your doctor promises that you have a very good chance at a long life. So you're planning for the future based on a bad past, but you need to be planning it based on a whole lot of blessings."

Crick closed his eyes and swallowed before he stood and crumpled his sandwich paper in one hand. That done, he moved a little closer to Deacon's chair. His game leg wouldn't let him squat, but he reached down for Deacon's hand and Deacon gave it, because it was Crick.

"Please, Deacon? I get that you need time to think, and I promise to give you some space, but... just stop fighting this, okay? If I can get everybody to get off your back, would you *think* about it and stop fighting it?"

Deacon nodded and smiled a little. "Yeah, Carrick James. Hell, if you could stop fighting the world, anything's possible."

Crick smiled at him, looking like the boy Deacon had fallen in love with. The smile deepened, widened, crinkled his eyes, cut grooves into his cheeks, and settled quietly all over his body.

That easily, Crick was the man who had come back from the war and who had stood solidly at Deacon's side for the last five and a half years.

Deacon swallowed and squeezed Crick's hand.

Yeah, Crick had earned better than Deacon's eternal pessimism. Deacon would try to live up to that.

Chapter 8

Mikhail: Sweetie, Bitchy, Grumpy, Doc, and Slutty

MIKHAIL sat at the little kitchen table, drinking more coffee than he knew what to do with in order to wake up. He'd eaten breakfast with the children in the larger dining room and overseen cleanup, and the coffee was his reward to himself—the Faire had been too hot and too crowded, and he was nearing thirty, and his body didn't react to that big clot of dancing in the marrow-boiling heat the way it had when his cop had first seen him five years before. The kitchen was pristine—clean, with new white tile and a stainless steel refrigerator and countertops. All of the appliances were big, shiny, and impersonal, and the floor was easy to clean. The plastic red-checked tablecloth was too, but the color at least was warm, and a big window opened up to the front lawn, with an epic view beyond of the absolute nothing that was Levee Oaks when it went unwatered in the summer, and that was warm too. All things considered, it could have been worse. So there he was, enjoying just a clear mirror fragment of peace, when even *that* was shattered.

"I don't give a *damn* what you *think* the little man said, you don't just shove your shit at me and tell me to wash it! That machine don't have a black people only sign and I ain't your nigger, bitch!"

Sweetie had made a name for herself at Promise House. She worked hard, kept quiet, and kept her nose clean. She'd do about anything to be able to go to Deacon's and pet the horses. Of course, she did all the other things too—everything from shoveling shit to washing out the troughs—as long as she got to ride Crick's horse at the end.

So, for Sweetie, chores, yes.

People, no.

People she didn't talk to much. Yeah, she'd been on the streets. Yeah, her moms had kicked her out 'cause her boyfriend wouldn't stop hitting on her. Yeah, sure, her grandmother had died and she'd ended up on the street before social services could do jack. So she'd put out for men, but hell, she ate, she was alive, who gave a flying fuck? Just let her do that thing, that quiet thing, that made people leave her the hell alone, and she would do whatever the hell she needed to. (She offered to put out for Shane, but since he revoked her Pulpit privilege for two days after that, she never put her body on the line again.)

So whatever was wiggling its gnarled claw up her ass at the moment, it had to be sharp, bony, and unwelcome.

Mikhail was afraid he knew exactly what it was.

"Sweetie, Missy, in here right now!" he snapped. His first dance instructor had been an old-school Russian, the kind who regarded children as chattel until they proved they could dance for him, and even then they were only as good as the muscles and sinews that bore them up. Mikhail had taught small children for much of his adult life, and he had never, not once, invoked his old dance master when teaching them how to point tiny feet and pudgy ankles.

But every now and then, as he dealt with the damaged adolescents at Promise House, he found the lessons his old dance master taught him had one useful application after all.

He could make these ungratefully tall children shake in their pretty sneakers should they need the voice of God to thunder in their ears.

Missy stalked in with squared shoulders and a fearsome scowl, her eyes shifting left and right as though she were looking for an angle. In general, she looked angry and sneaky and all of the things Mikhail had come to loathe about the girl in the past few days.

Sweetie slunk in with her arms crossed, looking at him from under lowered brows, her long body collapsed and slouching bonelessly in on itself as she waited for the verdict of the most feared authority figure at Promise House.

"Missy, I said you were to *ask* her how to use the washer and drier. If that was not the message you relayed, that is considered a lie."

Missy rolled her eyes. "I misunderstood."

"You lied," Mikhail said unequivocally. "You lied, and you tried to get another to do your work for you. You were scheduled to leave today and join in the shopping expedition to Wal-Mart, since you have no clothes of your own, but you will need to give your sizes to Kimmy, and she will shop for you."

"You can't do that!" Missy gasped, horrified. "That bitch don't know what I'm gonna wanna wear—"

"That 'bitch' is a friend of mine and my sister-in-law. You keep a civil tongue in your head while you are speaking to her." Mikhail frequently called her "cow woman," but Kimmy knew it for his own prickly way of saying "I love you." Missy did *not* mean the same thing Mikhail did. "And before," he cautioned, holding up a hand, "before you protest, asking me what I'm going to do about it, you may remember, upon your first night here, you signed a contract to obey the rules as we have set down. Part of that contract was no lying. Part of that contract was to be respectful of your roommates and the staff. So far, you have done swimmingly, no? Do you remember that contract?"

Missy swallowed, and her pale face—she had a hint of ginger in her hair and one of those redheaded complexions that blotched, as opposed to Benny's more sallow complexion that tanned nicely—grew patchy and flushed as she remembered what had been put in big letters, in case the more hardened of the children were not grateful for room, board, and a hand up in the world.

"It says you can place me in foster care or juvie or a homeless shelter or back home if you don't think we'll work out here," she said, and she did not look happy about that. Well, good. It was the first sense she had shown since she'd arrived.

"Do you remember some of the other things that could get you removed from Promise House?" he asked, implacable and angry.

"Fighting, drinking, smoking, tricking, drugs, sex, stealing, hurting the animals, destroying shit, skipping our counseling appointments...." She trailed off, and for the first time, Mikhail saw some meekness in the girl, which was good, since she'd shown nothing but hubris to date. "Generally not getting along." She swallowed, and Mikhail took his first real breath around her since her first day.

Her first day, she had arrived and demanded to see Kimmy or Mickey or whoever the fuck could give her a bed.

She had been left to sit outside on the porch until they could gather the contract and the appropriate documents. Most of the children were taken inside to where it was air-conditioned, but when Mikhail found out she'd been cautioned by Deacon not to call him Mickey, he made his own rule. (The fact that Shane had *told* her to call him Mickey was almost code. Mikhail could read his lover by now. This child needed not to be coddled and needed to be taught respect. Well, that was Mikhail's job. He was good at it.)

In the time it had taken to gather her paperwork, start a file, and activate the computer tablet to get her in their system, she had almost set the porch on fire by neglecting to put out her cigarette properly in the fulminating August heat.

When Mikhail had turned the hose on the porch, he'd made sure to give her a face full of water as well, as he had seen her brother do once to Jeff and Collin when they too had been acting like spoiled children.

They had taken it with more grace.

Missy had screeched and come roaring at him with fists and fingernails flying. Mikhail stood his ground, looking forward to one solid punch in self-defense. He was not squeamish about hitting women. If Lucas hadn't grabbed her around the waist and put her in a three-point restraint right there on the porch, Mikhail might have had the satisfaction of landing that punch too, and in the way of all feral pigs, this one might actually respect a predator mightier than herself.

Alas, Lucas *had* restrained her, and while her face had been pushed into the newly stained wood, Mikhail had squatted down and calmly explained what would be expected of her at Promise House.

The incident with the cigarettes and the restraints would not be counted against her, he said, feeling magnanimous, since she had not known the rules until this exact moment.

That had been the first day.

The second day, she'd slapped their poor little recovering drug addict, scratching his cheek until it bled, because he'd dared to ask her if she had done crank. He'd only been, he'd tried to explain to Mikhail, trying to encourage her.

"It's so hard, the first days," he'd sniffled, and Mikhail had actually put an arm around Eddie's shoulder. He'd worked so hard. He'd been with them for nearly two years, and he'd worked hard every day at staying clean. Mikhail worried for him. He would be exited in a year, and he would not be ready. Was there not some way to keep him there? Could they not find a cot for him, a way for him to stay at Promise House and live?

Mikhail knew which children would survive on their own, and Eddie was not one such. To see him destroyed by Missy's vicious temper... well, Mikhail had not liked her when she'd arrived.

When she'd stolen Emily's lipstick on day three, Shane had put her in the white room—a time-out room with the rules of the house written on the wall in indelible ink—for two hours. He'd tested her on them when she'd emerged.

If Mikhail had been there, instead of at the Faire in Gilroy, he would have petitioned for her to be removed right then and there.

But he hadn't been, and she'd kept her nose clean for days four and five.

This was day six.

Shane was currently sleeping in, because Mikhail had insisted, because he had stayed up pretty much for seventy-two hours during the weekend Mikhail had been gone. One of their counselors had been sick, and Shane had slept over to fill in for her. None of them slept well at Promise House—too many things could go wrong—which was why there was a rule and a rotation schedule, and generally, three days was too many.

When Mikhail and Kimmy arrived home only to find Lucas cooking dinner and Shane asleep on the couch, Mikhail read the entire staff the riot act.

He did this on occasion. It never occurred to anyone there he was not an actual employee, more of a volunteer. People didn't bother him with trifles; they did what he said and he was content.

So this morning, hearing Missy treating Sweetie with that much contempt? No. There was nothing good in that, and Mikhail would *not* let it slide. But she seemed to have learned *some* humility. Maybe enough to allow her to stay.

"Yes," he said, keeping his usual lip curl. It would not do to express hope. "You may go now to your room. Be pleased to keep your hands to your own belongings, and maybe spend some time writing an explanation to your counselor for today's incident."

"My *counselor!*" Missy protested. "But Kimmy's such a—"

"Disciplinarian," Mikhail said with a straight face. "Yes, my dear. She is. And you need that at this moment in your life, or you would, perhaps, be able to do laundry without getting into trouble. Which reminds me, go finish what you were doing in the laundry room while I talk to LeLauna. Thank you."

Missy glared at him, possibly wishing his entrails were being slowly roasted in the fires of purgatory while he watched. He was not interested in her petty schemes of revenge.

He looked at LeLauna and allowed his eyebrow to rise.

"Sorry, Mick—uhm, Mikhail," LeLauna said automatically, and he repressed a smile.

"That is wonderful. Perhaps you could tell me what you have done?"

LeLauna straightened up for a moment and tried to think. "I, uhm... I used foul language," she said proudly, and Mikhail rubbed at his mouth so he didn't smirk.

"This is true, because none of us here swear even a little, am I right?"

And LeLauna *did* smirk. "Kimmy's got a mouth like a sailor fucking a trucker," she said, rolling her eyes, and now Mikhail *did* smile, because it was true. Yes, the counselors tried not to swear so much in front of the children, but that did not mean they did not swear at *all.*

"Yes, well, she says all of the words her brother does not," Mikhail said staunchly, although Shane had been known to let the F-bomb slip out on occasion as well. "But that truly is not my point."

"And I'm waiting here!" Sweetie said, her narrow eyebrows arching.

"Don't be impertinent. The point is, she would have tried to con anybody. Black, white, yellow—there was no reason to respond with your race."

She flinched back. "It was just an expression—"

"Yes. And you are not in trouble for it. But there are so many troubles here in the air, yes? When that trouble is here, we should address it. Before it comes to visit, let us hope it does not visit. That is all I'm saying. If *she* had used that unfortunate word, we would be finding another place for her. Let us not introduce it into this place. It is like any other...." He fumbled, his English deserting him when he needed it most. "I do not let Dallas, Tony, Eddie, or Cooper say 'faggot', although they are gay. It opens a door, and beyond that door lies monsters."

She nodded carefully. "I hear you, Mikhail. If I use it, she can use it, and I don't like the way she'd use it."

"Yes. You are very clever. You will need to think of better words, is all."

There was a moment there when the corners of Sweetie's mouth pulled up, and Mikhail caught his breath. She was intensely beautiful when she smiled.

"I hear you. Can I go get my clothes out of there? 'Cause if she spits in them or somethin' gross, you're gonna wanna get rid of *me* next."

Mikhail did not correct her, but he did nod in dismissal and sink back down to the kitchen table to contemplate his neglected coffee.

He was washing his coffee cup in the sink when Kimmy came in. If they were performing, Mikhail would say she was playing a fairy or an elf sneaking in the woods—he recognized those graceful, quiet steps. They were part of the thing that could make someone with a mouth that sounded like a sailor fucking a trucker still seem graceful and elegant.

"I know you are here, cow woman," Mikhail said with a tired smile. "You are making a run to Wal-Mart, are you not?"

Kimmy grimaced. "God, I wish we could afford somewhere else."

Yes, well, you did not boycott the place that fed you, even if they stood against everything you stood for. "And I wish food fell down from trees. Why are you tiptoeing in like one of the outside cats? What have I ever done to you to make you think I cared, one way or another, if you are there behind me?"

Kimmy laughed, because they played this game of insult, and Mikhail was comforted. He was not as easy with all the bitterness Missy stirred up in him again as he used to be. He was happier now that he'd left most of that behind.

"I'm not tiptoeing because I'm *scared*, Mick... Mikhail," she said, catching herself up at the dreadful nickname that he loathed unless her brother was saying it. "I'm tiptoeing because I *want* something from you."

She said it with a smile, but her lower lip was out, and her round brown eyes were shiny, and her next step was not graceful at all. In fact, it was a little clumsy and it trembled, and Mikhail was abruptly concerned.

"Sit down, Kimberly, before you fall down. My God, I'm glad we are not performing—you would wrap those cow thighs around my neck and strangle me dead. What is the matter?"

Kimmy sagged into the chair pathetically, and Mikhail came up out of his own ruminations enough to realize she was wearing Lucas's old cargo shorts *and* T-shirt, like she was trying to minimize her body by swimming in those outrageously large clothes.

Like she was trying to hide.

He sat down next to her and bumped her shoulder. "Are you going to tell me or let me guess? I am *so* good at guessing the ways of people with breasts, am I not?"

Kimmy snickered quietly. "Oh, heaven forbid." The laughter died quickly. "It's... it's girl stuff," she said.

Mikhail resisted the urge to run out of the room screaming.

"Wonderful. Will I start menstruating from the telling of it? Why are you not talking to Amy and Benny?"

It was Kim's turn to grimace. "Because Amy and Benny are good girls," she said simply after a moment. "You know. *Good* girls. And you weren't a good boy. And that makes a difference."

For a moment Mikhail just blinked at her stupidly, because as much as he called Kimberly cow woman, he thought of her as the best of women. And then he got it.

"You mean you were a slut?" he asked, and her laughter was reassuring.

"Yeah, Mickey. I was a coke whore—and you knew me when."

Mikhail did remember her when. He had worried for her. She had been—like her brother, actually, very much so—so hungering for love that she attracted the worst people. Unlike her brother, Kimmy hadn't had the moral center, the solid sense of right and wrong, to hold her steady and give her purpose. And like Mikhail, when he had slid from dance to drugs to the streets at the age of fifteen, she had lived and breathed a profession in which it was better to be high than even a pound above the minimum weight to sustain life.

He swallowed hard, suddenly unwilling to banter with names. Not with Kimberly, who could flip him off while she was knitting a sweater for her brother.

"You were lost, Kimmy-love," Mikhail said, borrowing Jeff's pet name for her because it was better than cow-woman. "We were all so terribly lost. Amy and Benny—they know the worst of me. I am sure they know the worst of you. They still love us."

Kimmy looked away. She had such a pretty face—a high forehead that supported a fringe of bangs and the kind of smile that showed just a hint of her even white teeth when she wasn't planning on it. "Benny thinks Deacon's going to go through with it," she said randomly.

Mikhail grinned. Yes, Shane had come home talking about Deacon, who—characteristically—had injured himself when upset.

"So," Mikhail had asked his great lover as he'd come out of the shower that morning, "how did you help Deacon to the car?"

"Like this!" Shane had growled, and then the horrible man had *picked Mikhail up* in his arms, like a girl. But the things that had happened after *that* had no girls involved, and it was a *very* pleasant memory.

"Yes," he said, back in the kitchen with Kimmy. "He is still protesting— and still hobbling on crutches, I believe—but he will see sense eventually."

Kimmy nodded and clasped her hands tightly in front of her on the red-checked kitchen tablecloth, worrying her fingers knuckle by knuckle. "Why do you think it's seeing sense?" she asked, her voice almost whisper low, and Mikhail thought about it for the first time since Benny had called him and told him—complaining bitterly about Deacon's stubbornness, which he had taken for granted.

"Because he is a good man, and good men deserve children," Mikhail said after a moment. "I would… for Shane's sake alone, I would try to have one of ours, but the children here—they are his children instead, and I have my students, and we are good with that. But Deacon and Carrick—they live more guarded lives, I think. They need a child of their own."

"Good men deserve children," Kimmy whispered, and then, to Mikhail's horror, she wiped her face on the back of her hand, and he realized she had been quietly crying as he had nattered on.

"Oh, Kimberly—whatever I said, it was nonsense. You know me. I'm an ignorant Russian man who knows nothing about women or children or lady parts—do not listen to me! Look! I will go call Benny, or Amy, or—"

"I started my period today," Kimmy said, but there was a sob in the middle of it, and Mikhail made himself busy starting the kettle for tea and getting some Kleenex. It was a halfway house for runaways—there were at least two boxes of Kleenex per room, the nice kind with aloe in it, which was considerate and necessary.

He returned with the Kleenex, some leftover cupcakes from the night before, and a keen wish to be somewhere else.

"Here, eat one," he said, and Kimmy stuck out a flat tongue and licked off all of the pink icing first.

Mikhail shuddered. "I can't believe you just did that! That's appalling!"

"I's za beth par'," she said through a mouth full of sugar and lard. "'O we af any mil'?"

Mikhail swallowed hard on his rebelling stomach and got her a glass of milk. "No wonder you did coke," he said, truly stunned. "If your sweet tooth is that rabid, it's the only reason you are not *truly* a cow!"

Kimmy at least swallowed and washed it down with milk before she answered. "I started my period, Mikhail. I'm three weeks late."

Mikhail squinted at her. "I have no lady parts, soon-to-be-cow-woman. I do not know what this means."

Kimmy grabbed the Kleenex, blew her nose into it, and tried to clean up. It was hard—she put on makeup every morning, and now it was running into her eyes and all over her face.

Mikhail sniffed. "Come here. You have a raccoon face—it is not at all attractive." Mikhail took a clean tissue and started wiping under her eyes and cleaning off her cheeks. She had dark eyes and dark eyelashes, like her brother, and Mikhail thought it was a shame their parents were both cold, useless people, one of whom had died and the other of whom had not visited for either wedding. They had good bone structure and threw perfect specimens. If only that was what a person needed to be worth the air he or she breathed.

"God, I needed your sympathy, you snotty Russian bastard," Kimmy muttered, submitting to his care. "You have anything else to tell me? Do I look fat today? I know I'm all broken out—are my zits ready to pay rent or room and board?"

"The one between your eyes would like a class on Russian poetry, if you are not too busy, yes, that is very considerate of you. Now explain, please. From what I understand, you are upset about something that happens once a month and that you loathe." All women loathed it. For three days a month Promise House was like emotional Armageddon, and anybody with testicles and sense kept his head down and watched his back. "Why would you be upset that this event arrived?"

Kim took a shuddery breath and leaned forward, contemplating the other pink cupcake with blue icing from the haven of her crossed arms.

"Because there were two lines on the pee-stick test, Mikhail. For three weeks, I *was* pregnant."

Oh. Mikhail let out a deep breath. "I am sorry, Kimberly." Carefully he placed his hand between her shoulder blades and started to rub. She relaxed into his touch—they had been dance partners for many years, and part of that was easing the other's aches and pains. "Why did you not tell anybody?"

"That's the thing," she said quietly. "It's not the first time it's happened. Lucas and I—we've been trying for nearly a year."

Mikhail widened his eyes. Kimmy, who could ask him if her zits were ready to pay rent, hadn't *told* him? Hadn't told *anybody*?

"Why was this such a secret?" he asked, puzzled and hurt. "Why would you not—"

"I haven't even told Lucas after the first one," she whispered. "I just told him I wasn't regular, that's all."

And Mikhail heard the crushing loneliness then, of what it must be like to feel so lonely in a place where you were never alone.

"But *why?*" he asked, appalled. "Why would you not tell anyone! Not even *Lucas*? Kimmy!"

Lucas had been so patient. He'd arrived to take Martin home when Martin had run away to meet Jeff and find out if his brother really had been gay. Lucas and Kevin had been best friends—perhaps in the same way Deacon and Jon were best friends. Lucas had taken a job at Promise House, and, lost and adrift after leaving the Marines, he had found himself a quiet home. His courtship of Kimmy had been slow and patient, and Kimmy had, more often than not, been the one to put obstacles in his path. She had damage, the same as Mikhail had when he'd met Shane, and it took somebody truly worthy to deal with that damage, to minimize it, to help it become strength instead of allowing it to define a person.

Lucas—tall, burly, with a country boy's smile and hair he let down to his shoulders—was almost the anti-Kimmy. He rarely swore, was chivalrous as hell, and now that he was a full-time staff member at Promise House, it was clear the sweetness of his disposition was also ideal when working with the fractured children Shane and Kimmy attempted to make whole.

He looked at Kimmy the same way Shane looked at Mikhail—as though the light from Mikhail's smile was somewhat blinding. Mikhail was satisfied that finally, after watching Kimmy flounder through bad relationships and bad addictions, *here* was someone who could treat her well.

The fact that Kimmy would not tell her husband of these things was troubling.

"Why?" he asked again, and she had no more makeup to smear when the flood of tears released.

"Because," she sobbed, "it's my fault. My fault. Kurt gave me chlamydia, Mickey... *twice!*"

Mikhail actually felt his pulse pound. Kurt was her ex—and the one, Mikhail suspected, who had started Kimmy's drug use in the first place. She had, perhaps, experimented, but until Kurt, Mikhail had never seen her get stoned every day.

"Twice?" he asked, more than a little appalled. Very clearly Mikhail remembered the first times Shane had ever touched him, and how careful Mikhail had been about protecting the man from his past. God. Mikhail thought seriously about looking Kimmy's ex-fucker up and ripping his balls off.

"The second time, I didn't figure it out until rehab. At first we thought it was the detoxing, but it kept hurting and my fever was bad, so they checked me out. I was... I was so fucked up, I thought the last thing I should be worried about was having children. I could hardly take care of myself!" She forgot about the tissue and wiped her face on her palm, and Mikhail tended to her like he would to one of the children. He wiped her eyes and put the tissue in front of her nose to blow, and when she was not quite so gross with fluids in her sadness, he pulled her against his chest. He was wearing a tight T-shirt and plaid shorts today, like any American boy in the summer, so it was okay, the mess she was making on him. He tightened his arms and told himself that was all he was worried about, his pristine ironed white cotton T-shirt.

Sobs shook her body, and he was reminded of how thin she was, how much she dieted to keep herself in shape for dance.

"It is probably nothing," he said, wanting to believe it. "It is probably just your scrawny ass, that is all. Eat another cupcake, you will gain five pounds as I would, and you will be fine."

She shook her head against his chest. "I tried that," she confessed painfully. "I gained ten pounds over Christmas and kept it on for a few months. Remember that?"

Mikhail swallowed painfully. "I remember I thought you were beautiful, looking at Lucas at your wedding, and that you were foolish to worry about the weight with the dress. I remember that you looked very good in the antique color, and that white did not have enough character for you. I do not remember these things the way you do, Kimberly. I am sorry." Pfaw, the blind man that love had made of him. Kimberly, his friend, his sister—he would not have seen her look any way but beautiful.

She cried harder against his chest, and he grasped for something, anything to tell her. It was Shane, he thought pitifully, Shane who made everything all right. But Kimmy would not go to her brother, just like her brother had not gone to her when he had been in the hospital, recovering from wounds—twice.

"We will call the doctor," he said, sounding like he was sure. "Benny, she has a doctor for this, and we are on the same insurance for Promise House. He will see you, it will be fine. He will tell you there is a pill, or a shot, or you need to gain twenty pounds, or thirty. He will make it all right. Doctors do." It was a lie—he knew this. His mother had been a nurse, and Ylena Bayul had seen through the fraudulent hope the doctors had held out from the very beginning, from the moment she was diagnosed. She had seen the chest X-rays; she had read the reports. She knew who survived and who did not, and which side her diagnosis fell on. But Kimberly was sobbing on his chest, and he needed to tell her something, something shiny, to make it better, just for the moment, just for today.

It had been five years since Shane had come into their lives again, five years since he had told his sister he had a family and had told Mikhail he wished so badly to court him. So much had happened in five years—much of it good. But this last, most surprising thing was most unwelcome. Where, Mikhail thought wretchedly, comforting Kimmy on his chest, where had he and Kimmy placed their ever-present armor against heartbreak? They had possessed it, once, had slid it on so easily they were not even aware when others were throwing themselves against it and bleeding. And now, when they had let it chip away so those that they cared for would not be hurt, it was nowhere to be found, and the wounds were as fresh and as red as they had been when both of them had been brand-new and had no sins in the world to stain them.

Chapter 9

Crick: Thinking 'bout sneaky, but not

DEACON'S shoulders were pressed into the bed, his hands flailing against the
sheets. His ass was arched up off the bed. His still-sore ankle lay flat, but his
uninjured one pressed against the mattress as he spread his legs and groaned,
thrusting in measured strokes against the inside of Crick's mouth as Crick
squeezed the bottom half of his cock with his good hand.

Crick wanted to get off so bad, he thought he should get a medal for
giving this blow job fully clothed.

Deacon wasn't quite close enough, so Crick looked up and started running
his hand over Deacon's body, the tight, muscled tummy, the lean torso. For
fun, he tweaked one of Deacon's nipples as he swallowed the crown of his
cock, and Deacon's "Whoa!" plus a spurt of something salty in his mouth had
Crick pulling back, grabbing the small plastic cup from underneath his hip
with his game hand, and tightening those muscles with everything he had
while he beat Deacon off like mad.

Deacon's eyes flew open at the feeling of the cool plastic as it brushed his
crown, but that must have stimulated him too, because his head fell back with
a "Holy fucking Christ!" and he came solidly, three or four thick, clotty white
streams, right into the little plastic specimen cup Benny had brought Crick
from the doctor's office.

Deacon was still shuddering, lying on the bed naked, and closing his eyes
hard, then opening them quickly as he tried to get his bearings. Crick sat up
on his knees, his own hard-on aching in his jeans, and fumbled in his pocket
for the lid to the cup, which he screwed on *tight* so as not to spill any of the
captured swimmers.

"What in the hell?" Deacon snapped, sitting up and pulling the sheets over his crotch.

"Nice one, Deacon. The little sheet said I needed twenty milliliters, but I think there's way more in here."

"You're saving my jizz in a...." Realization dawned. "That's why no sex for the last three days? And the ambush this morning?"

Crick should have blushed, he really should have, but he was just so damned pleased with himself. "You would have put it off otherwise," he said frankly. "And besides, your ankle hurt too bad before now. It was perfect."

"Perfect," Deacon echoed flatly.

"Yeah. The sex thing was because of the ankle—well, until last night— and since, you know, I thought you'd get all self-conscious and pissed off if you knew you *had* to put it off for three days, I figured I'd tell you and then, you know, jump you."

Deacon narrowed his eyes and focused on Crick's face in that way he had when Crick had been in high school and had done something particularly dumbassed.

"Did we forget something, Carrick?" he asked with meaning, and Crick smiled dreamily.

"God, you were hot coming out of the shower," he said, meaning it. He'd had the little cup, and he had walked into the bedroom and locked the door behind him in case Benny got there early, because he'd called her at Drew's house that morning and promised the specimen in an hour. And then Deacon had hobbled out of the shower, his skin all pink from the heat as he toweled off his hair. His torso veed perfectly down to his hips, which had been cloaked in the towel. And suddenly, Crick didn't just *want* to touch him, Crick *had* to—it was his *job*.

Best. Job. *Ever.*

Crick had started with a kiss, palming the back of Deacon's head and taking over, devouring him with the sort of confidence that their time living together as lovers had given him. Deacon had devoured him right back, and Crick had shown the initiative for once. Deacon, who had been trying to make peace ever since their squabble at the hospital, let him, and... well. Opportunity, right?

Except....

"Yeah," Crick muttered, looking at the little cup like it had betrayed him when he hadn't expected it. "Sorry—I forgot to tell you that's what we were doing."

Deacon screwed his eyes shut and threw himself back on the pillows with a groan. At that moment there was a knock on the front door. Crick brightened and lunged for the door.

"Stay there!" he ordered. "And *stay naked*!"

"The hell I will!"

Crick turned and glared at him. "I mean it, Deacon. If you get up and get dressed and go out and hobble around and get in everybody's way, you'll leave me in here with a hard-on and a full bottle of lube." The thought made Crick shift and adjust himself. "Either way, I won't get much work done, but with you there to help, there *might* be food on the table for Sunday dinner."

Deacon's jaw dropped, and then his expression went slack and he got a little dreamy as well. He tried to pull himself out of it and get mad again—Crick could tell by the tightening of his eyes and the way his lower lip, which was normally sinfully full anyway, thrust out, but in a second Benny was going to open the door and look for the two of them, so Crick didn't have time to soothe him.

"Stay there—*please*!" Crick snapped, and then dodged out the door.

"Crick?" Benny was bent over, raiding the refrigerator. "Did you need me to get anything tonight? You said something about fried chicken, which, you know—fat! Do you want some skinless chicken breasts to broil for Deacon and anyone who doesn't like fried?"

"Yeah, sure, good idea. Is that what you're looking for?" Crick reached over her to the top of the fridge for the plastic bags and put the specimen cup in the first one he found.

"No," she said, straightening. "I'm *looking* for the specimen cup, which was supposed to be in the fridge—omigod."

"Well, yeah. If it was going to be more than an hour and a half, it had to be on ice, right?"

"Omigod."

"Well, it's what? Twenty minutes to the doctor's office? Go! It's fresh! Take it!"

Benny was usually so active, so animated, and she was just *standing* there, her blue eyes big as a lake, her wide mouth gaping slightly. "That's…

that's his *specimen*? You were just in there collecting his *specimen?*" she protested.

"*Yes!*" Crick danced from one foot to another. "And now it's time for him to collect *mine!*"

"Omigod!" Benny said after a moment. "Oh my *God!*"

"Benny, we've been having sex since I got home from Iraq—I don't know if that shocks you or not—"

"Jesus, Crick, *shut up!*" She'd turned bright red—so red her forehead was blotchy—and he could see sweat starting at her scalp where her hair was pulled back in a short ponytail.

Crick realized he was having fun. "Sure, sure, sure—take your jizz and go. We know when we're being used!" He laughed, holding the bag with the specimen cup high and above her head.

She leveled a glare at him meant to shrivel the pubes off his nuts, and if he wasn't so damned gleeful at having gotten Deacon this far in the process, it might have worked.

"Don't be a dick," she snapped.

"I'm not being a dick!" God, let a guy have a little fun! Jesus!

"You are being such a dick as to make a real dick look like a labia minora. Now give me my fucking semen and go get off! We've got real shit to talk about when you hit puberty, okay?"

Hell. Crick deflated and lowered his arm. She snatched the bag out of his hand with force, and then, remembering what she had, adjusted its position in her fingers.

"Yeah," he said, feeling cheated as his joy drained down his spine and into the floor. "I heard. She's at Promise House. Should we visit?"

Benny grimaced. "No—Mikhail told me she's being a complete and total—"

"Flaming twat," Crick muttered, echoing Deacon's words from when he was in the hospital.

"Yeah—except he said something absolutely vile-sounding in Russian that made a flaming twat sound like a skin condition and whatever Missy is being sound like Ebola virus."

"*God*, Benny, can you not open your mouth without saying something that turns my stomach?"

"*You*? I have to drive to the doctor's with semen in my front seat thinking about you having sex! You have this coming on general principle! Now we shouldn't visit, but should we let her know we give a shit?"

Crick grunted. "I'll think about it," he said, knowing it sounded callous but not able to do anything about it. They had tried—for the two years he'd been in Iraq, Benny and Deacon had tried, and for the five years he'd been back, they had *all* tried, to get hold of those girls and make them family. But the... the snake pit of pain and favoritism and abuse and bigotry that Missy came from... well, without Deacon and Parrish to bail Crick out, he wouldn't have been much to speak of either.

"Yeah, me too," Benny sighed. "We'll talk to Shane about it when her probationary period is over. All right, big brother. I gotta motor. I've got an ice chest in the front of the car. If I get this jizz to the doc in time, he can freeze it and use it for their holy and sainted purpose as daddy sperm and I don't ever have to know about you and Deacon having sex again."

Crick grimaced. "Yeah, well, five years, Benny—you might have figured out by now that nobody washes their sheets *that* often."

Benny shook her head and shuddered in disgust. "I'm outta here. I'd say tell Deacon hi for me, but I don't even want to be brought up in conversation when you do what you gotta do!"

Crick watched her go into the August heat—it was only eight in the morning and already eighty degrees outside—and some of his earlier joy came back. The Promise House kids were out there, feeding, watering, brushing, walking, mucking out stalls—all the things that needed to be done with the horses on a daily basis. Drew must have had Parry Angel, which meant Lucas was supervising and, for once, Deacon could sleep in.

But Crick wasn't going to let him do much sleeping. He closed his eyes for a moment and remembered the way Deacon bit his lower lip when he was coming, and smiled. There was a sudden tingle in his crotch, and an ache, and he thrust his hand down the front placket of his jeans and stroked, hardening and throbbing with just that much pressure.

Oh yes. Oh, oh *yes*!

"Deacon!" he called, heading toward the hallway, "you promised you'd still be naked!"

"I didn't promise any... thing... of the sort!" Deacon retorted, but his breath was coming short and it had the thready, desperate sound of an aroused man.

"And don't start without me!" Crick said indignantly. "That's not...."

He opened the door and saw Deacon, naked, legs spread, hand on himself while his eyes were closed. His cock was fully erect again, and Crick managed to finish his sentence on the jolt of irritation that surged through him.

"Fair," he said. "That's not fair." And he stripped as fast as his hands could accomplish the task. "You couldn't wait for round two?" he protested, and for a moment, Deacon's whole body shuddered, and Crick thought he might have seriously misjudged and Deacon was going to finish himself off without Crick's help. But he relaxed back against the bed with a happy sigh and opened hooded eyes.

"No, Carrick, I was getting myself ready for round two." With that, he reached under the pillow and pulled out the half-empty tube of lubricant, which he threw at Crick. "Now it's your turn to get ready."

Crick almost giggled, he was so happy. His worry about his sister fell away, and even his worry about what they were going to do with the results Benny brought back. Fact was, Deacon Winters was his most favorite person in the world, and they were going to spend some quality time together. Crick would put about anything on the back burner of his mind for quality time.

Chapter *10*

Deacon: Truth in Fiction

BY FRIDAY, Deacon was back to shoveling horseshit and riding the perpetrators—and just like when he'd recovered from his heart attack, he was happy enough to be back on his feet that shoveling horseshit looked good.

Sunday dinner seemed especially poignant—it was Martin's last dinner before he flew back home to his last year of high school, and Benny's last dinner before her last year of college started. And, of course, every dinner with Jon and Amy felt precious to the lot of them.

Everybody's favorite deserters spent this last dinner bickering over whether they were going to sell their house at Levee Oaks or keep it and use it when they came for vacations. The table conversation grew loud enough for Deacon to override the both of them and say of course they were keeping the house, but maybe, since it was damned huge, they could let someone move in and watch it for them and pay a minimal rent.

That seemed the perfect solution, and Deacon was able to finish his broiled chicken in peace. (It did not escape his notice that there were two kinds of chicken on the table, and that the fried kind was on the *other* side of the table. But he was replete with sex and well rested for once, and he wasn't going to argue with having to eat broiled, tender marinated chicken. Crick had done his job well.)

And not a soul—not one—mentioned anything about the baby.

Deacon's relief could have been written in fireworks and set to a big brass band.

God. Just a minute, a breath, for this idea to sink in.

And here, as he shoveled horseshit and straw, it was doing just that.

He'd been there when Parry Angel had been born. He'd held her first, as soon as the nurses had cleaned her up. She'd been ugly—all babies were ugly—and pink and wrinkled, but she hadn't cried a lot like most babies, and her blue eyes had actually seemed to focus. He'd handed her to a sweating, exhausted Benny and watched Benny become beautiful and grown all in one smile.

Next to seeing himself through Crick's eyes, or riding a horse hell-for-leather as fast as they both could go, it was about the closest thing to magic he could possibly imagine.

Since Crick wasn't going to sprout a uterus anytime soon, the idea of Benny having Deacon's child, with those little pieces of Crick—and even the pieces of Benny, whom he loved almost as much—made his chest hurt, made his breath come short.

He'd had a real heart attack before—this feeling was nothing like it.

There was only sweetness here.

He wanted it. He wanted it so badly. He knew what having a baby was like—the getting up early, the constant shift for child care, the worry that was so omnipresent you forgot it was there until it flared up. He, Parry, and Benny had gotten hit with the flu when Crick was gone, and had all ended up in the hospital. He'd held Parry when Benny couldn't, sung to her when his own throat was on fire, *willing* that little body to recover, to fight.

He knew that fear for the worst.

He'd lived through it.

That night, the worry, the fear—it had all been worth it. Every breath Parry had taken before or since had made it so.

He'd known it would be like this. It was one of the reasons he'd fought it so badly. He couldn't make Benny go through with it. He wouldn't beg her to give up a baby. But he wanted... oh, hells... he *yearned* for this baby.

The idea of telling Benny no was getting harder and harder to embrace.

So he welcomed this time in his own head, the quiet, the peace to align his thoughts and get his arguments in order. He could do this. He could live without this one thing he wanted most in the world besides Crick, if it meant Benny didn't have to break her heart.

He had that all firmed up in his head when Benny poked her head into the close yellow air of the stables.

He looked up and smiled. "Heya, Shorty! How's school?"

Benny made a face. "I'm taking a poetry class. I love it. It makes me want to go back and take all English classes and start all over again."

Deacon laughed. "Well, what's wrong with that? You got time!"

Benny shook her head. "Naw—I'm ready to be done. I'll take a few classes now and then read when I've got a sec." She came in wearing cargo shorts and a tank top and made herself comfortable on top of a bale of hay. She'd just gotten her hair cut shorter, so it was tousled and fluffy all over her head, and she didn't look much older than she had nearly seven years earlier, when Deacon had first taken her in.

"People say they're going to do that...," he cautioned, but she was ready for him.

"Yeah, well, I've watched you do it, Deacon. I can follow that example. Don't worry about it. I'm ready to be out of there, you know?"

Deacon shrugged and grinned at her. "I'm not ready for you to grow up, but you never seem to listen to me on that score."

She didn't smile back. "But you listen to me, right?"

Her face was earnest and calm, and his stomach sank.

"Yeah," he said, not wanting this conversation quite yet. "Every time. You know that, right?"

Benny nodded. "I do," she said, and her voice got rough, and he looked around in alarm for a cloth. Benny's heart sat on her sleeve every minute of every day. She would cry through this conversation if it was happy or sad, and....

She pulled a little minipack of Kleenex out of her pocket, and he smiled against the tightness in his throat. She knew herself too, apparently. And she was clever to boot.

"Look," he said, knowing his voice was portentous but not able to stop it. "Benny, I know you mean well—"

She held up a hand. "You need to hear me out," she said gently. "Please. Don't talk for this, okay, Deacon? Because I'm only going to say this once, and then you have to pretend we never had this conversation, all right?"

Deacon nodded seriously and leaned his weight on his pitchfork. "It'll be the secret conversation," he promised, trying to get her to smile.

She wiped her eyes and shook her head. "We can't laugh through this," she said, her voice surprisingly even. "Not even a little."

"Benny?" His stomach gave a tentative roil, and his chest started to ache even more. "Is this about the baby?"

She shook her head. "Only sort of." And in spite of her earlier words, she smiled at him, looking him full in the eyes. "Deacon, I'm in love with Drew, do you doubt that?"

He shook his head. He'd seen them together, seen them flirt, seen them kiss even. He'd seen that sweet, secret hope on Benny's face on the night she'd oh-so-casually mentioned she was going to Drew's cottage that evening and might not be back until morning.

"Not even a little."

She nodded. "Good. So you'll believe me when I say this next part, okay? Because if you believe I know I'm in love with Drew, you'll believe I know what I'm talking about, right?"

Deacon swallowed. "Yeah."

"Deacon Parrish Winters, my first love—my first *true* love—was you."

He had to fight not to shake his head and tell her she didn't know what she was talking about. She'd just proved it to him, didn't she? That she knew? If he believed her when she said she was in love with Drew, he had to believe her now.

"You did that really well," he said seriously, and she inclined her head modestly, like he'd just told her he was proud of her grades.

"Thanks. I've been thinking on it for a long time."

"Why tell me now?" Because this wasn't comfortable knowledge, not for either of them.

"Don't you see?" And her careful composure was slipping. She wiped her face with her Kleenex and some of her makeup came off with it. "I spent years trying not to be in love with you, Deacon. I'm not stupid. You started out being my teenage crush, and then you helped me with Parry and I was living with you—I *knew* what it would make me feel. But I also knew that nothing would make you... I don't know, find another place for us to live, get weird, whatever—just *go away*—like thinking you were hurting me just by being kind. So I made myself not love you. And it sort of worked, right? Because I let Drew in. I love him, for real. I want to marry him. I want to have his children, I want to watch him raise Parry—"

"Then why?" he asked. He'd leaned the pitchfork against the wall, but he couldn't stand still. He put his hands on the back of his head and paced, wanting to be anywhere, *anywhere* but here.

"Why what? Why tell you?"

"Why offer to… to have this baby! Because I have to tell you, Benny, knowing this about how you feel isn't going to make me any more comfortable with you carrying my child!"

"But don't you get it? *Look at me*, Deacon!"

He turned around and shook his head. She was crying, knees to her chest, chin resting on top, and wiping her face against her bare skin.

"I'm looking." His eyes burned, and his chest felt pressed almost flat. "Benny, I have loved you like—"

"A sister," she choked. "A daughter. A friend. I know this, Deacon. I know it in my heart. I've known from the very beginning that you have loved my brother like your mate, and everyone else is a real poor second. I understand that, okay? So this isn't about you. It's about me. It's about what I need to do to set myself free."

"Free?" Oh God. He didn't understand. He didn't get women on the best of days, but now he was lost, and he was hurt, and he wanted to talk to Crick at the same time he never wanted Crick to know this conversation had ever happened.

"Yeah. Free." Benny straightened, hopped off the hay bale, and then stood up. Her chin was up, her shoulders were back, she looked as self-possessed as Deacon had ever seen a person, much less the little girl he'd saved, and who had helped him save himself. "Don't you see, Deacon?" Still crying. She was still crying, and her blue eyes were puffy, and her breath was caught, but still, she had dignity. "All of this… this *mess*"—she gestured around her heart—"it's all the ways I love you. And I need to set it free. And I figure if I have this baby, I give all of *this*"—again that helpless gesture—"to that baby. And then I can give that baby to you. And you'll have it. You will have my love. And I'm free—I've given you everything I can, and I'm free to love Drew with all my heart, and love our children together, and to not worry that somehow, somewhere, I cheated you, because I was afraid that if you ever knew how I felt, you wouldn't let me love you at all…."

She was sobbing now, and he opened his arms and gestured, afraid to just hug her now that he knew, but unable to love her any differently than the girl he'd comforted when she was lost and alone and so in need of a grown-up who wouldn't let her down. She nodded and cried against his chest, and he remembered the first time he'd hugged her like this. She'd been pregnant and afraid and he could still smell the hair dye, because she'd dyed her hair every month back then, searching, searching for the identity that would help her be strong. He'd thought about how young she was, and how she still needed parenting, and how he was a shitty choice for it but he'd step up because she was Crick's sister, and she needed him.

She was strong now, and not young anymore, and now she was *his* sister, and she was in pain.

"Sh," he murmured into her hair. "I get it, Benny. I get it. You don't need to do it this way, but I get it."

"I do." She hiccupped. "I *do* need to do it this way. Please, Deacon? Please let me give this to you? It's all I can give you, and then...."

"Yeah," he said, hearing her. You didn't raise a girl like Benny without believing her when she stood up for herself and spoke. You didn't listen to her when she poured her heart out, without respecting that it was the truth. "Yeah, Benny. If this is the thing that'll let you and me be square, that'll let you be my sister forever, so there's nothing sitting between us?"

Benny looked up at him, her lashes spiked and her eyes red, and nodded. "This will do it," she said, and he held out his T-shirt so she could wipe her eyes on it. She did, and her nose for good measure, making him laugh. When she was done, she looked up at him again, and he lowered his head and kissed her softly, platonically, on the lips. He pulled back and met her eyes again to see if she'd understand.

She smiled a little. "That's as good as I'm gonna get," she said, and he nodded, because he couldn't think of anything else to say about that. "Fair enough," she filled in for him, and he crushed her to his chest again.

"It's gonna be the best baby," he said, because it was the only thing that made this moment bearable. The only thing that kept his heart from stopping then and there.

"Damned straight," she sniffled.

After a moment she pulled away, eyes somberly on his face. He pushed her hair back from her face and kissed her forehead before stepping back, because they both needed space.

"What do we do now?" he asked, thinking about specifics, and apparently so was she.

"Well, I made the appointment for next week. I've been taking the drugs, and they'll harvest my eggs then. Your swimmers will fertilize them, and then, when I'm right in the middle of my cycle, they'll throw the embryo in the oven and bake!"

Deacon took three steps back until he ran into the stall behind him and put his work boot square in a pile of horseshit. "*Jesus*, Benny! You got this shit *planned!*"

Benny hiccupped one last time and nodded militantly. "Well *yeah*, Deacon! I've been taking the fertility drugs since this started, so I figure I get pregnant in two weeks, and the baby's due in nine and a half months, which is one, maybe two weeks after finals and graduation, so I'll be done with school, and that'll give me three months to get rid of the baby weight, and Drew and I can get married next August or maybe September."

He knew his mouth was open and he couldn't see very well. "Jesus... I mean... *Jesus...*."

She smiled then, through the puffy eyes and swollen nose, and he saw her, the impish kid he'd known before Crick had taken off for Iraq, the little sister he'd loved since she was probably younger than Parry Angel herself.

"Deacon, I ain't fuckin' around. I'm ready for school to be over, you and Crick to be situated, and me and Drew to start living together on our own."

"You already pretty much live on your own," he corrected, and she looked sheepish, because they both knew that wasn't going to change while Drew went to school.

"Okay. Well, I'm ready to be a full-fledged grown-up now, okay?"

He started to laugh, helplessly, almost hysterically. "Benny, I don't know if you've *ever* been anything less."

She sniffed. "Well, come on. We need to tell Crick."

He took a deep breath and smiled slightly. "I've only got two more stables to muck. Want to lend a hand?"

And it was just like it had been before Crick had come back, when they'd been two refugees on a lifeboat, clinging together through the storm.

"Yeah," she said. "I wouldn't want you to fall asleep out here like you used to."

He winked and found the spare pitchfork in the corner. "Haven't done that in a while, Shorty."

"Well, after you have a baby in the house again, you might start," she said, like she was reminding him of something he didn't know.

His smile grew then, and he couldn't help it. A baby. A baby like Crick. All of his shortcomings were forgotten in the glow of Crick's little sister, so grown up his chest ached with it. "I can't wait," he said, and she beamed back.

They didn't say much after that, just worked companionably, side by side in the simple chore, until things were done right and they could go deal with all the excitement to follow.

CRICK jumped around the house, elbows and knees going in six different directions, so excited he woke the dog from under the house, and Mumford started running around the yard, barking in confusion. Crick, Deacon, and Benny ignored him completely, and Crick actually hugged his sister voluntarily, of his own free will.

And then reeled when she recited the same schedule to him that she had to Deacon.

"God, that's fast," he breathed, balancing himself against the back of a kitchen chair. All of that cavorting may have looked like fun, but it wasn't exactly easy for him, even now. "Can we do that?" He looked at Deacon. "Can we be ready for a baby that soon?"

His long dark hair was tousled and in his eyes, and he was wearing cut-offs that were too short and a tank-top that wasn't any longer, and he looked *so* earnest, just like he'd looked when he'd been nine years old and he wanted to help Deacon with the horses.

"Most people have less notice," Deacon said, swallowing on sentiment. Which was good, because it wasn't in him not to insert a little bit of practicality into this situation. "And," he said, looking seriously at Benny, "remember that there is no guarantee this baby is going to be as excited about a September wedding as you are. This takes a couple of tries sometimes, you know that, right?"

Benny grinned, undeterred. "Nope. Doc says we could probably populate Mars. It'll happen the first time. I'm sure of it."

Deacon cringed—actually cringed. "Benny, I don't want—"

She shook her head. "No. There will be no pessimism over this, okay?"

Crick nodded, actually agreeing with her. "Exactly. Let me ask Jeff—I'll bet he can tell us all sorts of reasons this will work, and—" Crick paused. "What?"

"Not tonight," Deacon said quietly, smiling. "Can it just be us tonight? Benny, Drew, Parry, you, and me? You can tell Jeff tomorrow, okay?"

Crick's air of being an overgrown puppy suddenly softened and grew still. "Yeah," he said, and ignoring his sister, he crossed over to where Deacon stood and kissed his forehead. "The whole world can know tomorrow. Tonight, it'll just be us."

Dinner was quiet but not subdued.

"Mommy," Parry asked, "you're going to get *fat*?"

"Not fat," Drew said hurriedly when Benny thrust out her lower lip in a little bit of hurt. "She's going to get beautiful!"

Deacon pursed his mouth in appreciation. "Good answer!"

Drew nodded emphatically—it had been a close call.

"So," Parry said, undeterred, "my mommy is having this baby, but it's not *really* going to be my brother or sister."

She narrowed her wide eyes, and she looked suspiciously at the grown-ups to see if they were having her on.

"It's going to be a baby for Deacon and Crick," Benny explained. "So you and me and Drew will all live together as a little family, and they'll have this baby to keep them company."

Uh-oh—those narrowed eyes were now accompanied by a pouty lower lip. "So I'm not going to be Deacon's only baby?"

Deacon reached across the table and ruffled her hair. "Now Angel, you will always be my girl. But you were such an *awesome* kid that when your mommy and Drew decided to be together, they wanted to give us a kid of our very own so we didn't miss you quite so much." Suddenly that sort of condescension that all adults have when they're trying to explain things to children fell away. "Crick and I will miss you *very* much now that you're going to live in the little house. Planning for the baby will help us not miss you so much."

God. Among other things, Benny and Drew were moving Benny and Parry into the mother-in-law cottage. There was enough room—it wasn't much smaller than the main house, because in the back of his mind, Deacon had sort of been planning for this contingency when he'd had it built.

Parry's lower lip began to wobble. "But... I'll still *see* you everyday, right? You're not going away like Lila, right?"

Deacon turned sideways and held his arms open, and Parry scrambled out of her chair and into them. Just like her mother, Deacon thought, and the idea was comforting. Parry was still a little girl, and he still had some time.

"Sh," he murmured. "Yeah, Angel. I'll be here. I'm coaching your soccer team, right? And Crick is your... what was it again, Crick?"

Crick winced. "Room mother," he confessed, and Deacon winced for him. When school started this year, someone had gotten a little overzealous while filling out the fifteen zillion little pieces of paper that came home with every grade school child anywhere in California.

"Yeah. We're not going anywhere for quite some time, okay?"

Parry nodded in his arms, but it took her some time before she was comfortable enough to back away from the table.

Crick and Benny shooed him away from cleanup, although that was usually protocol, and told Parry Angel she could dish up the berries and whipped cream for dessert. It wasn't until Crick gave Deacon a serious look and a head bob that Deacon realized he had one more uncomfortable conversation to go.

Drew was outside, leaning against the railing that wrapped around the porch. The dog was on the ground, chasing after his favorite toy, the tennis ball on the rope. Deacon knew the drill: Mumford would run the ball down, possibly flip ass over toes when he found it, and then prance around the lawn area with his tail up in the air, waving the unlikely fringe like a flag of victory. Then he'd curl his paws around it, gnaw on it, slobber on it, swallow some of the tennis ball, and *then* he'd return it to the person who had the honor of chucking that thing across the yard again.

"You know what we should get?" Drew said after watching the dog maul his toy with affection and drool.

"A Chihuahua?" Deacon asked, eyeballing the dog again. If possible, the damned thing had *grown* in the past year.

"Only if you're serving it to Mumford as dessert," Drew said, grinning. "No—one of those lever things that pitches a tennis ball. We get one of those things, pitch the ball halfway to Shane's, and by the time the damned dog got back here with it, he'd be too tired to drool."

"Good idea," Deacon said, smiling. "Next time I'm at the store—"

"No worries." Drew turned so his back was to the yard. "I'll have Benny pick one up. We told Parry she could have a kitten in the new house—Shane's got one ready."

Deacon smiled. "We've been thinking about doing that for a while—good for you!"

Drew showed his teeth a little, but he kept his eyes on Deacon's boots. "Well, it's good to have something to bring to the table, you know?"

Deacon groaned. "Drew, I don't know what to—"

Drew held up a hand, and Deacon knew that once again, this was going to be a time when the most important gift he could give was his attention.

"I'm not complaining," Drew said, looking him square in the eye. "You've been a stand-up boss—a stand-up friend—for the past six years. You've given me something I never thought I'd have after I left home—a family that just... just got me. That accepted me. That stood up for me. I'm not complaining, Deacon. I'm just saying, you're a hard act to follow."

Deacon opened his mouth to say he was flawed, to deny that he did, or had done, anything out of the ordinary, but Drew shook his head again.

"I love you like a brother," Drew said, "but I've got to thank you for letting her go. For letting *them* go. I don't think I could have forgiven you if you hadn't let her make things right."

Deacon sighed. "She didn't have to, you know that, right?"

"Oh yes she did. We both did." Drew palmed his head with his hand and wiped his forehead on his T-shirt. The last week of August, and dangerously hot, even now, so close to the delta—the breezes just were not doing it.

All of this honesty, Deacon thought miserably. He moved forward to lean and look out over the stupid dog, who was still drooling on his toy.

"Well," he said after a moment, "I'm grateful. I'm indebted. I don't know if you know what you've given us yet."

Drew turned around and looked out over the porch with him. You could see the barn from here, and six of the twelve divided fields, all of them faintly green, that the horses ran in. You could see the dirt practice ring where Crick had first shown up, a lanky, awkward nine-year-old, in awe, loving the horses so much Deacon could feel his yearning from where he'd stood on the rails of the ring. You could see the worn horse path to the rest of the property, most of it brown grass, but mown and maintained. If you followed that path beyond the rise the house and barn sat on, you could see the oak trees that marked Promise Rock. Of course, you could see the gravel road and the driveway too, but those things and where they took you had never been a part of Deacon's heart.

Drew leaned in and bumped him with a broad shoulder. "I know," he said quietly. "Don't think I don't know what this means to you. If it didn't mean so much, we wouldn't bother."

Deacon nodded. "Thank you," he said. "Just... thank you."

"Backatcha, boss. I don't know what we would have done if you hadn't said yes. It was the only way we knew of to eventually let this all go."

"But not right now," Deacon said, feeling pitiful.

Again, that comfortable shoulder bump. "We've got a few years, Deacon. Don't worry. We're not going to all run away at once."

"Thank God."

He said it with feeling, meaning every breath. The hope of the baby was wonderful, but it was just that: a hope. The certainty of things changing, of friends and family leaving—as they should—that was more real than the hope, for the moment, anyway.

Would that change? With enough peace, enough joy, would hope stop being the traitor at Deacon's table? Someday, maybe. Someday, maybe hope would be his friend.

Right now he eyed it, an old adversary, and begged his hope to stay loyal. So many people were counting on it, maybe just this once it could stand up for them. Just this once, it could serve them well.

Chapter 11

Jeff: Favor for a Friend

WHEN Jeff had first seen Shane, the big hairy Hoover, breaking his heart over Mikhail almost exactly five years ago, he'd been pretty sure no man was worth all that pain.

And then he'd met the little Ruskie diva bitch, and he'd been reluctantly impressed.

Mikhail wasn't a "nice guy." He was a *guy,* but nice was not in his makeup. He was blunt, sarcastic, superior, and often rude.

But once he considered you a friend, he was a mountain lion in a short man's clothing, and he would draw blood without remorse in order to protect you and the friendship. Jeff and Collin had seen it firsthand—and they'd come to treasure it.

But it was disconcerting to have that fierceness turned *on* you, instead of fighting *for* you.

"So Kimmy doesn't know I'm coming," Jeff said again, just to make sure.

"No. Nyet. Nein. Would you like me to say it in another language?" Mikhail snapped, looking uneasily toward the house. They were parked in front of Promise House, and Jeff couldn't figure out exactly why.

"Look, little man, you're the one who told me I had to take a day off—"

"Yes, yes, I made you take a day off. We will go for ice cream and knitting afterwards. Will that make you less obnoxious about doing this favor for me?"

Jeff was about to answer, but Mikhail was staring at the front door as though *willing* it to open, and muttering to himself.

"C'mon, Kimberly, c'mon. You are not a coward, I believe this, come *on!*"

"Well, since I'm driving, can I at least ask where I'm driving us all?"

Mikhail looked at him and grimaced, some of the iron in his spine melting in the early September heat. "Yes," he muttered. "The woman's doctor Bernice uses, you know where it is?"

Jeff widened his eyes. "You want me to take Kimmy to her *gynecology* appointment?" he squeaked.

"And me!" Mikhail turned a fierce gaze on Jeff, and Jeff was actually reassured. However bad this was, Jeff would not suffer alone.

"But why me?"

Mikhail let out a breath and then opened his mouth and startled Jeff badly by yelling. "Kimberly, you coward, get your cow-sized ass out here, we will be late!"

A pretty girl, African-American with exotic almond-shaped eyes, stuck her head out instead. "She says she's coming, and don't get your panties in a bunch."

Interesting, Jeff thought. You very rarely saw Mikhail's expression get that soft.

"Tell her I will bunch my panties however I wish, and that she has three minutes before I go in there and throw her over my shoulder."

And the young woman standing half inside the air-conditioned house had the nerve to smirk.

Mikhail sniffed. "You laugh. We do this several times a weekend, every weekend in the fall. Where do you think we go, and why do you think I come back so weary? Tell her that, and see if she does not move faster, yes, Sweetie?"

Jeff had to take several deep breaths to realize Sweetie was the girl's name, because the thought of Mikhail actually using an endearment turned the world on its end like a dizzy rooster.

And then he remembered where he'd heard that name before.

"Sweetie?" he asked. "Is that the girl Martin was crushing on?"

Mikhail looked startled and then pleased. "Oh was he?"

Jeff shrugged. "He talked about her a lot. Said she was pretty, said she was smart. I guess he got to know her when she worked her rotation at the garage."

Mikhail's tense expression eased up for a moment. "I knew he was a young man of worth. Will he write her, do you think?"

Jeff opened his mouth and closed it. "I... I have no idea...."

Mikhail looked at him with obvious impatience. "Well, does he write *you*?"

"Well *yes,* but that's e-mails on the computer!"

Mikhail's lips twitched in what Jeff knew to be his second-widest smile. "Then it is good. She asked for an hour's worth of computer time and an e-mail account for part of her privileges. There was no reason to do that. Her people have no computers. It was for him."

Jeff couldn't stop a cackle. "Why Mikhail, you old softie, you! It's like there's a closet romantic in the crusty Russian heart after all."

Ah, yes, there was that lip curl of disdain. "Fuck you. Fuck your cats. Fuck your supposed sense of humor, but don't fuck your husband, because he is a nice boy and deserves better. *Kimberly!* I *will* drag you out here by the hair, cow-woman, so get your ass in *gear!*"

"Jesus, Mikhail, don't twist your panties in a fuckin' knot!" Kimmy came out of the house like a barrel through a gate, and Jeff—who admitted he could sometimes joke his way out of all sensitivity whatsoever—got his first real inkling something was wrong.

Kimmy's eyes were red, her complexion was bad, and she'd lost weight—or so he assumed, because she was wearing some hideous red elastic jeans that looked like they could have fit her brother if he ever wanted to masquerade as a middle-aged woman from Florida. She stopped at the threshold and turned around to talk to someone inside, and Jeff muttered, "Hey, Mikhail—how long's she been like this?"

Mikhail sighed. "She's not using, if that's what you are thinking. But she *is* very sad, and that is why you're coming with us."

Jeff grimaced. "Which leads me back to my question. *Why* am I going again?" He still couldn't believe this was the reason Mikhail had called him up and insisted he take time off work. If Jeff hadn't loved Mikhail like a brother, he would have refused.

"To see if you've actually grown a uterus," Mikhail said without blinking, leaving Jeff to sputter, but not for long because Kimmy was walking down the stairs.

"WHY is he here again?" Kimmy asked, and Jeff met Mikhail's eyes in the rearview mirror of his Mini Cooper.

"See! That was *my* question too!"

Kimmy looked over her shoulder at Mikhail, and Jeff could only imagine the little man's contemptuous shrug.

"Someone will be needed," he said unflappably. "We will need a person who can translate medical speak into real speak. I know how these places are. When my mother was sick, she translated, and it worked well. But it is you, and the one medical person I know is Jeff, and since he's seen you at your worst, I took liberties. Sue me."

"God," Kimmy said with wonder, "how can he sound so bitchy when he's the one who's—"

Jeff gasped and caught Mikhail's steely, unrepentant glare in the rearview. "Don't say it, Kimmy-love," he murmured. "Don't say it. We'll just let him pretend his dick's bigger, and do what he says. It will make this whole thing less painful."

Mikhail rolled his eyes in the rearview and then looked away, his jaw clenched, and Jeff ignored him for the time being. "So," he said, forcing some cheer through the undercurrents of the car, "why are we going to the doctor's?"

In spite of the heat, Kimmy had brought her knitting, and she pulled out a sock in some sort of corn/bamboo fiber and began working, her movements nervous and twitchy at first and easing into grace after a mile. Jeff waited for her to answer. He was used to people finding their feet when they were dealing with medical problems. There was always that careful social boundary between a little information and totally TMI.

As they cleared Levee Oaks and turned right on Watt toward the freeway, Mikhail cleared his throat.

"You need to answer him, Kimberly." His voice had an odd pitch, a special note of tenderness that Jeff had only heard directed at Shane, and his carefully developed chest muscle squeezed.

"Please, hon? You're sort of scaring me."

"It's nothing life threatening," she said, but her throat was rough and she'd started out barely audible until she cleared out all of the overthinking that was blocking her wind.

"So...." Jebus! Kimmy was usually not this reticent about *anything.* Of course, the first time Jeff had met Kimmy, she'd been sitting on her lawn, surrounded by all her possessions, trying to breathe through the nose full of cocaine her ex-fucker had shoved in her face. Jeff figured once you pulled your shit together through *that,* you assumed shame was for pussies and got on with your life.

"So, I think the clammies destroyed my uterus," Kimmy said, her voice huskier than it should have been. "This visit is to get an ultrasound and see if there's a chance I can have a baby."

Jeff couldn't even think of a *sound* to make in response to that. The quiet in the car actually seemed to make it hotter, although the air conditioner was top rate.

"Have you been trying?" he asked quietly, and although it was a logical question, he hated himself when she wiped under her eyes with the back of her hand.

"Yeah," she said simply, and he didn't even want to know how long.

Jeff's specialty had always been to crack a joke, to make someone laugh, to take a shitty moment and make it lighter so the pain could have a chance to spread out and therefore not kill whomever it was aimed at.

"Well," he said now, looking at her knitting and wishing he'd thought to bring his own, "I hope you remembered to bring a sock for me. If I'd known we were going for tests, I would have brought my project bag."

He saw it out of the corner of his eye then: a smile. "Of course," she said with the ghost of a head bob that usually would have been filled with attitude. "It's never too early to start your Christmas knitting."

"Charming," Mikhail muttered from the back. "Next thing you know, we shall break out the pocket looms and become a family of textile workers like they have at the Faire."

"Those people seem really fuckin' happy," Kimmy said, and Mikhail's answer was classic Russian diva.

"How happy can they be? It is not like they dance."

"True that," Kimmy muttered.

Jeff had never done ballet, but he *had* been a club bunny once upon a time. Sometimes he would pull one of his favorite songs up on iTunes and dance in his kitchen when he was cleaning house. Sometimes Collin would join him.

"Word," he said dryly, and the incongruous slang lightened things up just a little bit more, and they could all breathe just long enough to get to the doctor's.

THEY all pretended Kimmy wasn't half-naked, getting her insides probed during the ultrasound, and the tech was very accommodating with a sheet at her middle while Mikhail and Jeff stood by her head, one on either side of her, holding her hand.

They all heard the tech's caught breath, and Jeff didn't need a specialist to tell him what the woman saw.

He saw it too.

The scarring was brutally extensive, twisting the surface of the uterus, making it impossible for any egg to implant, provided one could get past the swollen exit of either fallopian tube. It was not a picture of a womb that would give purchase to an embryo, much less nourish a fetus, and Jeff felt like the next fifteen minutes were a study in holding his breath.

The tech had to do her job too. She had a series of stations to photograph, each one a different horror show of what could happen when an untreated STD destroyed a once-healthy organ. Jeff could have stopped the procedure right then—he wanted to, because it was uncomfortable, and Kimmy was too embarrassed and irritated even to crack a sarcastic joke—but he didn't.

God, he didn't want to be the one to tell her.

One of the perks of physical therapy was that he got to be the cheerleader. He got to be the one telling people what they could do if only they tried.

He very, very rarely had to deliver bad news.

He didn't want to be the one to give her the bad news.

He let the doctor come in and do that for him.

Kimmy was dressed by then, and the fact that she hadn't kicked either of them out but had let Mikhail fasten her bra for her and hold her pants like he would for a child was enough to break Jeff's heart. But it was also enough to make him question: Kimmy was a strong woman. He didn't know particulars, but he got the feeling she and Shane hadn't grown up in the warmest of circumstances. It had left them vulnerable, he'd often thought. The two of them had both suffered through a series of dismal relationship failures before they found their mates. Shane had reacted by pursuing Mikhail with a single-mindedness that left all of his friends dizzy. Kimmy had reacted by pushing Lucas away. Jeff honestly believed if she hadn't finally found a place where she was happy and had family, she would have packed her bags and taken off for the hills when Lucas first arrived. But she had finally accepted his love. It had been precious, actually—Lucas, the earnest country boy, and Kimmy, the hardened woman of experience. Jeff and Collin had watched it eagerly, like teenagers at a movie and the best part had been that she'd been really happy.

Jeff wondered how that could have left her with no reserves now.

Because the woman who sat on the table seemed to have spent all her chutzpah on having the courage to fall in love, with nothing left for the ups and downs that followed.

"Yes," the doctor said, looking clinically sympathetic, "as you can see here, and here, and here, the scarification is too extensive to allow embryonic implantation...."

Jeff looked sharply at the doctor—a dry middle-aged man with crowded teeth, sparse blond hair, and a leathery tan—and then at Kimmy. Kimmy was so confused, he almost couldn't stand it. Her brown eyes were unfocused and her jaw was so tense he was amazed her teeth didn't crack. The white hand in his was clammy enough to make him shudder and squeezing enough to hurt.

"Look, Dr. Johnson...." He stopped. "Seriously. Johnson. It's like God was giving you a sign." He shook himself. "Look—tell her straight up. You don't need to shield her with the big words, we all know where this is heading, and she needs to grieve."

Dr. Johnson glared at him and snapped, "Her uterus is too scarred. She can't have children. Is that what you wanted me to say? People think that they can just screw around and have no consequences but—hey!"

The man was midsize, which was good because Mikhail didn't have to reach too far up to grab the back of his jacket, steer him around, and shove him toward the door.

"You've done your job. Now go," he said shortly.

For the first time, they saw some humanity in the doctor.

"But I have options!" he said a little desperately. "There's adoption agencies and surrogates—her ovaries are fine, there's still a chance for—"

"Good to know," Mikhail grudged. "Perhaps you could have told her that straight off before calling her a stupid slut. Here." He reached out and grabbed the chart out of the startled doctor's hand. "We have our own man who can speak this to her. You need to go."

And with that, he slammed the door in Dr. Johnson's face.

For a moment Jeff and Kimmy just stared at him, but Jeff had to hand it to the guy—he knew his Kimmy.

"Come here, cow-woman," he said softly. "You don't need to be brave for us."

And Kimmy threw herself into Mikhail's arms and cried. The room wasn't very big—Jeff was standing awkwardly when Mikhail thrust the charts at him around Kimmy's shoulders. "Put these down."

Jeff did, and then he found his own shirt yanked on as Mikhail pulled him into the hug. Oh. Oh yeah. This was what he was there for. He was taller than Mikhail and Kimmy by a good six inches, and he used them to drape his body over Kimmy's back and sandwich her in the only comfort he and Mikhail could offer.

THEY made it out of the doctor's office eventually, after stopping at the nurse's station so Jeff could ask for copies of everything so *he* could present the options to Kimmy when she was feeling less vulnerable. He had to grimace—God knew there were assholes in every profession, but he couldn't help contrasting this so-called Dr. Johnson with his own mentor and bestest adopted grand-uncle, Doc Herbert. Doc Herbert would have done this better, he thought wretchedly. Doc Herbert wouldn't have made her feel quite so awful. Some doctors made the rest of them look bad, and that was just the truth.

Nobody gave him directions when they got in the car, so he took some directions himself.

"Where are we going?" Kimmy asked, looking around with confusion. Normally he would have gotten back on the freeway, one way or another, to take them to Levee Oaks.

"Baskin Robbins," Jeff told her. "Or Starbucks, take your choice."

"Baskin Robbins," Mikhail ordered, his tone adamant. "She has not slept in days. Caffeine, we do not need."

"Kimmy!" Jeff grabbed her hand. "Honey. This is bad. I mean, I know you're sad, and it looks like you've been dwelling on this for a long time, but you're stronger than this! What does Lucas have to say?"

She didn't wail or fall apart—that would have been better. She just curled up in the front seat of the car, knees under her cheek, arms wrapped around her legs, making herself as small as she possibly could.

Jeff met Mikhail's eyes in the rearview mirror as he stopped at Eastern. He was thinking, *Oh shit! How can the GBFF fix this?* But that's not what Mikhail's eyes were saying.

No. It was perfectly clear from Mikhail's squared jaw and narrowed blue eyes that while Jeff was wondering how to fix things, *he* had decided that something had to be done. And because he was Mikhail, he had a plan.

Jeff pulled into the parking lot at BR and left Mikhail broiling in the back seat while he ran around the front, opened the door, and pulled Kimmy out. She went pliantly, and Mikhail scrambled after her. The fact that he didn't give Jeff the raw edge of his tongue was enough to tell Jeff how utterly fucked this whole situation was.

The line at Baskin Robbins was formidable, and Jeff tried not to whine with impatience. Nobody was staying to eat their ice cream, so once this cleared out, it would be them and their knitting, and maybe Kimmy would open up a little. He could wait that long. He could. The dejected slump of her shoulders and her thousand-yard stare didn't need him pummeling at her with his irritation, it needed gentleness, patience, love—

"Dammit, Kimmy," Jeff snapped. "You had better be studying the menu like it was the word of God, or I will order you diet fucking *everything.*"

The shock on her face was gratifying. "I actually have an excuse to break my diet and you wouldn't order me something with fudge brownie in it?"

Mikhail was standing to her right, and he gave a visceral shudder. "Oh God, I don't need to see this," he said, looking truly horrified. "Jeff, you know not what you do." He looked at Kimmy then and seemed to take in her rolled eyes and the obvious disgust on her face and came to some sort of internal decision. "I am going next door to the grocery store," he announced out of the blue. "Order me a…." He narrowed his eyes and looked Kimmy full on, like this was significant. "Order me a full-fat large caramel Turtle cappuccino freeze."

Jeff felt himself recoil, and Kimmy's expression was pure horror.

"Mikhail! You *never* order big! Not even on your birthday!"

Mikhail drew himself up to his full five feet six inches and gave her a level glare that actually intimidated the snot out of Jeff, much less the emotionally fragile Kimmy. "Yes, but in this instance I will *trust* that Shane will not mind seeing the worst of me when I am bloated like a pig."

And with that, he turned around and flounced off, ignoring Jeff's open mouth and Kimmy's furiously extended middle finger.

Jeff recovered himself first. "Put that away," he hissed. "There's kids in front of us."

"Fuck," she muttered and tucked her hand back under the arm holding the knitting.

Jeff smiled, because swearing was another good sign. "Excellent. That's my Kimmy-love. Now, do you have any idea what he was just talking about?"

Kimmy groaned. "God, yeah—but let's wait until I've got chocolate and carbs in front of me, okay?"

She was good to her word—three scoops of ice cream on a brownie coated with fudge and caramel and doused with nuts. Jeff looked at it while he was eating his two scoops of milk-free sorbet and actually felt cramps of lactose intolerance just from sitting at the same green Formica table.

"So…," he said, enjoying his diet not-ice-cream for once. Thinking about how long he'd have to work out to get rid of that monstrosity Kimmy was eating made him appreciate the fact that if he actually *did* eat it, Collin would have to wheel the television into the bathroom for the next five days, because he'd be stuck there and bored anything but shitless.

"So…." Kimmy rolled her eyes and took a huge bite of brownie and ice cream. It seemed to work—her entire body melted into the seat, and the tension Jeff had seen riding her jaw and shoulders since she'd gotten into the car at Promise House eased up. He waited for her to savor and swallow, and then heard her sigh.

"It's stupid," she muttered. "I just… you know, Lucas would be such a great father, right? I just… I hate to…." Her chin wobbled for a minute. "I hate that he's the one being screwed over because I was a fucking whore— *hey!*"

Jeff didn't realize Mikhail was back until he literally smacked her upside the head.

"Shut up and take it back," he muttered. His gigantic calorie-geddon was sitting in front of Kimmy. Mikhail grabbed it and pulled a mouthful through the straw with enough force to make Jeff a little jealous of Shane before he pulled his attention back to real life. "Scoot over," he ordered, and she glowered at him.

"Sit next to Jeff! You hit me!"

"Yes, yes I did, and I have not hit a woman since I was going into withdrawals and my mother tied me to the bed. Now scoot over or I will regale you with more stories of my youth."

Kimmy did, scowling at him warily, and he slid in next to her.

"I said take it back," he snapped, and both Jeff and Kimmy blinked.

"You were *serious*?" Jeff said, surprised, and then he cringed and wondered if Mikhail's glare had set the gel in his hair on fire.

"Did you understand what I said?"

"Yes—"

"Then I was serious. The only person who gets my jokes is Shane." He turned his body and his temper on Kimmy. "Now take it back."

Abruptly Kimmy's expression softened. "Mikhail, I know you think I'm being hard on myself—"

"Fuck that. You were being *inaccurate. I* was a whore, Kimmy. I allowed men to fuck me in back alleys on piles of trash so I could have enough money to fix."

Kimmy winced, and Jeff actually *saw* the moment when the counselor in her took over. "Mikhail, you know that was your addiction—"

"Yes. It was my addiction. But I was the one who was addicted, and it would be a lie to say I remember every trick, but when I wake up with the urge to vomit, I know what was in my nightmares. So you see, I *know* what it is to be a whore." His ferocity eased up for a moment. "And *you* know what it is to be fragile, and a victim to an asshole you trusted and who did not deserve you. I did not say it was a better memory, I said the word was inaccurate."

Jeff had never wanted to hug the petty little tyrant so badly in his life.

Mikhail looked up and met his eyes, and suddenly Jeff too was absolved of any sins he had ever committed thanks to Mikhail's precision.

"Jeff and Collin, they deal with the aftermath of their sexual history every day. But no one—not one of us—has ever thought worse of them for the virus they carry. How you could think Lucas would blame you for the blind malice of a brainless virus, I will never know, but you must stop it this instant, do you hear me?"

Kimmy was crying again, but it was a different brand of tears. "It's different—"

"That's bullshit," Mikhail said implacably. And then his face and voice *truly* softened. He took a brief sip of his melting frappé and reached next to him and grabbed Kimmy's hand. "You need to talk to him," he said softly, and Jeff watched Kimmy put her spoon down and lean her head on Mikhail's shoulder.

"I don't know how to tell him," she whispered, and suddenly so much was made clear.

"You haven't *told* him?" Jeff asked, and before Kimmy could retort, Mikhail straightened up.

"You don't have to," he said, kissing her on the top of the head. "I did. He's here. You need to trust your husband, Kimberly. He won't let you down."

Before Kimmy could sputter or give in to outrage or whatever her reaction would have been, Mikhail slid back out of the booth and grabbed his frappé first and Jeff's elbow second.

"We'll see you at home. Jeff will help me for the rest of the day— otherwise Crick will have to come help at Promise House, which is a bad thing."

And with that, Mikhail dragged Jeff out of the store and into the stifling heat. They passed Lucas on the way, and he looked sad and frustrated—but not devastated and not angry. However, it was obvious Mikhail wasn't taking any chances.

"You promised," he said sternly.

Lucas nodded, his longish blond hair brushing his shoulders and his red-rimmed country blue eyes sober. "Thanks for calling me. I don't see why—"

"She will tell you when she's ready," Mikhail said shortly. "Asking her now will not help."

"Well, what does she need from me?" Lucas asked.

Jeff recognized that sound. Collin wanted to fix things for him. Whenever Jeff complained about the cats or the house or work, Collin wanted to step in and make it better. Lucas wanted to fix this.

"She needs you to love her, and she needs you to listen, and she needs you to not ever say she'd be a better woman if she could have children!"

Lucas took a step back, his massively muscular body actually recoiling from Mikhail's words. "I don't think that—"

"Good. Then you will be fine."

They stopped and watched as Lucas slid into the booth next to Kimmy. She wouldn't look at him at first, and Jeff's heart quailed. Lucas leaned in and talked to her while she was stuffing her face with ice cream, and after a moment she looked up—and gave him a bite.

Lucas took the ice cream in his mouth and swallowed, then grinned at her and said something.

And Kimmy gave him a soft, sad little smile.

"Good," said Mikhail. "It will be okay."

A few minutes later the Mini Cooper was buzzing through the blinding heat when Jeff remembered something important.

"That thing you said, about me and Collin?"

"Yes?"

"That was really nice."

Mikhail shrugged and sniffed. "Again, inaccurate. I spoke only the truth."

Jeff laughed. "You know what the truth is?"

"I am quivering with curiosity."

"The truth is that you constantly talk about not being worthy of your cop. And I swear to God, Mikhail, of all of us, you are probably the only one who is."

Mikhail's eyes widened with shock. "Lies!" he snapped. "I never suspected you of being cruel!"

Jeff shook his head. "All true. I swear on my God."

Mikhail was looking out the window at side of the road. They were nearing Levee Oaks now, and the landscape was parched yellow and brown, practically smoking from the heat.

"If it is true, then perhaps your God exists," he said quietly. "Benny is going to have Deacon's baby."

The non sequitur almost threw Jeff off, but he was getting better at following Mikhail's brain. "I know. Crick called me this morning."

"Yes, Deacon told Shane. They will keep running, I think, even when Jon is gone. But Benny's pregnancy, it will be hard on her." Hard on Kimmy. *Brutal* on Kimmy.

"Maybe," Jeff said, thinking that for many other women, the jealousy might be divisive. "Maybe it will be a healing thing."

Mikhail looked at him then and smiled just enough to be encouraging. "Healing is good," he said. "We obviously all have wounds that are still healing."

"We'll hope," Jeff told him optimistically, and Mikhail's smile grew musing.

"I didn't used to believe in that either," he said. "Amazing what the world can bring."

Jeff had to agree with him.

Chapter *12*

Deacon: Goal!

PARRY ANGEL was six, which meant her soccer team now had a goalie and keepers and forwards.

Deacon had coached the week before from the sidelines, on crutches, trying not to be frustrated that he couldn't get in there and play. That was when he'd put his angel in as a forward, imagining she would be the best goal scorer and lead the team to victory. Her first try, she had dribbled the ball up to the other team's forward and passed it to him.

He'd said thank you and scored in the opposite direction.

Deacon asked her why she did that, and she told him that she'd *had* her turn, and now it was someone else's. Since the other team was a whole bunch of new people, she was just trying to make them welcome.

Collin spit out his vitamin water when she said this, and they spent the entire next practice—when Deacon could actually *play* with the kids— explaining the dynamics of soccer. Deacon was appalled at the number of kids who found this to be new information.

"But why can't we all follow the ball!" one kid wailed, and Deacon had a brain flash.

"Because this way," he said, "you can all take *turns* handling the ball."

All those little faces lit up, and Collin just shook his head. "The killer instinct is dead," he muttered to Deacon, and Deacon looked at those grubby faces, excited, hopeful, eager to please—

"Cheyenne, honey, get your finger out of your nose. Your mom told me not to let you do that."

The little girl with the masses of blonde hair looked crestfallen, but she finished her excavation, popped the proceeds in her mouth, and looked back at Deacon expectantly.

Deacon turned to Collin and said, "Well, some things they still go after," and left Collin to struggle for breath before he introduced them to the time-honored game of Sharks and Minnows to help them get the idea of "Us Keep Ball/Them Lose Ball."

Collin recovered himself enough to run into the fray and start helping this one dribble and encouraging the other one to compete for the ball. The parents on the side of field looked up once in a while from their reading/texting/homework/laptops and cheered their kids on. Deacon had come to appreciate the casual indifference a lot of them had to the actual *game* of soccer—most of these parents weren't there to foment budding soccer stars. *Most* of them were there because their kid had excess energy after school, and they thought a team sport would teach the kid all sorts of things that the kid wouldn't get in the backyard by himself. Deacon figured that depended on which backyard they had, and enjoyed the fact that he had yet to experience one of those people who yelled at the refs, the coach, and the kids on the field about how everyone was stupid except for the bright and shining fruit of his or her loins.

Which was just as well, because Parry Angel and Cheyenne were currently picking the last of the tiny summer daisies that grew up in the badly maintained school field, and Tyler and Treven were.... Oh Jesus. What *were* they doing?

Deacon stopped suddenly and squinted as both boys—the little blond one with the wide, guileless brown eyes and the one with the dark skin, curly hair, and dimples—grabbed the sides of their silky soccer shorts and pulled them up into their little crotches and swiveled their hips.

"Hey, Collin?"

Collin came over from getting the little girls to try to get the ball from the clot of "minnows" in the center of the field, and looked where he was looking. "Are those kids...?"

"Yeah," Deacon said, caught between horror and humor. "I think they are."

They looked at each other, at a loss, when suddenly Megan's voice shrieked over the rest of the chaos on the field.

"Jesus *Christ*, Tyler! Give your wiener a rest and play soccer!"

Collin was laughing so hard he tried to sit down, but Deacon grabbed his hand and hauled him to his feet. "This was *your* idea!" he hissed. "You stand up and go coach that little masturbator like a man! Shit!"

Now Collin was on his back, howling, and Megan was stalking up to them, shaking her head.

"I'm sorry, Deacon," she said, bulldozing her embarrassment like she'd bulldozed Deacon's objections to coaching. "His teacher said it's something ADHD boys do sometimes. It's like they get bored and it's the world's greatest toy."

"And it's portable too!" Collin gasped before banging his head back down on the ground.

Deacon pinched the bridge of his nose and tried to summon some sort of response. "Well," he said after a moment, "can't really blame the boy, but, yeah. We may want to have a talk about doing that in public." Treven was looking at Tyler in confusion now, but unlike his friend, *he* was still apparently playing the wiener game with his shorts. "And, uhm...." He looked over to where Treven's father was watching his son, head tilted to the side, with pretty much the same expression Deacon and Collin had just worn.

Dad's eyes widened and he shouted, "Dammit, Trev, leave that thing alone!" at about the same time Deacon told Megan, "You may want to talk to Trev's dad about, maybe, not yelling at him in front of the other kids."

Collin was laughing on the inhale now, making a sound like a strangling seal. "Eeeeeeeehhhhhhhhhhhhh... *hoooooooooooo*... eeeeeeeeeeeehhhhh...."

Megan worried her lower lip and nodded, obviously considering the suggestion. The two little boys had been (thank *God!*) largely ignored by the rest of the kids on the field, and when Deacon called, "Trev, Ty, c'mere and be minnows!" they dropped their equipment, as it were, and ran into the circle with their... uhm, other balls.

Deacon took two steps (gingerly, because his ankle was still a little shaky) toward the center of the grass circle when Megan said, "You know, Deacon, you're a brave man. Most men would think twice about fatherhood after coaching a soccer team first!"

Deacon turned toward her, feeling a flush along every capillary. "Benny told you that?" he asked, and Megan's nod was enthusiastic.

"Oh yeah! We've got a pool going on whether your swimmers are gonna take the first time or the second!"

Collin had been recovering himself and struggling to sit up, but when he heard that, his blue eyes nearly bugged out of his head and he said, "Take the first time—he's good for it!" before collapsing back on the ground.

"You know," Deacon said, trying for dignity, "I think if I could deal with this asshole as my copilot, I could pretty much deal with anything!"

"Hey!" It was hard for Collin to be indignant when he was still flat on his back on the crappy overgrown grass.

"Hey, Collin," Deacon said meanly. "*Wiener!*"

"Heeeeeeeeeeeeeeeee...."

"Jesus...." Deacon finally made it to the middle of the field and declared the shark team the winner (because the shark team *always* won, it was the point of the game) and then said, "Okay, kids, goalie drills! Everyone set your balls down and get in formation—"

"Eeeeeeeehhhhhhhh...."

"Deacon?" Parry Angel asked when they were all in line, trying hard to get the ball past Tyler, whom Deacon had named goalie for this go round, figuring he didn't want that kid standing still *ever*, much less in line.

"Yeah?"

"What's wrong with Uncle Collin?"

"He's refusing to grow up," Deacon said, although it was hard when that infectious laughter was still ringing through the soccer field.

"Can I do that?"

Deacon looked at her wistfully. "You can try, Angel, but if you don't grow up, you'll never get to ride Crick's horse, remember?"

Because that was the deal. She could ride the biggest horse in the stable when she was eight, if she kept her grades up and didn't get in trouble at school. Of course Parry loved school, so that wasn't a problem, but Deacon just wanted some time to get used to the idea of seeing his angel on that monstrosity.

She sighed. "Okay. But unless something else good comes along, I'm stopping at eight!"

"Deal," he told her soberly. Because of course other good things would come along. Second grade, third grade, field trips to the zoo, family trips to the ocean, best friends, slumber parties, favorite movies, and boys—it was all looming on the horizon for her, and Deacon would get to be a part of it.

But Drew would get to be a bigger part of it, and for the first time since Drew and Benny started talking about moving out—and making plans for a distant future—that thought didn't hurt nearly as bad.

DEACON'S plan was to drop Parry off at the cottage, which was something he was getting more and more used to, and he enjoyed looking around the little yard surrounding the little house. He'd laid in sod after he'd had the house built, and put a little picket fence around it, thinking even then Andrew and Benny might live in it some day and he wanted it to be perfect. Parry's toys were out in the lawn now—sun-bleached Barbies, a little blue wading pool with a tiny slide, and a bottle of bubbles near the front stoop—and he liked the way the place looked like the home of a young couple getting established in the world.

He did not, however, care for the rusted-out car parked in the driveway. The make and model had changed from time to time in the past few years, but Deacon knew the owners of that car.

He'd loathed them since Crick was nine years old.

"Angel," Deacon said quietly, "I don't want to leave you here in the truck, but if I ask you to sit in the shade on the other side, can you stay there until Crick or Drew gets here?"

Parry nodded soberly. Deacon wasn't sure if she remembered the time her grandfather had shown up at The Pulpit after a tent revival and tried to kidnap her, but she had—wisely, it seemed—sure picked up on everybody's reservations about Crick and Benny's family.

Deacon pulled out his phone and started to dial Crick, and then he saw the cloud of dust as Crick and Flower Princess rode to the rescue.

"Awesome," Deacon muttered.

Parry looked where he was looking and squealed, *"Flower!"*

"Yup. Here. Wait in the shade of the pickup. I'll be right back."

Deacon waved to Crick, pointed at Parry, and waited for Crick's nod. As soon as he gave it, Deacon vaulted the little white fence and charged into that damned house.

He slowed down as he entered, wanting to hear what he was walking into. He closed the door gently and looked around the neat little kitchen. There was a mudroom around back, because the one in The Pulpit was right off the kitchen, and Deacon sort of hated that and he wanted it different for Benny and Drew.

The carpeting was dark blue, and Deacon winced when he saw the mud tracking across the white tile and Benny's new carpeting. Damn her family— damn them all. He peered into the living room, where the people inside were too enmeshed in their own drama to notice him, for which he was grateful.

Step-Bob hadn't aged well. Five years before, Deacon had beaten him into the hospital—he'd never gotten his nose straightened or his teeth replaced. His face was red and rough from alcoholism and his eyes were decidedly yellow. Deacon had heard he'd been taken from the drunk tank to the hospital a couple of times for throwing up blood, and right now he looked like breathing was a chore. His sweaty, rank, irritated presence felt like an abomination in the little room with furniture Benny had picked out special because green was Drew's favorite color. There was a crushed beer can on a lace doily Benny had spent a month on, because it had apparently been a challenge. Deacon wanted to strangle the guy for that alone, not to mention what he'd done to his children, but not here. Not in Benny and Drew's home. Not here.

"Are you telling me you haven't even *seen* your sister since she went to that place? How do know they're not molesting her or mind-wiping her or—"

"She's been there for weeks, Melanie," Andrew said. He sounded faintly out of breath, and Deacon figured Drew had probably seen Melanie's car pull down The Pulpit driveway, called for Crick, and then cut across the horse fields to be here so Benny didn't have to be alone with her family. "If you cared so much about the girl's whereabouts, why didn't you track her down after she'd run away?"

"Girl was out whorin'" came a gruff, blurry, masculine reply, and Deacon narrowed his eyes. Great. Step-Bob was *very* drunk. "Just like her sisters."

"I haven't seen her, because they asked me not to see her, because the more contact she has with this family, the worse of a human being she becomes," Benny said sharply. "If you want to contact her, write her a letter, like Crick and I've been doing. But don't mess with her life. She's having a hard enough time as it is."

It was true—the reports they'd heard from Shane and Mikhail weren't encouraging. The pinch-faced, bitter girl who had passed Deacon on the road three weeks ago was not automatically going to become Miss Congeniality— Deacon knew that. But his disappointment that Crick and Benny's sister should turn out to be such a singularly unpleasant human being was bilious and bitter.

"Well, those people are making her do all sorts of things she shouldn't be, making her work with homos and druggies and ni—"

"Don't say it," Benny growled, and Deacon stepped into the front room from the kitchen in time to see Drew with his dark-skinned hand on her arm, trying to pull her back.

"Benny, they're just trying to piss you off," he said gently, and Benny bared her teeth and growled like a rabid terrier.

"They succeeded," she snarled. "Now get out of my house. You want your youngest back at home, learn how to be her fucking parent!"

"You mind your mouth, girl!" Bob snapped, and without pause backhanded his daughter in her own home.

Benny's head snapped back and Drew caught her, and Deacon tried not to become an animal.

The last time Step-Bob had laid a hand on a member of Deacon's family, he'd beaten the man into the hospital. He couldn't do that in Benny's living room.

He had Bob's arm twisted behind his back before he even finished the thought. "Drew, is she okay?" he asked, and Drew looked up, his eyes blazing. Benny was nodding and pretending her face wasn't swelling, and Bob was hollering up a storm.

Deacon twisted his arm harder and ground out, "Shut. Up." And that stopped damned quick. Melanie opened her mouth to protest, but Deacon glared at her. She stopped, and he took a deep breath. "Crick's got Angel outside. How about you call the cops, and I'll escort Bob here to the front porch."

"You'll kill him!" Melanie squealed. "You'll kill him, Deacon Winters, I know you will—"

"Shut up, Mama," Benny snapped, and Melanie looked surprised when she found herself obeying her daughter's command.

"I'm not killing anyone," Deacon growled. "But we *are* calling the cops, and we *are* filing a restraining order. You two aren't getting anywhere near this family again, and if you do, I want the law on our side."

They were big words, and Deacon had every intention of keeping them. He frog-marched Bob out to the back porch, Melanie yipping at his heels, and he stood up on the top stoop for a minute. Behind him, he heard Drew simultaneously talking on the phone while getting ice for Benny's cheek, and he remembered again why he wasn't letting his temper get the better of him and beating Step-Bob senseless.

The heat on the front porch was considerable. The full import of the 102-degree day was just waiting there to smack Bob in the face with the setting sun, and Deacon squinted past it to see Crick and Parry riding away, which was a blessing.

He'd no more than thought that when Step-Bob gave a groan, staggered down the two steps to the front lawn, threw up, and passed out, convulsing at Deacon's feet.

Melanie ran down the porch and to his side, screaming his name, and Deacon shook his head, the anger draining out of him completely.

He popped back in the front door and said quietly, but with a voice that carried, "Drew?"

Drew looked up from the phone, and Deacon pulled him over with a nod. "You still on the phone with 911?"

"Yeah?"

"Tell 'em to send an ambulance. Bob just collapsed—he's seizing on the front lawn."

Drew's eyes widened and then narrowed. "He couldn't have done this at home, on his umpteenth beer?" he asked savagely, and Deacon shrugged and shook his head. From outside, there was a harsh burst of sobbing from Melanie, and a part of Deacon actually felt a little bad for the two of them.

He would have felt better about that sympathy if they hadn't, characteristically, tried to spread some more of the goddamned pain.

"Apparently we don't get a say," Deacon said neutrally, and Drew crossed his eyes. Deacon suppressed a laugh and looked beyond Drew to the living room.

"Let her sit until the cops get here," he said quietly. "Crick's got Parry for the night. She didn't see a damned thing."

Andrew nodded. "Best news I've heard all day."

Deacon thought wistfully about the story of the little boys and their soccer shorts, and how he'd been planning to tell Benny and Drew that when he came in. Another day, of course, but damn. It was a real shame to have this one ruined.

BOB ended up going to the hospital, but Deacon filed the restraining order anyway. The policeman who took his statement was Shane's old partner, Calvin Armbruster, and Deacon was grateful. Calvin liked Deacon's family— in fact, as far as Deacon knew, he and Shane still got together once a month for a beer and some gossip. More than once, Calvin had turned a runaway or a kid heading for juvie toward Shane's center, which was a trick Deacon was pretty sure he'd learned from Shane himself.

When Calvin left—after seeing Benny's bruised cheek and confirming Deacon's version of events—Deacon brought her some iced tea while Drew started dinner.

"You all right, Shorty?" he asked, and she rewarded him with a wry smile.

"Yeah, Deacon, I'm fine." She'd had worse was what she meant, but neither of them brought that up.

He reached across the table and grabbed her hand, and she squeezed. He heard a suspicious sound and looked up to see her dragging the back of her hand across her cheek. "I was so excited," she mumbled, like she needed an excuse to be sad. "I was going to tell you that I took the little test tonight, and we can go in tomorrow for the insemination instead of Monday."

Deacon hauled in a surprised breath. "Oh man," he muttered. "I—"

Benny shrugged. "I know—you've got to meet with the Ren Faire people tomorrow, I made your schedule. But you don't really need to be there, do ya, chief? Your part's already done."

She tried to smile winningly at him, but he still shook his head. "Well, I guess the good news is that I know Drew's boss, so he's free to come with you."

Drew grimaced. "Why thank you, Deacon. Tell my boss that's damned human of him."

A wave of self-consciousness washed over him. Awesome. He'd just given the guy time off to go watch a doctor get his girlfriend pregnant with his boss's baby. Well, fuck. There *was* no good way to put that, was there.

He looked at Benny, who was scowling at Drew, and decided that at this very moment, his one job—his *only* job—was to get out of their hair.

"I'm glad you're okay," he said quietly to Benny. "If Melanie ever comes up here again, don't open the door, just call the cops and then me, okay?"

He stood up and moved toward the door, and suddenly Benny was hugging him and crying, and he just rocked her like he had when she'd been a teenager and life had seemed too hard.

"It's okay—you don't have to go tomorrow," he said softly, and Benny shook her head.

"I want to go tomorrow," she told him, sniffling. "It's just... I was so happy. And Drew was happy too, and... and now it's all twisted and... dammit, why did they have to remind me how fucked up I really am?"

"Stop that," Deacon said sternly, pulling back to look at her. "This baby you're so hell-bent on having? That there was some of the raw materials. Now, what they chose to do with those materials, that's their problem. But the fact is, they gave you good building blocks, Benny. You are pretty and you are smart, and you are kind. You and your brother are creative, and you're clever and you work hard—all the things I would want from a baby, you have. So you forget them, okay? Fuck. Them. All the doubts I had, all the hang-ups that held me back, and the *one* thing I never, ever doubted was you."

Benny smiled at him brilliantly through her haze of sudden tears, and he wondered if she'd been taking hormones for the egg extraction, because as emotional as Benny was, she also usually managed to hold it together. "Love you, Deacon."

"Love you too, Shorty."

Deacon looked at Drew and felt another stab of guilt. "You can take the whole day off if you want it," he offered and saw Drew looking at them while he stirred the spaghetti sauce.

"No," he said quietly, like he'd come to terms with something. "Man, I take one day off, and you will find some way to fuck yourself up. I know it. I'll be damned if you do it on my watch."

Deacon shrugged. "That's the truth," he said, and then he winked. "Enjoy your night without Parry," he told them kindly. "I'm pretty sure Crick made something awesome for dessert." He didn't add that he knew Crick had, because Crick had been making *them* a special dinner, but that was okay. He and Crick would get lots of quiet nights between this one and the baby. From the looks of things, Benny and Drew needed tonight.

As Deacon left the house, Drew was hovering over Benny, giving her some more ice to hold on her cheek, and the sun was hanging over the horizon like a giant maw, threatening to devour Deacon's days whole.

Deacon drove straight into the gaping golden cavern, because that was where Crick was.

LATER that night, after Parry was asleep and dinner cleaned up, he sat on the couch with one leg along the back and one leg touching the ground. Crick leaned back against his chest in the space between, watching television, and Deacon read from an e-reader he held in the hand resting along the back of the couch. His other hand settled on Crick's shoulder. Crick was watching *American Horror Story*, which actually freaked Deacon the hell out, so he was relieved to immerse himself in the musings of the late great Christopher Hitchens.

Suddenly Crick paused the television in the middle of some girl crawling on the ceiling with her head on backward, and sat up from his position of being sprawled all over Deacon. Sometimes he sat in the corner and knit, the stitches painful and flawed, but tonight his hand was cramping, and Deacon was secretly a little grateful. He liked snuggling in all its forms, but he was reluctant to impose on Crick's time. The knitting was physical therapy—they both knew it.

But right now, Crick turned awkwardly in his arms, and Deacon pulled back and smiled a little, because they were face-to-face and close enough to strain his vision.

"Something on your mind, Carrick?"

"You ever wish I was a girl?"

Deacon blinked. "For fuck's sake no?"

"Are you sure?"

"Am I here?"

Crick made a little grunt of frustration and tried to squirm away. Deacon didn't let him. Crick's shoulders were still wide and muscled, and the way they felt under Deacon's hands went straight to his heart. He could probably touch Crick forever—his bare skin, the warmth pulsing underneath it, the life quivering in every sinew.

After a few moments of squirming, Crick settled down and allowed himself to be petted.

"I'm being serious," he muttered.

Deacon laced his fingers behind Crick's neck and leaned forward and kissed his forehead. "Would it be easier if I'd loved someone with a uterus? Sure. But Benny has a uterus, and she's still got your parents—that didn't solve a damn thing. Amy's got a uterus, and I let her go. I loved you more."

Deacon smiled fully, thinking about the baby, how maybe it would have the shape of Crick's eyes, since that was both Crick's thing and Benny's. Maybe it would have Benny's stubborn chin, or that arch that both of them had to their noses. But it wouldn't have Crick's brown eyes, and that might be unfortunate, but it wasn't a tragedy. "I love you more," he said, his voice soft.

Crick smiled and pushed himself against the couch with his toes so he could lift up and kiss Deacon on the mouth. Deacon opened and let Crick in, and the moment was sacred, hushed, and holy.

For that moment, it was hope.

Chapter *13*

Benny: About Women

CRICK actually went in with her, as well as Drew, which might have *sounded* nice when he first offered, but it had the potential to be a colossal pain in the ass.

Seriously, bring your stupid brother to your artificial insemination—how fucking weird was that, right?

Except Crick was… well, he started out by bringing a quilt of Parry Angel's they had left at The Pulpit. When Benny raised her eyebrows at him, Crick shrugged.

"They're going to cover you up with something. I thought it would be more comfortable than the whole paper thing. I mean, this thing'll wash, and, you know, it won't be…."

"Cold," she said, understanding, and Crick shrugged.

"Yeah. Speaking of cold and private, any news?"

Drew grunted in general disgust, and Benny looked at him wryly before turning her attention to the road. Drew could drive, but it wasn't easy or comfortable with his prosthetic leg. Crick could drive too, but his injured hand made it hard as well. Apparently she was driving herself to her own medical procedure, which was sort of funny when you thought about it. She'd have to talk to Deacon about getting the car adapted with one of those accelerators they put on the steering wheel, at least before the baby was ready to be born.

"Benny?"

She stopped her mind meandering and answered Crick's question. "Melanie called me this morning. He's probably got a week to live, maybe two. His liver's been going downhill for years now, and it's just up and quit on him."

"Fuuuuuck...." The word wasn't being wasted on sentiment, Benny was well aware.

"I vote we do jack and shit," Benny said calmly about the man who fathered her. Well, "fathered" was too strong a word.

"Benny, don't do that for me," Crick said reluctantly, and her heart started to swell a little as he spoke, because he was being unselfish and noble, and that was something Crick hadn't always been good at.

"I'm not. He wasn't great to me either, remember?"

"Yeah, but there were moments, you know?"

Yeah, she knew. She remembered Bob telling her she was smart once, when she'd been being mean to Missy, or even when she'd gotten into trouble for mouthing off to the teacher. She'd learned, though. She'd made her first-grade teacher cry once with her mouth, and it had occurred to her that Bob's idea of a good girl might not really be good. She'd tried to stick with the idea of a good girl that didn't make anyone cry, and that worked better.

"Yeah, but not enough," Benny said with decision. "It's easy to be good to a baby that you don't have to take care of. Say it's cute, give it beer, you're father of the fucking year. No." She shook her head and tried to put her thoughts into words. What she had to say was not flattering to her Zen inner life—but it was the truth.

"Crick, about all I can feel about this is relief. He will *never* show up again to scare my daughter. I could give a fuck whether or not he approves of Drew or Deacon or you—but this way, I don't have to hear it or see it or fight it. It will simply be taken out of the world."

Drew's warm hand on her knee was a comfort, but even more surprising was Crick's hand on her shoulder.

"Do you want to tell him that while he's still alive?" Crick asked, and for a moment, she thought about it. How relieving would that be, to just… just….

Just spew word vomit at a dying asshole?

"Closure," she said, thinking about it. "Maybe. Can we talk about something else?"

Crick made a pained sound, and Benny grimaced.

"No, we're not going to talk about Missy either," she said seriously. "I want to talk about something fun and happy that reminds me that not everything in our lives is fucked up. Got any suggestions?"

Suddenly Crick started to giggle, like, uncontrollably giggle.

"Did Deacon tell you about coaching Parry's soccer team and the two boys and the shorts?"

Sometimes her stupid brother really *was* a godsend. By the time Benny pulled up in front of the clinic, she and Drew were laughing so hard they could barely breathe, and Crick was cracking up through the rest of the story.

"So Collin told me that he tried to get serious, right, and he was recovering, and then Deacon walked up to him and said, 'wiener!' and he was just fucking *done!*"

"Omigod!" Benny gasped, putting the brake on and leaning on Drew. She loved watching him laugh. "That's precious. That is just fucking precious!" Then she started to laugh in a whole other way.

"What?" Crick asked, sliding out of the back of the car.

"I know what I'm gonna curse you with," she said, feeling happy and free and excited about the future—even the next nine months of misery, just to give the fruits of her labor (literally!) to her stupid brother.

"Curse me? What the hell are you going to curse me for?"

"Because. It's a mother's prerogative. I'm going to wish a *boy* on you, big brother. I could wish a sweet, tractable little girl, but nope, when this baby takes, I'm going to hope with all my heart it's a *boy.*" She let out a chuckle that even *she* had to admit was evil, and she caught Drew and Crick's alarmed glances as they trekked through the parking lot in the fierce heat.

"I don't know, Bernice," Drew said, working to draw even with her. "That laugh right there did *not* speak well of your gender."

Benny twinkled up at him. "Oh, honey, it doesn't need to. For the next nine months, I'm the thing that spawns. My gender is well protected."

Drew pulled her into the shade and looked suddenly, unaccountably sober. "Go check us in, willya, Crick?" he asked, and Crick nodded and walked in without arguing or anything. It really was like they were adults, wasn't it?

"What's the matter?" Oh, please, let Drew not be having second thoughts about this. Not now. Not when this really *might* not be the last time they had to come in and implant. Not now when they'd almost started what might be a long, painful thing.

"I just want you to know," he said, fidgeting for a moment. He sighed and reached into his pocket. "Look. You're more than an oven. And I know that you know that. You know that Deacon and Crick love you for more than what you're about to do. But I don't know if you realize that even while you're cooking this baby up, *I* will still love you for you. The baby will be part of you, yes, and it won't be mine, and I'll admit that'll be a little hard. But I will still be loving *you* for you. Does that make sense?"

She smiled at him, just grinned, because that was how much she loved him. "Yeah," she said softly. "That's about the most perfect thing you could say."

Drew looked uncomfortable. "God. Wow. Proposing to you is going to suck if I've got to top *that!*"

She rolled her eyes. "Really? You think you have the option of proposing to me now? We're getting married in a *year*, Drew. If you're going to pop the question, you need to do it before I get the timeline going for how I'm going to fit into the dress."

She turned around and sauntered into the building, and Drew spun on his prosthetic leg and thumped after her. "We're getting married in a year? And you didn't even wait for me to propose?"

"Crick didn't propose to Deacon," she said logically. "Remember? We just sprung the wedding on Deacon and made him say something sweet. I'm taking it easy on you. I'm giving you a year to think it over."

Drew's smile about blinded her, and he seized her hand and kissed her, right there in front of the receptionist's counter. "I'm gonna have something that makes you speechless," he said seriously, and she winked.

"You'd better. If you've got a year's head start, I expect some goddamned poetry!"

He laughed and kissed her again, and she made sure the receptionist knew they were there.

LATER, during the procedure itself, she lay back and let herself be probed and inseminated by the cold tool thing they used (there was a name for it, but the whole thing was sort of unpleasant and invasive, even if it was damned quick). She reflected for a minute that even the impersonal procedure couldn't take away some of the mystery of what they were doing.

"How does the swimmer know?" she asked. "And which egg did it choose to go for? I mean, is it a big popularity contest or a swimmer race or—"

"Benny?" Crick said, his voice strangely hushed as he looked at the little camera they were using to guide the syringe.

"Yeah?"

"They're going to make you pregnant with Deacon's baby. This is a big fucking deal. Can we all have a little bit of quiet and say a quick prayer this will work?"

And just that quickly, she had her answer to all of her stupid questions.

"Sure," she said, waiting while the thing inside her jerked. "It's a mystery. It's like all babies. It's a mystery, and all we can do is pray."

She closed her eyes then and ignored the fact that this wasn't making love with Drew, whom she adored, and this wasn't conceiving a child in the traditional mommy/daddy/baby makes three sense.

It all came down to the same thing.

It was a mystery. It was a random chance meeting of one particular sperm from a crowd and one particular egg from whichever ones popped out of the party room to look for adventure. It was hope that things would develop to the point where there was a real human being in there, and not just a collection of cells, and some more hope that the whole thing would coalesce and cook until done, and pop out pissed off and viable and ready to keep growing.

So it might not have been a traditional baby, but there was a breathless hush when the procedure happened.

There was a little respect for the mystery.

SHE wasn't stupid. She waited until the pee-stick test read positive for a week before she called the doctor and had it confirmed.

And she waited until she had it confirmed before she told anybody else.

She told Drew first, and he kissed her and held her hand and said, "Holy shit, it's gonna be a bumpy ride."

She thanked him for his optimism and then moved on to stage two.

She called an emergency knitting meeting with Amy and Kimmy, because those were her women friends, and while Amy was moving, she would still be on text alert 24/7, and Kimmy was going to be up on base, so she needed to be in the know as well.

Benny hadn't *had* female friends last time she'd done this. It had been her and Deacon, reading religiously from *What to Expect While You're Expecting* while they both wrote letters to her stupid brother and pretended Deacon wasn't focusing all of his energy on her and her impending baby to make it through the first couple months of sobriety. Amy had been there, in a sense, but Benny hadn't trusted her like she'd trusted Deacon. It had taken a year before she could sit and knit with the older woman and not expect to be judged or censured or lectured in some way.

But the trust had come.

So she was actually looking forward to this, even though Kimmy worked over the weekend, so they had to go to Promise House, and it was a Monday afternoon, so Parry Angel didn't have soccer practice and had to come as well.

They arrived, and Parry asked if she could sit on the front porch and play on her iPod. (Deacon spoiled her rotten—but in this case, the iPod was the electronic babysitter that masqueraded as learning software. Benny was a fan.) Benny could see her through the window and said that was fine, and she went into the kitchen to where Kimmy and Amy were already waiting.

Kimmy looked—well, gorgeous, because she really was, with those big brown eyes in her delicate face and the waves of gold and brown hair—but also pale and a little sad. She smiled at Benny, though, and offered her chocolate-chip oatmeal cookies and milk, and Benny sank down at the kitchen table gratefully.

Amy looked tired, and Benny had a sudden guilty thought that she'd been sort of consumed with the Deacon's baby thing and had maybe missed some stuff in her friends' lives.

So she asked about them first.

"How's moving?" she said as she dug for her knitting. She'd been planning this cream-colored baby blanket with lots of cables and eyelets since she'd first proposed this idea to Drew. She'd cast on after the doctor's appointment and had started the beginning of the complex pattern, but she needed her pattern book open and a chance to actually sit down and concentrate in order to work on it. A knitting day was the perfect time to work. "And where's your children?"

Amy laughed a little and made a deliberate stitch in what was obviously a bright-red sweater for Jon-Jon. "The kids are with my mother, who hasn't stopped crying since we announced we were going. I think she's trying to teach them Spanish in two months, because every time Lila comes home, she knows four more words."

Benny grimaced. "Well, you know, Deacon, Crick, and I will teach her to swear, if you'd rather she learned that!"

Amy laughed, surprised, and patted Benny's hand. "No, sweetie—I'm pretty sure Jon's got that covered. But thank you." She sobered. "God, nobody in DC is going to knit. You know that, right? I'm going to be explaining to all these new people how it helps me concentrate and they're going to think I'm rude and—" She stopped with a deep breath like she was reminding herself of something. Then she let the breath go all the way. "It's going to suck," she said after a moment. "I mean, I get the going for our careers and all, and Deacon was right—it's the sort of thing Jon and I always dreamed of doing—but we're leaving our friends and...."

"It's going to suck." Benny's heart fell a little bit. Crap. Who wanted to give good news when your friend was all buried in a funk of her own, right? She looked outside and saw one of the Promise House girls was outside with Parry. Even though the girl was dark skinned and nothing at all like her sister, for a moment Benny's heart gave a startled lurch.

"Kimmy, Missy's not here, right?"

Kimmy jerked a little like she'd been daydreaming over her sock as Amy had spoken, and she blinked. "No—no. Missy is at the homeless shelter today, giving out food. It's the only place that'll take her right now."

Benny grunted. "Did you tell her about Bob?"

"Yeah." Kimmy narrowed her focus and glared at her sock. "She said 'Fuck him. It's not like he loved us anyway.' Stone cold, but you know?"

"First sensible thing she's said since she got here?" Benny actually felt some sisterly affection for her now. That's exactly how Benny had felt.

"Yup." Kimmy wrinkled her nose. "Sorry, Benny. I shouldn't be that way about a resident."

Benny turned her gaze back to her knitting, making sure the yarn was coming smoothly from the bag so she didn't have to put it on the kitchen table. "Crick and I haven't been allowed to see her for a couple of years," she said, wondering why she felt so compelled to apologize for this. "We...."

"You were getting on with your lives," Kimmy said gently. "It's okay. You all had your own problems—it's what families do."

Benny smiled at her, feeling some better, and she thought maybe now would be a good time to fill them in.

"Uhm, speaking of families and moving on and...." She trailed off and grinned, so happy she couldn't quite contain it.

Amy guessed first. "Yeah?" she said, bouncing up and down. "Jon said you'd gone to see the doctor, so... so *yeah*?"

Benny did a little chair dance, knitting needles and all. "Yeah!"

Kimmy looked completely nonplussed. "I'm sorry—what doctor?"

"I'm pregnant!" she said, fully expecting Kimmy to celebrate with her. "I got inseminated, and I'm going to have Deacon and Crick's baby!"

Kimmy's expression was not quite what Benny expected. She blinked rapidly a couple of times and then pulled in her lower lip to keep it from wobbling. "Deacon and Crick's baby?"

Amy looked at her worriedly. "Yeah, hon. This was sort of big news— Crick and Benny had to do some fast talking to get Deacon to agree."

Kimmy sucked in a breath. "I'm sorry," she said, giving a pale smile. "I'd forgotten about that.. Congratulations... that's...." Her voice wobbled. "That's generous of you," she managed. Suddenly she dropped the sock she was working on and stood up, and Benny watched her, hurt and a little alarmed.

"Kimmy?"

Kimmy shook her head. "I'm sorry. I... I'll be back in a minute, okay?"

She practically ran out of the room, and Benny shared a helpless look with Amy. "Maybe you'd better go check on her. I... I don't know what I said...?"

Amy grimaced. "I've got sort of a suspicion." She got up and followed Kimmy, and Benny stood up unhappily. She wandered to the front door and stuck her head out, and saw the girl she'd seen out with Parry was sitting next to her, a skein of acrylic yarn in her lap, making little yarn dolls for Parry to play with.

"Oh, aren't those clever," she said, sort of at a loss. "Can I help you make those?"

The girl looked up at her, startled, sort of like Benny had been when Amy had first sat down and knit with her.

"Yes, ma'am," she said, and Benny had to look behind her to see if the girl was talking to somebody else.

"Do you make clothes for them?" Benny asked, taking the skein of light-coffee-colored yarn and wrapping it around her fingers the way she saw the girl do.

"Yeah, Sweetie," Parry said excitedly. "Clothes! Can we make clothes?"

Sweetie—apparently that was her name—looked a little embarrassed. "We'd need some felt and scissors and a glue gun," she said, shrugging. "That's how my nana did it."

"Maybe we can bring that stuff by next week," Benny said, and then she remembered why she was out here. "That is, if Kimmy's up for it."

Sweetie suddenly looked at Benny with an uncomfortably adult expression. "I don't think it's anything you did," she said, and Benny fought the temptation to squirm.

"Yeah?"

"Yeah. She's been... I mean, she hides it real good, but there's something sad going on. I don't think...." Sweetie shrugged. "It ain't my place to bear tales, right?"

Benny was dying to know. She was. But she remembered how hard it had been to know right from wrong. She'd been pregnant and desperate and watching Deacon wander into the liquor store while she just *wished* he would look at her, hanging on the corner, hoping for a handout. It had only been a week, but she'd stolen during that week. She'd cried.

Doing right after that—it had seemed such a huge thing.

"That's probably a good idea," Benny said, feeling noble. "It would hurt Kimmy's feelings, and we don't want that."

She and Parry immersed themselves in the fun of tying the little dolls around the neck and waist, and of making the little bundles for the arms, and, for the boys, splitting off the legs. It was soothing, and although Sweetie wasn't much on conversation, some of the hurt washed away. Kimmy was really good at pointing out when something wasn't your fault. It wasn't Benny's fault her parents sucked ass. It wasn't Benny's fault Deacon was a little too wonderful not to fall for, even if she knew better. It wasn't Benny's fault something had hurt Kimmy when Benny hadn't been trying.

Kimmy would know that, right? She'd know whatever Benny had done, she hadn't been trying? For a moment, Benny fought that terrible childish fear, that heart-sinking moment of knowing you'd done something wrong.

But Amy came out then, and although her eyes were wet, she smiled at Benny reassuringly.

"It's okay, hon. I think today just wasn't a great day for us to come over."

Benny bit her lip against the disappointment. "Yeah, okay."

Amy plopped down on the porch steps at Benny's feet. "Those are *darling*—can I make?"

Sweetie raised her eyebrows like she hadn't been expecting to host a crafting party just by being nice to a little girl. "Yeah, sure. Be my guest."

Amy took the yarn and started to wind her own bit around her fingers. "So," she said, "when are you due?"

Benny breathed a sigh of relief. She wanted to celebrate so badly. "About a week after finals," she said. "The end of May."

Amy nodded. "I can't wait to tell Jon—he'll be so relieved."

"It won't replace you guys," Benny said, fighting off irrational tears. Not now. She could cry when they moved, but not right now.

Amy shook her head. "No, I know it. But it'll be good for Deacon to have something to look forward to. Something to plan." She stopped winding the yarn and very practically broke it with a sharp jerk between her hands. "So," she said, her eyes twinkling a little. "Do I get to know how you convinced him this was a good idea?"

Benny's blush took her completely unaware. *I told him it was the way I could stop being in love with him and live my own life.* Mortified, she shook her head, and to her relief, Amy didn't look hurt at all. Instead, she patted Benny's knee.

"So see, baby? Secrets, things we're afraid of seeing the daylight—that's part of being a woman, you know? You'll tell me when you're ready. Kimmy will face us when she's ready. It'll all be okay."

Benny wiped under her eyes with the back of her hand and pulled out the yarn scissors from her knitting kit and snipped her yarn neatly.

"Of course," she said, her voice only a little thick. "Sweetie, do you want us to bring you some felt and a glue gun next time we come by?"

Sweetie blinked at them. "Yeah," she said, surprised. "That would be really nice. And more yarn if you got it—and maybe some needles. I seen Kimmy knitting. I wouldn't mind doing it myself."

Benny grinned. "Deal," she said, and they all kept working quietly in the suffocating heat.

KIMMY came out eventually, and they had a stilted conversation about the weather with a hope for a cool-down while they pretended Benny had not somehow accidentally broken her friend's heart.

At the end, though, Kimmy went to give Benny a departing hug, and it was long and hard. "I'm really happy for you," she said quietly into Benny's ear. "I am. And I'm happy for Deacon. I think what you're doing, it's a good thing. Let me know if you need anything, okay?"

Benny nodded and wiped her eyes and then smiled brilliantly. "You too."

Kimmy's smile was a little stronger than it had been. "Yeah."

By the time Benny got to The Pulpit to tell Deacon, she was pretty sure she could do this surrogacy thing, sisterhood or not.

Deacon

"REALLY?"

"I told you!"

The ginormous chestnut gelding Deacon was leading around the ring jerked against his halter, and Deacon cast the animal a stern look. Pickles subsided, and Deacon nodded his head decisively. Pickles had a good future as a jousting horse—he was generally calm and obedient, and he had a streak of vanity as wide as his dinner-plate-sized feet.

"The first time?"

Benny grinned from her perch on the side of the metal pipe fence that surrounded the practice ring. Deacon had a flash to her brother doing the exact same thing when he'd been barely older than Parry Angel, and to Benny watching him as he worked when she'd come to live with him, and to Parry herself, who could watch Deacon work a horse for hours.

But Benny wasn't a child, and Deacon's sense of time telescoped shut, leaving him with this moment, and this one alone.

"Yeah," she said, quietly, her lip curled up cockily like she knew she'd done a good job.

"You're pregnant the first try? How often does that happen?"

"About 20 percent of the time. Would you like a math lesson now, or can we start jumping up and down?"

Deacon felt his cheeks stretch in a smile. He couldn't help it. "Let me get the halter here so I don't scare the fuck out of old Pickles, and I'll hop the fence and celebrate, how's that?"

Deacon called a halt to the horse's paces and unhooked the bridle from the halter. He took a few steps from the horse, scaled the fence in two steps and a vault, and landed on his feet in the dust not far from Benny.

"C'mere, Shorty," he said, still grinning, and her smile at him was gold like September.

"Yeah?" she asked, nodding, and he nodded back.

"Yeah."

"Yeah?"

He picked her up and hugged her so tight he probably cut off her breath, and spun her in a circle while she laugh-cried on his shoulder. "*Yes! Yes!* Hot *damn*, Benny, you, me, your brother, we're gonna have a *baby!*"

That moment under the heartbreak of an autumn blue sky, Benny shrieking happily in his arms, was etched as cleanly as one of Crick's sketches, as perfect as the day.

THE moment he told Crick was not quite as poetic.

"Yeah? That worked?" Crick said, looking over the refrigerator at him.

"What do you mean it worked? You were there!"

Crick shook his head. "Well, yeah. But, you know. It was a thing up my sister's hoo-ha."

Deacon scowled. "Okay. For the rest of our lives together, you will never again utter that phrase. Ever. I need your word on it. This is a *baby. Our* baby.

If you ever call it a thing up your sister's hoo-ha again, I swear, I'll never eat your cooking again."

Crick straightened up over the refrigerator. "Take that back!" He looked seriously alarmed, but Deacon wasn't backing down.

"I will not! This is important—this is our *baby*!"

Crick looked vaguely uncomfortable. "But, you know. She needs to see the doctor, and it may not take. It's… you know. We've got nine months to go, Deacon. Maybe don't celebrate just yet."

Deacon swallowed hard against his disappointment. "Well, yeah. I'm not stupid. We talked about this. We've seen how this goes. I just thought…." He curled one corner of his lip in self-deprecation. "You know… we could be happy?"

The expression in Crick's brown eyes was a painful mixture of hope and anxiety. "I want so badly for you to be happy," he said, pulling the milk out of the door with a jerk. He was using his lame hand, which meant he was working all of his muscles extra hard just to hold it. Deacon wondered how many small chores he did like this to challenge himself, to help shore up the body that would, every now and then, up and betray him out of the blue. "I do."

Deacon took his life in both hands and ventured past the invisible line in the kitchen that was marked by the table. Very gently he reached down and took the milk from Crick's grasp and set it on the counter.

Crick watched him, one eyebrow cocked. He was actually almost docile when Deacon nudged him back so he could shut the refrigerator door. They were standing close, and Deacon had to smile when Crick grabbed his hips and pushed at him until Deacon was backed up against the counter and Crick was leaning against him.

"See," Deacon said soberly, "here's the thing."

The thing was, Crick's eyes were lit up inside, no matter how serious the occasion was, and the corners of his mouth were quirking up too. The thing was, Deacon was remembering for the thousandth time that day and the millionth time that week and the billionth time that month how much he loved this man and wanted to give him the world.

"Thrill me," Crick said, and Deacon winked.

"Every night, I give it my best shot. But about the thing. When your sister came to live with me the first time, she'd been… well, she hadn't been eating right, and she'd been sleeping on the street, and—yeah, we were worried. We took her to the doctor and got her extra supplements, and I swear, she drank about a gallon of milk a day, but… you know. One night I heard her crying, and I went in to see what was wrong."

Crick was looking at him avidly, and Deacon realized this story hadn't made it to his letters or phone calls. Benny wouldn't have told Crick, and Deacon had been too busy trying to mask the aftermath of addiction and recovery. This was a gift. A tiny puzzle piece of the life Deacon and Benny had lived without Crick, that Deacon could gift him in a story.

"She was worried," Deacon said bluntly. "This baby—it had become our project, you know? We were working on making *her* healthy and happy so the baby could be healthy and happy, and she was worried. Not just about the baby. She was worried that if she miscarried the baby, the two of us… well, we wouldn't have anything to keep us together, you know?"

Crick nodded. "Yeah. I know. She wanted to belong—even *I* could figure that out from half a world away."

Deacon leaned forward and traced the line of Crick's jaw with his nose. Crick's reaction was electric and immediate. He groaned and relaxed against Deacon a little further, and Deacon reached behind him to grab two healthy handfuls of Crick's ass. Tight as usual, Deacon thought with another smile. The luxury of doing this every day was still not a thing Deacon took for granted, and the animal touch was comforting as he resumed his story.

"Yeah. But there I was, and I've got a terrified teenager on my hands, crying her eyes out, and most of her fear really was for her baby. So I tell her what the doctor said—that after the first three months, she had less of a chance of miscarriage—she knew this, right?"

Crick nodded, still listening. His dark hair fell into his eyes, and Deacon pushed it back.

"But you know how smart she is. She pointed out that late pregnancy miscarriages still happen, and then she pointed out that babies die during labor, and then that the boy babies especially get low blood sugar or infection, and then I remembered that toddlers have a tendency to escape and stick their fingers in light sockets or run into traffic or fall off of refrigerators, and then we both talked about all the damned stupid things you'd done as you'd grown up, and then… then it just hit us. You were in Iraq, and we worried about you every second of every day."

Crick swallowed audibly. "This isn't very reassuring, dickhead."

Deacon felt that joy in him, the feeling that had welled up without hesitation in front of Benny. "That's the point. Don't you see? From the minute that swimmer found a home, we were going to worry. This ride gets faster and scarier and trickier, and the loops get higher, and there's more of them, and the entire fucking roller coaster is just going to go zooming down the track at Mach fucking *twelve*, and *that's* parenthood. Taking Parry out to the soccer field and hoping she doesn't get trampled searching for earthworms is scary. Putting her in the car is scary. There *is* no end to being the daddies, Crick. We enjoy the ride, or we spend every fucking second expecting to have our hearts ripped out of our chests. Dammit—I say we enjoy the fucking ride!"

Crick had closed his eyes near the end, and Deacon could see about six different emotions struggling to take over his face. The expression that won, though—that was Deacon's favorite.

It was a lopsided smile so full of excitement it couldn't bother to be straight.

"Hey, Deacon!"

"What?" But Deacon knew.

"We're gonna be daddies!"

Deacon nodded. "We're gonna be daddies."

"We're gonna be the fuckin' daddies!"

"Yeah we are."

Crick's mouth came down on his, and Deacon opened and let him in. The kiss went on forever, through the kitchen, into the bedroom, where it became naked and sweaty and loud. An hour later, they emerged, freshly showered, and put the milk back in the refrigerator. Crick gave cooking a rest and microwaved some chicken breasts for sandwiches, which they ate sitting kitty-corner to each other at the table.

They didn't stop smiling until they went to bed after television and fell asleep, Deacon in his place as big spoon, Crick holding Deacon's hand to his chest, both of them conceding that sometimes, you just got to be happy, and worry could happen tomorrow.

BY OCTOBER the weather had given them a bit of a break, and although Benny hadn't quite begun to show, she had gotten (in her brother's words) fatter.

Her middle finger was still elegant when extended. Drew had made a point to tell her that too, because her bird really was awesome. Especially given they were on the soccer field, cheering Parry Angel on in one of her last games when she flipped Crick off, and Deacon was a little embarrassed.

Then she kissed Drew right there on the sidelines, the kind of kiss that spurred other parents to go home and spawn other children, and Deacon's embarrassment faded. He wasn't going to begrudge them that, especially not because—

"Go, Angel, go!"

"Omigod, is that her? Does my baby have the ball?"

"Dammit, Parry, don't stop now!" That last was from Crick, because if he wasn't swearing he wasn't living, but most of the other cheers were from, well, everybody. Jeff, Collin, Shane, Mikhail, Jon, Amy, Lucas, and Kimmy—all of whom had had shown up this night, because sometimes a crucial nexus just forms in the fabric of time and everybody gets to see that moment when—

"Really?" Collin said blankly, and the entire Pulpit group stopped jumping and cheering abruptly.

"Angel...." Deacon's voice trailed off, and they all watched as Parry stopped in what was about to be a run for their first goal of the game and kicked the ball to the forward of the other team. On purpose. Because she was Parry's friend at school.

Sherrilyn took the ball and ran hell for leather in the other direction, and Parry turned a smiling face at her entire family.

"See, Deacon! I shared!"

Deacon's mouth fell slowly open, and all of the parents—every last one of them behind the sideline—made the time-honored sound of being helplessly cuted out. "Aw...."

Deacon pulled up a green smile, pleased that the torches and pitchforks were staying buried under the floorboards. "Nice job, Angel," he said. "Maybe next time, Sherrilyn could share with you, do you think?"

"Not on your life, faggot!"

The voice was from one of the parents on the other side of the field, and as soon as they heard it, when all of the parents on Deacon's team were still frozen in shock, the ref went stalking across the field.

"Oh my," Collin said, and Deacon had to agree with him.

"That nice man went and got himself a red card." Deacon's mind boggled.

"Do you think they're getting different training than when I was in school?" Collin asked, and Deacon heard Crick snort.

"Damned different than when *I* was in school," he agreed.

"Different's not bad," Jon muttered, and the entire Pulpit contingent watched in awed silence as the seventeen-year-old ref gave the parent the red card and then patiently explained to the coach of the other team that hate speech would cause the team to forfeit the game.

"Didn't say it was bad," Crick said, his eyes, like all of theirs, glued to the little drama on the other side of the field. "Just weird."

"Weird can be good," Mikhail said, and Deacon heard the rumble of Shane clearing his throat. Mikhail's voice softened. "Very, very good."

The ref trotted out to the middle of the field then, assembled the players, and cautioned them all to play by the rules. Across the field, the offending parent was stalking off, muttering to himself and throwing his hands up in the air—but he was leaving. The ref double-checked to make sure, blew her whistle, and play resumed.

Deacon resumed his goal in coaching the group of little kids in how to accept a graceful defeat at the hands of a more bloodthirsty enemy. And then there was juice and cookies.

As Deacon gathered up the unbelievable amount of crap that went with this job—the banner, the wagonload of extra soccer balls, the duffel with the team roster and the first aid kit, the ice chest full of waters, and the giant pop-up shade Shane carried at his side like it wouldn't usually take two men to do that—he heard a shrill voice. Benny was crouched down next to Parry Angel and assuring her that nobody was mad at her for sharing the ball. Deacon saw her stiffen and look around, wild-eyed, for where her mother was bobbing and weaving across the soccer field, wailing loudly.

Deacon and Drew met eyes. "Get them to the car."

"Yes sir," Drew said.

Deacon used to hate the way the young private deferred to him, but not right at this moment.

"Deacon...," Crick said warningly, but Deacon wasn't having it.

"Not here. Not now. You guys go. I'll deal with her."

"But she's my—"

"She's everyone's problem, Crick. Get your sister and Parry out of here. Leave me the truck and we'll meet at the ice cream place."

Crick growled, but like Drew, he knew an order when he heard one.

Deacon finished grabbing his crap, giving a distracted nod to the parents who were congratulating him on the solid loss, all the while aware that Melanie Coats was getting closer by the scream. He looked up when he could no longer avoid her, and glanced apologetically at Megan.

"Hon, can I talk to you about the game in a few? I've got some ugly family business to attend to."

Megan nodded. "I know—but if you let me stall her, you can get out of here too."

Behind him, he heard Shane chortle, and that's when he realized Drew and Crick had done what he'd asked and gotten the girls out of there, and Amy had joined them, but that everyone else had stayed.

He grinned at Megan then and nodded reassuringly at the other parents. "Your support is really wonderful, thank you. But don't worry, we've got this."

He swung the coach's bag over his hip and walked up to talk to Crick's mother.

"What do you want?"

Melanie looked around him almost desperately, and he didn't blame her. He wasn't sure they'd had a conversation in more than ten years that hadn't resulted in an arrest or a hospitalization. Either Deacon or his father had been the protector of two of her children—the storm break between Crick and Benny and their parents that kept them safe from the crash of unstable people mired in their addictions instead of their family.

"I'm not talking to you." She glared at him, her eyes red-rimmed, and he let out a sigh. He could guess.

"When'd he die?"

She sniffled, and he regarded her impassively. There was not enough pity in the world, not for him to feel any for her. She'd hurt Crick, she'd hurt Benny, and she'd hurt Parry. It might not make him a saint, but he wasn't going to worry about sainthood—he was going to worry about his people.

"Two days ago," she snapped. "The funeral is next weekend. Are you going to be decent and let my family come?"

Deacon shook his head. "Lady, if I have my way, we will be hell and gone from Levee Oaks next weekend. You could not pay me enough to put my family through that kind of pain."

Deacon had been wrong. Apparently he *could* feel pity.

"How come they get to be your family?" she asked plaintively. "My girls have gone, my boy's a faggot—how come you get to have my people? That's not fair!"

Deacon felt the weight of his own people at his back. "It's what we make it," he said simply. "I'm sorry for your loss. May your church be the solace you always dreamed it would be."

He turned then, and Shane and Jeff each took a step sideways. Jon had the E-Z UP, Mikhail had the soccer balls, and Collin was coming back from getting signed off with the ref. Megan and Shannon were both standing with a contingent of parents, glaring at someone whom, as far as Deacon knew, they had never met.

"Hey," Megan said out of the blue, "how did you know they were here? I mean, here we were, playing soccer. We've never seen you at practice before—what the hell are you doing here, anyway?"

Melanie blinked at her. "I… well, everyone knows what his truck looks like! I saw all the cars—"

"And you decided to come here and tell the family about a death," Shannon said, looking at Megan. Both of them had their arms crossed.

"Classy," Megan sniped, her long face showing disdain in a way Deacon never would have guessed.

"Sounds like something my family would do," Shannon said thoughtfully. She curled her lip and shook her head, and her clown-car-red hair frizzed around her ears. "Now *there's* something to strive for. You need help, coach?"

Both women were looking at Deacon expectantly, their kids coming up to them with their hands full of cookies and juice boxes, and Deacon's grin was full and heartfelt.

"You guys are awesome. We're going to the frostie for ice cream—you want to meet us there?"

They met eyes and shook their heads regretfully. "Sorry—we've got pizza night. It's a tradition—but thanks for asking!"

And that was it. No beatings, no screamings, no hysterics. Melanie was left alone, no scene to make, as the business of a productive community streamed around her.

Deacon was mildly surprised to realize he hadn't even thought of having a panic attack, and not once had he blushed. Interesting. Melanie might have been stuck in her place in the world, but Deacon, it seemed, was making progress.

He had no doubt the support of the people who followed him to Collin's mom's shop to have ice cream were much of the reason why.

Chapter *14*

Crick: Like Sand in the Hourglass

THEY spent the weekend of Bob's funeral at the beach in Monterey.

Not everybody could make it, but Jon and Amy could, and so could Drew and Benny. Mikhail and Kimmy were going to join them on the way home, since Gilroy and the Faire were less than an hour away, so family, but family small, and Crick was relieved.

He hadn't been to the beach with Deacon since they'd gone to Seattle five years ago to visit the family of his friend who had been killed in Iraq.

The beach at Monterey was a little warmer than the beach at Seattle, but it was still sandy and, on this day, saturated with sun.

Parry's soccer games were on Friday nights, and the family had packed up in three different cars and caravanned down early the next morning.

It had been Deacon's idea—he'd proposed it in the ice cream shop after Parry's soccer game the week before.

They'd had the plans halfway made before they were done with ice cream—Jeff, Collin, and Shane were professing to be green with envy—and it wasn't until then that Crick saw the relieved, almost secretive look on Deacon's face and realized something was up.

"What did Melanie want?" he asked during a quiet moment as the rest of the family chattered around them, and Deacon just looked at him.

Crick knew then. It wasn't so much a lightbulb as a series of connections. Crick's eyes widened. "So, next week…?"

Deacon didn't meet his look. "It would just be really great," he said quietly, "if no one in this family had to hurt any more because of that man. I was going to tell Benny before we split up."

"Yeah," Crick said. "Okay."

He knew. He knew Benny was going to sniffle on Deacon in spite of how well-adjusted she'd seemed the day they'd visited the clinic. You didn't just say good-bye to someone in your life like that without tears, even if they were tears of frustration or anger for what this person *should* have meant to you, if only he hadn't been a reeking, venomous douche bag.

There had to have been *something* about Bob Coats that had seemed decent and human, twenty-odd years ago when Crick's mother had first met him. *Something* must have seemed worth having. Bob had held down a job then—had he appeared to be a good provider? Crick couldn't remember if he'd been handsome before the years of drinking had taken their toll in coarsened skin and exploded veins. Had there been a time when it had looked like Bob would be a good father? Did Melanie think that even if he wouldn't be a good father to the son she had, maybe he'd be a good father to the children she'd have with him?

Something, Crick thought wretchedly, watching Benny cry on Deacon in front of the town frostie while Drew held Parry Angel and looked at Crick in resignation. Something to give him a reason for why the man had been able to father children and then destroy them.

Well, maybe not destroy.

Benny gave a little hiccup and then took a step back, wiping her face on her sleeve. A half smile played at her wide mouth. "So, the beach at Monterey, huh?"

Deacon shrugged, but he didn't look embarrassed. "I've had worse ideas."

Benny stood on tiptoes and kissed his cheek. "I've been there for some. I think it sounds like a wonderful idea." She turned to Drew and her daughter. "You guys ready? Mommy's done being sad."

Drew snorted. "As if!"

"Hush, or I'm going back in there for more ice cream."

Drew's cheeks widened in a patently insincere smile. "I think you should. Ice cream is good for you. You need more ice cream."

Benny giggled and kissed him over Parry's head; she was leaning against his leg in a casual gesture of trust. "Home. Let's go home and scare up something better than ice cream, okay?"

"But Mama, there is *nothing* better than ice cream!" Parry said soberly, and they were still discussing the benefits of frosty desserts when they got into Benny's car and drove away.

Deacon turned to get in the truck when Crick stopped him with a kiss. That Deacon's cheeks colored was actually sort of charming. Crick knew there would still be panic attacks and shyness, but for some reason, telling a bunch of little kids on the soccer field which direction to run, and then talking to their mamas about team photos and snack, seemed to have given Deacon just the slightest edge over the thing that had shaped his life. Either that or he'd just extended his definition of family. Crick deepened the kiss and pinned Deacon, helpless and hungry, against the side of the truck, sighing and relaxing when Deacon's hands came up to cup his neck and pull him even closer.

Crick ground up against him, and Deacon pulled away, resting his forehead on Crick's shoulder and gasping for air.

"That was awesome. What'd I do?"

"Are we really going to Monterey?"

"Yeah. Why not? We've got the money, we've got people to take over for a couple of days. I call time-out. Let's go play. I mean"—there was barely a hitch in his voice, but Crick heard what wasn't there—"Jon and Amy aren't going to be here forever."

Crick dropped a kiss in his hair. "How bugnuts do you think the dog is right now?"

Deacon let a laugh escape. "The technology to measure that dog's psychosis has not yet been invented."

"Yeah. Should we take him to the beach with us?"

"God, what a pain in the ass!"

"Yeah, but should we?"

Deacon smiled a little. "Please?"

AND so it was that now, even as Crick watched from his little kick-back sand seat next to a sleeping Parry, he could see Jon and Deacon throwing the stick for the giant Labra-donkey that lived under their porch. Mumford had ridden down in the pickup with Deacon and Crick, his head hanging out the open window in the back, his tail thumping against Crick's head for pretty much the entire three-hour trip. Once they arrived at the beach, he took off for parts unknown practically before the truck stopped. Deacon ignored him.

"Aren't you going after him?" Crick asked, struggling with the chair and the blanket and umbrella. Deacon had the ice chest and the beach bag and the useless fucking lead for the dumbass dog.

"Nope."

"Why not?"

"Because he can run faster than me."

"What if he bites someone?"

"He hardly chews his food."

Crick had to concede—Mumford had an amazingly soft mouth. His ancestors had obviously been bred as bird dogs, because the dumb animal had been mouthing the same stuffed toy for almost three years. It was stinky and drool saturated, but there wasn't a bald spot on it.

"What if he knocks someone over?"

"Hard to do that when you're in the water," Deacon said, and sure enough, the dog was a quarter of a mile away, paddling like he owned the freakin' ocean.

"What if a whale eats him?" Crick asked, because the plaintive rhythm of the questions was fun, that's why.

"I would actually *pay* someone to take a picture of that."

"Okay, what if a *shark* eats him?"

"Then we give thanks to his stupid spirit for warning us before we threw the kids in."

"The kids aren't going to swim!" Crick protested. Not in Monterey, where the water was fucking cold, especially in October!

"No, but they have life jackets on for a reason. It'd be nice to know that if they get swept away, they're not just bobbing there like a really big lure."

Crick glared at Deacon for a moment, outraged, and then he saw that full mouth fighting so hard against a grin that he was tempted to drop all his shit and slug him.

"You bastard."

"You were asking for it."

"I'm gonna beat you once I dump this crap, you know that."

"You'd have to catch me first."

"I will seriously pummel you until you bleed."

"What'd he do now?" Jon asked, laughing as he carried his own armload of crap through the parking lot with them. Drew and Benny had apparently hit all the lights—they'd been there for a good half hour, and Benny had called Crick and said they staked out a place by the dunes so they could back up into the shade of the overlook. The sun was hot enough to make walking through the parking lot uncomfortable, and for a minute, Crick had the time-honored response to going to the beach: looking at a picture in an air-conditioned room would be a lot more fun.

But a picture wouldn't smell like yarrow and salt water, and a picture wouldn't have the roar-swish sound beyond the dunes. Crick got a firmer grip on his chairs and blanket and gave thanks he wasn't Amy, who had Lila by one hand, a beach bag over one shoulder, and Jon-Jon on her hip.

And then it occurred to him.

In a year, he *would* be Amy, except with only one kid. The conflict of excitement and terror that crashed over him left him without any words.

Which was fine, because for the moment, Jon was taking care of all of the silences.

"Forget what Deacon did now, what the hell is your dog doing?"

"Being shark bait," Deacon said, with that same deadpan delivery.

Jon snorted. "I don't know if he'd pass the interview for that job. He has to be smart enough to bleed."

Deacon snickered like a little kid. "Then you should go swimming too—you'd fail that interview in a hot second!"

"Me? I am wounded! Wounded, I tell you!"

"Mommy! Daddy's hurt!"

Lila tugged at Amy's hand and tried to escape to go check on her father, who was so close to collapsing from laughter Crick wanted to kick him.

"Daddy's not hurt, sweetheart," Amy said sweetly, glaring at her husband. "He's just stupid. He's like that a lot."

"Oooh, Mommy! We're not allowed to say 'stupid' in school. That's a *bad word!*"

By now Jon and Deacon were laughing so hard they could barely breathe, and one thing and one thing only was stopping Crick from kicking one of

Jon's feet behind his other one to send him sprawling: God, they both needed this.

Jon and Deacon giving each other shit, laughing—they needed this memory of them, of their families, of a good time untainted by worry.

Deacon ran with the stupid dog and with Jon and the kids until the kids wandered off and started building sand castles because they were tired. The dog collapsed on the sand next to them, and eventually the girls ended up asleep on the big sandy dog, covered with a towel so they didn't burn. Parry's curly brown hair stuck out wildly next to Lila's straight blonde fuzz. Jon-Jon was currently curled in a ball next to Amy, quietly drooling on her leg.

Benny and Drew had played, and sat and sunned themselves—and then left quietly, with Deacon's blessing, to go have some quiet time in their hotel room. Drew had brought a special prosthetic made for sand, but that didn't mean walking in it was a picnic, and Crick envied him the ability to say, "Nope! I've had enough! Play without me!" Crick couldn't do it. Crick's leg ached, and his arm too, and he was content to hang out under the umbrella next to the girls and read a book while Jon and Deacon pushed each other into the water (which was still ice-fucking-cold) and threw the Frisbee, making seemingly impossible catches against the red light of the sun on the water.

"You know," Amy said, startling him because he'd thought she was asleep, "you're the only reason we can leave him."

Crick looked at dainty, dark-haired, vibrant little Amy and felt a distinct pang of sadness. He loved her like a sister—and since he loved his sister a helluva lot, that was saying something. He could remember, like a hazy dream, the jealousy he'd harbored when she and Deacon had dated in high school, but that emotion didn't really exist now. What was left was gratitude. She and Jon had helped keep Deacon together when he'd been gone. They'd helped them keep their home together after he'd come back, and things had been rough and on the verge of collapse for oh so long. Crick and Amy knitted together, watched movies together, and met sometimes in the morning for coffee when their husbands were out running, a pastime that baffled them both.

And she hadn't talked about the fact their house was almost empty of furniture, down to the bare minimum of toys, and that very soon it would be vacant, ready to be rented out to the two kids from Promise House who were on the verge of turning eighteen but who still needed the family that Shane's family provided.

"Yeah?" Crick said, answering Amy like all this wasn't lying heavy on his heart. "Then I sort of wish I was still a fuckup. If you guys taking off is the result of me being competent, that's like rewarding someone for a good job by kicking them in the balls."

Amy cracked up quietly into her book. "Asshole. You couldn't let us leave without trying to make me feel like shit, could you?"

"No," Crick told her seriously. "I was just waiting for the right time."

"Well, excellent, Carrick! We're all happy, it's been a good day—kick me in the balls!"

Crick laughed, because she was just as snarky as Jon. "We're going to miss the holy hell out of you. They've been inseparable for almost thirty years—I don't know what he's going to do without Jon."

Amy sighed a little. "Yeah, same with Jon. Deacon's his conscience. When we were in school, he always used to complain that without Deacon, he could have cheated his way into college."

Crick watched the two of them horsing around and had a sudden, vicious moment of relief. If Jon had been even the slightest bit inclined toward men, Crick's life might have been very, very different.

"Jon is his laughter," he said after a moment, because this was the thing Jon had that Crick didn't. Deacon had never blushed in front of Jon, and they'd never fought. (Although Crick was aware of some harsh words spoken when Deacon was having his heart attack—Deacon claimed not to remember.) Jon was easiness and laughter and the simple assumption life didn't have to be that frickin' hard. It was something Deacon sorely needed. "It's going to be a lot harder to keep him from taking life so damned seriously without Jon here."

"Yeah," Amy said, and her smile was pure affection. "But you guys— you've got Shane and Jeff and everyone. And you're going to have a *baby*—I know you think you know, but no one *ever* knows the difference that makes."

Crick shrugged. "I've got a good picture," he said, thinking of Amy with her hands full. "It's gonna be a challenge."

Amy nodded. "It is. And you know, we've got computers and stuff. We can Skype in the mornings, you can ask me stuff. It's a little easier to keep up with each other than it was when you were in Iraq."

Crick nodded. "Which is good. You've seen my parenting role models, right?"

Amy regarded him soberly. "Parrish Winters was a good man."

Grimace. "Yeah, but he wasn't there when I was as little as Jon-Jon."

"No—but you've seen your sister and Deacon and Drew with Parry. You've got a good start, hon. But"—because he was obviously about to dump crazy insecurity on their gorgeous day—"I'll be there. Your sister will be there. Deacon will *definitely* be there."

Crick blinked and laughed a little. "Would you believe I forgot that last part?"

Surprisingly enough, she laughed. "Yeah—everybody does. You know, the first week after Jon was born, I was a mess. All hormones and I was finally off of bed rest, and I was just absolutely certain that I had to make up for being on my ass for months by being the world's perfect mommy, you know?"

Crick shook his head. "I had no idea. No men were allowed in your inner sanctum until Jon-Jon was two months old."

Amy clapped her hand over her mouth and scrambled to sit up, holding Jon-Jon's head until she could rest him gently on the ground. "Right? *Right?* Because I was just that crazy! Anyway, one night I just lost it—Lila dumped potpourri on the ground and I had a *cow*, became a hysterical shrieking crazy bitch, and Jon came home and Lila was crying and the baby was crying and dinner was burning on the stove. And it was like—like, sudden clarity. He turned off the stove, made me sit down and nurse Jon-Jon, and made mac and cheese and hot dogs for Lila. And then he fed me some, and I realized I hadn't eaten *all day*, because I'd been trying to clean the bathroom with two kids in the house. So there I was, scarfing fat in a bowl over Jon-Jon's head, and he was eating like a champ, and Jon was making Lila laugh, 'cause that's what he does, and it hits me—"

"You needed a maid?"

Amy giggled. "Well, yeah. Being a lawyer has its perks, and Shane's kids work for cheap. But more than that."

"You needed help?" He wasn't stupid.

"Yeah. And some people have to go it alone—that boggles me. Single mothers? They get all the respect in the world. Because you've got to admit, as hard as it's going to be, you're not going to be doing it alone."

Crick looked out again at Deacon and Jon. "Deacon's worried that I might have to someday," he said shocking himself with the rawness of that. He looked up at Amy and saw she was sad—but unsurprised.

"Yeah," she said softly. "We don't have guarantees. But think about it this way. If the worst happens, would you rather be parenting alone, or would you rather just be alone?"

He grunted. She was fearless. She'd been fearless when she was in high school, dragging Deacon to dances or riding a horse out to Promise Rock to go skinny-dipping with Deacon. (Deacon thought Crick didn't know about that. Crick let him keep his illusions.)

"Yeah," he said. "It always sort of comes down to that."

"Yes, it does."

"Sort of a no-brainer."

"Yup. And since you have proved you actually have a brain...." She raised her eyebrows impishly, and he rolled his eyes in response.

"It's not like I was going to suddenly call a halt to the whole thing anyway," he said with some injured dignity, and Amy laughed.

"I should hope *not.*" She stood up, brushing the sand off her shorts. "Now help me get all packed up. You and I can get the kids back to the hotel for a bath before dinner, and the boys can stay and bond."

Crick nodded and had a sudden thought. "Oh, oh hell. What are we going to do with the damned dog when we're all out eating?"

"Silly puppy." Amy smacked his cheek lightly with a cool, dusty hand. "You and Deacon are going to stay at the hotel and have sex, and we're going to bring you takeout!"

"I'm gonna make you somethin' *extra* special for Christmas!" he said playfully, and just that sudden, Amy was serious again.

"You'd damned well better. 'Cause I'm going to be missing the holy hell out of you people while we're gone."

There didn't seem to be much more to say to that. Amy offered Crick a hand and he took it, relying on her tiny, vital body to heft him up. She didn't let him down. He started packing stuff up, leaving the kids and their sun umbrella until the very end.

"Hey, Amy," he said after a minute, and she looked at him over her shoulder as she put the last of the trash in a small bag and then tucked it into the ice chest to get rid of later. "How come we don't know any tall women?"

Amy shook her head. "Like I would know the answer to that. Collin's sisters—they're all Amazons. Those moms on the soccer team—thereyago. Jesus, Crick, the things that come out of your mouth."

Crick would explain it to Deacon later—after they'd gotten back and showered and the dog had passed out and Crick had given Deacon a first-class blow job on the hotel bed, rushing it only a little because he wanted to finish before dinner came knocking on the door of their room.

"Why don't we know any big women?" Deacon asked, covering his eyes with one hand while trying to pull his boxers up around his hips with the other. Crick helped him out there—his lame hand wasn't great with fine motor skills, but he had enough strength to slip it under Deacon's scrawny ass and lift it up while Deacon pulled.

"Yeah."

"We *do* know big women," Deacon said, looking at him sort of laughing and helpless, once they got him dressed. "They're just all big on the inside and tiny on the outside. How's that?"

Crick shook his head and flopped on the mattress next to Deacon. He'd shot off in his shorts, because watching Deacon play in the sun on the shore had made him half-mast and aching for pretty much all day. "It's weird. I'm sort of hoping Parry Angel is at least five foot seven. And if our kid's a girl, maybe she'll get to be, you know, closer to your height than Benny's."

Deacon's hair had grown long enough to fall a little across his forehead. Crick liked it like that, but he knew it wouldn't last. He pushed at it, though, so he could feel it against his palm, and Deacon took him seriously in a way that had always surprised Crick—but it had also made sure Crick could probably not love another human being the way he loved Deacon Winters.

"Why is this important?" he asked after a moment, and Crick wondered if he would ever get tired of looking into Deacon's green eyes.

"Because babies are small," he said after a moment. "Babies are small, and I'm big, and my hand is lame, and I'm hoping this baby will be big so I'm less afraid to hold it."

"It's not going to pop out toddler-sized," Deacon said, but he wasn't laughing when he said it. "It's going to come out the size of a Chihuahua, and wrinkled and helpless. And yeah—we're going to have to do some work on how you'll manage when you're alone. But you won't be alone too much, Carrick, you know that. I work long hours, yeah, but Benny and I managed, and you and me—we can do the same."

It was so very close to the reassurances Amy had given that he wanted to smile. His people knew him.

"Okay," he murmured. "I'll trust you."

Deacon blinded him with a smile and then leaned forward to kiss Crick, and that was pretty damned awesome. It might even have gotten somewhere, but someone knocked on the door. After pulling on their sweats in a damned hurry, they opened the room to Jon and Drew with an armload of takeout for Deacon and Crick and plans to order a violent movie on cable while the girls had a slumber party in Jon and Amy's room.

But the conversation, that stuck with Crick. It lasted through whale watching the next morning, which was pretty amazing for Crick but not so amazing for Deacon, who spent much of his time in the back of the boat, chumming the waters and assuring the little kids he was going to be just fine. Eventually Deacon put a clamper on his gag reflex, and when the gray whale dove under their ship to slap the water in front of them with his massive, massey tail, he was one of the first to run around the other side, Parry Angel in his arms, to watch the animal as it surfaced, the water sliding slick and shiny off of its soft hide.

That was a man, Crick thought, and although he'd known this his whole life, it came to him now in a big way that the things that made a man a good man, period, also went into making a good mate and a good father.

It wasn't until much, much later, after the drive home when the exhausted dog (who had been allowed on the whale-watching boat but who had spent the entire time dozing in the cabin) had fallen asleep in the living room and he and Deacon were falling asleep in their own bed, that it occurred to him: Deacon's plan for the weekend had been completely successful.

He'd call Benny the next day and confirm, but he was pretty sure neither one of them had thought of Step-Bob once the entire weekend.

Parrish Winters, yes. Jon and Drew, yes. Bob Coats, no.

For some reason that, of all things, reassured Crick more than anything else. His stepdad had been a shitty role model, that was for sure, but Crick had moved past that when he was nine years old.

It had just taken him twenty years to realize how far beyond it he really was.

Chapter *15*

Shane: Favorite Dish

SHANE and Kimmy had lived through some lonely-assed holidays.

When they were children, more often than not, their parents had been traveling, and they'd been at home with the help. The "help" had been competent but not warm, and as such, they both remembered gourmet turkey, five-star dressing, and stifling evenings of reading in the same room together, until Kimmy got old enough to sneak out and go clubbing.

Even after Shane met Mikhail and become part of The Pulpit family, his luck with holidays hadn't been great. Their first Thanksgiving, Mikhail spent the night with his mother and her church, because she was dying, and Shane had been devoted to courting him slowly. That Christmas, Mikhail and Ylena had been on a cruise, because it was Mikhail's last promise to his mother, and Shane had been recovering from a knife wound, because that's what he'd done as a policeman. He'd gotten hurt a lot.

The next year, they'd started Promise House, and Shane (and Kimmy and Mikhail) had resolved for all of that to change.

Their first Thanksgiving, Shane and Mickey busted their asses to make sure the kids all got the full meal treatment from top to bottom, and Kimmy stayed with them to eat it. Shane and Mickey planned to eat at The Pulpit, and that had turned out to be frightening because the night before Thanksgiving was the moment Deacon's heart took to just give out. Shane had been the one to sit down and talk Deacon into admitting that maybe, just maybe, there was a problem, and that once Benny arrived, Deacon could possibly let the family handle things. Getting inside people's heads to find out what they did—that had turned out to be Shane's best thing, which pretty much made up for the fact it made him just a little bit weirder than the average bear. (He'd liked that turn of phrase, but Mickey hadn't—Shane had reluctantly put it away, along with any ideas of waxing his chest, because Mickey didn't like that either.)

That Christmas Collin was recovering from the flu, and Jeff was trying very hard not to let all of that dying and living scare the holy Jebus out of him (as Jeff would say), and that was a tough time too.

But the Thanksgivings *after* that—well, Shane, Mickey, Kimmy, and Lucas had pretty much put together a game plan to make the holidays not suck for a bunch of kids who knew *exactly* how shitty Thanksgiving and Christmas could be.

One of the first things they did was ask the kids what side dish they wanted to help cook for Thanksgiving dinner.

It had been Mikhail's idea, sort of. Shane had asked him before their wedding if he ever missed his mother's Russian cooking. It had been the third or fourth time he'd asked—Shane was still trying valiantly to cook in those days—and Mikhail had wrinkled his pert little nose.

"Borscht? Are you high? I think you must be high. How about *you* overcook cabbage and stuff it with ground-up pigs' feet, and then tell me if that sounds like a good idea to *you*!"

"That's not the recipe for borscht." Shane knew—he'd looked it up.

Mikhail grunted. "Well, it should be. No. I told you. American food. In fact...." Mikhail's face softened with memory here, and Shane was enthralled. "My best holiday meal was probably meatloaf. We had just moved from Brighton Beach to California, and *Mutti* wanted to celebrate the American Thanksgiving. We didn't know about turkey and pilgrims and pumpkin pie so much—and I... I remember I really wanted red meat. It seemed to be everywhere. So *Mutti* asked a friend from church and made us meatloaf for Thanksgiving." Mikhail's smile was... small, on his pointed face, and nostalgic, and Shane was sharply reminded of Ylena Bayul, who had been compassionate and dry and who had desperately loved her son. "It was a very good recipe," he said after a moment. "There was soup and bread crumbs and ketchup. I should like to have it again sometime."

So Shane tried to make it for him, just a side dish of it, for Thanksgiving. The recipe turned out too dry, of course, because Shane couldn't cook boiled water, but Mikhail ate it with that same small nostalgic smile, and some of the kids had asked for some, because *they* remembered a time when meatloaf had made *them* happy.

The next Thanksgiving, the week leading up to it, Shane had asked every kid at Promise House what his or her favorite holiday dish was. And then he and Kimmy and the other two counselors spent the rest of the week mining that one good memory—a good food during a holiday—to remind the kids life wasn't all that bad, and that holidays were worth celebrating.

The last Thanksgiving had been the best ever. Shane and Mikhail had regretfully passed on the gathering at The Pulpit (Lucas and Kimmy had gone instead), but the kids had been *so* grateful, because each of them hadn't just contributed a *dish*, each kid had contributed a *memory*.

This year they were doing the same thing, but the results weren't quite so spectacular—at least not with Melissa Coats, they weren't.

"I don't give a shit," she snapped when Shane asked her what side dish she'd like to have at her meal.

"Really?" Shane liked food—a little too much, but all that good running with Deacon was starting to pay off, and you could hardly tell at all.

"Yeah, really. It's food. Someone cooks it. You eat it. Meal over."

"So no one ever tried to make the holidays special for you?"

Missy scowled. Since her father's funeral—which she had refused to attend, even if it would have given her a day off of chores, which she loathed—her attitude had gotten more sour but less violent. It was, Mikhail said in distaste, like she'd turned into a simmering cauldron of bile. You never knew when she would bubble up and get you, but she wasn't likely to set the house on fire.

"Yeah, I guess," she grudged. "Not lately, but…." She gnawed on her lower lip. "You know, Crick made us dinner once. It must have been right before he got kicked out. He… well, it was one of those boneless turkey breasts, but he cooked it, and baked potatoes, and… and he made that green bean stuff with the soup. I think Deacon helped him." She frowned, but in memory and not in bitchiness. "Yeah. He must have, because there was stuffing, and Crick didn't know how to make stuffing. But… but that was real good. Bob was out drinking, and Melanie told us we could have a sit-down if we wanted, so Benny and Crystal and me, we made place mats with office paper and crayons and… I remember that. They let me cut out leaves and color them orange. It was… it was nice. It was holidays like the kids talked about at school."

Shane's heart caught. For a moment, right *this* moment, Missy's face relaxed, and she looked a little like Benny and a little like Crick, and a little like someone Shane could care about out of kindness and not just duty.

"The green bean casserole stuff was my favorite," she said after a moment of consideration. "Bob came home and finished off the stuffing and threw it all back up, but the casserole… I ate that the next morning for breakfast." And then she looked up at Shane. "Could we…." She shook her head. "I'm sorry. That's stupid—"

"No. No. We could have some made. Just like you remember it."

For a moment the girl's narrow, pinched face was wide open and vulnerable, and then it closed down as she remembered the whole world could go fuck itself. "Yeah, well, if you don't have anything better to do, feel free."

Shane sighed as she shoved away from the kitchen table and stalked out to her room, but he was actually a little pleased. It was a sign. It was a start. It had taken nearly three months, but finally, *finally*, they had proof of intelligent life inside.

That done, he went and found Sweetie.

He'd saved Sweetie for last, actually, not because he was afraid of problems but because, well, he'd had a feeling Mikhail would want to do it. When he'd brought it up the night before, lying in bed and talking randomly like they did sometimes, Mikhail had given a trademark sniff.

"Why should I want to involve myself in your holiday plans? I shall be there to eat the food, is that not enough?"

Shane had hmmed and hugged Mikhail just a little bit tighter. He had not grown, or even gained an ounce, in the past four years. His stomach was still tight and wiry, and his entire little body still vibrated with the things he didn't say. "You really like her, don't you, Mickey?"

"Getting attached is not a good idea," he said. The words were practical, but Shane heard the underlying hurt.

"You really made a difference to Kimmy, you know that, right?"

Shane could also hear Mikhail's hard swallow, even in the dark. "She will still not talk to Benny, and I cannot fix it."

"That's not ours to fix. That's Kimmy's. She will or she won't—but you were there when she needed you."

Mikhail didn't pretend to Shane—at least not for long. Not anymore. He turned in Shane's arms, dislodging the furry brown Jensen Ackles, who still regarded Mikhail as his favorite human. Mikhail's breath was warm against Shane's neck, and Shane dropped a kiss on that wildly curly hair out of need. God, Mikhail in his arms? Even if all they were doing was this—talking about their day—it was as good now as it had been that first night. Better, even, because Shane had no doubts now that Mikhail was there to stay.

"You say that because you love me," Mikhail sighed. "That is very kind of you, but it does not fix what's broken."

Shane reached under the covers for Mikhail's hand and brought it, flat-palmed, to his stomach. Scar tissue from being shot, from being stabbed—Mickey would know the placement of every scar. Sometimes, when Shane was falling asleep after making love, he had to still Mikhail's restless fingers, because too often Mickey liked to dwell on what he almost lost instead of on the man he held in his arms every night.

"Sometimes it takes a while to get fixed," Shane said, his voice weighted with the dark, and Mikhail's hand balled into a fist.

"It is not comforting that you are wise when…." Again, that audible gulp. Shane could even finish his sentence. Mikhail was hurt and helpless because one of the few people he allowed himself to love was miserable.

Shane slanted his mouth over Mikhail's full and vulnerable one, and that sigh, that giving up of all his defenses, was something Shane treasured every time he heard it. Mikhail answered him, mouth open, legs spreading. He rolled to his back and shimmied out of his underwear, and Shane rolled on top of him, careful because he was really very much larger than Mikhail.

But sometimes Mikhail liked to be covered by Shane's body, sheltered by his shoulders, and kept warm in the dark. It was never said between them, but Shane knew, could read the ease of his body, the way he became supple and needy.

Another thing about Mikhail: sometimes, especially as they grew older, penetration was not his goal.

Sometimes it was enough that their bodies, naked and vulnerable, rubbed up together. Shane would kiss his stomach, his ribs, his chest, his neck, and then grasp their cocks together and simply thrust, and Mikhail would melt, fall apart, and come in a roll and shiver. Those were the times he needed Shane more than he needed the sex, and took the sex because he didn't know how to fill the need any other way.

He made sexy noises, uninhibited, when Shane kissed his collarbone and his neck, and the spurt of his come scalded Shane's hand, drove him up, pitched him higher. With a sudden impish lunge, Mickey arched his back and pulled one of Shane's nipples into his mouth. Shane groaned and Mikhail nipped, and that was it, he was spilling between them. Mikhail kept making those sexy groans in his ear as they frotted desperately for that one... last... spasm....

"Auuuughhh...." Shane's own voice echoed back to him from the hollow of Mikhail's neck, and he released their cocks and rolled to the side, wiping his hand on the towel they'd learned to stash under the pillows. He used the same towel on his Mikhail's stomach and then his own, and Mickey grabbed a wet wipe from the end table and finished the job.

"So'd that work?" he panted, and Mikhail let out a sweaty laugh from his shoulder.

"Did your magic cock take away all my worries?" he asked acidly, and Shane grinned.

"Why yes, yes I *do* have a magic cock, why do you ask?"

Mikhail thumped him fondly on the bicep. "Exasperating man! You know what I was saying—"

"Yes," Shane rumbled, tucking him more securely on his shoulder, right where all that curly blond hair and attitude belonged. "You were saying that us getting it on cannot possibly help Kimmy, but that's where you're wrong."

"You know how I love it when you tell me I'm wrong."

Shane grabbed at his groin again. "Why? Is it giving you wood? We could do something with that!"

"Hey!" Mikhail smacked at his hand, and Shane rolled backward, laughing. Mikhail sat up and smacked him on the top of the head, and Robert Downey Jr., the cat who slept on the foot of the bed, finally had enough, so he hissed and bailed off the bed in frustration. "You are either being deliberately dense—"

"Or...."

Mikhail grunted and settled down again. "Get over here. Your life is not in danger and I need a pillow."

"Yes, sir, I live to do your bidding."

"Stop it."

"Of course."

Mikhail settled in, cuddling like a supple, sinewy cat. "You are insufferable, you know that?"

"I know I love you, and for fifteen—"

"Five—"

"Ten minutes, you weren't thinking about Kimmy or any of the kids at Promise House—"

"As if I would!"

"And for ten—"

"Eight—"

"Nine minutes, you knew one thing, and one thing only."

"That your cock is so big you could have posed nude and lived off the proceeds for the rest of your life?"

Shane snorted. "As. If. No, you knew that I love you."

Mikhail took a deep breath. "I would say that you are very wise, but I have said it too much. Your head will get big, and you will not be able to fit through the door, and our grand love affair will be over."

"We're married, Mickey. It's not over until my head explodes or you kick me out on my ass. Even if my head explodes, my ghost will haunt you, and you're stuck."

Mikhail lifted his head and repositioned his cheek against Shane's chest. "Then I will take my chances with the exploding head. You're very wise. I needed reminding."

"I love you. We can give to the people we love, but that's not going to change us, okay?"

"Yes. Yes. But have I mentioned how mad I am at you?"

"Not right this moment. What'd I do now?"

Mikhail's voice grew very small, like it only did when he was confessing something true, and something close to his heart. "You did not tell me how much it hurt when you leave your heart open like you do. It hurts, Shane. You're strong and you're used to it, but until you, I had only ever loved one person, and now I love more, and it hurts…." His voice thickened, and Shane breathed hush against his temple.

"Sh… we'll make it better, Mickey. I swear. I swear we'll make it better."

"You never said how this helped Kimmy," Mikhail muttered when he'd gotten himself together enough to talk.

"If we're strong, we can be strong for other people. I'm not strong unless I've had my time with you."

"I'm not strong at all," Mikhail said bleakly, and Shane ran his fingers through that wild hair.

"That's not true. Not even a little."

"Yes? Look at me, falling apart on you—"

"I'm not strong without you. You make me better. Sometimes I think it's just so I can be there for you, and sometimes, when I'm dealing with the kids, I realize that there's a bigger reason for all this strength. It's the way love works, Mickey. It doesn't fix everything, and it's not foolproof, but it can make life just a little bit better."

"You make me tired," Mikhail said, curling tighter against him. It was early November and the nights had finally gotten cold. They were waiting for the thermostat in the house to kick on at midnight, but in the meantime, the heat they radiated under the covers was the heat they had.

"Good. You need your sleep."

"I love you, Cop. You know that, right?"

"Love you too, Mickey. Does it make you feel better to know I don't ever doubt it?"

"Yes. As long as you keep trying to earn it, that makes me feel just fine."

Shane smiled as he fell into dreams.

BUT he woke up in the morning resolved to have this conversation himself, instead of letting Mikhail do it.

"Hey, Sweetie, do you mind turning that off for a minute? You can have makeup time when we're done talking."

Sweetie turned around then and looked at him full in the face. "Can we leave it on so I don't have to shut down all my browsers?"

Shane laughed. "Yeah, sure. No worries."

"Thanks. Is this the food question? Because I was starting to think you'd forgotten me, and that would suck because I've got a good one!"

God, she was delightful. After Missy and all of that concentrated bitterness, it was just so much fun to talk to a kid who had taken what Promise House had to offer and run with it. She still preferred the stables to anywhere else, but every job she'd tried her hand at had requested her back. She was smart, she was quiet, and she didn't mind working hard. Shane let her go to The Pulpit, though—partly out of favoritism, and partly because he only wanted the kids he trusted the most to be there.

"Excellent," he said, crossing his arms and smiling. "Thrill me."

Sweetie nodded decisively. "Shrimp and grits," she said. "Mm-hmm. It's a staple in the South, right? And my grandma, that's where she came from, and she was raising us before…." Sweetie looked away, and Shane cursed her solid guards. He'd heard—barely—that her grandmother had died, and that the woman had been looking after more than one grandkid. But Sweetie's mother hadn't come back to claim her, and Sweetie had been on her own before Social Services had a chance to intervene.

"So, she made you shrimp and grits?"

Sweetie swallowed and nodded. "It's real rich, you need butter and spices and such. But she'd make us go to the grocery store and buy fresh shrimp, and you know that shit's hard to find, and then grits, and it took for*ever*, because that shit's in the specialty section. Anyway, we'd have turkey and shrimp and grits like everyone else had dressing. She even used spiced grits to stuff the turkey. I don't know if they did that in the South—I think she might have just been trying to stretch her money, right? So she didn't have to buy the dressing in the box? But she added onions and celery, and it tasted real good too. Anyway, yeah. If we get our choice, I want shrimp and grits for Thanksgiving."

Shane grinned. "I think that sounds great," he said. "But you may have to help us make it, because honestly? I'll bet you're the only soul I know who knows how."

Sweetie shook her head. "No, no—that's not true. Martin can make it. He said his brother used to make it too, so that guy—you know, the tall one who calls everyone sugar? Yeah, he can make it too. Martin said so. He said he was almost sure of it—but you had to ask… shit, I'm sorry, I can't remember his name—"

"Jeff," Shane said, trying to fit Martin into his worldview of Sweetie at Promise House. "Jeff—and I'll ask him. I'm pretty sure he'd be happy to." And, a*ha*, a teaching moment, something Shane could give this girl that she hadn't let him before. "It makes him feel good when he can remember something nice about Kevin."

Sweetie caught her breath. "Even though he's dead?"

"Well, yeah," Shane said, thinking about Mikhail's mother. "Those memories, they're all we've got when someone passes. Anything we have that gives them back to us, that's precious, right?"

"But…." Sweetie swallowed. "He's got… you know. He's *married*, he's got a whole new man. Isn't that… isn't that disloyal?"

God. It was easy to tell yourself she thought this way because she was young, but Shane knew—anyone could believe this. Human beings had been telling themselves terrible stories about sin and betrayal since the species began.

"No," he said softly. "Not if he's glad for who Collin is. It's okay if he misses Kevin. That doesn't mean what he has with Collin is any less important."

Sweetie nodded. "Oh," she said, her voice small. She blinked hard a couple of times. "I… I'm gonna go back and finish my e-mail, is that okay?"

"Yeah, sure. Thanks for telling me your favorite dish—it'll make Thanksgiving a lot better."

She let out a little sound. "Uhm, you know our counseling days?"

Yes. He knew. When the kids weren't working, they were counseling. Keeping them busy solved three-quarters of their problems.

"How can I forget?" he asked dryly, and she grimaced.

"Yeah, well, how come none of this comes up during *those*?"

Shane had been in the room with Sweetie. "You're a tough nut, darlin'. We've been spending the last three months just trying to find the right key."

"Humph. Well I guess you know now," she said, turning around and dismissing him.

He barely refrained from doing a fist pump of triumph. Yup, he knew.

Shrimp and grits.

THERE was a whole other Thanksgiving planning meeting at The Pulpit that Sunday. Given that everybody who *wanted* to eat at The Pulpit sometimes had other obligations, it had to be timed with military precision, as did who was bringing what. That sort of thing made Shane's head swim, but Benny and Jeff sat at the table sharing a legal pad and a pen and got everyone's input with so much competence, Shane was mildly surprised they didn't do it tech, with a computer and a spreadsheet and some sort of alarm that said, "Abort! Abort! Abort! Too many people are bringing pie! Someone needs ice cream, stat!"

"Okay," Benny said after taking a pull on the glass of milk at her elbow, "here's what we got. Jeff and Collin are going to Collin's mother's for pie, but they can make dinner."

"And Collin's mother is donating a pumpkin cheesecake so she can have her baby boy for the evening," Jeff chirped.

Benny looked at him with big eyes. "Oh God—is that as *amazing* as it sounds?"

Jeff nodded and did a double wrist-flap with a twist. "Oh, honey—there is *no* comparison. I would sell my soul for just one bite! Would you like us to bring you some?"

Benny whimpered and made puppy-dog eyes, and Jeff pretended to be blind.

"Oh, God, no! Not the puppy-dog eyes! You had me at 'pregnant woman', precious, no need for overkill!"

"I'm trying not to milk the pregnant thing until I can't move anymore," Benny said, and Shane thought that might be never. Benny's figure was a little fuller, and her hair was a little shinier (not in a good way—the poor kid's hair was stringy), but she still looked pretty energetic and very, very well.

Shane was relieved. They'd all worried over Amy with Jon-Jon, and it was nice to see that *this* pregnancy, this gift, was going okay. Nobody wanted Benny to have a rough pregnancy anyway, but *especially* not this time.

And Jeff was *so* not on board with anything that didn't make her the center of attention. "Don't want to milk it?" Jeff's voice rose shrilly. "Sister, you are our *queen*. You are like grand girl-pooh-bah of all the gay boys in this room—and that's a lot of gay! Don't just *milk* it, sausage it, egg it, pancake it—Benny, my love, you get the whole grand slam of gay breakfasts out of this one! You should get pumpkin cheesecake every *day*—"

"Except then I couldn't fit out of the house," Benny said dryly, and Jeff sniffed and put his hands on his hips. For once, Shane didn't think he was being overdramatic.

"Okay." Jeff pouted, sinking down next to her. "Fine. You get low-fat cheesecake, but the kind that tastes like full-fat, so you can pretend it's good."

"Well, it's good to know you celebrate the human oven," Benny said dryly. "I promise to gestate to the best of my ability."

Jeff stood up so fast his chair shot out behind him. "No," he said, shaking his head. "No, no, no, no, no... you do not even get to *joke* about this, girlfriend—this is not... you just...." Jeff threw his hands up in frustration and then turned to Shane of all people to help him out. "Talk to her!" he snapped. "Don't just stand there like a taxidermist's wet dream, *talk* to her! Counsel! Be... be all Zen and shit! Make her see!"

And with that, Jeff flounced out, and Shane watched him go in surprise.

"His mom's getting worse," Collin said, and Shane turned to Jeff's husband in sudden understanding. Collin was, well, young—twenty-seven, which was younger than Mikhail, who was nearing thirty. But he was still beautiful with his blond hair caught back in a ponytail and his blue eyes serious for once. He'd looked like a pro on the soccer field next to Deacon, and very much like a grown-up on the day he'd been married. He looked grown-up now.

"Ah," Shane said, thinking about Jeff's quiet crusade to keep touch with a mother who couldn't remember, from one day to the next, whether her son was still in high school or grown and graduated from college and married to a man. "So maybe Jeff's the one who needs to be counseled."

Collin lifted a shoulder. "Couldn't hurt. Not that we want her to think she's just an incubator, but, you know…."

Shane looked over to the table, where Crick was smacking Benny upside the head. "'Just an oven' my *ass*. I swear to Christ the oven never nagged me to cook a fucking *flan* for dessert. Did you all hear that? A *flan*. Like I'm gonna know what to do with *that* shit. You will get fruit sorbet and like it, Ms. 'I'm just an oven', and you'll sit down and knit while Deacon helps me with the cooking too!"

"Oh *hell* no!" Collin said, suddenly shifting his attention. "Jeff will help you with the cooking."

"You haven't even *seen* my cooking!" Deacon said, surprised. He was leaning against the back counter, wearing jeans and a hooded sweatshirt and looking unfairly young. His long feet were bare on the tile of the floor, and he was drinking a flavored water because Crick wouldn't let him have soda on general principle.

"Yeah, but I don't have to be a genius to know that you'll find some way to either hurt yourself doing it or poison us all trying. No. Leave the cooking to the pros and just… just feed the horses and be Deacon, and the world will be a better place."

"I *have* tasted your cooking, Deacon," Benny said drily. "Collin's got the right idea. Besides, Jeff does, like, gourmet stuff. He can be my wingman any time."

"Why is not Amy doing the cooking?" Mikhail asked from the living room. He was perched on the arm of the recliner so he could scratch the dog's ass with his toes. It was a rainy, cold November day, and *nobody* wanted that dog to get too wet—least of all the dog.

"All her shit's packed," Benny said shortly, and Shane remembered that Jon and Amy weren't here, in this room, for exactly that reason. Most of the people here had spent the week helping them pack a big-assed shipping crate with the majority of their stuff, and they were sending it today, so it would be at their new house in a DC suburb the day after Thanksgiving.

"Fuck," Mikhail said succinctly. "So, have we given any thought to some sort of gift for them? A parting gift?"

"Yeah," Benny sighed. "Jeff and I are knitting blankets, and my useless brother is drawing them a pretty picture."

"So that's two months of my precious art time, boiled down to a kindergartner with a crayon. It's almost poetic."

Benny let out an exaggerated sigh. "My brother the artist spent his time wanking off on paper—how's that, Crick? Feel better about that?"

"Yeah. Much."

Shane laughed a little at the byplay and then looked behind his shoulder, toward the door. Quietly, he wandered out to the front porch, grabbing Jeff's coat and his own from the line of hooks in front of the door.

Three years ago, before Collin, Jeff would have been out here smoking his one cigarette per day. But he'd given up even that vice with Collin and was instead warming his hands and bouncing on his toes and gazing out to the pasturelands under the gray light from the dense storm clouds overhead. A wicked wind was pulling Jeff's hair from its carefully arranged product 'do, and it was cold enough to make Shane's balls shrivel.

Shane dropped Jeff's coat on his shoulders and was rewarded with a scowl.

"God, man-mountain, sneak up on a guy!"

Shane shrugged. "I'm like Mumford's gas. Silent but deadly."

Jeff guffawed so loud he clapped his hand over his mouth, probably in surprise. "Omigod! *Shane!* That was good, and almost completely socially acceptable. You *have* improved."

Shane rolled his eyes. "What're the gray hairs for if we don't get better with age?"

"Speak for yourself, big bear man. I'm going Grecian Formula all the way."

"That's *way* too much trouble. I'd rather just grow old with dignity—"

"That would be a first," Jeff snarked, and Shane let him. "Since when has dignity been your strong point?"

"It hasn't, but if I'm growing older, I'd like to try new things."

Some of the snark went out of Jeff's sails. "I hate new things," he said, and Shane could hear bitterness.

"Tell me about it," he said, but he was totally, completely sincere.

He leaned out against the porch railing and looked at the sky, and in spite of the chill, the sailing-ship clouds mesmerized him in a tumultuous, perilous way. The sun was going down behind them, and the billows were bruise colored but tinged with transcendent gray, and there was something cleansing about the rain-laden wind.

Jeff joined him against the railing, inhaling deeply. "Mom hated winter," he said. "She loved the heat and the sunshine and sweating and gardening. Every morning she wakes up and asks me when it's going to be summer. Even in July."

"It's a cruel disease," Shane said truthfully. "I haven't met one survivor who hasn't been pissed off."

Jeff turned to him appreciatively. "Thank you! Seriously—*thank you.* No 'I'm sorry!', no 'sucks for both of you!'—just 'dude, be pissed off!'. God, you totally get shit, don't you?"

The twelve-year-old giggle caught him off guard. "I get *some*," he said, "I don't know if I get *shit.*"

Jeff's chortle surprised him too. "And damn, it's not like getting some doesn't make getting shit any easier, right?"

Shane couldn't even follow the sentence, but he could follow the sentiment. "Hell yes. Getting some makes taking shit a *hell* of a lot easier. You getting some, Jeffy?"

"As often as I can."

"He's wearing you out, isn't he?"

"As. If." Jeff's sniff was intentionally haughty, but even in the dark twilight, Shane could see his sweet brown eyes crinkling in the corners. "It's sort of a dead heat right now," he confided, and Shane's laugh boomed across the porch.

The laughter faded and they both resumed their sentinel watch of the wrestling clouds. Shane leaned sideways and bumped Jeff's shoulder.

"You know you can talk to me about it any time, right?"

"I just did, big man. You made me feel a shit ton better, and then we told sex jokes. Best. Shrink. Ever."

Shane's self-deprecating laugh hurt. "It's going to get worse, you know." Jeff was a tough nut to crack. Three years ago, he'd been holding on to himself with both hands, and he'd still almost disintegrated under pressure. Three years of love and the picket fence he'd wanted for his entire life had made him a little less brittle and a little easier to shape.

"The worst thing," Jeff said, sighing and sagging a little against the railing, "is my father. He keeps thinking I'm going to come back and head the family again, meet a nice girl and settle down."

"Didn't you just marry a guy?"

"Yup. Dad pretended he didn't get the invite."

Shane pursed his lips. He'd known Jeff's father hadn't shown up, but he hadn't known how bad it was. "Well, you want to make a visit up to Coloma, you don't just have to take Collin, you know. Me and Deacon, we make an impression."

Jeff grinned. "Yup. You're so butch, he couldn't miss the gay when he sees me!"

Shane grinned back, knowing that's not what Jeff needed. Jeff's sigh indicated he knew it too.

"I was so happy," he said. "Dad talked to me. I mean, we were still arguing, but it was communication, right? But it's still the same communication: 'Dad, I'm gay.' 'No, son, you're not, because that would mean you're going to Hell.' 'Dad, I'm still gay, but I don't think I'm going to Hell.' 'No, son, you're not gay, because I said so, and my word goes.'" Jeff snorted.

Shane threw an arm over his shoulders and hugged. God, of all the things—when he'd first started counseling, he'd tried so very hard to maintain a personal distance. But the first time a kid had felt comfortable enough to just throw her arms around his neck and hug him, he'd had his own little breakthrough.

Sometimes, a little personal contact was really all someone needed to get through the day.

"You know," Shane said, making his voice deliberately portentous, "sometimes, when a person isn't going to see you for what you are, you have to limit the relationship to what he knows."

"Sounds wise, oh mountain-on-the-Lama-Dalai, but what the fuck does it mean?"

This was going to sound cold-blooded, there was no two ways about it. "It means you have a full life. You have a husband, you have a job, you have a family—if I recall, you made that more than clear to him. If he can't invite you and your husband to a family meeting, you give your apologies and don't go."

"Well *duh*—"

"But you let it end there," Shane told him gently. "You don't argue, you don't try to change him, you just don't see him on his terms. In short, you let him go."

The fact that Jeff didn't even pay attention to his hairstyle when he ran his fingers through his hair meant he was well and truly thinking about it.

"I let it go," he said, waving his chin like it was just that easy.

"Yup."

"What do I do then? I mean, it sounds like what I'm doing now except—"

"Except now you keep thinking about how to change his mind. You're not going to do that, Jeffy. Think about it. Martin had to do this when he went home. He goes home, he says, 'I have friends who are gay, don't be disrespectful', and then he walks away. If he didn't do that, he wouldn't have made it through high school, you know that, right?"

Jeff sighed. Shane knew Martin was coming for Christmas, because Sweetie had told him, half-shy, half-afraid. She'd been trying to figure out a present for him, and Shane had told her he'd set Kimmy on that, because she was good at that. He also knew Jeff lived for the boy's visits. Shane, Mickey, Kimmy, and Lucas—they had the kids at Promise House. Jeff had Martin. The fact that his old lover's little brother wanted to be a part of Jeff and Collin's family was something Jeff took a lot of pride in—and he should. He'd had to work damned hard to forge that relationship, and Shane never forgot it.

"Well, we all know that kid is emotionally more mature than I am anyway, right?"

Shane nodded soberly. "Think about it, Jeffy. I hate to see you hurting."

Jeff sighed. "Yeah—but don't worry. Jon's going to leave and we're all going to be so busy watching after Deacon, you won't hardly notice me."

Shane felt a certain pride. "We're still running together. He talks when he runs."

"Wonderful. He talks when he runs. Excellent. Crick will be thrilled—he'll take up jogging."

Shane chuckled. "He talks more now—you know it."

"Yes, yes, I do. But we're all getting so fucking grown-up now. How am I going to give anybody shit when they keep outgrowing their flaws?"

"I still don't wax my chest—how's that?"

"Awesome, Cousin It. Let's go inside before you weave a cloak for me out of your chest hair, okay?"

It was officially dark and officially cold, and Shane had no problem with that.

PEOPLE with heads for details and better minds than his put together Thanksgiving—Shane's job was to relay the schedule and the cooking agenda. Which meant that being a touchstone to his family was not over by a long shot.

"Kim?"

Kimmy was in the TV room, watching *The Walking Dead* with a really bloodthirsty group of teenagers. She grimaced at him, annoyed—this was one of her favorite shows. "Now?"

"Don't whine—it's the commercial. Give me three minutes, you can watch zombies blow up again, okay?"

She pouted and turned to one of the boys who had just arrived. "Tony, do me a favor and pause that if I'm not back, okay?"

Tony let out a whine that actually made Shane proud—that was a kid's whine. That meant he was happy. "But—"

"Three minutes, I promise."

"I'll hold you to it!" Tony was Hispanic and slightly built, but he could grumble like a pro. "Jesus, woman, don't you want to see if the cute guy gets blown up?"

"I do," Kimmy muttered to Shane. "Now hurry up! Lucas is coming to get me as soon as this show's over."

"It's Thanksgiving, okay? You said you wanted me to give you the deets, here they are!"

Kimmy grimaced and smacked her forehead with her palm. "Dammit. I was going to go over there with you tonight. God—Benny—she's going to think I hate her."

"Well, she's confused, yes"—because Shane hadn't missed the look of disappointment when he and Mickey walked through the door without Kimmy—"but she knows something is up. Why don't you just tell her?"

Kimmy grunted. "Yeah, well, I think I'm ready to do that *now*, but… but *now* she'll be so hurt and—"

"So you're going to just let a perfectly good friendship lapse because you're afraid to talk about it? Jesus Christ, Kimmy!"

Kimmy narrowed her eyes. "Patient much, big brother?"

They were twins. "Yeah," he said, scowling. "I'm plenty patient. But this? You are fucking loved. Jesus—we see kids all the time who are afraid of not being loved, and you are *loved* and you're blowing it off for your pride, and I just want to… to…."

"To yank my hair and steal my yarn?"

Well, yeah. He'd had more mature moments. Shane ducked his head. "*I* love you. Isn't that enough?"

Kimmy's expression softened. "Yeah. Yeah."

"She's going to need a girlfriend. I can be a lot of things, sweetheart, but I don't have the ovaries for that job."

Kimmy stood on tiptoe to kiss his cheek, reminding the both of them that they might be twins, but they were about as alike as chocolate and cheese.

"You do your best," she said. "Now my show's starting, and Mikhail is fidgeting in the kitchen. He's going to start making them clean the corners of the stainless steel, and we almost had a rebellion the last time he did that. Take him home, okay?"

Shane looked up and met Mikhail's eyes. That vulpine, moody face lightened up fondly, and Shane took a deep, cleansing breath. Family and friends, children and grown-ups—he could be there for everyone he needed to be as long as Mickey was his home.

"Will do."

Mikhail's hand slid into his as they walked out of Promise House, both of them glad that their shift was the next day.

"That was a big sigh," Mikhail assessed as they walked out to the car.

"I was letting the weight of the world off my shoulders," Shane said, smiling a little.

"Good." Mikhail nodded sharply. "It will be there in the morning, and I cannot give you a back rub when it's there."

Shane laughed and squinted into the fog. He was glad home was less than two miles away. Right now it was the only place he wanted to be.

Chapter 16

Jon and Deacon:
Brothers Against the Wind

JON walked through Deacon's house, and it was ringingly empty. The old plaid couches were thick with dust, and the ratty carpet was soiled with too many boots and no broom. Booze bottles sat everywhere.

Patrick, Deacon's hired man, had told him that Deacon was sick and in the house, and that he was being stubborn about help. Bring Valium, he'd said—Deacon had told him to have Jon bring Valium. Jon hadn't seen Deacon since the night Deacon had gotten back from seeing Crick in Georgia. It had been a good night—a big bottle of vodka, lots of talking about high school, a debrief about the wedding, how's married life, that sort of thing. Jon had seen Deacon relax a little, let go, had thought vodka agreed with him. Hoped they'd have some more.

But Jon had been busy setting up business, and Deacon—well, he'd sort of dropped off the map. Jon had been a little relieved, actually. It hurt to see the guy missing Crick so badly when Jon himself wanted to beat the living shit out of the kid. Kid who'd run off and do a thing like that—he didn't deserve Deacon.

Looking at all the bottles—vodka, scotch, rum, bourbon, pinot noir, of all things—Jon felt a sudden, terrible acid sinking in the pit of his stomach.

He didn't want to see where this trail of glass and despair led.

"Deacon?"

Jon barely heard the lecture on benzos and alcoholism that followed. Deacon was naked, skeletal, and crouching in a bathtub, covered in his own filth. He had bandages on his hand and his nose was swollen, and his lank hair was in his eyes, and he sat there and told Jon it wasn't Jon's fault—Jon had given him his first drink, and Deacon had just kept drinking.

And all Jon knew was that his friend—his perfect, beautiful, shy, and fragile friend—was a breath away from hell, and everyone in his life had left him. Deacon would rather they left him than see him like this.

Jon would rather see him like this than think of him alone.

JON sat up in bed, breathing hard, sweating in the fine hotel sheets. He looked wildly around the room, trying to get his bearings, and he was relieved when Amy pushed her tangled dark hair back from her eyes and looked at him in the faint ambient light that came from under the hotel room door.

"Bad dream?" she murmured, and Jon folded himself over her. God, he loved how tiny she was, compact, but soft on the edges. Pregnancy had changed her body, but he hadn't minded. He'd liked the changes—for some reason they made that worship in her eyes when she looked at him even sweeter. She'd had his children. She was sharing his life. Jon, the class-A fuckup, and Amy, the smart girl in class, and here they were holding hands like little kids and getting on a plane and starting a grand adventure.

But first he had to get past that bathroom door.

"Deacon," he muttered. He'd had this dream before, and he didn't hide anything from his wife.

"Me too," she said softly.

Amy hadn't seen the worst of it. Jon had cleaned a lot of that up before he'd called her, just so he could pull himself together while Deacon slept off the first Valium and the purging and the DTs. But she'd seen him afterward, hollow-eyed, ribs showing through his shirt, pants that wouldn't stay up, the bruises on his face and arms from running into doorways bright and vivid on his pale skin. A little piece of both of them was going to be stuck in Parrish Winters's house, cleaning up booze bottles and crying helpless tears, for maybe the rest of their lives.

"It's stupid," he said, hating himself. Every time he had that dream, had that fear, it seemed like betrayal of the worst sort. Deacon had needed help up twice in his life, and that had been the first time. He'd spent every moment after that proving to the world he was one of the strongest people Jon knew.

"It is," she said softly. "It's not fair."

Jon let out a strangled laugh, relieved because she seemed to read his mind. "I want to dream about him healthy," he said, meaning it. "I want *my heart* to remember that he's happy, and we can leave him now, and we're not deserting him, we're just... just relocating. I mean, is that so much to ask? Whatdowegottado?"

Amy laughed for real by his side, and he was grateful the kids were sleeping at The Pulpit the last couple days before Thanksgiving, because that meant they could have this conversation and not be worried about being overheard.

"He's going to be fine," she said firmly.

"Yeah? Tell my stupid subconscious that," he muttered.

She sighed and pushed herself up on her elbow. "You know, Jon, we don't have any kids in this hotel room."

Jon felt a reluctant smile start. "Distracting me with sex is absolutely shameless," he told her.

"What's the matter?" She pouted adorably. "Don't you wanna?"

"Am I breathing?"

She put her hand to his groin to check. "Yes," she said with a squeeze.

"Then I wanna."

"Good." She shifted on the bed and brushed her lips over his. "When we're done," she said soberly, "try to imagine him with a baby in his arms. It'll help."

Jon filed that away for later and opened his mouth, all the better to take advantage of the smartest stupid woman in the world. She was a brilliant attorney, of that there was no doubt, but he would forever wonder how she came to be stupid enough to marry *him*.

THE kids were used to sleeping at The Pulpit, which was awesome, because it meant they were nice and relaxed by the time Thanksgiving rolled around.

There hadn't been enough room for Jon and Amy to stay, as much as Jon knew Deacon would have liked it, which is why they'd been in the hotel for the past couple of days. That meant that Thanksgiving night after dinner, they stayed in the living room, talking with the entire family and pretending like this wasn't their last night in their hometown.

Jon and Amy tried to make light of it—they'd left for college, right? Six years? The two of them had spent a couple of years dating other people, and then Amy had cried on Jon's shoulder for the last time and Jon had taken his courage in both hands and kissed his best friend's girl.

And she'd been his girl ever since.

But the whole time they were in college, screwing around (Jon) or dating around (Amy), they came home during their breaks and spent their summers and their Christmases—and even some of their spring breaks and Thanksgivings—in Levee Oaks. And most of that time was spent with Deacon.

Amy had family she rarely spoke to, but she was at The Pulpit at least twice a week. Jon's parents got Christmas dinner with Jon and his family, but Deacon's family got Christmas Eve and the post-Santa Christmas brunch. Their daughter was named for Carrick's friend who died in the service, and their son was Jonathan Parrish Levins.

The three of them had known each other since kindergarten.

No, Amy hadn't been in their inner circle in kindergarten, but she'd loved Deacon since middle school. Jon had loved him forever.

So the two of them sat in the new living room—which was still hard to look at because Jon had loved the plaid furniture and ugly green carpet in the old living room—and listened to Deacon's extended family talk about the past five years, and Jon and Amy laughed, but they didn't participate all that much.

Part of it was that they were tired—they'd been quietly closing up their practice, closing up their lives, separating themselves from day care, school, family, and home. It was a lot of work, and even Amy, with her famous organizational skills, couldn't get it all done in one swoop. They were content to sit, Jon on the recliner, his tiny wife in his lap, and let the conversation of the past five years of weddings and babies, of meetings and partings and fights and romances, wash over them.

Part of it was that the past five years had flown by—but Jon and Amy had older stories to tell. If Jon thought about it, he would have imagined this moment full of Jon himself, leading the party, telling the best stories, making all of his friends laugh, and giving them a glimpse of Deacon that maybe they hadn't had.

But that was the other part.

Those memories, he was coming to realize, had become private.

Many of them involved Crick, but others did not. Many of them involved Amy, but some, a precious few, were his and Deacon's and only his and Deacon's, and suddenly he was clutching those memories with all the force of a child clutching a beloved stuffed rabbit.

Others might think that rabbit was a toy, meant to be discarded with the approach of adulthood, but Jon knew the truth: that toy was *real*, as nothing else in his life had ever been or would ever be again.

At the end of the evening, after Jeff and Collin left for pie and Shane and Mikhail left so they could make it back the next morning to help transport the luggage and people to the airport, Amy went back to kiss Jon-Jon, Lila, and Parry good night, and Jon hung out on the porch with the man who had taught him how to be a man.

There were not enough words.

They stood side by side and looked into the deep fog.

"Gotta be careful driving," Deacon said. "Gonna suck out there."

"Yeah."

"Plane doesn't leave until one, right? We'll get you to the airport at eleven. Plenty of time for breakfast—Benny's been planning it."

"We gonna get presents?" Of course they were. Benny was the worst secret-keeper at Levee Oaks. Yeah, part of her time had gone to the baby blanket that pretty much boggled Jon with its delicacy, but he'd seen her working on a piecemeal project, and she'd lied unconvincingly that it was for Shane.

If it had been for Shane, it would have been green.

It was, instead, the colors of sand and sky, and everybody knew those were the colors both Jon and Amy loved the most.

"No," Deacon said, seeming to ignore the chill wind that threatened to cut through the fog. "No one loves you, no one will miss you, and only good boys get presents. Go away and spoil your wife, she's your only hope."

"No," Jon said quietly. "I would have been a cheating little scam artist who lost my wad on Wall Street if it wasn't for you."

The truth is so simple and so real. Deacon gaped at him.

"You remember me in grade school, Deacon?" Jon asked, and Deacon's smile was sweet and, God help them both, young and soft.

"You were lazy," Deacon said, laughing. "God, you copied my homework more than you copied the board."

"Right?" It wasn't the sort of sound that needed an answer. "And I was entitled. I was an entitled little fucker, and you didn't once call me on it."

Deacon shrugged and turned his face to the wind. You couldn't see the pastureland from here—hell, visibility was so bad, you could barely see the barn—but Deacon probably knew where every horse and every fence and every blade of grass was, because he'd put his hands on all of them on this little spot of property, and made them his own.

"You were my friend. You know that's all I ever wanted."

Jon closed his eyes, remembering their one abortive kiss in junior high. Deacon's hair had been longer then, but it was that same lovely dark blond, and his face had been thinner in adolescence, and his wrists and ankles skinnier too. It was two years before Crick Francis had come to watch Deacon work a horse, and five years before Amy and Deacon would finally go steady, breaking Jon's heart just a little.

They had sat on Promise Rock after swimming, the spring sun hard and bright and heating the granite to the point where it stung to the touch. Jon had reached down to adjust himself because his swim trunks had made him hard.

Deacon saw him and rolled his eyes.

"God, I know health class says those things are supposed to wake up right about now, but seriously. Is yours as woke up as mine?"

Jon was so relieved *someone* was talking about this that he didn't even bother with embarrassment.

"God, all the fucking time!" Swearing was new to them. They indulged in it a lot. "I am sporting wood *every minute* of *every day*. I swear, a girl so much as looks at me, and suddenly that thing is just all happy on its own."

Deacon looked down at his hands as they dangled between his knees. "It doesn't just happen with girls," he confessed, and Jon's eyes widened.

"Don't tell that to anyone else but me," he snapped, because they both knew the word "fag" and they both knew how hard life was for the kids who got called that word. Deacon didn't hardly talk to the *teachers*. How hard would it be if he walked down the hallways and people shouted that word at him?

Deacon wasn't surprised, though, and he scowled at Jon. "How stupid do you think I am?"

Even then, stupid and self-involved, Jon knew Deacon talked to two people in his life. One was his father, and the other was Jon. *Sometimes* he talked to Patrick, his father's hired man, but mostly, it was Jon.

"It's private," Jon agreed and thought that his friend, the one who urged him to do his algebra and helped him with his spelling, was beautiful. He still had freckles, and his nose really was absurdly, adorably small. Jon could look at him for hours, because his lower lip was girl pretty, and here, in the sun, his eyelashes were blond and his green eyes were almost gray, and his smile was sweet like that Amy girl's who'd had a crush on Deacon since forever.

It would be so much easier if Deacon were a girl.

"Boys?" Jon asked, suddenly curious. Jon liked people, and he definitely liked girls. But *God.* People obsessed over his family's money all the fucking time. *Nice shirt, Jon-boy, Mommy buy that? Hey, Jonny, go buy a clue!* But not Deacon.

Deacon loved him (and Jon was young enough that he didn't need to differentiate between loves) because Jon made him laugh and liked riding the horses and never asked him what happened to his mother or why he was living with his dad. (Jon couldn't actually believe people asked that. Apparently there were some dads who didn't stay. Jon had seen Parrish Winters with his son and it had never entered his mind.)

So, well, yeah. If Deacon was going to keep his thing for boys a secret, Jon was in. Why couldn't they keep this secret together? Why couldn't it be Jon's secret too, and he wouldn't have to worry about finding a girl or his wood going off at the wrong time? He wouldn't have to worry about Deacon only liking him for his money, or about being laughed at, or about Deacon saying mean things behind his back.

Deacon *loved* him. Deacon was loyal. Deacon would *never* betray him.

Deacon was safe.

Wouldn't it be great if Jon could have that calm and that comfort and that safety, all in the same person?

"Boys?" Jon said again. "Like… would you like me?"

Deacon flushed (a not uncommon occurrence, this was true) and looked at him sideways. "Why wouldn't I?"

Jon flushed too—he wasn't above being vain. "So, who else?"

"Amy Gonzalez," Deacon said promptly. "She's nice to us at lunch."

Jon nodded. She was a little... uhm, sporty for him, almost a frightening bundle of energy, when Jon was rather proud of how perfect he was in his laziness. Besides, he *definitely* liked tits, and as of yet, Amy didn't have any.

"Niceness counts," Jon said. It was true. He wanted to say something funny, something bright, that would make Deacon laugh and take away this uncomfortable question between them. But he couldn't. He could hear the horses they'd ridden out whuffling softly in the shade, and the burble of water, and the whoosh of a hot wind through the drying grasses of the pasturelands, but he couldn't think of one funny thing to say.

"Counts for what?"

Oh great—there went his plan for laziness.

"The person you want to...." Jon blushed again. "You know. Get wood around. They have to be nice. It's got to be someone you...." Oh geez. "You know. Someone you trust." This made him sound like such a weenie, but he didn't keep secrets from Deacon. Deacon had picked *him* out in kindergarten. Jon had been feeling lost and alone and forgotten—had, in fact, been crying in the boys' room because he missed his parents—and Deacon had promised him *this place* if only he'd stop crying.

Deacon had made it sound like Disneyland, only better, and at first, Jon had been a little disappointed. Swim? That was all? Sit on the rocks? Read a book? The best part of the trip had been riding a horse in front of Parrish, while Deacon had gotten to ride his own. But then, as Parrish had played with them, splashed them with water, made sure they had buckets and shovels, Jon had become enmeshed in Deacon's game of (what else?) cowboys and displaced Native Americans.

By the end of the day, Jon had been convinced that Promise Rock was the world's most perfect place. There was sunshine and water, earth and sky, lunch and exercise, and people who wanted to hear *everything* Jon had to say.

Jon started to think of good things—the *best* things—so Deacon and Parrish would laugh for him. Deacon was a nice kid, but he was too serious. Jon wanted to make him less serious.

And he was certainly serious that day in middle school, sitting on a sun-heated rock and talking about boners that wouldn't go away.

"Jon?" Deacon asked, uncertain, and Jon realized he was leaning close enough to see the brown speckles in Deacon's green eyes.

"It would be great," Jon said, hoping so hard. "We wouldn't have to worry about girls or...." He swallowed. He was too young to throw out the word "rejection" and too old to say "getting hurt" without embarrassment.

Deacon leaned into the kiss then, and Jon closed his eyes and thought hard about tits, and Deacon's lips moved over his, and then Deacon's tongue swept inside, and Jon hoped, hoped so hard, and…

And he caught a strand of scent—warm boy, sweat—and he suddenly couldn't kiss at all.

He pulled away slowly, not able to meet his friend's eyes.

"You don't feel it, do you." It wasn't a question.

"I'm sorry," Jon whispered.

Deacon pulled back and shook his head. His smile was so gentle. For the rest of his life, Jon would remember that forgiving, accepting smile.

"It's not your fault," Deacon said. "If I had tits, I'm sure you'd be all over me."

Jon nodded fervently. "I would," he said, relieved. "I'd totally bang you in a hot second!" He had no idea what "banging" meant at that point in his life. Between a spotty health education in fifth grade, movies, and the word itself, he had some sort of hazy idea of getting naked with someone and having his dick explode—but everyone said it was better than that, so he had hope it wouldn't get bloody.

Deacon laughed softly. "As long as you don't care that I like boys too, I don't care if you don't."

It took Jon a minute to figure out what that meant, and when he got it, he was a little shocked. "I will beat the shit out of anyone who picks on you for this," he said soberly, and Deacon shrugged.

"No one will know," he said. "It's not anyone's business."

But it was Jon's now. Jon would have taken that to his grave.

As he'd have also taken that faint, wistful stirring in his groin, before he'd realized that no amount of wishing would let him kiss Deacon the same way he wanted to kiss people with tits.

Jon opened his eyes as an adult in a cold gray November, and knew they were burning. "Our lives would have been so much easier if I'd been gay," he said frankly, and Deacon snorted and shook his head.

"I've always been a stop on your way," Deacon said quietly, and Jon hated him because he believed this. "You—you and Amy—I knew when you left for college that you were meant for something bigger than Levee Oaks. I…." He shrugged, and Jon remembered the cold sweats, the times he'd answered a question with perfect composure in class and then had a meltdown behind the school building, or even gotten sick, afterward. He remembered the time Deacon was scheduled to give a speech during an assembly and he'd actually *begged* Jon to pull the fire alarm so he didn't have to. Jon had tried to pay someone to do it too (he knew he'd get caught—all his teachers looked at him first when something went wrong), but Deacon had felt bad then about asking him to get in trouble, and had given the speech anyway. They'd both played a football game that night, and Jon, Deacon, and Amy had gone on to the dance afterward. Jon and Amy had both been in the car on the drive home when Deacon—finally free of all the things he knew he was supposed to do—pulled over and got out of the car, then slid down the side, shaking so bad he bit his tongue.

It had always seemed so unfair—the smartest of them, the brightest and best, had been maimed and folded in a tiny box of his own fears. Jon had come home for Parrish Winters's funeral. He'd seen Crick hovering over Deacon's back, solicitous and protective, and he'd let out a sigh of relief. *Someone* had Deacon's back when Jon was gone.

"It's like God made you that way," Jon said slowly now, "so you could stay here and make this place better, because no one else could have."

Deacon rolled his eyes. "That's the stupidest—"

"Please," Jon said, suddenly not ashamed of how raw he felt inside, "don't say it's stupid. Let me make fantasies about you here. Let me fucking idolize you. Amy would have been fine without me, and she may even have been fine without you, but me? I would have been fucking useless. I'd be shoving my parents' money up my nose right now, if I hadn't killed myself by wrapping a car or a plane or a train around a tree before I even graduated from high school. I... I spent a lot of time worried about leaving you behind, and... and now that I'm about to leave you behind for real, it's like... like finally hitting me, you know?"

Deacon quirked a corner of his mouth up, and Jon knew he was going to try to make a joke to talk Jon down. "That Levee Oaks is the most boring place on Earth?" he said, and Jon obliged him with a weak laugh.

"I knew that. You know what I didn't realize? Don't answer that"—because he saw that lip quirk again and he wanted to get this out. "I realized that I was just as worried about what would happen to me when I left you as I was worried about what would happen to you. You—you have *friends* in there, Deacon. You've got family. You're going to be okay." Jon felt tears threaten again, and he wiped them distractedly, because he knew of all people, even his wife, the one person he could cry in front of was Deacon. "But I'm not. Man, how am I supposed to go do something great without you there to keep me honest, how am I—"

Deacon hugged him. It was fast and hard, and Jon wrapped his arms around his friend's shoulders and clung.

"You're going to be fine," Deacon told him, and Jon hung on to those words tightly. "You're going to be better than fine. You're going to be great. You and Amy—there's no words for how good you're going to be."

"You bastard," Jon whispered. "You're not going to miss us at all."

Deacon cuffed him upside the head and then resumed the hug. "I take that back. Amy's going to be fine. You're still the stupidest asshole on the planet."

"You knew I was stupid," Jon muttered, and suddenly it was okay. Deacon would miss him. Miss him and his wife and their family just as much as he would miss Deacon. He needed that. He needed to know that the one person who had known him all his life would still miss him, still know him, would never let him go.

DEACON didn't *dream* about things, per se. No, he woke up in a pulse-pounding sweat about them, his worst nightmares actually flashing across his eyes as he was awake.

When Crick had been gone, right after Parry had been born, it had happened almost nightly, sometimes twice a night. He'd wake up gasping for air and think, *Crick's dead, I'm drunk again, I dropped the baby, Benny's on the streets, Jon left me, holy fuck* Crick's dead!

It happened less often now, but it still happened.

Benny lost the baby, Jon left me, Mikhail left Shane, Jeff's getting sick, holy fuck Crick's dead!

Or, this chilly November a.m., *Jon left me, Jon left me, Jon left me, I failed I failed I failed I failed, oh holy fuck,* Crick's dead!

Even as he sweated his anxieties out in the cold dark, Deacon was aware that some fears didn't get any better, and they tended to repeat. This night, though, he could put the one about Crick away for a bit, because Crick was patting his knee and mumbling.

"Deacon… Deacon, calm down and get the phone."

"The phone?"

"Yeah, man, it's ringing on the charger."

"Fuck...."

Deacon fumbled for it and turned it on without looking at the number. "You can't sleep either?"

"I call it off. I'll call the shipping company in the morning and we'll stay here. I'll buy another house for Shane's kids. We can start up the practice again. It was a shitty idea. They don't really want me. We'll stay here, it's fine—"

"Are you having a panic attack in a hotel bathroom?" Because Jon's rant had a tinny, echoing sound to it, and Deacon couldn't imagine him saying these things out loud to Amy.

"The hotel stairwell. We should have gotten a better hotel. I'm freezing my ass off!"

Deacon smiled. "If you'd wanted a good hotel, you would have gone farther than Levee Oaks. Get dressed. I'll meet you in front. Is all your shit packed?"

"Yeah." Jon sounded relieved to have it taken out of his hands.

"Good. I'll have you back before Amy wakes up."

Jon laughed. "Remember when I used to sneak over to your house in the middle of the night?"

Deacon made an affirmative grunt. It didn't count as sneaking when his parents didn't notice he was gone.

"It'll be like that," Jon said, and he sounded miserable and panicked, and if anyone could identify with that, it was Deacon.

"Whereyagoin'?" Crick slurred as Deacon got out of bed and turned on the lamp.

"Jon needs talking down."

Crick sat up and squinted at him in the dim yellow light. "I *knew* he was too quiet tonight," he muttered, and Deacon grunted in agreement. He hadn't told Crick about the rather desperate hug before Amy had come out and they'd left for the evening.

"He did this before he left for college too," he said, although he doubted Jon would remember. He and Amy had gotten hammered, and Deacon had driven them both back to The Pulpit that night. For the entire trip home, Jon had adamantly claimed he was going to live in Deacon's stables for the rest of his life, and they wouldn't be able to make him leave. He'd still been a little drunk the next morning when Deacon and Parrish had driven him to the airport. (Amy had been completely hungover by that time, and she'd claimed ever since that it was the last time she'd ever gotten *that* drunk, ever.)

He'd never told Deacon in so many words, but Deacon was pretty sure the reason he'd gotten on the plane was that Deacon promised him he could come home.

Deacon slid on his jeans and a hooded sweatshirt and denim jacket. Benny and Crick kept trying to get him to wear a bigger, denser jacket, something with a lining—something that hadn't been fashionable twenty, thirty years ago—but Deacon liked simple.

"Put on a scarf and gloves or I'm coming to nag you," Crick said stubbornly, and Deacon grimaced. Of course, being married was never simple.

"No hat?" he sniped.

Crick narrowed his eyes. "It's on top of your scarf on the dresser." Crick had made them both, in sort of a sand/green combination that Deacon would have expected to see on Shane. "I figured you'd use your common sense."

"But why do I need to when you're so good at using it for me," Deacon said sweetly, grabbing the stuff and putting it on. He snagged his wallet and keys from the nightstand and leaned over to kiss Crick.

Crick kissed him back, and for a moment, bed looked *really* tempting, but Deacon resisted. He turned off the lamp and paused at the doorway.

"Go to sleep, baby," he said, his voice low and throaty. "It's going to be an early morning."

"You're sure Jon will be there?"

"Yup."

"'Kay." Crick was snuggling under the covers as Deacon shut the door.

Deacon trotted to the mudroom for his tennis shoes and was down the steps and into the truck before even the dog knew he was gone. It occurred to him, as he was driving his father's old Chevy pickup down the road, that pretty much any adventure he and Jon had survived had happened in this pickup truck. There was something to be said for a vehicle that lasted—even if it did look like a primered shoebox full of rubble.

Jon was waiting outside the hotel when he drove up, and Amy must not have woken up, because his head was bare and so were his hands.

That was okay. Crick had put an extra set of woolens on the front seat of the truck for when Deacon forgot. Deacon didn't even think about laughing—

every stitch of the wool fabric was a painful testament to Crick's courage, and his love.

"Here," Deacon grunted as Jon opened the door. "You're going to freeze your ass off."

Hooded sweatshirt, denim jacket, and tennis shoes. Jon could afford a better coat too.

"I have a real coat—you know it's like twenty degrees in DC right now." Jon was jamming the hat on over his ears and wrapping the scarf around his neck, though. The fingerless mittens too, although he tucked his fingers inside the mitt part. These were navy blue, as stolid as you could get—Crick had made them before the green set and had stuck with conservative colors until he knew Deacon would wear them.

Deacon nodded. "I know it. I'm sure Amy has already bought the entire snow wardrobe for the lot of you. Jon-Jon's toes aren't going to see sunshine until it's warm enough to keep them pink."

Jon smiled appreciatively. Who wouldn't? Pink baby toes were fucking adorable, there were no two ways about it. "Where we going, Cochise?"

"To 7-Eleven to get coffee, first." There hadn't been any made, and Deacon had guessed Jon wouldn't appreciate waiting in the cold for it to drip out. Deacon pulled into the parking lot of the 7-Eleven, and they both ran in, surprising the hell out of the bored night clerk, who had run in from the bathroom when he'd heard the bell. The man reeked of pot—and so did the 7-Eleven.

It was weird how their voices echoed around the little store as they asked each other stupid stuff—"Cream? Sugar? Do you want hot chocolate in yours?"

Jon did, actually, and Deacon tried not to make gagging noises. Jon also wanted ice cream in his, so Deacon went up to the guy—midtwenties, long stringy hair, still reeking of weed—and asked him for lottery tickets to distract him.

The guy squinted at Deacon under a fluorescent light that flickered and strobed, and then said, "I really couldn't give a shit about two ounces of ice cream. Are you sure you want the tickets?"

Jon guffawed across the store, and Deacon laughed and bought two anyway, as well as the coffees, and a big bag of M&M's.

"Why are we getting chocolate?" Jon asked as they grabbed their shit and exited.

"If I'm going to be up *before* crotch-of-the-fucking-dawn a.m., I'd better get something out of it," Deacon shot back, and Jon shrugged.

"Well, you *could* have had chocolate coffee ice cream with a Bailey's-flavored creamer in it," he said with dignity, and Deacon shoved a handful of M&M's in his mouth and tried not to think too hard about what his friend was drinking.

"I could have had my thumb dislocated too, which also would have made me throw up, but I could have kept my dignity," he complained in disgust, and Jon's cackle was worth the spots still dancing in front of their eyes from the bad fluorescent lights.

"Where are we going? You still haven't told me."

Deacon grunted. One of the best things about his and Jon's friendship was that Jon did most of the talking. From kindergarten to the present, Deacon had always been able to listen to his friend chatter—half the time his stories weren't accurate, but since the changes made them funnier, Deacon didn't care. His one-liners were legendary, and he probably could have performed standup on a regular basis if he wasn't the one who laughed until he couldn't stand.

But Deacon had told Crick his friend needed talking down, and that meant Deacon actually had to open his mouth and talk. The injustice needed another handful of M&M's to be palatable in any form.

Deacon finished chewing and said, "The day they told us Crick was wounded, I rode out to Promise Rock. Did I ever tell you that?"

"No," Jon said, quietly enough that Deacon knew he'd picked up on how this wasn't garden variety conversation.

"Yeah. See, Benny, she got really freaked out. I'd taken the gun with me because of the rattlesnakes, right? You remember, right after the flood, the fuckers were everywhere? Anyway, she thought...."

He heard Jon swallow. "I know what she thought," Jon said quietly. "You were a mess."

Deacon had to concede he had been.

He took a right at M Street to drive to The Pulpit, and prepared himself for the almost invisible turnoff to the service road that ran between Deacon's property and Promise House property. Deacon had a key to the gate so they didn't always have to take the horses out to Promise Rock, which had been nice of Shane. He'd also maintained the side road, which was good—Deacon had once broken an axle racing down that road trying to keep Crick from doing something stupid. He'd failed, and Crick had ended up going to Iraq anyway, so it was nice to see that some things changed for the better, even if stopping Crick from being stupid was no longer an item Deacon needed on his to-do list.

"But see, she didn't need to worry that day," he said. He made the turn carefully, because maintained or not, the road was still dirt, and the empty truck could fishtail with the biggest flounder in the stream.

"No?"

Deacon couldn't look at him, because he had to pick his way over the road—it was easy to veer into the weeds if you weren't careful, because there weren't any lights or reflectors out here. In fact, the closest streetlight was about two miles away, back by the 7-Eleven, and if he turned around on a clear night, he could see it. Not tonight, though. The fog was still thick in places, passing in clumps as the wind blew it.

So he couldn't look at Jon to read his expression, but he did know what that one careful syllable meant.

"No," he answered quietly. "I had too much to live for, even then. And Crick has too much to live for to not go on without me."

Jon grunted. "That's good to know," he said.

"It doesn't just go away because you don't see that person every day," Deacon said, wishing words were easier for him. "It wouldn't go away if one of us died. It won't go away if you're not two miles down the road. It doesn't just go away. Not for me, anyway."

"Me neither," Jon said, but he didn't sound certain. They were both quiet then as Deacon negotiated the road, and after about ten minutes, he pulled up to the gate. The fog from the irrigation stream was too dense for them to see, so he just let the engine idle for the heater, and put the truck in park.

"So," Deacon said quietly, "I came out here that day. I came out here, and I remembered you and Amy and Parrish and Benny and Parry. And Crick. And out here, it was okay that it was all memories. That's what this place is. It's a promise that there will be more memories. It's a promise that love will live on."

"I know that," Jon muttered. "I've officiated four weddings here."

"And been to your own. And you'll be back for Benny and Drew's wedding. And, God willing, for Parry Angel's too. It's not going away, Jon."

Deacon could hear Jon's swallow across the car.

"I just don't...." Swallow. "I don't ever want to be just some guy you knew. I don't ever want to say to myself, 'Gee, I wonder what happened to Deacon. He used to be my whole world, but now we never talk.'"

Deacon sighed. There were no guarantees. They both knew that. "It may be like that someday," he admitted. The thought made his throat raw. "I hope not. I don't have so many friends I can forget the one who hasn't left me in twenty-seven years. I like to think we'll see each other Christmases and weddings and birthdays. We'll e-mail and Twitter and Skype and all that shit, and fifty years ago, we would have written letters like they do in textbooks. I promise you, Jon, I'm not going to let my best friend go without trying to keep him close."

Jon sighed from his end of the cab. "I promise you, Deacon, I won't let you go either."

Deacon risked a look at him, sipping his impossible dessert thing and looking sleepy and a little less like a runaway bride.

"You're my brother, and I love you," he said, and Jon smiled and looked at him in the eyes.

"You're my brother, and I love you," he replied. "And if you ever tell another human being about this lame, stupid, sorry conversation, I'll hire ninja assassins to kill you in your sleep."

"Understood. You ready to go to bed yet? I would wager we both have people who would be willing to warm our feet up when we get back."

Jon grunted. "You got your iPod plugged into the radio?"

"Yeah."

"Here, let me see it."

Deacon handed it over, and after a minimum of fuss, Jon set it down and Deacon turned up the sound.

Three Doors Down's "Kryptonite" filled the cab of the truck, and Deacon rolled his eyes. The summer after high school graduation, they had played that song until they'd both known it by heart.

"Asshole."

Jon started out singing about how he didn't care what happened, as long as "you'll be my friend in the end."

Deacon laughed and caved to the inevitable. "If I go crazy, will you still call me Superman...."

He lost track of how many times Jon repeated that damned song, and they sang it at the top of their lungs. But sometime before the sky turned gray and the fog started to get thicker, silence fell and Jon said, "We can go now, Deacon. It's okay. I'm out of the crazy."

Deacon nodded and backed the truck around. "For now," he conceded. "I'm sure in the morning, you'll be a complete moron again."

"You should talk. You're going to hurt yourself as soon as the plane takes off, you know that?"

"Why wait until then? I'm sure I'll burn myself cooking breakfast. Jeff'll be there. He can bandage me right up."

Jon started to giggle. "And if you sprain your ankle, Shane can pick you up like a girl, and this time we'll get *pictures.*"

"Nice. We can make it easy on him. We'll have him pick up Benny and photoshop you in. Crick can have them on ten different websites before you land in DC."

Jon chortled. "Great! I'll send it to my new boss, and we can come home!"

Deacon couldn't banter back. "Just as long as you know you can always come home," he said.

Jon made a suspicious sniffling sound. "I need some fucking sleep."

"Or you just need some—"

"Don't say it," Jon warned, and the banter was back on.

When Deacon pulled up in front of the hotel, Jon hopped out and paused before closing the door. Deacon was afraid he'd have to talk again—but not Jon. "Yeah," he said, looking Deacon in the eyes.

"Yeah."

"See you in the morning, Deacon."

"Try to be on time—the airport with kids ain't a picnic."

"Yeah, yeah. 'Night."

The door slammed shut, and Deacon turned the pickup around and drove home. He wouldn't remember until Jon and the kids left the next morning that Jon had taken his spare hat, mitts, and scarf, but Crick was probably planning a new set for Christmas, so that was okay.

He'd need a nap the next day after dropping everybody off, and the much-planned morning brunch would be a blur. (Jon confessed that it had been for him too, when he called to tell them they'd all arrived safe in DC.) Deacon didn't care. As he slid next to Crick for a scant hour of sleep, he knew he might still wake up in cold sweats but that Jon and Amy leaving him wouldn't be on his list of things to fear.

They'd never leave him. The memory of them would always be at Promise Rock.

AMY was sort of wonderful, Jon thought four days later. Their stuff had arrived, she'd put an army of movers to work, and in very short order they had a home, one with their familiar stuff in it, one that made sense and that was nearly completely unpacked.

The agreement was Amy would work for the firm for two days a week as Jon's assistant, at least at the beginning, so that she could make sure the kids were going to be okay. The plan for Monday was she'd spend that day getting the kids set up in school and day care, and Jon was going to visit the office for the preliminary tour and intros. He'd spent a long time the night before sitting on Lila's bed and reading her the storybook Parry Angel had written her, the one about the two princesses who played together and never forgot each other, and Lila had stopped crying after three days of a wobbly chin, and promised him she'd try to be happy at school the next day. Jon-Jon hadn't let a thing disturb him from his chow and his crib, and for that, Jon could only be grateful.

Amy kissed him warmly as he left, bundled in his coat and the scarf, hat, and gloves he'd unrepentantly stolen from Deacon's truck.

"You're not going to wear the leather gloves?" she asked, wrapping her robe against the terrible chill from the open door. Her piquant little face was still frowzy with sleep, and the caveman part of him sort of wished she could send him off every day like this, but that was only because he hadn't yet missed her company and her sharp professionalism in the office.

"No," he said, grinning. "I stole these fair and square, and the leather ones are just a reason to give them back."

"Oh," she said, nodding like she understood. She probably did. He was pretty sure there wasn't much his wife didn't know, and what there was, she could learn if she had the schematics and a screwdriver.

He arrived at the office after a forty-five-minute commute that involved a train and a bus, both of which were unfamiliar to him as a California driver, and he was grateful Amy would be there at least two days a week for the company. The office building was small and old—on his first fact-finding trips out, he'd come to understand that small and old actually meant prestigious in this neck of the woods, and so did dark and intimidating. He tried to switch the word "intimidating" to "stuffy," but it didn't make him any less tongue-tied when his new boss, an older man with creases in his smoker's face that rivaled the irrigation ditches of a healthy Martian colony, introduced him to the office almost as soon as he walked in.

The whole firm was gathered around a table, a group of experienced veterans of the civil rights war, and Jon suddenly felt totally outclassed.

"So, Mr. Levins," said one of the men sitting down. He was a partner in the firm, and although he was younger than Mr. Cosgrove, he was still about twenty years older than Jon. "Give us some background on how you came to work here—tell us anything you think is relevant, and then we can start with the Monday briefing, okay?"

Jon nodded, and although this wasn't entirely unexpected, for a moment he thought his mouth (the only thing that had never stopped working for him) would finally let him down. He was the youngest person in the room. Most of these people had been fighting for civil rights since before he'd graduated from high school, and most of them were part of the LGBTQ community. Who in the fuck was he to come in and take his place in their ranks? He tugged nervously at his Looney Tunes tie and realized he'd left the gloves on, the ones Crick had made Deacon. He pulled them off and smiled at the room.

"Hi. My name is Jon Levins," he said, remembering this was one of his best skills. "When I was five years old, Deacon Parrish Winters made me his best friend. I idolized that kid through grade school, through junior high, through high school—he's the best friend I've ever had. He's my brother. The love of his life is a man. You would not *believe* what they've had to endure to be together."

He kept talking. His new coworkers nodded and smiled. He'd say later that once again, Deacon had saved his ass. Deacon would tell him that once more, Jon had saved his own ass.

Jon took it as a sign, a promise, that Deacon wasn't going anywhere, but he didn't tell Deacon that. Deacon could still call him a stupid asshole from three thousand miles away.

Chapter *17*

Crick: She Moves in Mysterious Ways

"OH YEAH," Andrew said, watching Crick's sister walk toward the stables from the driveway, "the titty fairy has arrived."

"I just threw up in my mouth a little."

Crick had come outside to dump eggshells and coffee grounds in the compost pile. It was his first time outside that day, and the hard blue of the November sky, as well as the savage, dancing wind, made him reluctant to go back in. Andrew was pulling hay bales off the delivery truck and stacking them against the wall, so that gave him a windbreak *and* a warm wall with sun, and Crick was taking a break.

Drew cast him an annoyed look now. "Hey—you and Deacon are going to go home with the cute wrinkly thing—I gotta take my bennies where I can get them."

Crick looked at his, well, admittedly voluptuous sister, and tried to see the downside of taking the *giant* opening Drew had just given him.

"You already got all the Benny you need," he said, full of himself. "And in another few months, you're going to have even *more* Benny than you can handle!" He didn't even quail under Drew's disgusted glare.

"You know, you're not the only one who was hauling that travois through the fucking desert, Lieu—"

"I was the one who wasn't going to get you killed, Private Blood-loss," Crick zinged again, practically hopping he was so happy to get a few in edgewise. Yeah, so Deacon was the "older, more mature" partner. Crick had long since accepted he'd be putting his size-fourteen feet in his mouth whenever it opened—he was used to it by now.

"Yeah, there was that. And I have to admit, you're *mildly* less irritating than Private Andy—"

"I am deeply wounded by that." When Drew paused to ogle Benny, he leaned over the corner of the truck with his hooks already set in the next hay bale. He leaned back on his good leg and, using it like a pivot, pulled his prosthetic foot up and whirled around to drop the bale on the ground next to his last stack.

"Wounded?" Drew panted, and Crick felt a sudden pang—he used to help do this. He'd tried, a couple of times actually, since he'd come back, but his hand still didn't grip hard enough, and his leg would still give under the weight of the bale.

He swallowed against that sadness and pulled his attention back to the bright day and his sister's tired—yet happy—look as she came to brief them on her last doctor's appointment.

"Yes! I'm wounded that I'm only mildly better company than Private Andy. I mean, my boyfriend—"

"Husband—"

"He was my boyfriend at the time! Anyway, he gave you a job, and I gave you a girlfriend—"

"Fiancée—"

"I see no ring!"

Drew grunted and glared, his pink lower lip thrusting out considerably. "There is a plan for a ring. God, could she move any slower?"

Crick looked up. "Crap. No. And she looks like she's in pain. C'mon."

Drew dropped his hay bale back into the truck bed, and both of them hustled across the gravel driveway (as though either of them could hustle!) to see how she was doing.

"I'm fine," Benny grunted, and Drew and Crick both met panicked glances and took her left toward the porch.

"What'd the doctor say?" Crick asked, and Benny sighed.

"He said I needed to rest more," she admitted, and Andrew growled loud enough for Crick to know they'd had this discussion before.

"I told you—I told you everything you did for Thanksgiving—"

"It happens, Drew!" she snapped, and that's when Crick knew she *really* didn't feel well.

"Well, we can make sure it doesn't happen anymore," he said firmly. "Soccer season's over, I can pick Parry up from school and drop her off—we've got it covered, Benny."

"Ugh," Benny muttered, and the two of them helped her up the porch steps one step at a time. "Look, guys—you're right. You can take over." She paused then and took a breath before waving them both off. "I'm fine. Tired, a little breakthrough bleeding—I just need to rest for a couple of weeks. The doctor told me to come back in two weeks after getting lots of sleep, and she was pretty sure it would be all right."

"But Benny," Crick said, "you look like hell."

"Fucking nice," she snapped. "Want to know how you look?"

"I could look like a baboon's butt," Crick retorted, "and who gives a fuck! I'm worried about you. Deacon told me this wasn't a picnic. Do you think I just signed on to do this without worrying about you?"

She grunted and leaned against Drew again. "God. Just when I want to kill you, you turn around and act like...."

"A baboon's butt?" Crick smirked, wanting to see her smile.

She did, and snuggled softly into Drew's arms for a minute before straightening and trying to make it up the stairs.

She got one foot on the next step, and the only warning they had was the pounding of boots.

"Jesus, Shorty," Deacon said. He stopped next to Benny and bent to heft her up. Drew helped her into his arms, and Benny leaned against Deacon's chest in a way she hadn't even done with Drew.

"I'm fine," she said quietly as he hefted her up across the porch, and Crick and Drew could both hear her talking to him, softly and without expletives or insults, explaining what the doctor had told her. The door closed behind them, and Crick and Andrew found themselves struggling up after him and grunting.

"Wow—it's like helping her is his superpower," Crick said in awe.

"Great," Drew muttered. "Chopped liver. I love that."

"Yeah, I know the feeling."

"It's not the... same...."

Crick had stopped to glare at him as soon as the words started coming out of his mouth, and Drew paused and swallowed. "Yeah. I'm sorry. You're right. It's *exactly* the same, isn't it?"

Crick nodded grimly. "Yup. But you know what's different at the end of the day?"

Drew gave a frustrated sigh. "She's going home with me."

"Yup. And he's staying here with me."

Drew took another deep breath and turned to look at him. "Man, but tell me sometimes it doesn't chew up your guts, right?"

Crick paused and stared at the closed door. "It does," he confessed, because it was something he hadn't let himself think about until just this minute. "But then, sometimes I feel the same way about you."

"Because of my sister?"

Crick closed his eyes and remembered some of his good humor. And that he'd never *met* Drew's sisters. "No, Drew—because of *all* of it. Remember when they were sick? All of them were in the hospital, and Deacon... I guess he just *escaped* to come talk to me on the computer because that was his date, and you know, the military didn't fuck around? You remember that?"

Drew shifted. "God," he said. "You know, Lieu, I could have not thought about that for pretty much the rest of my life."

"Yeah, well at least you were here for it—"

"Do you know... man, Crick, Parry was the worst. If anyone ever tells me I don't love that kid like my own, I'll kill 'em. I was in the hospital and she... she was so tiny, and they had all those tubes in her body, and she was just so still... and Benny, she'd just wake up every five minutes and say, 'Oh crap! Where's my baby!'. They had to *sedate* her, did you know that? Because she wouldn't sleep enough to let her body heal. And while we're all freaking the fuck out in *that* room, Deacon just gets up, and pulls the IV out of his arm, and drives away. I'd forgotten he had the keys—I had to catch a *cab*."

The sky was still hard and bright, but it wasn't fun any longer. "So, have you noticed that everybody waited until I'm scared to death about having a baby to tell me how shitty things got when I was away in Iraq?"

Drew had the gall to laugh. "That's not true."

"Well, maybe not. But see, you and Deacon—you've done this before. And I missed it. I *missed* it. Hell—I helped *cause* it, and you and Benny and Jon, you all cleaned up my mess. I'm just...." He looked away. Drew had been a good friend—and a good man to his sister—and he didn't want to get maudlin. "I'm just grateful. I don't have any worries about Deacon loving my sister best. I mean, think about it. If that was going to happen, wouldn't it have happened when I was gone, and he was hurting, and they were both so fucking miserable?"

Drew swallowed and studied his boots. Sometimes Crick had to remind himself that there wasn't a real leg in one of those boots, because Drew was so good at using his body. "She wasn't a grown-up then."

"Yeah. Yeah. But Deacon's five years older than I am. He...." Crick flushed. "He waited. He tried to get me to go away to college, and I went away to the army instead, but... but he *waited*. He was *celibate!*" Crick's voice cracked on the word, because the fact was, Deacon liked sex—Deacon *loved* sex. Once Crick had come home and healed, and they'd learned how to take liberties with each other, Deacon had been as sexual a person as Crick had ever known. But only with people he trusted. Amy, probably (Crick had never asked her—and since she seemed truly in love with Jon, it didn't seem fair to drag back up), but Crick—Crick for sure. And Deacon had put off sex for Crick. For one of the few times in his life, Crick was actually embarrassed about having to put his foot in his mouth in order to bare his soul.

"Look, Drew. I can see... I mean, I think he's awesome because he's *my guy*, but... I know. I know how you'd think he's a threat—"

"Not because he wants to be!"

"But the thing is, he wouldn't be *doing* this if he thought it would hurt us, okay? He had to sign papers and... you know, spooge in a cup—and you *know* nobody thinks of all of the bad things that can happen like he can."

"Including—" Drew cut himself off, and Crick shook his head.

Drew sighed.

It just felt so disloyal even to say—Crick knew.

"Okay—I *know* what it's like to be the second banana. I'm the fourth of seven, Crick, did you know that?"

Crick wrinkled his nose. "God. No, I didn't know that—you don't talk about home—"

"That's because I'm *nobody* at home. Nobody knew I was gone, nobody knew I came back—nobody gave a shit when I left again. I send my parents a letter a month—they still ask me how I can wear a prosthetic in the army."

"Ouch."

"Yeah—but you know what? I was important to *Deacon*, and damned if I wasn't important to him. And your sister...." Drew looked him in the eyes, and Crick realized, seeing that broad, kind face, just how much of that loyalty he took for granted. Deacon, not so much. Deacon didn't equate giving Drew a job and a home to hauling a travois through the desert—but Crick was pretty sure Drew held the two of them equal parts accountable for saving his life.

"My sister?"

Drew's smile went lopsided. "She just... just treated me like I was important. They listened to my war stories and gave me a job, and just like that, I was family. And she just... just *saw* me, you know? She always knew where I was, what I was doing—whether I'd eaten. She *loved* me, before she even knew I was in love with her. I... I want to give you this baby. If I could, I'd carry it for her, but I can't. I can just... just *rent* her out and... and watch her be in pain, and I know... hell, if the worst happens here, Crick, she's going to do it again...."

Crick winced. "We won't expect her to—you know that. This... we love her, dammit! We love you both!"

"You think I don't know that? I just... I want to start a life with her, that's all!"

"Look—let's just go inside and you'll—"

"Jesus, Andrew!" Deacon stomped out onto the porch and grinned—but gently, Crick noticed, which meant that he wasn't stupid. "That girl won't take help from anyone but you. I hate to spare you, but do you think you could go get her some water and some lunch?" His grunt of disgust was real this time. "She seems to think I can't boil water."

Drew smiled. "You can't boil water. The only one who cooks worse is Shane."

"Well then, save her," Deacon said and took a few steps down the stairs while Drew walked in.

As soon as he heard the door close, he looked toward Crick, who suddenly wanted to kiss him so badly.

Deacon didn't give him a chance. He took two steps in and palmed the back of Crick's neck to pull him down for a kiss.

Crick opened his mouth and moved in, treasuring the warmth of his body, the taste of him, the feel of his tongue. He wrapped his arms around Deacon's shoulders and engulfed him, embraced him, held him close.

"How is she?" he asked when Deacon let him up for air.

"Tired," Deacon said. "Remembering that she's not invincible, and she's not fifteen either. She needs to drink milk and take lunch breaks and... you know. All that shit your sister *so* does not do well."

"We'll take care of her," Crick said with some conviction, and Deacon grimaced.

"She needs a girl."

Crick blinked. "All the gay men in the world and you need a girl?"

"*She* needs a girl. Someone to talk to. Even Drew tends to freak out about the girlie parts, and from what I understand, he *likes* those parts."

"Amy—"

"Is across the country, starting a new life."

"I... there's something going on with Kimmy. I don't know. Jeff said it's sort of private."

"Well, he's *your* best friend—ask him! Besides, you know he loves—"

They said it in tandem.

"He loves Benny, yeah. Yeah, I'll ask him. You know, rally the troops. Get her a girl to talk to. Whatever."

Deacon grinned, and although the worry lines stayed at the corner of his eyes, he wouldn't be Deacon if they didn't. Deacon kissed him again and then took a step back and looked up.

"You know, we've got some gas heaters. Ask your sister if she wants her knitting brought outside after Parry gets home. It really is a beautiful day."

"Deacon—" Crick's misgivings suddenly bubbled up to the forefront.

"Yeah?"

"Aren't you... I mean, you know. Worried about the baby?"

Deacon stopped, and Crick could have kicked himself. "Well, yeah," he said softly. "But... at the moment, the baby is a hope. A good one. One with some teeth. But your sister, we love her now."

Crick nodded. "We do. Here—let me go ask her about knitting on the porch."

JEFF stopped by after work with a stuffed bear, some chocolate, and premium merino yarn in a color that reminded Crick of the November sky.

And Kimmy, looking miserable and sad in the passenger seat.

"Lookie you, Mr. Care Package," Crick said, helping Jeff unload the back of the car. He'd been doing laundry most of the day. When Benny and Parry had called to him from the porch that Jeff was there, it had been, once again, the call to slack off from what amounted to an extra busy day.

"Yeah, well, Collin's coming over with dinner and a bunch of frozen dinners for their fridge. They'll be balls to the walls with broccoli cheese potatoes and beef bourguignon."

"Fancy!"

"Yeah, that's Collin. He's Mr. Culture."

Crick snickered, like he was supposed to. "So if he's bringing dinner, what's in the cooler?" It was one of those soft-back affairs with a strap to go over the shoulder—they usually came in black, but Jeff had found one in nipple-piercing pink. Jeff took it from him and looped it over his head so the strap was across his chest.

"Two kinds of pie," Jeff said seriously. "And a shit-ton of this premium organic orange juice, with calcium. She'll love it." Jeff *loved* sweets—but very often his drug regimen left him sensitive to them. The pie? That was for Benny and Parry, and Benny and Parry only. It was very typically Jeff.

"Well, this is much appreciated—she's knitting right now. Did you guys bring yours because...." Crick looked at Kimmy, still huddled in the front, and then at Jeff, who was glaring at her.

"Heifer, get out here," Jeff snapped, and Kimmy crossed her arms and glared back.

"No!"

"Look, we talked about this—"

"I changed my mind."

"Because *why?*" Jeff had just picked up the teddy bear and his yarn bag, and he flapped both of them in the air because that's what he would do with his hands anyway. Crick lunged and caught a ball of really sweet silk cashmere in purple and orange before it could hit the dusty gravel of the driveway. Go good hand!

But Kimmy didn't notice his heroic save—she was still arguing with Jeff. "Because look at her, there with her kid, and I'm like... like...."

"Like the Scarlet fucking Weiner. Get your ass out of that car and go be a friend!"

"She needs better friends!"

"Well, tough, because God cursed her with you!"

And then Jeff turned to Crick and betrayed every confidence Crick had ever given. "Crick, you asshole, tell her about Germany!"

Crick's mouth fell open. "I'm sorry?"

"Tell her about Germany! And Deacon, the night of the flood! And coming out at a funeral and in the middle of court and... uhm. Yeah."

Crick floundered and realized maybe this was how people felt about *him* when suddenly his mouth just opened up and vomited out some shit it shouldn't. "After we eat this pie, I'm never speaking to you again!"

"Oh bullshit. You love me. You forgive me. Get that part over with and *sit in my fucking car and bare your soul!*"

Crick stared at him as Jeff flounced away with a teddy bear in one hand, a knitting bag in the other, a portable ice chest slung over his shoulder, and enough swish in his ass to power the Sunset Strip.

Crick watched Benny wave and smile and welcome Jeff up to the porch. Jeff blew a bubble in Parry Angel's ear and looked very seriously at her craft project (something that involved a lot of glue and foam pieces) and then presented the teddy bear and yarn before going into the house with the food.

Fuck.

For an asshole, he really *was* a good guy. He wouldn't ask if there wasn't a reason.

Crick sighed. The shadows were long and it was getting chillier—the windbreak offered by the Mini Cooper's interior was welcome.

"So, why am I telling you about one of the shittiest things I've ever done?" he asked, sliding in carefully. He was surprised at the legroom, although he shouldn't have been, because Jeff was over six feet tall as well, but still. The car didn't look that big on the outside.

And Kimmy usually looked bigger.

It wasn't that she'd lost weight—although there was some of that—but Crick had never seen her so... diminished. Crick had always thought she was a pretty woman, and even though Crick had seen Shane's sister during one of the worst days of her life, he'd always gotten the impression of strength and humor.

There were lines in her face, around her mouth, and a sort of miserable defensiveness in her shoulders.

"I have no idea why," she said now, but when she turned to him, the corners of her mouth were turned up a little. "Who knows why Jeff does anything?"

Crick looked across the yard. Jeff must have cracked a joke on his way back to the porch, because Benny was laughing at something he'd said, and Crick had an answer.

"Because his heart is actually bigger than his mouth." Oh God. "So, here goes, you ready? It's short."

"Hit me."

"So, I'm in Germany, and I'm halfway through my tour, and I've got leave. And Deacon and Benny are here, and Benny just had the baby without me, and things haven't fallen to shit yet, but Deacon isn't doing well. Any idiot can see it from six thousand miles away. Anyway, so I end up in Germany on leave, and… and…." He remembered the pounding music, the girl dragging him away from the strip club. Her brother, Stefan, blue eyes, gapped front teeth, who had listened to stories about Deacon for most of the night before he finally just quieted Crick with a kiss.

"It was a night," he said into the silence of the car. "I confessed to Deacon the next morning. He… he was awesome. I mean, I don't know how he felt in real time, but… but for me? It was like… it kept me sane, right?"

Kimmy was looking at him with big eyes, and for a minute he couldn't place her expression. When he was talking about it to Deacon later, because he told Deacon everything, he said she was looking at him a little like Crick looked at Deacon. Like he was a hero.

"I know the feeling," she said quietly.

"So, that was me in Germany. With Deacon…." Crick cringed. Well, fuck. The whole town knew, right?

"Deacon *cheated* on you?" She sounded horrified, and Crick knew he needed to make sure she understood.

"Not… he wasn't quite in his right mind, see?" Crick gripped Jeff's steering wheel and then reconsidered. Was that black stuff leather? Holy cow, did Jeff have a *kid leather* steering wheel cover? Damn, that was nice, wasn't it?

Kimmy cleared her throat, and he sighed, wishing he could talk about all-leather interiors. God. This had been hard enough when they'd told each *other*. "He hadn't heard from me in three days—my phone got lost, I hadn't even texted—and he'd been working. Benny said he'd been awake for pretty much seventy-two hours, loading sandbags near the levee to keep the place from flooding. So he's coming back from the sandbag place, and the truck stalls in front of a bar. He orders a 7UP, goes to take a leak, and the girl who wanted him all through high school spiked his drink."

Kimmy groaned, and Crick shrugged. "Yeah. I mean, it's worse than that—you know he hadn't eaten, and you know about the alcoholism, and he hadn't had a drink in a year and a half. So when it hit him… it was bad. Not so bad he didn't say my name in bed, though—which sort of sucked, because she was cheating on her boyfriend, who was a cop who tried to beat the hell out of Deacon when he got out of there. And then there was a trial, and, so, you know, that's how the whole town knows Deacon's gay."

By now Kimmy was covering her mouth and trying to hold back horrified laughter. "Oh my God!"

Crick shook his head. This was where the history lesson ended. "The day got worse," he said after a minute. "A lot worse. But… but, you see? It *got worse*. I mean… the cheating, that was bad, and… and sex isn't small, but… but it's not *everything*, you see?"

Kimmy nodded. "Yeah. Yeah, I see." She looked up at the porch again, and Benny and Parry and Jeff all had their knitting out, and Jeff was holding a full needle of stitches in one hand and gesturing with the empty needle in the other. "How much does Benny know?" she asked quietly.

Crick blinked. Whatever reason he was doing this, he didn't know what Benny had to do with it. "All of it?" he said, thinking. "Yeah. Yeah—she was there when I texted Deacon from Germany. She… I guess she'd been calling Deacon the entire blackout because she'd come back from her grandma's in Natomas and was trying to find out where he'd gone. So, yeah. I guess Benny knows the whole thing. Why?"

Kimmy sighed. "You know, your sister looks at me like I'm a grown-up."

Crick looked at her sideways, leaving off his contemplation of Jeff's steering wheel. "You are a grown-up," he said. She was, right? Shane was older than Deacon, so Kimmy was older than Deacon, and if Crick was—holy crap, was Crick *really* twenty-seven? Yes, yes he was, so Kimmy was— "You're like, what? Thirty-seven?"

Kimmy's sharp look was almost reassuring. "Thirty-six, asshole, and has life taught you *nothing*?"

Crick shrugged. "I've got Amy, I've got Benny, and I've got Melanie. Amy doesn't give a shit how old she is, Benny isn't old enough to give a shit how old she is, and I haven't given a shit about Melanie for over ten years. What is it with women and their age, anyway?"

"We're supposed to get less attractive with age," Kimmy said dryly. "But you're right—since I wasn't that attractive to you in the first place, I guess I'll settle for old crone—"

"Oh Jesus, shut up!" Crick snapped. "Look—this is all girl shit, right? Well, this is all above my pay grade. You need to talk to *Benny* about this, and I need to stop telling you the worst things that Deacon and I ever did, because that shit's just depressing! Are you going to talk to my sister or not? Because I need to know how many people to cook for and—hey!"

Kimmy seized his head firmly in her hands and pulled him sideways for a big, squishy kiss on his cheek, just like a maiden aunt.

"You're awesome," she said, and he turned to see a decidedly Kimmy look on her pretty face. "You and Deacon, you're wonderful. Don't worry about the worst shit you've ever done. You've made up for it since. It's my turn to do the same thing, okay? Yeah, I'm staying for dinner, and Lucas'll probably come join me. Go cook, and tell Jeff he needs to go inside so you can be gayfriends, okay?"

Crick leaned his forehead against the steering wheel, where the softness of the cover once again reminded him that Jeff had shopping down to an art *and* a science.

"Okay," he muttered. "I'm confused. Holy Christ am I confused. But if you can make my sister feel better, I'll tell you any secret you want. My first blowjob, when Deacon and I got laid—"

"Oh hell, junior, get out of the fucking car!" Kimmy hopped out, looking surprisingly light on her feet for someone who had looked tired and sad just moments before. Crick struggled out after her and limped gamely across the driveway to the porch.

"Did you girls talk?" Jeff asked smugly—but he was also looking at Kimmy with something like relief.

"Uncle Crick's not a girl," Parry corrected. "He's a boy. Deacon said so."

Crick looked at his niece in horror. "You had to ask?"

"You screamed at the casserole and your voice got funny," Parry said forthrightly. "I thought you were a girl."

"No," Crick said, closing his eyes against Jeff, who was laughing so hard he was beating the side of the porch couch in an effort to breathe. "*Uncle*

Crick. I'm a boy. And Uncle Jeff is too, but he might not be if he doesn't get his ass inside."

Benny made a little whimpering noise, and Crick sighed. Yeah, yeah, the whole reason he'd had that little confessional with Kimmy was to get Benny a girlfriend. Yes. A girl. That was what this was about.

"You want to come inside with me?" he asked Parry, and sent his sister a dark look. "We can talk more about girls and boys inside."

"Can't I just watch *SpongeBob*?" Parry asked plaintively. "I'm tired of knitting!"

Oh thank God. "Good. I'm tired of talking about girls and boys. *SpongeBob* sounds *awesome.*"

Parry hopped up and left her yarn and needles and bits of foam and glue for her mother to pick up, and Crick didn't even reprimand her. He *did* cast a hairy eyeball at Jeff, who was fanning his face to recover from his laughing fit. "You can come in when you've decided which side of the fence *you're* on, Twinkles," he said sourly, and Jeff, true to being Jeff, busted up laughing again.

He came in shortly and talked to Crick while Crick fixed dinner, but in the meantime, Crick figured he'd had about enough of girls to last him an entire week.

Chapter 18

Collin: Interlude with Sex

COLLIN hadn't shot his chef wad with the beef bourguignon. The garage had been slow, so when Jeff had called him in a tizzy about Benny, he'd taken the half day off to cook.

Joshua, his "employee," had taken the time off too.

Of course, there were plusses and minuses to having Joshua in their house, helping Collin cook.

"What in the fuck is that?" Joshua asked while Collin was slicing carrots with one of those fancy cheese grater thingies.

Collin almost shaved the tips of his fingers off as he looked over his shoulder. "I don't know, Joshua, they appear to be cats."

Catherine the Great Big Pain in the Ass was lying on the kitchen table. On her back. Her paws spread to the side, the long fur on her stomach clumping after its last cleaning, and twin lines of drool tracking from her mouth. Constantine the Terrible was sitting next to her head, staring at Joshua with unblinking censure from his slightly bugged eyes. It was true, they'd moved almost three years ago, but Collin still got the feeling the cats blamed *him* for the place with more space and the bigger scratching post and the big room with the kitty-nirvana carpet-covered catnip-saturated apartment complex that sat in the sun most days of the year.

A thing they deigned to use *only* when neither Jeff nor Collin were present. The rooms were covered in fur, but they'd actually installed a little computer camera in the room to see if they should maybe move the kitty condo out doors. The proof was shocking, all right. As soon as the door closed behind Jeff and Collin, the cats went into the kitty room, they played, they scampered (which was hard since both of them were pushing twenty pounds), they beat the holy hell out of each other, and then they each found separate quarters and slept.

And then, when either Jeff or Collin's car rumbled into the driveway, they both beat it out of the cat room, to be found either asleep on the couch or (more usually) on any clothes Jeff had tried on and discarded on the bed that morning.

Jeff had been appalled—he'd threatened to evict them both—but that had done it for Collin. Collin had only *thought* he loved the cats at that point. He saw the video of the duplicitous little fuckers and he *knew* he was thoroughly in love. After all, Collin had been voted among his friends as most likely to sneak out of his mother's house, steal a car, get laid, and get back home before the car was reported missing, the come was dry, and breakfast was served.

That fact that he'd been voted most likely to do this *after* he'd done it only made him more ensorcelled. Oh yeah, those fur-barfing, cock-blocking, clothes-shredding little bastards were dear to his heart—he was *never* getting rid of them.

"I know what they are," Joshua said now. "What in the fuck are they doing on the kitchen table?"

Collin stopped slicing carrots and took a small bit of seasoned ground turkey from the pan, breaking it into two pieces.

"Waiting for treats," he said indulgently. He moved to the table, leaned forward, and touched noses with Con, who narrowed his bulging green eyes in acknowledgment of Collin's presence and took the little bit of meat from his fingers. Collin then took his life in one hand and scratched his big fat princess's splayed fuzzy tummy. This move was a fifty-fifty proposition— sometimes she purred, sometimes she tried to eat him. Today she purred before awkwardly rolling to her front and meowing piteously until Collin gave her the treat he had in his other hand.

"That is *so* fucking unsanitary!" Joshua complained, really appalled, and Collin grinned at him.

"Joshua, if Jeff and I aren't worried about catching anything from them, I think we're safe."

"I think you're suicidal. Remind me never to eat at *your* house again!"

"What about the food we bring to my mom's?"

Joshua made a rather disparaging grunt. Collin's mother, Natalie, invited *everyone* to her family gatherings, including Collin's "hired man" and his wife *and* their grandchildren. Of course, so did Deacon, so the two families had a lot of really awesome, really *big* gatherings, but the fact was, Jeff and Collin's cooking was always welcome.

"Yeah, well, Don't Ask, Don't Tell worked for the military for a long time. As long as I don't know you guys brought it, I won't think of giant fur balls on the kitchen table."

Collin pursed his lips and glared but decided he didn't feel that political. Joshua was a friend, and he didn't want to get into a smackdown about the damned cats.

"Deal," he grudged. "So, that's beef bourguignon cooking for tomorrow, broccoli cheese casserole for tonight, chicken casserole for the rest of the week, and my mom says she's got lunches nailed—she's right down the block from the school. Crick's gonna drop by on his way to get sandwiches."

"Sounds like you've got them girls taken care of right nice," Joshua said, and Collin smiled, all rancor forgotten. Joshua had wandered by the garage when Collin was starting his business; a veteran parent and grandparent, he'd been bored with retirement and had proceeded to give his two cents plus a Ben Franklin on Collin's life ever since. He'd worked for damned near free until Collin could afford to pay him, and one compliment from his sour-lined cantankerous mouth was measured by the platinum ounce.

"Thank you," Collin said, refusing to gloat in his obvious victory over being an adult in a community. With a little bit of begging, he'd gotten Deacon to stay mum about the whole wiener incident (although Crick knew—that was a given, just like everyone knew what they told Jeff was relayed to Collin verbatim, with commentary), and for the most part, he'd been feeling right smug about his foray into committed domestic life. The fact that he'd been doing it for two and a half years notwithstanding, that whole "husband" thing came with responsibilities.

"So when're you going to have one of your own?" Joshua asked, and Collin barely escaped with his skin this time.

"Dammit, Joshua! Why you gotta do that?"

"Because I'm nosy." And unrepentant.

"Jeff and I are fine," Collin said, remembering his complacency at the end of summer. "We have Martin—he's coming to live in town after graduation. He'll be our son."

"And you two have done a fine job riding his folks' coattails, I'll give you that."

Collin grimaced but didn't argue. Yeah, Martin's parents weren't excited about the gay thing—but they *did* let Martin come over whenever Jeff and Collin sent a ticket. They *had* started talking about Martin's older brother, who had been killed in the line of duty, as though he was a hero and not a shameful secret. So, well, maybe the boy's manners and sense of basic decency had been instilled before Jeff and Collin had come along, but still, Collin had taught him cars and business, right?

"Next you're going to tell me he's almost grown," Collin muttered, and *that* idea didn't sit well either. Martin still felt like a kid to him—Collin was reluctant to let him go.

"Not until you are," Joshua said, wrinkling his upper lip and sucking his dentures. It would be a really revolting habit, but Joshua saved it for when he was making a point about Collin's lack of maturity.

Well, point made.

"I have nieces," Collin defended, thinking about Kelsey and Allison coming to his house every so often in their princess dresses and jeans. He should get them and Parry together—they went to different schools, but Parry had been pining for Lila, and….

"And they're just proof," Joshua said, stealing a carrot and gesturing with it.

"Proof of what?" But Collin knew.

"Boy, you let your cats sleep on your table. You adopted your boyfriend's ex-boyfriend's little brother. You plan play dates for children that involve cartoons and ice cream. You coached a soccer team of the world's *sorriest* soccer players—I mean, I love that Parry kid, but I don't think she kicked the ball in the right direction even *once*. You know where this is heading, right?"

Joshua was leaning back against the counter, and Collin found he couldn't look at him.

"To two men with HIV *not* getting custody of a kid?" he said quietly, and Joshua threw the carrot at him.

"What in the *hell*—"

"Do you know why gay men have dogs and cats?" Joshua asked him, and Collin looked at his fur babies, who were both sprawled across the kitchen table with utter abandon.

"Because we have no spines and the fuckers just move in?"

Joshua stole another carrot just to throw it at his head. Collin ducked, caught it, and threw it back.

"*Stop* that!" he complained, and Joshua shook his head.

"Because everybody wants somebody to love," he said irritably. "Before we had kids, the wife moved an entire forest in our house, and then she planted one outside, and then she got a little dog that went booby-diving if she so much as went to the bathroom. That woman made a sling for that little fucker before those things were for sale at pet stores. You and Jeff? You got a good home. You got family. You got qualifications. Of all the people on the planet, I'd think the two of you would be looking for ways that you *can* instead of ways that you *can't.*"

Collin shooed the old man out of the way and started stirring the broth for the chicken basil soup he was making for his own dinner. He threw the carrots in and turned to the giant thirty-five cubic foot refrigerator Jeff had *insisted* they get so they could house enough fresh produce for an entire army. He pulled out some celery and some onions and turned back around to the cutting board, chewing on what he wanted to say.

"Jeff thinks he's old," Collin said apologetically.

"Not since he met you."

"But... I don't know. Deacon and Crick—what they're doing with Benny, that's not a picnic." And that was the crux of it, wasn't it? He'd seen Kimmy over the past couple months, and he'd been there when Amy had been sick. One of his sisters had *multiple* miscarriages, and he'd been there when her heart had broken, every time.

"Now you're thinking," Joshua acknowledged. "You're right. That's the hard part. The hope. You two gotta decide if you're up for the hope and the disappointment right there, because that's the hard part."

Collin stopped slicing onions and looked hard at Joshua. "Your kids all moved away, didn't they?" he asked, and Joshua shrugged.

"Yeah, well, maybe I used to be an irascible bastard. You learn shit when you get old."

Collin nodded. "You ever think about going to visit?"

Josh shrugged. "The missus goes. She tells me about them. She tells them I've mellowed. I guess when they believe her, I'll get visitors." He looked at Collin soberly. "It'd be nice to get visitors in the home, you know?"

Collin raised his eyebrows, just as sober. "No guarantees Jeff and I will live that long."

Again, that iron-bodied little shrug. "None that I will. You want guarantees, go to a bank—but you better be holding a gun, because you and I have both seen how that ends!"

Collin laughed a little, but it sounded far away to his own ears. He kept making soup, and about the time he had it all settled down to cook, the casserole was done, and the beef bourguignon would be ready the next day.

"I'll take the casserole over," Joshua declared. "You're shitty company right now anyway."

Collin shrugged because it was true. "Send Jeff back here when you get there!"

Joshua wrapped the casserole dish up in tinfoil and old bath towels and let himself out. He must have been true to his word, though, because Jeff was home in half an hour, running in talking a mile a minute, hanging up his yarn bag, throwing his coat and scarf over the peg in the hallway that was really too small to hold that much shit.

"So Kimmy almost made me drag her out by the hair, the heifer, but Crick got in there and talked her out of the crazy car and into the house. I didn't know he had it in him, but boyfriend must have skills, because she was all kinds of fucking stubborn. And it seemed to work too, because she and Benny didn't shut up for, like, an hour. Then Deacon came up the porch and played hero and carried Benny inside so she could eat at the couch, and baby, it was all movies and fibergasm after that, right?"

"Jeffy nirvana and time well spent," Collin said, smiling at him. Jeffy swished into the kitchen, bringing with him cold November air and a hint of his aftershave, which was surprisingly dark for someone who liked to claim he had more air than iron in his spine. (This was a complete fabrication, of course. Collin knew few people as strong as Jeff Beauchamp-Waters, but Jeff didn't like people to think about him that way. It messed up his hair—at least that's what he claimed.)

Collin's stomach clenched at the scent, though. Jeff also smelled like he'd been cooking in the kitchen with Crick, and there must have been bacon involved, and that was one of Collin's favorite foods *ever*.

But it was more than that. It was that it was *Jeff*, and the way he smiled at Collin and dished all the news—that was *home*.

You told the truth at home.

"So," he said quietly, smiling at Jeff with all his heart so Jeff wouldn't worry. "So Benny's going to be okay?"

Jeff nodded and poked into the soup. After Joshua had left, Collin had rolled out some pasta with some fresh Romano and made little tortellini dumplings. As soon as Jeff had come in, Collin emptied them from the bowl to the boiling soup, and they'd be done in about two minutes.

"Yeah. Crick and Deacon were so worried, though. And not just about the baby, either. You could tell." Jeff sniffed at the soup and tried an experimental sip of the broth. Collin had gone a little bit spicy, but since the chicken broth was mostly mild and he'd stayed away from too much salt, he figured the spice should be okay. "*Nice,*" Jeff said and turned his head to grin.

Collin captured his mouth effortlessly, and very carefully he moved Jeff away from all combustibles and pushed him back against the opposite counter for a very deep, very fulfilling kiss.

Ah, Jeff—his mouth was hot and wet, and he whimpered and gave almost immediately. Collin shivered and spread his hand at Jeff's throat, feeling his Adam's apple bob at the vee of his thumb and forefinger. Jeff brought his hands up to frame Collin's face and push back his hair, which had been falling out of his queue. Collin used his other hand to reach behind Jeff and pull him tighter so their groins ground up together, and he could feel Jeff responding, just as fast and just as hard as Collin had come to expect him to be over the last few years.

Jeff groaned and frotted closer, and Collin pulled back for a minute because taking him on the kitchen table would mean moving the cats, and they might not go willingly.

They panted and rubbed their lips gently along cheekbones and jawlines, and Collin heard the glug of soup that was perilously close to simmering over.

"Oh crap!" He pulled away quickly and turned the gas burner off under the soup, then stirred it once for good measure to make sure all of the tortellini didn't end up on the bottom of the stew pot.

Jeff moved up behind him as he worked, coming just close enough to rub his hands along Collin's backside.

"Wow," he sighed, his voice dreamy as only Collin's boy-princess could get. "That was amazing—what brought that on?"

Collin blurted out the five words designed to shrink the boner of any man, gay or straight, who had ever existed on the planet.

"I want to have kids," he said, stepping sideways so he could lean against the uncluttered counter instead of the stove.

Jeff rucked up his shirt and started planting little kisses on his suddenly bare shoulder blades. "Yeah?"

"Ye—eah…," Collin sighed, as those kisses lined up his spine.

"That's gonna be a tough one, Sparky. You know that, right? Lots of applications, lots of waiting, lots of scoping out the old house for the authorities… you know how that goes, right?"

But Jeff wasn't mad or outraged… or even put off. He was dropping gentle kisses on the back of Collin's neck now, and when he pulled the sweater up past Collin's armpits and hefted it over his head, Collin let him, barely shivering in the stove-heated air of the kitchen. Jeff pressed up against his back and kissed the side of Collin's neck, by his ear.

"You've thought about this," Collin managed, and Jeff trilled in his ear.

"Watching you coach soccer was a real revelation," he rumbled. "You were such a good dad, and those kids would have actually learned to play if only you'd asked them!"

Collin choked back a laugh, and then just choked as Jeff thrust his hands down the front of Collin's jeans, in front of his belt.

"I can't believe this is turning you on!" He wasn't complaining, but he couldn't believe it either.

"You turn me on," Jeff purred, and he did the two hand-knead, one on the shaft, one on the man-i-folds, and Collin tried to wrap his brain around Jeffy-the-incurable-gossip and Jeffy-the-man-eater, but failed. He pulled Jeff's hands out of his pants so he could turn around and kiss his brown-eyed boy again.

"You're funny," Collin purred, pulling them groin-to-groin because he knew Jeff would wrap one leg around his thighs and try to climb him like a tree.

"Funny ha-ha or funny I-want-you-more-than-soup?" Jeff asked, and this time Collin stuck his hands down *Jeff's* pants to knead his skinny backside, because skinny or not, it was just *so* sensitive. Jeff purred and started rubbing Collin's chest. Collin's blond hair started growing on his chest as he neared thirty. He'd offered to wax, but Jeff had growled sexy about Daddy bears, and the fact that Collin was ten years younger seemed even less of an obstacle in light of that growing blond patch of fur between Collin's pecs.

"Funny that I thought this would scare you shitless. You're the man who didn't think he had a future, remember?"

Jeff pulled back and narrowed lazy brown eyes at him. "You're the moron who told me I did, remember? If I'm going to have a future with you, Sparky, I'm thinking it needs to be the best future we can make it."

Collin nodded soberly. "It's... I mean, it's going to be hard. All the shit you had to do for Kimmy—we're going to need that."

Jeff hmmed and leaned forward to hook his chin on Collin's shoulder and tilted his head against Collin's cheek. He and Collin were nearly the same height, so he had to bow his back a little to make that happen, but Collin felt the boneless, trusting way his Jeffy leaned into him, and there was a total faith there. Collin could bear his weight.

"We should probably save all of our drama until Benny's done and married, you know that, right?"

Collin closed his eyes tight. It was like they had the same brain sometimes. "We can look into it before then and, you know, have our ducks in a row."

"Mmm-hmm...." Jeff pulled back and kissed him again, and that quickly, the moment became hot. "Great, Sparky. Ducks in a row. Think we can get our ducks off before that soup gets cold?"

The kisses—strong, intense, wet kisses—kept going out of the kitchen, all the way down the hallway, and into the bedroom. When they got to the bedroom, Collin paused.

Jeff was wearing a nice cashmere cardigan, gray, with little cables running up and down like long snakes—a metaphor that made Jeff's upper lip crinkle in terror every time Collin used it. The buttons were made of polished wood, and the yarn was fingering weight cashmere/merino/alpaca, hand spun, hand dyed, and overdyed with a subtle indigo shimmer. Collin would normally neither know nor give a ripe shit about all of those details, but Jeff had knitted the sweater just for Collin, and Collin knew he stole it on days when he wanted comfort, or cheering up, or just to feel good about himself.

So Collin stood there, listening to Jeff's breath coming in quick pants and feeling Jeff's hands kneading his shoulders and his chest, while very carefully, with utmost respect, he unbuttoned his husband's boyfriend sweater, one wooden button at a time.

"Could you do this any slower?" Jeff complained as Collin got down to the buttons right over the placket of Jeff's slacks.

"Nope," Collin breathed. Underneath the cardigan was a simple white T-shirt, and Collin could see the definition of Jeff's waxed chest underneath. After the last button had popped free and Jeff had shrugged out of the sweater and draped it over the bedroom chair, Collin lowered his head and suckled one shell-pink nipple into his mouth through that white T-shirt. He felt the hard tremble in Jeff's biceps as Jeff grabbed his head and urged him to suck harder.

"*Oh sweet Jebus!*" Jeff tugged at Collin's hair, but Collin sat it out and enjoyed the sting. When the wave passed, Jeff started pulling at Collin's sweatshirt with bony, careless fingers. "Naked, Sparky, *now!*"

Collin moved his hands to Jeff's belt, and when that was done he fumbled with the stays of Jeff's slacks.

"Naked?" Jeff whimpered, and Collin obliged him, letting go of the nipple and ducking so Jeff could pull the sweatshirt and shirt over his head. Collin went to shove Jeff's pants down and Jeff went to work Collin's nipple, and there was that awkward tangle of limbs that can sometimes make catastrophe of even the hottest passion. Collin led, though—that's what he did. That's what Jeff had needed so badly from the moment Collin had looked at him, as an adult, and said, "I want you."

"Here, Jeffy," Collin murmured, holding his shoulders. He kissed his lips tenderly, and down his jaw, and then down his throat. One kiss at a time (and a couple of sucks guaranteed to leave marks on Jeff's pale skin), he moved down Jeff's body, pulling the slacks down and letting Jeff lean on him while he removed his loafers.

"You're still not naked," Jeff whispered, but his voice was breathy, and when Collin ran a pointed tongue from his balls to the tip of his cock, Jeff stopped trying to make sense altogether. "*Nungh….*"

Collin took Jeff's whole erection into his mouth, and Jeff's noise went deep throat too.

"*Whoa….*"

Collin chuckled around his length and swallowed, then wrapped his fist around it and started stroking while he sucked on the head. Jeff's noises got louder and his hands on Collin's shoulders, neck, and face moved in frenetic patterns while Collin concentrated his efforts. He wrapped one arm around Jeff's thighs and pulled him deeper and deeper until Jeff finally found his voice.

"I got one go, here," he rasped. "How about you get busy and *fuck me!*"

"Mummf ngo!" Collin let Jeff's cock slurp out of his mouth with a pop. "One go! As if!" But he kissed his way back up, and this time, he let Jeff pop open the fly of his jeans and get rid of *his* pants and boxers. He kept his hands firmly on Jeff's skinny little hips, though, as he stepped out of everything, letting his moccasins go as he did.

Jeff let out a little moan and took his mouth again, wrapping his arms around Collin's shoulders with an almost absurd grace to keep from going too fast.

That little flick of his wrist, the way those long-fingered hands stayed lightly fisted—those moments when Jeff seemed the most delicate were the ones when Collin loved having Jeff's hard, wiry body against him the most.

Collin took as much of his mouth as humanly possible. He dominated, thrusting his tongue inside, tasting, mastering, until a pliant sigh told him Jeffy was his, his for the taking, the using, the needing.

Jeff backed up until he could sit on the bed, and Collin let him scoot backward and push the navy-blue comforter and sheets down. At the head of the bed, he spread out on the sheets, his knees splayed, his cock hard between his thighs, and his fingers plucking restlessly on his nipples.

Collin took a deep breath and prayed for fortitude before grabbing for the end table and the condoms and lubricant.

Some nights he took his time and teased Jeff, massaged his rim, spread him open and licked him until he screamed, but not tonight.

Tonight was all about need, and possession, and, yes, about having hot, sweaty chimp sex before the fresh pasta turned to glue in the bottom of the soup pot.

Collin was so quick and so practiced with the glove and the love by now, as he covered Jeff's body and poised his erection at Jeff's entrance, he actually looked down and checked to make sure he and Jeff were being as safe as possible. The sight of it—Jeff's pale flesh, the dark hair at his groin, Collin's body about to penetrate him—drove Collin into his body with a groan.

The speed, the force, the urgency—that was sex with *Jeff*, and as Collin rode him, fast, hard, until he felt prickles of sweat chilling on the back of his neck, Collin stopped thinking about the goodness of it and started *living* it. He lived the beauty of Jeff's kiss-swollen lips as he took them, bruised them, made them red and puffy instead of pink and lean. Every sexy little grunt/whimper Jeff made when Collin surged forward into his body sent goose bumps along the back of Collin's arms, down his spine, down the crease of his ass and straight to his balls. He *lived* those chills, *lived* Jeff's strong fingers pulling on his nipples, *lived* Jeff's half-closed eyes, his frantic breaths as he lost himself in the passion.

Collin growled and sat back on his knees, pulling Jeff's hips up so they could stay joined. It was time to close his eyes and fuck like a champion, time to make Jeffy scream. "Grab your cock, Jeffy," Collin panted. "I'm almost there."

Jeff did, and Jeff's strokes were hard and slow, no matter how bullet-fast the fuck. And then Collin's head tilted back all on its own, and his eyes closed, and it was all sex, exploding through his body, even as Jeff cried out on a spurt of come.

Jeff's convulsions around his body were all Collin needed, and he groaned from the pit of his stomach and fell forward, not minding the wet mess between them. He wanted to kiss Jeff again, kiss him hard, tremble down from the peak with him, because that was always the best way, and Jeff kissed him back the same.

Eventually Collin sighed and rolled sideways, trying to get himself together enough to clean up and go get dinner. He startled awake a few minutes later, when Jeff thrust a wet washcloth in his hand.

"Easy, Sparky," Jeff chided, and when Collin opened his eyes, he saw Jeff was wearing his sweats too.

"Jeffy," he mumbled, washing himself off and disposing of the condom, "how come you keep stealing my clothes?"

"Because I like wearing you on my skin. Did you expect another answer?"

Collin chuckled weakly and was rewarded by his boxer shorts and a clean pair of Jeff's sweats hitting him across the chest.

"Get dressed—I'll go stir the soup."

Collin mumbled in protest. He'd been going to set the table and make everything all formal, the way Jeff did when he was trying to make a big deal about a night in. Martin was coming for Christmas next week, and he was going to stay at Jeff and Collin's for the last time. He'd been making polite noises about inviting Sweetie over to Jeff's house, as well as singing "My Girl" on the phone whenever he talked about her, so Collin was counting on his and Jeff's Christmas being relatively sex-free. When Martin came in the summer, he was moving into Collin's old room above his mother's house, and the thought was both happy and sad. Collin and Jeff could sacrifice some romance to have their kid brother/adopted son living under their roof for Christmas.

Jeff knew this, because he leaned over the bed and laid a sweet kiss on Collin's lips. "Don't worry about romance, baby," he said, his brown eyes warm and his curly hair impossibly tousled. "After that performance, you haz it. I'd rather eat soup standing at the sink with you after sex than have the whole candlelight dinner without it any day. Hands down. No contest. Okay?"

Collin smiled and palmed the back of his head forward for another kiss.

The pasta would be glue by the time they got to the soup, but the taste wasn't bad, and Jeff was right. Some things made eating soup standing up over the sink better than the full-court romance press.

Mostly Jeff made it that way. Collin made sure to tell him so—and Jeff made sure Collin was aware that he already knew.

Chapter 19

Deacon: Calms and Storms

DEACON sat in the living room with the laptop balanced on his knees and Benny looking over his shoulder. They were all grateful Benny had been almost finished with her finals when she was put on bed rest; she'd been able to submit most of her work via computer, although Drew had needed to drive to Sac State and drop her paper off in the office of one holdout who thought pregnant women were faking it for the sympathy and computers were a passing fad.

The bad part was that although she'd dominated the computer for two weeks, she'd been too busy with schoolwork to do any Christmas shopping. With a two-week hard deadline on *that* project, Deacon was the one who thought to bring her the credit card so she could go to town.

Benny had asked for his input, the way she had from the very beginning when it had just been the two of them ordering for Jon and Amy, as well as Crick's care package overseas.

Deacon had ordered for Benny on his own that year, and put Crick's name on all the tags. Girl stuff—he remembered that. Girl stuff. Amy had given him suggestions—mostly things like mani-pedis, gift certificates to her favorite stores, beauty products. Girl stuff. It had been hard; he'd helped Crick raise her and her sisters, and he'd still remembered buying her things like Barbie dolls and Hello Kitty backpacks. But for that first Christmas, she'd been expecting a baby of her own. In the end, his best gift had been a teddy bear. He'd told her she could give it to Parry when she was born, but he'd seen both rooms after they'd been painted and redecorated for the two of them: Benny's room had the teddy bear, propped up on the pillow. It was one of the more expensive ones, with the exquisitely soft fur and the old-fashioned face, sewn with darts and tiny beaded eyes. He'd even had a little vest and tie, and Deacon remembered Benny's resignation when she had to get new clothes for the bear because Parry wouldn't stop undressing him.

So this time, her on the couch, pregnant, ordering Christmas gifts, talking hesitantly about the future—this was déjà vu.

"Oh...." Benny's whine hadn't changed in the intervening seven years, either.

"I know, Shorty. I'm sorry."

"But... but... oh, man! Look at that bike! It's *perfect.*"

Deacon nodded. It was. Sturdy, with training wheels and a matching pink-and-blue helmet and pads, it was exactly the right size and skill level to teach Parry how to ride a bike.

"I don't know how we'd give her anywhere to ride," he said apologetically. "I can make it a project this summer, lay down a concrete driveway between here and the cottage—that should do it—but in the meantime...."

Benny humphed. "In the meantime, she'd have that awesome bike, and she'd have to wait on us to take her to the school on the weekends."

Deacon shrugged. "Well, her birthday's in February. Maybe we can lay down the concrete between now and then."

Benny rolled her eyes and slugged him softly in the shoulder. "Maybe you've got better things to do with your time. When are you going to paint the baby's room?"

Deacon colored. He and Crick had talked about this. A lot.

"Well, see," he said, embarrassed as he always was about small intimacies, "Crick needs to decide on a color. I keep telling him he needs to, because he's the one who gets the decorator credit, right? But he keeps telling me that he's not feeling the color scheme." Deacon frowned and squinted at her. "Do you have any idea what that means?"

Benny wrinkled her nose. "I think it means he doesn't want to commit until he's sure the baby's going to be okay."

Yup. "I was pretty sure that's what it meant," he confirmed. "Jesus, and *I'm* supposed to be the pessimist."

Benny giggled and rested her cheek on his shoulder. "Yeah, you are. Why aren't you, by the way?"

Deacon looked away from her and studied the corner of the television. "I am," he admitted. "I just don't do it so much in front of you."

Benny laughed softly. "That's not all of it," she said, because she knew him, and he shot her a quick grin.

"I was here the first time, remember?" he said, and her eyes got a little shiny.

"Duh, Deacon. It was my best Christmas at the time, and it was still shitty."

He put his arm behind her shoulders and dropped a kiss on her soft hair. Sure, Crick said it was getting greasy with pregnancy, but Deacon didn't see it that way. He thought she looked beautiful, spots and all.

"Yeah. But you have always been… I don't know. Indomitable," he said, liking the word. "I mean… it was like you just *decided,* and you were a grown-up. You've been a grown-up ever since."

She laughed a little. "Yeah. But you were the one person in my life who ever let me be a kid. It was like I had permission to screw up, and that… I guess it made it so I wanted to try three times as hard not to screw up for you."

He thought about that for a minute. "Parrish used to fuss about that," he said slowly. "He used to tell me I was a good kid, but that didn't mean I had to be perfect." He found himself smiling softly, remembering a pair of fine brown eyes and a narrow little face looking at him from the bars of the practice ring. "And then Crick came along and he started screwing up enough for the both of us, so Parrish stopped his campaign to let me be a bad kid."

Benny hmmed like she wasn't saying everything on her mind.

"What?" he asked, irritated, because people did this to him all the time.

Her returning look was wry. "You forget sometimes," she said quietly. "I know all your secrets, Deacon. I know about your mother." The woman who drank herself to death in front of him. He'd read the psychology homework she'd given him, about how it was common for a child whose parent spun out of control to try to get a little of that back. "I know that you worked your whole life to be the good kid."

Deacon swallowed, suddenly irritated with how much still bothered him. Didn't passing thirty have its privileges? "Well, I blew that to hell, didn't I?" he asked dryly, and Benny kissed his shoulder.

"Don't you see?" she said, suddenly so serious he had to set the laptop on the coffee table as courtesy.

"See what? That we're no closer to finding Parry a present than we were before?"

"Well, yeah." She was as disheartened as he was—they wanted something *big* this year, something that said she was still going to be loved the same, even if Uncles Deacon and Crick had something else to occupy their time. "But that's not what I'm talking about. Remember what you said? When I was pregnant?"

"Wasn't it mostly 'whine whine whine, Crick, why did you leave me?'"

She laughed and slugged him again. "Jesus, be serious. When I was looking for a name, we picked Parry for your dad and Angela for me—you said it was a way of seeing the best of me, remember?"

Of course he did. "Yeah."

"So what are you going to name your baby, Deacon?"

"Do we really—"

"Yes."

"You are damned bossy for someone who's supposed to be weak and helpless."

"You taught me to *never* be weak and helpless," she said, trying to look stern. She wasn't a stern parent. Parry was well behaved, but mostly because Benny tried to read her mind and figure out what was making her fractious before she got out of hand. Parry was the kid who had a snack and a juice box if she had to take a trip with Mama to the store, and the one who got enough sleep every night so she wouldn't be too tired to operate in the morning. So Benny's stern look didn't really frighten Deacon, but just like Benny had said, knowing you could get away with something and *wanting* to get away with something were two different things.

"So I did," he said. Crick was at the grocery store, and Deacon suddenly, irrationally, wanted him very much. During those two years apart, talking about small things like this had been lost. Every word coming out of their mouths had needed to be of utmost importance. Over the past five years, Deacon had gotten used to small moments, little jokes, being able to hassle Crick on the phone when he got too anal retentive with dinner, or being able to tell him how soccer practice or breaking a horse had gone. Suddenly he wanted *Crick* to have this conversation with, even though Crick had told him—verbatim—that if he was the type of guy to give a shit about names, he would have killed his mother in her sleep for naming her first daughter Bernice, and he would never have approved of a little girl named Parry Angel.

So it was up to Deacon. He actually already had sort of a plan.

"Well, I think we already decided on a boy's name when you were pregnant with Parry," he said apologetically, and her eyes widened.

"Carrick Parrish or Carrick Deacon?"

They both cringed.

"Carrick Parrish would be child abuse," she conceded, and he nodded.

"How about James Deacon—JD for short," Deacon told her, and now *she* was the one who looked like she remembered ancient history.

"Awesome. Now a girl's name."

Oh God. His mother's name? Surely not. And as for naming her after anyone else?

"It would have to be...." He sighed and felt self-conscious. "All the strong women in my life," he said seriously, "they're going to do strong things. I don't know if I could name a baby after Amy—for one thing, Crick would be jealous as hell—"

"And things are hard enough!"

"Amen, but for another, Amy will *always* be Amy to me. I don't want another girl to take that place. I'd name her Bernice—"

"But I'd kill you."

"And Crick would help," he affirmed. "But it's more than that. It's that... that a baby named James wouldn't ever be *Carrick* James. But a baby named Bernice would have no choice but to be just like you." Oh God. This was convoluted and painful. "I guess all the girls in my life have just been fresh air, and we'd need a name that was like *that.*"

He looked sideways to see that Benny was looking at him avidly. "Go on!" She batted her big blue eyes at him, and he kissed her forehead.

"Daisy," he said, thinking of the tiny wild ones and not the big domestic ones in gardens. "Daisy Sky. Something wild and perfect and... and able to live up to all the girls I know."

Benny put a hand over her mouth. "Oh, dammit, Deacon! I don't know which one I want it to be now!"

Deacon would never preen, but he did flush a little, pleased. "Well, if it's a boy," he said soberly, "you could keep Daisy Sky to name one of Drew's children, right?"

She blinked then, slowly, and her eyes suddenly spilled over. "God," she said, wiping the back of her hand across her face. "I... I'd forgotten, you know?"

"Forgotten?"

"I'm... I'm so geared up to... to giving this baby away," she said, her voice thick, "I'd forgotten. Drew and I... we'll have children. I...." Suddenly she was full-tilt sobbing, and Deacon could only wrap his arms around her tighter.

She fell asleep soon after that, and when Crick got home, they had a quiet dinner. Drew had Parry Angel out seeing a kid's movie, and Benny was staying the night on their couch. When Crick saw her curled up, still in her loosest pair of drawstring jammies to accommodate her tummy, and clutching the softest blanket they had to her chest, he kissed her forehead, which was something Deacon wasn't sure he'd ever seen Crick do for his sister.

"She's exhausted," Crick murmured. "And she looks like she's been crying."

Deacon nodded, feeling slightly awful. "Yeah, well, we picked out baby names," he said, digging into his tuna sandwich. They used low-fat mayo, which sucked, but he also used mustard, curry, chili powder, celery, onions, Bac-Os, and pickles. It was the one thing he could cook that people actually liked, and he'd made it for Crick, with some leftover soup, so Crick wouldn't have to come home and cook one more goddamned time.

Crick had a sudden look of sadness and then one of absolute horror.

Deacon took a hard swallow of his sandwich. "I would *love* to know what just passed through your pointy little head."

Crick put down his sandwich and actually appeared off his feed. Deacon would have checked the calendar for an apocalypse, except he could see out the window, and at present, there were no frogs raining down from above.

"It just hit me," he said, still seeming a little frightened.

"What just hit you? That your sister's going to have to give up the baby? That was part of the plan—we both knew it would suck for her going in, which makes us selfish bastards, and that's just hitting you *now*?"

Crick glared at him, and Deacon watched him heft his game hand—which was the one closest to Deacon at this moment—like he was thinking about whether or not he had the wherewithal to smack Deacon in the head.

"No, asshole. See, first I thought that, but *then* I thought that Benny could change her mind, and we'd have to let her, because it's her baby too, and then

I got *worried*, because that would suck, because it would so totally hurt, and then I thought that once she'd made the decision and the baby was ours, we wouldn't have to worry about it, and *then* I realized that, no, we'd just have to worry about the baby for the rest. Of its. Life."

Deacon blinked at him. "Yeah. Didn't we talk about this?"

Crick nodded, that horror still there. "But it just hit me again! We're going to be worried forever. We have *honestly* gotten on the train that there's no going off."

Deacon nodded. "Carrick James, you need to paint that baby's room."

"*What?*"

"Yup. Make a decision. Get on the fucking train and stop just looking at how fast it's moving, okay?"

Crick opened and closed his mouth a couple of times, and Deacon stood up and kissed his forehead. "If it's a boy, it's James Deacon, JD for short. If it's a girl, we'll name her Daisy Sky."

"Daisy Sky?" Crick sounded surprised but not adamantly opposed, so Deacon was hopeful.

"Yes. Daisy Sky. Because if it's a girl, she's going to be very individual here. No past."

Crick grunted. "Now I'm sort of hoping it's a girl."

"Well, yeah. That'd be nice." He thought about Crick, with big eyes and hope, watching him work a chestnut horse that first day. Thought about all the ways Crick could have gone wrong, and what an amazing person he was now. "But sometimes," Deacon said slowly, looking at the man who shared his bed and his life and no longer jumped into things with both feet without looking, "it's good to learn from past mistakes. Sometimes, that kind of strength is what gets you through."

Crick scowled at him and took a big bite of his sandwich. "That is way too fucking deep for me. Eat, dammit. This shit is good."

But later that night, when Mumford was lying next to Benny's couch playing watchdog and the rest of the house was dark and quiet, Crick came behind Deacon as they were undressing, and slid a subtle arm around Deacon's waist.

"I'll paint the room after Christmas," he murmured.

Deacon turned his head to kiss that spot under his ear where his jaw started, and Crick's long body went limp and warm over Deacon's back.

"What're you gonna paint?" he asked, and Crick nuzzled his temple.

"A field of daisies, a big horse, a seashore, and sky."

Deacon closed his eyes and couldn't imagine it, but he knew he couldn't see the world the way Crick did in his pictures. He relied on Crick sometimes for a view of a wider world, and he was always pleasantly surprised at what Crick came up with.

The picture Crick had given him at their wedding, complete with the signature of their family on the matte border, still sat in a place of honor on their wall. It showed Deacon breaking horses; holding Parry; nuzzling Crick's old horse, Comet; and lying, exhausted and covered in mud, on the kitchen floor. The way Crick saw Deacon alone, as so much bigger than the man Deacon had always thought himself to be, was proof that Crick's vision couldn't be trusted for truth but could *always* be trusted for beauty.

"It sounds like freedom" is what he said, thinking carefully. "It sounds like big and wide and far away. I like it. Get the baby thinking outside The Pulpit."

Crick made a hurt sound. "It's not even born and you're planning on making it leave?"

Deacon turned and cupped the back of Crick's head and brought him down for the kind of kiss that would make Crick's knees go weak. "I'm planning for this baby to *fly*," he said, and then he made good on that promise of a kiss.

Crick tasted so good, so solid, and Deacon kissed him harder. With the width of his chest and the fierceness of his kisses, he pressed Crick back against the mattress until he was on his back, gazing dreamily up at Deacon, pliant and happy and ready to do anything.

Sometimes, Deacon loved him best like this. Crick had always been so passionate, even as a child. Deacon loved short-circuiting his brain with sex and tenderness and then just having his way. That wide motormouth would be still for everything except kisses and gasps, and wrapping around Deacon's cock when the mood suited.

Right now, Deacon's mood ran more to pulling off Crick's clothes and wrapping *his* mouth around *Crick's* cock, and letting that long body thrash around for a bit on the bed while Crick made soft, helpless noises into the air above him. Crick grounded himself, knotted his hands in Deacon's hair, and Deacon suddenly craved the taste of him more than anything. Crick filling his mouth, filling his senses, filling his throat with come—Deacon needed it, loved it, wrapped his arms around Crick's thighs and sucked for it, and Crick had never been slow about giving.

He muffled his cry behind his hand, and Deacon shuddered, holding on to his own orgasm from sheer force of will as Crick let loose in his mouth. Deacon never got over the sharp difference in the taste of Crick's come, the texture of it in the back of his throat, the bitterness that slid down his tongue.

Nights like this, swallowing it down was the most natural thing in the world.

Crick stopped bucking and Deacon pulled away, wiping his mouth with the back of his hand. Crick cupped his cheek with a sweaty palm, and Deacon grinned at him.

"Ready for round two?"

Crick's smile was a lot looser, sloppy and buzzing and dirty. "Haven't you learned by now?" he asked, spreading his knees. He undulated a little on the sheets as Deacon backed away enough to strip down. "I'm *always* ready for round two."

Deacon loved feeling wicked. What he hadn't told Benny—what only Crick knew—was that when they were together, skin to skin, that was the baddest boy Deacon ever needed to be. He crawled up the bed, his erection bobbing under his body, and gestured imperiously for the lube they kept under the pillow. Crick handed it off, and Deacon greased his cock quickly and then thrust his wet fingers around Crick's rim to stretch him. Hearing Crick cry out, watching him thrash some more at the mercy of those fingers—that was worth the time to prep, even if Crick sometimes wanted it without. (Crick was always delightfully dirty—Deacon loved that about him in bed.) But Deacon couldn't last that long, and he replaced his fingers with his cock damned fast.

And then, as Crick's body embraced him in the soft and the wet and the heat, time slowed down.

It all felt so good, being inside his lover, Crick's hands on his chest, the limpid, trusting look in Crick's eyes. Deacon couldn't just thrust blindly now, he had to move slow, move long, take the time to kiss Crick's cheeks, his bicep, the scarred parts of his forearm, to the lame hand Crick was rubbing against his shoulder. He loved all of it: the scars, the strength, the dirty, and now, the pliant and sweet—it was all Crick. Being wrapped up in Crick right now was like his destiny, his reward.

Crick started shaking, a sure sign Deacon had built him up to a second climax. Deacon pushed up and hauled Crick's hips up, and there, right there, with Crick's sweet spot under his crown, it was time to just pound the holy hell out of him.

Crick held back cries, making them whimpers and grunts, and Deacon thrust faster, faster, until his vision went black and he fell on top of Crick, still thrusting, while Crick wrapped his legs around Deacon's thighs and his arms around Deacon's shoulders and held on.

That feeling again—being inside, enveloped, held close—that sent Deacon over the edge, and he muffled his noises in Crick's shoulder so they wouldn't wake Benny up. He kept thrusting on his own, unable to stop the push and the tremble of aftermath for quite some time.

Crick's spend slid between their stomachs, sticky and warmed by their skin, and Deacon laughed/groaned into the hollow of Crick's neck.

"Baby, if you were any hotter, you'd kill me."

Crick didn't laugh.

Deacon pulled back and saw that Crick's lower lip was quivering and his eyes were shiny. "What?"

Crick shook his head. "All those years," he said, his voice rough. "I found this place escaping church. Deacon, I swear, this is the closest to God I ever feel."

And now *Deacon's* eyes were burning, and he buried his face in Crick's neck again. "Amen," he whispered, and finally, finally, he felt Crick's wide chest shudder in laughter.

They cleaned off and made it into sweats to sleep, and that's where they were, cocooned in each other, happy and unprepared for disaster, when the phone rang in the charger.

It was Mikhail, frantic and upset.

"She is gone—you need to find her!"

"Who's gone?" Deacon mumbled, squinting at the clock. Eleven. Okay, so that was two hours of sleep. That made sense. "Who do I need to find?"

"She's gone—she trusted us and that... that...." Mikhail said a word in Russian that sounded *really* vile and unrepeatable in English, and Deacon swung his legs up over the bed.

"Who?"

"You called her a 'flaming twat'!" Mikhail spat. "She... she lied, and there was a terrible fight, and now she is gone." Mikhail's voice broke a little. "My cop, he is calling other cops, but... but she is gone, and I am worried."

"Here, Mickey." Shane's voice was gentle. "Give me the phone."

"Hey, Shane." Deacon stood up and found a clean pair of socks and his sweatshirt. His denim jacket was hanging in the mudroom, and it was cold enough for the watch cap Jon *hadn't* stolen, so he grabbed that. Crick used to have nightmares when he got back from Iraq—not so much anymore. For the past few years, he slept like he had as a child, limbs draped over the bed in a passable impersonation of a drugged puppy, and that's what he was doing now. Not so much as a twitch.

"One of our girls ran away. She's... she's usually real stable, but I guess her and Crick's sister got into it, and... well...."

Deacon remembered Crick taking off in a fury because he hadn't understood what Deacon had been trying to give him.

"Kids are stupid," he said, feeling that one in his gut. "Who is it?"

"Sweetie."

He didn't realize he'd made a noise until Crick startled in his sleep, splanging outward and then pulling those long limbs in to his chest.

"I know her," Deacon said numbly. He remembered the girl, dark like a shadow, hiding in the stable and cleaning like her life depended on it. In the past few months it had gotten so he could walk in there and she wouldn't startle, and they'd work in companionable silence, bound together by the common belief that horses were better to be around than people.

"Yeah, well, she's a good kid. We want her back."

Deacon swallowed. Mikhail seemed to think he could do something. God, he was supposedly going to be a parent—couldn't he *do* something?

"I'll call the soccer moms," he said, feeling stupid even as he said it. "Can you send me a picture of her? If the police don't find her by morning, we'll put out fliers asking for her to come back."

Shane exhaled. "Good. Good. I wouldn't have thought of that."

"Have Jeff call hospitals—it's really foggy out there, Shane. She could get...."

"Yeah. Yeah, I know."

Hit by a car. The fog had lingered all day, and between the time Crick walked in and the time they'd gone to bed, it had become deadly—the kind of fog where a flashlight or a headlight just sent back a sheet of white blindness.

"Yeah." Shane's voice sank. "Fuck. Mickey—Mickey, we've got to tell Martin."

"Martin?" Deacon felt a little lost by the three-way, but Shane pitched his voice for Deacon this time.

"The boy and Sweetie—I guess they've been e-mailing. There was some sort of misunderstanding involving Crick's sister... oh *fuck*—Mickey, get back here! Deacon, I gotta go. Get here when you can and we'll put together a game plan, okay?"

"On it."

Deacon grabbed the truck keys from the table and headed for the door.

"Hey!" Crick grumbled, sitting up. "Where's my kiss?"

Deacon was going to snap something snarky at him, and then he remembered the boy who had taken off on a misunderstanding and who had stayed in the army because he'd given his word.

He turned around and captured Crick's mouth with his own. "I love you, Carrick James. In case I forgot to say it today."

Crick kissed him back. "You never forget to say it. Love you back. Be safe—it's ugly out there tonight."

Deacon grunted. He and Shane had installed lights on the connecting road between Deacon's property and Promise House for nights just like this. "I know it," he said quietly. "Be listening for Benny, okay?"

"Yeah. I'll be listening for you too."

He would be too. Since the heart attack—hell, since he'd come back from Iraq—Crick had learned to worry.

"Get some sleep. Call ya when I can."

And Deacon pulled away from a warm man in his bed one more time to help a friend in need.

Chapter 20

Mikhail: Unsuccessful Heart Transplants

MIKHAIL had been caught blindsided. He'd heard the girls quarrelling and had stepped in. Usually Missy was the aggressor, but this time he actually had to pull Sweetie off of her.

Given that the girl didn't have any warnings on her record, Mikhail didn't bother with the "this is how you stand in the house" speech.

"What in the holy mother of hell is wrong with you!"

He glared at the two of them, not sparing any sympathy for the hanks of strawberry hair hanging from Sweetie's shaking fingers or the scratches that patterned Missy's face.

"I don't know what happened," Missy snapped, folding her arms in front of her. "She just went crazy. You know how those people—"

"Shut up," Mikhail snarled, suddenly far angrier than he had ever imagined being at one of the children at Promise House. "You will go to your room and we will hear your story then."

"Well, fine," the girl hissed. "You stay here and talk with little Miss Perfect here. I'm gonna go pack."

Mikhail turned his back on her with a flounce, because she didn't own the franchise on that dish, and looked at Sweetie, unhappy and confused. "Sweetie, I—"

"LeLauna," she said, her jaw mutinous. "When you all call me Sweetie, I can't hardly breathe for fear of fucking that shit up."

"Yes, of course," he said, uncertain. "LeLauna. I... I don't understand. You are smarter than this. I know you are. What did she say? What would make you so mad—"

"I'm not a saint!" She realized she had big hunks of Missy's hair in her hand, and she threw them down on the carpet. "Stop treating me like I'm smart or I'm better than something! We both know I'm just a ragged-ass whore! *You* know what I am! I offered to blow you for a fucking sandwich!"

"Yes, but you declined to bend over, which shows that even then you had sense."

"Aw...." For a moment the girl's lower lip wobbled, and Mikhail was relieved. She would cry. She would cry, and then he could get Shane and Kimmy, who dealt best with tears, and it would be better. But she was tough, Sweetie was. For five months she had been quiet and self-contained, and she wasn't going to let him in now. "Aw, fuck you," she said in disgust. "You're not cute, and neither am I!"

He was suddenly very afraid for them both. "I don't understand—you have friends here who think much of you—"

"Well, don't! I'm trash, and we're all gonna know it!" And with that, she stalked off to her room.

She was sullen and uncommunicative during dinner—Mikhail and Shane exchanged glances when she stood up and dropped what amounted to a full plate of food in the sink. Missy refused to come out of her room and had flat out ignored everybody who'd knocked on her door. At one point she'd screamed, "Sweetie'll squeal on me. That bitch loves to kiss your asses!" but after that, they heard nothing but silence.

After dinner cleanup, Shane looked at him and said, "You know it's got to be you."

Mikhail frowned at him, uncomfortable. "I am not great with baring my soul," he said. "She will need me to do it."

Shane snorted. "You're *awesome* at it when it's needed. And yes. She *will* need you to do it."

Except she was gone. Her covers were untouched, her drawers were open, and her few possessions all gone. Shane remembered she'd had one of the reusable grocery bags in her room, and Mikhail was stricken.

"A grocery bag? She could fit all of us in a grocery bag and just walk away?"

Shane... the look in his eyes was too terrible to see, so Mikhail turned away. It was Mikhail's fault. He had handled it badly. He had thought to let them cool off, thought to talk about it later, thought to give himself some time before he spilled all of his stupid secrets in front of this girl. This girl was not Kimmy—Kimmy knew all of the bad about Mikhail, and they were equals. This girl—she was his *charge*. It was his job to help her grow, not to tell her the bad things he had done.

Unless, of course, those things would help her heal.

"We must find her," he said, not sure where to walk or what to look at. He was wringing his hands, and he didn't know it until Shane took them both in his. Shane's hands were startlingly warm, and Mikhail recognized the iciness of his own shock.

"We'll do our best," Shane said, and even then, when Mikhail needed reassurance the most, he recognized his cop's inability to lie. He did not say, *We will find her.* He said, *We'll try.*

"She is out there all alone, and... and she is so *stupid,* she did not know we cared for her!"

Shane pulled him in for a brief, hard hug. "Did you know I cared for *you?*" he asked.

Mikhail was mashed against his hard chest, but he still tried to answer. "Yes," he mumbled. "But I did not think I was...."

"Yeah," Shane sighed. "Now excuse me while I call Calvin. He'll tell his guys to keep an eye out."

Shane called Calvin, and while he was doing that, Mikhail called Deacon. Deacon would help, he thought numbly. Deacon was the man they all depended on. Deacon could help make things right.

Shane had to take the phone away from him, because he was ranting, but when he was forced to listen to them talk, he found some peace and a moment to think. It was when Shane repeated something about getting Jeff to help that Mikhail suddenly understood.

Martin.

Shane had the same idea too, but not in time to keep Mikhail from storming off to Missy's room to *drag* an answer from the girl, willingness to talk or no.

"*What* did you say to her!" Mikhail snarled, yanking the door open. He worked out constantly, danced in the fall, and still, he should have been surprised at how easy it was to break the lock on the door.

"None of your goddamned business!" Missy screamed.

Later, details would hit Mikhail. The small trinkets she kept on her dresser, and how they were things Benny and Crick had mentioned giving her. The fact that her pillow wore the day's makeup, including the dark mascara, where she'd been crying, escaped him then as well. All he knew was that she had hurt someone important to him, and she needed to pay.

"What did you say?" Mikhail demanded again. "She was excited today—she was going to see Martin tomorrow because his plane came in this afternoon. She was... she was *talking*. Do you know? You drip venom all day and all night, do you *know* how often that girl talked?"

"Never." Missy sneered. "Conceited bitch didn't talk to fucking *no one*. So fucking lonely here, and she was too good to be my friend! She was like the rest of us—nobody here's a saint, we *all* put out for food and a place to sleep. She didn't have no cause to be all high and mighty around us!"

Mikhail's eyes narrowed. He and Shane, they did not think like other people. They did not go in straight lines. They chased conversations around corners and under tables. "Is that what you said?" Mikhail asked, figuring hard. "Did you say she wasn't worth it? Did you threaten to tell Martin she was a whore?"

Behind him he heard Shane and Kimmy, and probably Lucas and the other counselors there, because he had done the unthinkable and had breached a resident's room. Mikhail wasn't even an employee, technically—everybody else had a key, because the children weren't always safe by themselves, but Mikhail, he was not supposed to be there.

"Her and her damned boyfriend," Missy muttered, her voice breaking. "Wasn't that nice for her, when boys won't give me the time of the day. Prissy bitch. Why shouldn't I?" She shored up her voice with acid then, and he would not, *could* not, see that her chin was quivering, and she was sorry, sorry and miserable and unable to find the words to grow into any compassion she'd managed to scrape together. "Yeah, I told her she was a whore, and that Martin would fuck her and leave her, or fuck her and beat her, because that's what men *did*. Wasn't my fault she was too stupid to know how to use them before they used her. Wasn't *my* fault she's fucking gone! She's probably happy to get the hell out of here too, with the rules and the chores—she's probably laughing her ass off and getting drunk and getting laid, because God knows that's what *I'd* like to be doing, and you fuckers won't fucking let me—"

Her voice was rising hysterically, and Mikhail wasn't even aware he'd raised his hand to her until Shane caught his wrist midblow. Missy just stood there, grinning in triumph, ready to take the blow, to love it, because it was something she'd done her damnedest to earn, and Mikhail whirled on his cop in fury. His other fist cocked back and was ready to fly, and Shane just stood there, sorrow in his eyes, waiting for the blow to land.

Mikhail's whole body went still. For a moment, he even stopped breathing.

"I'm sorry," he said into the hollow silence. "This is not helping. Excuse me. I will get out of your way."

He did not see what happened next in that room. He went instead to sit on the porch and look out into the night. He couldn't see anything, just the white face of the fog staring blankly back, daring him to peer any farther to where secrets were rabid, hidden, and dark.

He was still sitting there a half an hour later when Shane came out and laid a blanket on his shoulders.

Mikhail's teeth were chattering by then, but he tried to throw the blanket off.

Shane clamped his hands down then, keeping it wrapped, and for once, he sounded on the verge of his formidable patience. "Don't be stupid, Mickey. It's freezing out here, and you don't even have a sweatshirt on."

Mikhail stopped resisting. He *was* being stupid. "I am no better than the damned children," he said, his jaw tight with cold. "You should not waste your time with me. You should try to find Sweetie instead."

"Deacon's on his way," Shane told him. "If it's taken him this long to get here, it's because the fog is insane. We can't look for her in this. We'll have to wait until morning."

Mikhail nodded and thought of the girl out in this cold. "She has a good jacket," he said randomly. He'd taken her to Wal-Mart and told her to pick one out. She'd shyly picked one with a fur collar, in brown, and he'd told her it was a good choice. "I almost got one in purple," she'd said, "but that seemed a bit flashy, you know what I mean?"

He thought of that now and wished she *had* gotten it in purple. Or neon pink, or green. "Brown will be hard to spot," he mumbled, almost to himself.

Shane sat down on the top porch step and wrapped an arm around his shoulders.

"I'm sorry," Mikhail murmured. "I almost… I almost… I swore I'd never hurt you again, and you almost let me—how could you let me do that?" he accused, because it was easier than remembering what he'd almost done.

"Because you weren't lashing out at me, Mickey," Shane said patiently. "Baby, I'd do about anything if you forgive yourself."

"When she's home." Once upon a time, Mikhail would not have felt any hope at all, only worry. Once upon a time, he would have written the girl off as a lost cause and let her wander into the fog without caring. It was her fault, was it not? For not trusting? For not having faith? But he had been the one who hadn't trusted, who hadn't had faith, and someone had believed in *him* until things had worked out. He had a little hope now, didn't he? He had hope that somehow, this girl would come to her senses. Somehow, she would come home.

DEACON arrived, and between Shane's resources and records and Deacon's community ties, they had some reassurance that in the morning, a picture of Sweetie would be posted all over town. Megan-the-wonder-soccer-mom had a friend who lived in nearby Natomas, and she'd be posting fliers as well. Jeff had given Sweetie's description to every hospital in the area, and between Jeff and Shane, they'd managed to get word out to the shelters that Sweetie was *always* welcome home.

Mikhail had nothing to do. He brought them coffee and water, gave them snacks from the kitchen after the first hour, and curled up into a ball on the couch after that. Normally, this would have been his and Shane's night to go home, but when Mikhail woke up in the morning, Shane pulled him into his big, bear-sized embrace, and Mikhail slept in his husband's arms.

Much of him was still broken, but that—that gave him hope: it might someday be fixed.

Hope was thin on the ground. He needed all he could get.

Martin arrived that day, and the look on his face when he realized Sweetie had gone and was not coming back—at least not on her own—was something Mikhail would carry with him for maybe the rest of his life.

"Why?" he said quietly to Jeff. "Why would she go? I don't understand. We were going to meet—we had…." His voice choked. "We had *plans*."

Mikhail walked up to the boy—the giant of a boy, really, the almost-man—and awkwardly patted his shoulder. "It…." Oh God. He'd failed Sweetie in this. He needed to pony up for this boy.

"When you are broken," he said carefully, "you do not realize where your weaknesses are."

Martin looked at him blankly, and Mikhail grimaced. Oh, what he would give if only all the people he loved could follow his brain like Shane could.

"Sweetie, she and I—we did some things on the street to survive," Mikhail mumbled. "Things that we were not proud of. I used them to scare Shane away. I am guessing...." Mikhail looked at Martin for confirmation. "I am guessing she didn't tell you these things?"

Martin shook his head slowly, his long, handsome dark face impassive. "She didn't," he said softly. "I guessed, but I didn't pry."

Mikhail nodded. "Because you are a good, respectful boy. That is as it should be. They were her secrets to tell. But... but someone else, in a... fit of irritation, told her that you wouldn't like her anymore—"

"But that's *bullshit*—"

"Yes," Mikhail said, patting his cheek sadly. "It is. You are a boy of worth, I have said that already. But Sweetie... she didn't trust herself. She... you will have to trust me on this, Martin. She believed that you were too good for her, and so she left. Probably so she did not have to endure your good-bye."

"But I wouldn't have *said* good-bye!" The boy was angry, and Mikhail could not blame him. His heart was open and bleeding, and all Mikhail was giving him were the fears of a panicked child.

"No," Mikhail said softly. "No. You would not have. But she didn't know that. Doing the things she's done to survive, it breaks you in unexpected places. None of us knew where she was weak or how she would break. She never *told* anybody where her weaknesses were. And so when they were attacked—"

"She broke," Martin murmured.

Jeff had been standing at his shoulder the entire time, helplessly patting his back. Martin held on for a moment, because he was a man, and men were stubborn about being strong, but he wiped his face once, twice, a third time, and then Jeff was there, like he had been for his family so very often, hugging the boy who probably topped him by three inches, and murmuring into his ear like he was small.

Mikhail could do nothing but walk away and let Jeff comfort him, and be grateful they all still had Jeff.

THEY tried to keep their sadness from Deacon's house at Christmas. The fliers, the phone calls, they continued, but there was nothing. Nobody had heard anything. Nobody had seen anything. One slender, dark-skinned girl could, apparently, flit in the shadows of the world, never to be heard from again.

Mikhail and Missy avoided each other. They made no eye contact at dinner; there was no pretense of her trying to please him or him trying to exert authority over her. At one point, Missy yelled at one of the younger boys right in front of Mikhail—something about not pawing her shit for drugs. Mikhail took the boy in the kitchen for ice cream and dispatched Miriam, one of the other counselors, to deal with Missy. It wasn't until Christmas came and went without any dramatics from that end of the house that Mikhail realized she had probably been trying to get his attention.

He wouldn't have cared if he had known.

He wanted nothing to do with her. Nothing at all.

He hadn't realized, though, how much this attitude had seeped into everything he did until they were standing outside of Deacon's on Christmas morning and Shane gave him the presents for Benny and Parry Angel. "Try not to look like the Grim Reaper when you give them to her, okay, Mikhail?"

That had brought him up short. Shane *never* called him by his given name.

"Do I look that bad?" he asked suddenly, aware of the misty morning in the familiar Pulpit driveway. Deacon had fresh gravel poured, so it was not as muddy as it used to be, but he could not look at his toes forever.

He looked up instead and watched Shane try to answer his question before averting his face. Mikhail felt a little thrill of panic. Was that *hurt*? Was his cop *hurt*?

"What... what have I done?" he asked suddenly, upset like he hadn't known he could be.

Shane shrugged and tried a sad smile. "She's been gone for two weeks, Mickey. It's Christmas morning. You got me a new belt with a nice belt buckle, and that was great. Do you remember what I got you?"

Mikhail actually had to think about it. "Pots," he said decisively. "Because it was getting hard to cook on that old shit we have at home."

"And...."

For a moment he went blank, and then: "Satellite radio," he said, and felt smaller than shit on a shoe. "So I can dance in our home." He swallowed and looked at his feet in new boots from Kimmy. "They were wonderful gifts. I did not hardly say 'thank you', did I."

Shane shook his head no. "I understand," he mumbled. "She was special—"

"No," Mikhail said. They hadn't yet shut the doors on the GTO, and there was probably some important car reason to do that, but for the moment, it served Mikhail's purpose. First he set his stuff down in the car. Then he took Shane's pile of gifts and put them down too. "I don't think you do."

He stood on tiptoe and took Shane's face between his hands. He had warm mittens Crick had knitted him the year before, and the circle of giving was one more thing he had forgotten in the past two weeks.

"You… you have given me so many wonderful things," Mikhail said through a raspy throat. "You have given me a family, and you have given me hope. I saw that girl, and…." He swallowed and closed his eyes. "I liked her," he said hoarsely. "I liked her. I cannot lie about that. She was such a sweet child. I wanted to give to her the same things you have given me." He opened his eyes. "When I failed, I… I realized how much hope I'd had, and it hurts…."

"Sh…." Shane comforted him, as he always did, arms around his shoulders, big, burly chest pulling Mikhail into its warmth. He remembered Martin, and how Martin had cried helplessly, guilelessly as a child, and how Sweetie would not. How was it, he wondered wretchedly through the tears, that he had to learn this same lesson again and again and again?

And then it *really* hit him. If it took him this long to learn this lesson, how long would it take Sweetie? How lucky was he to have found Shane, to have believed in him in time?

His tears were still silent, but they hurt more, and Shane held him, disregarding time, disregarding being late for Christmas breakfast, because these lessons were a long time in the making, and they needed the respect of Mikhail's broken heart to drill them in just right.

HE BARELY remembered going in after that, or giving gifts. He found himself stashed in a corner of the couch, balancing a plate of food on his lap, and eating because Shane had growled at him to eat, dammit, it was fucking Christmas.

He was very aware he could have spent Christmas at home with a microwaved dinner, sitting on the couch and looking out into the drizzle, and he would have felt just as festive as he did here on Deacon's couch.

But Benny wouldn't let him get away with that shit either.

One moment he was on a corner of the couch, staring sightlessly as Parry Angel showed everyone her brand-new wide-wheeled scooter with girl-chattering excitement. The next moment Benny was practically in his lap, leaning her head against his shoulder and cuddling.

"Is there something you wanted?" he asked dryly, and she made a negative sound.

"Not so much, no."

"You're just going to sit there and impose on my personal space."

"Yes. Your personal space was taking over the house. It was distracting. Pretty soon we all would have been pushed out the front door, and it would have just been you, a cranky little Russian bastard, ignoring my brother's best cooking."

Mikhail looked down and saw that, among other things—and there was always a lot—Crick had made meatloaf.

"Why is there meatloaf?" he mumbled, taking a bite. Crick's meatloaf was moist, with sourdough breadcrumbs and onion soup. It wasn't Ylena's, but it had been cooked in stewed tomatoes, and it was, in fact, very good.

"Because Shane asked if Crick could make it, special. He said he tried a couple of times, but he didn't think it was good enough."

Mikhail felt his eyes burn, which was foolish, because he'd just spent an interminable amount of time crying on Shane as it was.

"His meatloaf is fine," Mikhail said, taking a bite of Crick's excellent meatloaf anyway. "What he does is always good enough."

"Yeah, but I think he felt like he needed some help," Benny said softly, and Mikhail looked at her for real.

"How are you, little one? You are looking very 'glowy'."

Benny's smile was less tired than it had been, although her complexion was still a little shiny, and her hair, although freshly washed, looked stringy again. Pregnancy was not always kind. "*I* am going to be off bed rest in time for next semester, and I'm very, very happy about that."

Mikhail nodded and kissed the top of her head as it rested on his shoulder.

"So am I," he said, meaning it. "And the baby? The baby is good?" For the first time in two weeks, he managed to pull himself out of his own misery. The baby... *Deacon's* baby. Deacon, who had arrived out of the fog to give them good suggestions and call everyone he knew for more. Deacon, who had given Shane a home before Mikhail had arrived, and this girl was giving him something that he'd obviously hungered for.

Benny nodded and something fresh and sweet blew through Mikhail's soul—even with the undertone of sadness behind it. "Yeah. Little fish is doing fine."

"Little fish?"

Benny patted her stomach affectionately. She had a bump there, it was true, but no extra roundness. "Yeah. Kimmy started calling it that since Deacon and Crick don't want to know the sex."

Mikhail thought rather wretchedly that Kimmy would probably have gotten fat, and the image sent an unexpected pang through him.

"Kimmy has been visiting, yes?" Mikhail had noticed it dimly. Jeff had been doing a victory dance about it until…. Mikhail looked up and saw Jeff and Collin huddling over Martin's massive shoulders like nervous parents. Yes. Yes, everybody had his hurts. When had Mikhail forgotten this?

Benny nodded. "Yeah. She's been keeping me sane, you know? Talking about hope." Benny's voice dropped. "She was so hurt when I got pregnant—"

"It wasn't your fault," Mikhail said firmly, and Benny patted his knee.

"I know. She told me. But it was like, as soon as there was a possibility that I could lose the baby, she realized that I could hurt like her, and she was right here, being my friend."

She reached out and clasped his hand, and he had a sudden flood of memories, of all the times the two of them had watched Parry play and talked about everything from learning to drive to the newest recipes to stretching exercises Benny could pass on to Crick. If Deacon was the father of their little family and Kimmy was his sister, then Benny would be… well, she'd be the simplest thing, would she not?

"I'm sorry," he said, weaving their fingers together. "You have been a very good friend to me, and I have not returned the favor."

"Yeah, you have," she said quietly. "You've had a full plate, Mickey. But I'm glad to talk to you now."

Mikhail tightened his fingers. "You know, I should like nothing so much as to hear about you. Tell me again, why do they not want to know the sex of the child? That seems silly to me. How are we to buy baby clothes if we don't know?"

Benny giggled. "I've been thinking about that. The doctor can *tell* me, right? I mean, the fish is swimming around in *my* belly. So I'm thinking that I tell one person, right? And when I go into labor, that one person tells the whole freakin' world who's *not* Deacon and Crick, and then you all can decorate the house. What do you think?"

A sudden thumping pushed at Mikhail's chest. "You would tell me?" he asked hopefully. Amy was not there. Kimmy... well, Kimmy had been trying to coax him out of his shell too. This was obviously not the first plate of meatloaf Mikhail had been given in the past two weeks.

Benny laughed, and he closed his eyes. When he had first moved into Shane's home, before Kimmy and before Promise House, Mikhail had visited often. He had learned to treasure Benny's laughter.

"Of course," she said, and then she lowered her voice to a whisper. "Is it okay if I tell Kimmy too? And that way it will be you, Shane, and Kimmy, and *someone* will remember the house."

"Perhaps we can buy clothes too," he said, smiling. "Although... well, Jeff would buy something on the way to visit you anyway, yes?"

"Yes," she affirmed. "And that way, we can have the baby shower and people will bring unisex clothes and the important stuff, right?"

Mikhail blinked. "What do they need?"

"Oh, everything! Car seats, cribs, strollers—all of that stuff goes out of code almost before you buy it. Standard operating procedure is to throw a shower, make a list, and then buy the stuff people don't give you."

Mikhail smiled a little. "How was your shower with Parry?"

Benny's face grew... well, sad. "I didn't get a shower," she said, trying to smile. "Deacon, Jon, and Amy all took me shopping, and Jon and Deacon took turns fighting over the tab. Every now and then Amy would dive in and get one, because I guess she still had her own bank account then. Deacon had me pick out paint for the rooms earlier—the two of us spent a week cleaning out Crick and Deacon's old rooms and... well, you know what they look like now, except seven years ago, the paint was fresh, and you don't have all the times Parry found Sharpies and played artist on the walls."

"That sounds...."

"Small," Benny said, looking at the crowded living room. "It was small. It was before Andrew and Shane and Jeff, before you and Collin and Kimmy and Lucas. It was small."

They both looked at the people sitting and talking, eating the buffet Crick and Jeff had set out on the counter, playing with Parry Angel, and making sure that she never, not once, had cause to miss her shadow, Lila, who had been there from the time she was eighteen months old. Drew was there most often, and Parry had no trouble wrapping her arms around his waist and hugging him like the father he so obviously was.

"I was missing Jon and Amy," he confessed, looking at his plate. The meatloaf had disappeared. Shane would be pleased. "Now, I see that it's as though Deacon surrounded himself with people so he could let people go if he needed to." He turned to her. "Does it not seem that way to you?"

Benny laughed a little, as though she knew something she couldn't articulate. "It's why I decided to have the baby," she confided quietly. "So we'd never really leave."

Mikhail opened his mouth, caught by the simple beauty of that, by the simple sacrifice. His eyes burned again, and he felt wretched, utterly wretched.

At that moment the phone rang, and he jerked, breathing hard, which he'd been doing since Sweetie disappeared.

"It's Jon," Benny said unnecessarily. Crick had picked up the phone at the wall, and his whoop of excitement bounced off the walls. For a moment Mikhail saw Crick—who was about Mikhail's own age—as a young man with more enthusiasm and passion than good sense, and his heart stuttered. He looked sideways at Benny, and for the first time since that wretched girl had pounded up the stairs like a poisoned cow, he saw the resemblance between Missy and her sister.

Finally, he had a moment of compassion for someone so angry she would *say* hideous things, *do* hideous things, because the bile in her belly was so corrosive that she would slaughter villages just to spite the world.

"What?" Benny asked, looking at him.

He shook his head. "Would you...." He sighed. "Never mind. I am still not feeling that charitable."

"Wow. That was cryptic." Benny shrugged, short hair flying carelessly, and the illusion of Missy was dispelled. Mikhail shook his head and wondered bitterly when Benny had grown older than him.

Shane caught his eye from the kitchen then, and Mikhail took a deep breath, body filling with oxygen. In three steps, Shane had crossed the room and was reaching to take his plate.

"Thank you," Mikhail said quietly.

Shane only smiled a little. "You ate!"

"I guilted him out about the meatloaf," Benny said cheerfully. "He's little. If he skips a couple of meals, we'll see right through him."

"It was very good meatloaf," Mikhail said with dignity. "How are Jon and Amy?"

Shane looked over at where Crick was on the phone, talking extra loud and gesticulating wildly with his least-coordinated hand. "I am thinking they're doing pretty good," Shane said, laughing. "Jon called us this morning, remember?"

Mikhail looked at him blankly.

"You were outside feeding the dogs—I don't think you registered I was on the phone when you came in."

Oh yes. Mikhail had been feeding the big hairy beasts and picking up after them. It was his Christmas present to Shane, who usually got up early to do that chore. He remembered that now—he'd done it every Christmas they'd shared together, except the one he spent on the ship with his mother.

"I was distracted, *lubime*," he murmured, because *Chert*, that was obvious, was it not? "So… is there anything new?"

Shane chuckled. "Amy said that Jon put on twenty pounds in the first month. She's started kicking him out of bed early so he can hit the gym at the law offices. She also said that Lila misses dance lessons with you and that Jon-Jon's first word was 'dammit'. Apparently the folks in DC did not think it was as funny as she did."

Benny laughed. "I *know*. Did she tell you about the time Jon forgot and parked the car in the driveway instead of the garage? *Three* people came to make sure their garage door opener hadn't busted. And *then* they asked her if she was getting a divorce, because her husband seemed to have left all his clothes in the car!"

Shane was laughing openly now. "I heard that one—and then…." Shane's smile died a little and his mouth twitched. "When she told the group of women what she and Jon did for a living."

Benny caught his mood, and Mikhail did too. "What happened?"

"Well, Lila wasn't invited back to playgroup, for one thing," Shane said quietly, and Benny growled and rolled her eyes.

"What did Amy do?" she asked, and Shane blinked.

"What do you mean, what did she do?"

"Well, it's *Amy*. She doesn't take that sort of thing lying down." Benny nodded. "She'll get some sort of revenge. You'll see. Nobody fucks with Amy's kids. She'll be pissed."

"Why did she not tell *you* this story?" Mikhail asked, and Shane's next breath sounded strangled.

"You heard her, Mickey—Benny's demanding action, and maybe Amy feels like sitting this one out!"

Mikhail thought about them, about Jon and the wonderful things he had said at their wedding, and about Amy, who let her handsome, lazy husband get away with nothing.

"She will do something," he decided. "That one, she is a fighter."

Shane nodded. "I think you're probably right. But you two, don't give her any grief about it. She'll get her feet under her in a little while, okay?"

Shane stood up and squeezed Mikhail's knee before taking his plate to the sink. Mikhail turned in time to see Benny sticking out her tongue and crossing her eyes.

"What in the *hell*!"

"I love him," Benny said matter-of-factly, "but even *you* have to admit he comes off like your favorite teacher sometimes."

Mikhail was watching Shane's bottom, which filled out his good jeans. "I have to admit no such thing," he said seriously. "I did not ever want to be nailed to the wall by *any* teacher, favorite or otherwise."

Benny cackled with glee, and Parry ran up to her mother to see why the happiness.

"She was laughing because I was being silly, bunny girl," Mikhail said. Parry's curly hair was up in two ponytails for Christmas, one with a green tinsel-spangled ribbon and the other spangled red. She was wearing an old-style plaid dress, with a white lace bib and a tie in the back, and a white lace cardigan, and white Mary Jane shoes. Every Norman Rockwell fantasy Mikhail had ever had about Christmas in America was dressed like this little girl sitting on his lap, and yet Mikhail knew that the little girl's happy childhood had not come easily. Every adult in the room, including Kimmy and Lucas, who had come latest to the party, had participated in her growing up.

"You have not told me about your favorite present today, Angel," Mikhail said soberly. "Why am I the only one who has not seen it?"

Parry's face fell. "Drew made me put it out on the porch. He said it could be dangerous to Mommy if she got up to pee."

Mikhail masked a smile. He'd seen her riding the thing around the living room and into walls and into people. He thought—not for the first time—that Benny had chosen very well when she'd picked Drew to be Parry's father. His own mother had never found a man worthy, and he had to admit, after the time spent with Shane's children, Missy not least among them, that better no father at all than the wrong one.

"That is probably *exactly* why he had you put it outside," he told her, setting his mouth in serious lines. He looked sideways and saw that Benny was flashing through the TV menu, and when she stopped, she grinned at Parry with a combination of delight and relief.

"Look, Angel—they're playing *Tangled* on Disney. You want to sit here with me and Uncle Mickey and watch it?" Benny patted the space next to her. Reflexively, Mikhail tightened his grip around Parry's shoulders.

"She can stay on me." He wanted that very badly.

Benny nodded and leaned back against him while he angled his body so Parry could lay her head on his shoulder and settle in to watch. The noise from the kitchen leveled off to a quiet rumble, and Mikhail thought that maybe Jon and Amy were about to wrap up their call.

"Oh, hey—Mikhail!" Benny whispered, right when he was settling in.

"Wha—" Suddenly the hand not steadying Parry was dragged down and thrust flat against the front of Benny's black yoga pants. He felt the heat of her body, and then, unexpectedly, a flickering little *thwap* of pressure against his palm.

An honest smile stretched his cheeks. "It is kicking?" he asked, and it was a brand-new thing, a glowing, wonderful thing, and none of the sadness that had suffused him could taint it.

"Yeah," Benny whispered, and he closed his eyes, everything concentrating on that flicker against his palm. "Deacon already felt it, but Crick hasn't. I think Deacon teared up, but don't tell anyone."

"That... that is *amazing*," Mikhail said.

Benny hmmed in her throat—and then just left his hand there, on her stomach, until his arm cramped and he had to drag it away.

He needed this, he thought, his chest sore. All of the things that Benny and Parry were to him, he needed this. Shane had given him pots and music and those had been nice, but they weren't his real gifts. His real gifts were that moment at the car, lost and found in Shane's arms while he remembered the taste of grief, and this right here: joy and family pressing against him until the grief faded and he could breathe again.

Chapter 21

Benny: When Blood Tells

ONCE she had permission to get off the couch and resume her regular scheduled life, Benny remembered that she *loved* being pregnant.

She did.

She'd thought, at twenty-two, that she was exaggerating the memory that she'd carried at fifteen, and through all of the bullshit of the first trimester—the nausea, the boobie-geddon, the *wildly* massive mood swings, the revulsion to *any* foods but popcorn, steak, and strawberries—it had all come flooding back to her.

When you were pregnant, you woke up *every* morning with the certainty that something wonderful was around the corner.

It didn't matter how shitty life was in reality, there was that *promise* of something wonderful that could come. When she was fifteen, she hadn't recognized it at first. Part of that was that she started out living on the street, in fear that her father would find out that she was pregnant. It didn't seem rational, didn't seem sane, that she would wake up and think about that burgeoning, alien thing in her stomach and be happy about it. She hadn't *done* anything to put it there. She'd woken up after a party sore and achy, and in two weeks she'd been thrown down the pregnancy hole.

But that didn't stop the feeling of *something wonderful* that had followed—especially after Deacon had gotten her off the streets, away from her parents, and she'd discovered what living with someone who gave a crap was actually like.

She hadn't expected that anticipation this time. That *something wonderful* wasn't meant for her—why would she feel that excitement about it? It was a burden, something to be borne but not enjoyed. Right?

She didn't trust that feeling—not this time. This time, there would be pain, the terrible roller-coaster plunge and horror of labor, and there would be... nothing. A sore body, breasts that needed to be emptied, blood that would need to be sloughed off, and... and then what?

Her, and Drew, and Parry. Her tiny, sprouting family, and nothing else.

There would be no *something wonderful* after this—at least that's what she told herself. The singing thing inside her didn't seem to believe that, and she had difficulty telling it to fuck off.

But on days like this one, her first week back to school, she was having no trouble at all telling *someone* to fuck off, and that was the truth.

"What do you mean, I can't get in the class?" she asked her evaluator. "I signed up, I registered on time, I was *on the roll sheet.* I need these four classes to graduate—how is it this one isn't available?"

The evaluator was a middle-aged woman with short graying hair, thick black-framed glasses, and the sort of rabbity expression of someone who was accustomed to wanting to run away because of her own incompetence. (That last was purely a guess on Benny's part, but she'd put honest-to-God money on it being a damned good guess.)

"I'm sorry, Miss Coats, but someone with a higher priority bumped you out of the class—"

"There's a higher priority than graduating senior?"

The woman cringed. "I don't understand why the computer did it either. You can go wait for people to drop out—you're not far down on the list, but you know there are no guarantees!"

Benny let out a growl of frustration. Her back hurt, her neck hurt, and her head hurt. She needed food, and she needed a nap, and she needed this little woman with no spine to get out of her fucking way and let her get an education.

"I am five months pregnant. Do you know what that means?"

The woman's eyes opened and closed and then focused with laser intensity on Benny's expanding midsection. "That maybe now isn't the best time to finish your degree?" she asked, like that might possibly be the right answer.

Benny thought her eyes were going to pop out of her head and roll on the floor. "Wrong answer!" she growled. "It means that sitting on the ground while I'm waiting to get a spot in the class is going to be a *colossal* pain in the ass, and I don't mean that in the good, fuck-me-harder way, either! Do you think that maybe, just *maybe*, you could check your computer again and see if there's maybe a junior or a sophomore who could be bumped down, since *they're* stuck in this hellhole for at *least* another two years?"

Hellhole was unfair. The Sacramento State campus was actually very pretty, once you got over how close the buildings had gotten as the student population had grown larger. Trees grew over the river, and a wide, generous green opened out in front of the library. Drew was, in fact, playing with Parry on the green now, because Parry had this Monday off for some inexplicable reason, and Benny had been reluctant to just leave her at home. It was like a holiday for her, and since Benny didn't actually *have* any Monday classes, she figured they could go down to the school while Benny cleared this up, and then maybe take Parry to the railroad museum in Old Town, or to Sutter's Fort or the Crocker Art Gallery or something.

She left it up to Drew to choose, since he was coming down with her, when she knew *he* had things at the ranch he wanted to do too. The business had gotten big enough—and they had enough horses to care for—that he and Deacon had started divvying up tasks. There were some things Drew couldn't do—he was very agile on the prosthetic, but agile didn't always cut it when you were dealing with a monster stallion with an anger management problem. But there were some things—breaking the gentler horses, putting the babies through their paces in the ring—that he *could* do, and that he took pride in doing. Since Deacon had given him more and more autonomy, he'd gotten less and less enthusiastic about going back to school, and Benny wasn't sure what to think about that.

On the one hand, she'd been proud of his ambition. On the other, she was proud of The Pulpit and of what the four of them—her, Deacon, Drew, and Crick—had made of it. It was a thriving business—and one of the few successful horse-training operations that had survived after the crash. She knew that some of that was the canny investments she'd made when they'd started working in the black instead of the red, but most of it was... was *them*. It was Deacon and Drew and the way they treated the kids who were paid to come help them. It was Deacon's philosophy of kindness and strength and not cruelty and domination, and the way he favored the gentle animals over the pretty ones. It was the way Crick dealt with the people (blunt asshole that he could be) and the way Benny ran the books and Drew filled in all the spaces in between.

If Drew was happy at The Pulpit, Benny wasn't going to object to living her life there and raising Drew's children.

And watching the one inside her continue to grow.

She couldn't lie to herself that the baby, the *something wonderful*, was part of her motivation for wanting to stay. Deacon would want to watch Parry grow—that was never in any doubt—but that she would want to watch this child grow too? Even though she would only be "Auntie Benny" to this one, that was starting to loom in her mind as something important.

How stupid would it be if she had this baby to make it possible for her and Drew to leave The Pulpit, but it became one of the reasons they decided to stay?

That irritation was spilling over into her little interview now, and she didn't think she could contain it.

"Do you not understand?" Benny leaned over the desk, scrabbling on the woman's blotter like she was trying to find flesh under her fingers. "Don't you get it? I *need for things to be settled*. And they're not going to be. My boyfriend may or may not go back to school after we get married. We may or may not continue to live in the same house. I may or may not be able to let my stupid brother and his awesome husband have this baby. All of this shit is up in the air, but the one thing, the one *goddamned thing* that *wasn't* up in the air, was whether or not I was going to *have this class*. Do you think you could maybe fix that for me? Do ya? Maybe? Maybe could I just take this fucking class and get my education?"

"Did you say your brother's *husband*?" the little woman asked.

"*Ergh*—hey!"

"We're awfully sorry, Mrs. Abrams," Drew said, taking her by the shoulders and almost physically lifting her out of the chair. "She can take the class next semester. Is it offered online?"

"Drew—"

"Let the woman answer, Bernice—is the class offered online?"

"Why yes," said the evaluator, looking shaken. Benny had no idea why she'd be so puzzled—after what Benny had dealt with today, she was sure all *sorts* of people must threaten Mrs. Abrams with imminent physical danger. Crick would have driven the woman shrieking from her desk in *half* the time it took Benny to lose her temper.

"Can we have the information? We can get Benny signed up this summer, and in the meantime, maybe you can look into when she'd be able to apply for graduation."

"Oh, yes… of course."

Mrs. Abrams looked relieved, and as far as Benny could tell, she *should* be relieved, because Drew's surprise arrival had *totally* gotten her off the hook.

"But Drew—" Benny was going to object, and then she saw Parry waiting not so patiently at Drew's side, with the Frisbee they'd been playing with in her hand. That was when Benny realized that they were both cold and their clothes were coated with mist. The gray sky that had shrouded their trip down must have finally decided to drop and give rain.

After a few more minutes, and the woman's business card, and a finalizing of Benny's schedule with only nine units, taken on Tuesday and Thursday of the semester, Benny, Drew, and Parry were on their way.

"Don't pout, Bernice," Drew said on their way out to the car. It had started raining, and Benny pulled two little umbrellas out of her purse. Parry had the bright pink umbrella in front of them, and Benny and Drew held one with Monet colored flowers, just a couple of steps behind. The rain wasn't falling that hard, and they'd bundled well. The walk—under the trees, around the buildings, between the wide lawns—actually felt sort of pleasant. Or it would have been, if she wasn't in a shit-kicker of a mood.

"I'm starving," she snapped, and he shoulder-bumped her in spite of her crappy attitude.

"There's orange juice and crackers in the car," he said gently. "I packed."

Benny brightened considerably. "Yeah? That was sweet. I was going to put some in my purse, but—"

"There wasn't enough room with the umbrellas. I get that. But see? We work good together—right?"

She nodded and shoulder-bumped him in return—and to warn him about a pile of slippery leaves up ahead. Parry just went gamucking through them, but Drew couldn't sense the changes under his prosthetic foot, and she didn't want him to slip. Together they walked around the hazard, and when they got back on the path, she realized she had sighed away some of her tension.

"I'm not going to be done until next semester," she said, and Drew didn't argue.

"Nope. But this way, you can take more of those poetry classes you've been whining about."

"But...." She waved the hand *not* holding the umbrella. "But... you know... we were going to...."

Drew sighed. "How upset would you be," he asked after a moment, "if, you know, that AHT and veterinarian thing didn't happen?"

It so exactly mirrored what she'd been thinking that she actually felt *guilty*, like she'd somehow beamed her secret hopes to him by telepathy. Or maybe just really clear signals—it wasn't like she'd ever kept her heart's desires under lock and key.

"But... but...," she sputtered now, trying to think of a good reason to make him go out and do something he apparently wasn't excited about anymore. "But you *wanted* us to be on our own. You *longed* to go do something autonomous, remember?"

Drew's sigh sounded almost as guilty as Benny's wild heart flail a moment ago. "Yeah," he confessed, "yeah. But... I don't know. I was... I'm not as jealous now, I guess. All that insecurity, all of that doubt about having you to myself—that's no longer an issue."

Benny felt an acute moment of unfairness. "But... but if all that was going to go away, why did I do *this*?" she asked, gesturing to her swollen, irritable, unhappy body.

Drew wrapped a reassuring arm around her waist. "Don't you get it, Benny? You were right. *This*"—and he squeezed her thickening middle—"is *exactly* the reason I can stay. *This* is going to be the part of you that Deacon and Crick get, and it's going to be *awesome*. Just because it's not going to be my baby, do you think I don't want to see it grow?"

Oh fuck. Oh hell. Oh *no*!

"Benny, are you crying?"

They had gotten out to the parking lot by now, and Benny was looking around their section for her car, the nice safe gold sedan Deacon had bought her not long after she'd had Parry Angel. "Shut up," she muttered.

"Benny?"

Parry had found the car, and she was standing next to it, staring up through her umbrella to see the pattern the rain made when it fell on the pink surface through the fabric.

Benny wiped her eyes with the damp sleeve of her coat. "Orange juice," she muttered. "I need orange juice. And crackers. And a big chocolate cake."

"Benny," Drew muttered, tightening his arm around her waist. "*Talk* to me!"

Benny turned toward him and looked up, thinking that everything about his dark-skinned rectangular face was especially dear today. She cupped his cheek and pulled him down for a quick kiss that got a little deeper and a little deeper, until Parry's plaintive "Momm-eeeee!" reminded them both where they were.

"You're perfect," she said hoarsely. "You're perfect, and you're awesome, and you're right. I really *did* want to take those classes in poetry and politics."

She hurried then, to go help Parry get in the car (although Parry didn't need much help these days—she could pretty much sit in the car seat and do the belts all by herself), and let Drew muddle through all the rest on his own.

THAT was a nice moment—and it helped her get through the next few months. Parry's birthday party was in February, and although Lila was *sorely* missed, Parry got to invite other friends to Chuck E. Cheese, and that seemed to make her happy beyond all reason. She went to sleep that night in a brand-new princess bed with pink sheets, and newly painted pink walls in her room in the cottage, and Benny and Drew retired to make happy, triumphant love. Their little girl was seven, and they'd made her happy, and damn if that wasn't to celebrate.

And as it seemed to be every year since she'd been born, Parry's birthday was a harbinger of spring. Spring at The Pulpit was always something special—when Mother Nature wasn't trying to kill them dead, that is.

This go-round, spring was actually pretty mild. Not as much rain as people would have liked, but it often seemed that when there *was* enough rain, there was actually *more* than enough rain, and the world went straight to shit. The year before, there had been flooding—not quite as bad as the year Crick was gone, but enough to give them all a scare.

The rain that day lasted a week and then went away. What followed was February clear and dry and so cold *Deacon* actually remembered his hat and gloves.

The first week of March, though, the rains came back—and didn't go away for another three weeks. Drew and Deacon came in and pretty much shed mud in the mudroom, and the dog got away from them and ran into the living room and shook twice, leaving little brown pellets all over the couch and walls like a shotgun blast. Everything in The Pulpit and Benny and Drew's house started taking on a mild brown patina from all the damned dirt tracked in and out, but since Drew and Crick were doing the cleaning, Benny managed not to get into a tizzy about it.

Benny spent Monday, Wednesday, and Friday working at The Pulpit, answering the phone and doing the books in between doing her homework. Crick took on Parry Angel duty, right down to stopping at the frosty a couple of times a week for a treat, and Benny began to see the pattern for the next semester, and maybe the semester after that one.

It didn't seem so bad.

Especially on Saturday, when most of the riding lesson clients cancelled because of the rain. Deacon stayed outside for a couple of hours to work some of the more high-spirited horses who would go apeshit without workouts, but he sent Drew inside and the kids back to Promise House as soon as the stables were mucked and the horses fed.

Kimmy came by, Jeff in tow, and Crick plopped down on a couch next to Benny, and they sat and drank some sort of coffee/chocolate thing Crick had experimented with, knitted quietly, and listened to the rain.

Drew was on the floor, helping Parry put together a puzzle, and the television was on quietly—Parry had seen *Tangled* so often she knew it by heart (Benny wished Crick would stop saying Flynn Ryder *really* belonged with Prince Phillip at the end).

Her stomach was big enough to set her knitting down on when she went to take a drink of chocolate *without* the coffee, and she had one of those O pillows under her ass to help stave off the hemorrhoids. With all her comfort needs attended to, it was a perfect moment.

Until Kimmy brought up the one subject guaranteed to kill a moment, shoot it in the heart, strangle it, and stomp on it, dead.

"Benny?"

"Yeah?" The baby blanket was coming along—not as fast as Benny usually went, but that time on her ass had given her an edge.

"You think you and Crick might be ready to talk to your sister?"

Benny dropped a stitch and spent longer than she needed to finding it and fishing it back up through the delicate white wool. Crick wisely put down *his* knitting, because his stitches were painstaking enough without losing them.

When she had her knitting situated (and didn't have an excuse not to broach the problem), she rested it on her stomach and tentatively looked at Crick.

Crick was regarding her patiently, like he'd been waiting for her to make eye contact. Whatever he saw there, he was the one who took the lead.

"Is she still a flaming twat?" he asked, and Kimmy hurriedly covered her mouth with her sleeve as she spit out hot chocolate coffee or whatever the hell Crick had been pouring down their throats that made Benny need to pee.

Benny didn't even check the floor to see if Parry had heard. She'd heard, and Drew's strangled "Dammit, Crick!" proved it.

Kimmy wiped her mouth and shook her head. "Okay. How you're not straight and we're not dating, I will *never* know. But yeah. She's still not sweetness and light, okay? If you can imagine his mouth on the girl from *The Exorcist*, well, then, there you go."

"And we want to talk to her why?"

Crick smacked her with his lame hand—*hard.*

"Dammit, Crick!"

"Oh, sure, but flaming twa—twinkie is a bad thing to call someone!"

"You *hit* me!"

"She's our sister!"

Benny whimpered. "Well, is it so bad I've been pretending she's not?"

When she'd first come to The Pulpit, she'd wanted nothing more than for Missy and Crystal to come live with her. She had it *good*. For the first time in her life, she had comfort, and someone who cared, and a reason to work in school and a room that didn't smell like piss and mildew. She'd wanted that for them too.

But seven years had passed. When she and Crick had been sending them hopeful gifts, that had been one thing. But this wasn't a gift or an "I missed you so much." Benny and Crick had gotten out, and Crystal and Missy hadn't. It wasn't their fault—never had been—but bearing the brunt of Missy's hate because Benny had gotten out of the house was just not something she wanted on her plate right now.

"No," Kimmy murmured, and that quickly she went from just being a friend to being on the clock. "Benny, it's not so bad. You and Crick tried, and there had to come a time when you moved on with what you had. But... this whole Sweetie thing—"

"Has there been any word?" For Mikhail's sake, please?

Kimmy shook her head no. "And see, Mikhail—they used to fight like cats and dogs. Sweetie was his favorite, we all knew it, but your sister—it was like she went out of her way to piss him off."

"Mission accomplished," Benny said, because, well, *duh*!

Kimmy shook her head. "No. You don't understand. She thought she was doing it because she hated him, but really?" Kimmy put down her knitting for a minute so she could try to talk with her hands. "You don't see the dynamic at Promise House. I'm not a leader—I've *never* been the leader. But I can be a good little soldier, and I'm fine with that."

"Well, yeah," Benny said, thinking about it for the first time. "Shane's the leader—he's the big daddy bear—"

"And Mikhail, whether he sees it or not, is the mama. Well, from what I know about your house growing up, *nobody* wanted the daddy bear's attention, am I right?"

"That would be damned accurate," Crick said evenly, and Benny winced.

"Good. But what about mama bear?"

"We... we *wanted* it," Benny said, and then she looked at her brother. "But, you know, Crick sort of filled in. She... she was really just... I don't know. Void. Not there. Absent."

Kimmy nodded like she'd known this. "Well, for a little while, Missy had a mama bear that gave a shit."

And Benny got it. "Oh. Oh no."

Kimmy's voice got a little thick. "He... he tries to hide it, but he's still so hurt. When he opens his mouth to ask a kid to do something, you can see—sometimes he's asking for Sweetie, and then he remembers, and he has to find another name. He... he almost hit her, the night Sweetie disappeared. Shane stopped him, but... you didn't see his face, Benny. It was like... like when he shut down the part that wanted to kill your sister, he shut down any part that could have given a shit. And she... she misses it. She misses *him*. And she's given up trying to get his attention. She doesn't act out anymore, but... she doesn't wash her hair anymore. We have to remind her to brush her teeth. She's... she's...."

"Void," Benny repeated dully. "Absent. Not really there."

Kimmy nodded. "Exactly."

Benny sighed and resumed her knitting thoughtfully. Next to her, Crick did the same.

"We could come and see her, right?"

Kimmy smiled a little. "Yeah. That would be great. Tomorrow the kids are all going to the mall—it's sort of a special event. Everyone has money saved, and it's a good chance for them to go get something that they really want. We've got a chaperone for every two kids—do one of you want to go?"

"I'll go," Crick said quietly, throwing his yarn.

Benny looked at him, feeling hormonal and weepy and grateful. "Yeah?"

Crick patted her arm gently, taking the sting out of where he'd thrown his hand at her before. "You said it yourself, Benny. I was the mama bear. That sounds like what she needs."

Benny gave it up and let her eyes flood over. She grabbed his gnarled hand and brought it to her lips and kissed it. Her stupid useless brother. Deacon may have saved her when she needed it, but damn if Crick hadn't tried to do it before then.

"You were the best mama bear a girl could have," she said, and Crick wiped carefully under her eyes with his thumb.

"Practice," he said with a little smile.

They both picked up their knitting at the same time. It wasn't until she heard Jeff snoring in the corner of the couch that she looked up and realized he'd been asleep through the entire exchange, and she choked back a giggle. Kimmy and Crick giggled too, and until Deacon walked in, the only sounds were the low babble of the television, their needles, and the rain.

Chapter 22

Crick: Things to Wake Up To

HE DID what Kimmy had asked, right? He showed up with his wallet and the little sedan Deacon had bought for him when he'd returned from Iraq, prepared to be the good big brother and spend time with his sister.

Kimmy greeted him as he pulled up. She made the little finger-up gesture, and he unclicked the car door. She hopped in and said, "Keep it idling, hon. I think you'll be turning around to go home."

"What?"

"I'm sorry." Kimmy actually leaned against his arm, and since the car was in park, he humored her and gave her a one-armed hug. "She... she stole something this morning. It was something stupid—a book one of the other kids was reading—and she left it on her dresser. Normally this would be her third strike—we should already be sending her to juvie—but...."

Crick filled in the blank. "That's what she wants," he said sadly.

"Yeah," Kimmy murmured.

"Well, can I talk to her?"

"She's in the timeout room," Kimmy explained. "It's not going to do much good, but it's the punishment we set out, right? Marion is going to stay and watch her, and, well...."

Crick looked up and saw the rest of the residents lined up on the porch. They were talking animatedly, and behind him, Shane, Mikhail, and Lucas were all waiting to move their vehicles into place to pick up kids. He wondered which lucky bastards got to ride in Shane's GTO, and at the same time he wondered which poor fuckers would have to ride in the giant Chevy van Mikhail had nicknamed The Purple Brick. And then he put that aside and wondered, "What should I do?"

"Come by next week," Kimmy said. "We'll set up a time and not warn her until an hour before. In a way, the fact that she did this is a good thing."

"Explain the hell out of that!" Crick snapped and then felt bad.

Kimmy toyed with the end of her waist-length braid and shrugged. "It's the first sign of life we've seen from her since December. She was actively trying to get away from you."

Crick groaned and leaned his head against the steering wheel. It was a basic Saturn sedan, gold on the outside, cream on the inside, vinyl steering wheel cover. All things considered, his discussion in Jeff's Mini Cooper had been a lot more fun. "Wonderful. Fucking wonderful. You know I'm going to be a father soon, right? And this kid—who I raised until she was, like, nine—won't talk to me. Why was it we didn't come see her earlier?"

"Because your family situation was six kinds of fucked up," Kimmy said. "And she didn't want to see you then either. That's what the place is for, Crick—they say they don't want to deal with it, we sign the papers that say we respect that. Your stepdad died, and, well, Shane and I just keep putting off having her sign a new agreement, so we can do stupid shit like try to get her to talk to you."

Crick nodded. "Stupid shit. This was stupid shit. Do you think Benny would want to keep that baby? She's a good mom. She'll be fine. I mean, who wouldn't want Deacon's baby? Ouch!"

"Stop being an asshole. You don't mean any of that, so stop saying it. The situation is fucked. What can I say? This is the first time her accountability for her actions has ever stared her in the eyes and spit in her face. She's not taking it well."

"Yeah, well, welcome to the fucking family."

Kimmy gave a surprisingly kind smile. "The human family, Crick. We all fuck up. Sometimes the consequences are...." Her voice dropped. "Out of proportion. Out of proportion for our original sin. I mean, look at the frickin' Bible, right? All they did was eat an apple."

Crick actually smiled at that—and then Kimmy got out and he went home.

THAT had been the last time he'd tried—and the last time anyone had talked about it either. Of course, it was weird the way that stuff could come back and kick you in the ass.

"Crick! Crick! Wake up!"

Crick squeezed his eyes shut and opened them again. "Benny, what in the hell—?"

"Look—you can *see* it kick this time! Look!"

Crick grunted. Yeah, sure, that's what she'd been saying for the past month, and Deacon had actually seen it. "You woke me up to tell me the baby's kicking? Aren't you *tired*?"

Being tired was the whole reason Benny had stayed over. They'd painted Parry's old room and turned it into the baby's room that weekend, and it hadn't turned out bad. The field of daisies stretched along all four walls, with the crash of the sea beyond it. A horse stood in the middle of one wall, ankle-deep in daisies, and everything three feet from the ceiling and up was a cobalt sky blue with big puffy clouds. A girl or a boy, this baby was going to have something to *see* when it laid in the crib.

The crib actually arrived when they were in the middle of painting.

Deacon had assembled it, and the changing table as well—and that was a whole other story. While he'd been putting the crib together, Drew had cleared out Benny's old room, and they'd debated whether or not to leave Benny's bed there or to make it a playroom. They'd decided to split the difference, but Crick needed to paint *that* one too, so they left the bed in the center of the room and, well, Crick had more work to do that weekend.

His game arm and leg ached, his back ached from compensating for them, and his good arm ached from painting. His head ached from the paint fumes (in spite of the open window into the rainy night), and his stomach muscles ached from... hell. From holding up everything else.

And he was still in better shape than Deacon.

The only thing that had driven Deacon inside to help them with the rooms had been getting stepped on by the damned horse. His boots had stopped some of it—although his instep was pretty damned bruised—but the horse had been shod and the shoe had sliced through his jeans and peeled the skin off his shin to the bone.

Drew had the horse in the pen and Deacon in the truck to the ER before Crick even knew he was hurt. Benny had stuck her head outside to call for lunch and they were gone. She put on her mud boots to lead the horse into the stable and then rubbed him down before returning back to Crick's chicken soup waiting for her at the table with Parry. (Parry *loved* painting with them. She *especially* loved the little shower cap Benny bought her to keep paint out of her hair. There had been an incident when they'd been getting the mother-in-law cottage ready that none of them were likely to forget soon.)

"Where'd they go?" she asked, and it wasn't until *then* that Crick actually thought to call them.

The news that Deacon was in the hospital getting stitches seriously pissed him off.

"Put Deacon on the phone," Crick growled, and Drew hadn't laughed at all.

"No, sir. That would violate a direct order from the boss."

"A direct order from the boss? Who does he think is cooking for him, goddammit! The man who runs the kitchen rules the world! Drew? Drew? He hung up on me!" Crick said, looking at his sister in outrage.

Benny shrugged. "I don't blame him," she said reasonably. "You've been a total asshole since you went...." She grimaced.

Since the aborted shopping trip with Missy. Wonderful.

Missy had been busy working for the past week—Kimmy said that of all the things, her work ethic had improved, and so far her employers hadn't complained once—and Crick hadn't had a chance to see her again. Deacon had proposed they do the baby rooms this weekend, and Benny had been surprisingly eager to assist.

It had been a pretty decent day too. Until Drew hung up on him.

"I have *not* been a total asshole!" he snapped, and if Benny's skeptical eyebrow hadn't told him that he'd *just* been a total asshole, Parry's snicker did it for her. "Okay. Maybe I've been a partial asshole. Does he really need to run away from me?"

"Well," Benny said slowly, "maybe he's worried too—you ever think of that?"

Crick regarded her blankly. "I'm more than a total asshole. I'm like *six* total assholes all rolled into one. *God*, Benny—how could I forget that... that... he's *Deacon*?"

Deacon, who knew everything—Sweetie, Missy, Crick's fears about being a parent, Benny's fears about giving up the baby—but who didn't *talk* about his own problems. Seven years ago, Crick had worried his ass off—and for good reason—about Deacon's propensity for keeping things close to the vest. Three years ago, it had almost killed him. Deacon was doing better in that department, but same as anyone else, he did not get better almost overnight.

So Crick had been troubled, a total asshole sunk in his own head, snarling at everyone unless he was painting, and Deacon had just... been Deacon. Making shit go, keeping it all together, and not letting anyone worry about him.

Until a horse practically maimed him with one careless step.

Or that's what it looked like when he hobbled in, his jeans ripped off at the knee, a big swathing bandage wrapped around his calf.

"You have got to be shitting me," Crick said, rushing up to him, and Deacon waved him off.

"It looks worse than it is," he said easily. "The doctor said inside activity, nothing too big. We had lunch on the way home—put me to work now, or the painkillers will kick my ass to the couch!"

Crick stood there, getting ready to rip Deacon raw with his temper, when some of that newfound-daddy maturity kicked in, and he took a better look at the way Deacon was holding his jaw.

He was in pain, painkillers or no, and he wanted a way to stay useful. Crick nodded. "Can you put together the crib?" he asked. "It arrived when you were gone."

So Deacon didn't say much for the rest of the day, but he had by God gotten shit done.

Crick tried not to resent the hell out of him for it.

Deacon went to bed early that night, after taking a pill from *both* of the bottles Drew had filled for him. He'd had to ask Crick for help with the bandage, though, because the other one had gotten torn and displaced during his workout. Crick needed to help Deacon put a plastic bag over his shin, and Deacon hadn't met his eyes the entire time.

"Have I really been so awful?" Crick asked quietly, remembering everything he'd done—snapping at Parry; throwing the ball over the house so the big furry donkey just sat there and stared at the roof of the house for an hour, waiting for it back; drinking Benny's orange juice and telling her to suck it up. Well, that last one had been mostly brotherly pique, but still.

"You've been mad," Deacon said. "And thoughtful. You didn't need *me* spilling crazy all over your freshly painted room."

Crick grunted. "So you had me spill paint in it instead. Very clever, Machiavelli—did you ever think that *your* crazy distracts me from *my* crazy? Or that maybe if I saw your crazy, my crazy wouldn't sound so bad? I mean, hello, that thing is fricking spazzing out in her stomach 24/7, and pretty soon it's going to be living in our house. Maybe I'd like to know that's freaking you out too, right? Maybe it would be just *fucking swell* if you'd cop to a few real human feelings like being scared out of your goddamned mind!"

Deacon's short, sharp laugh did not reassure. "Carrick, you've seen me living in fear for most of my life. I'm not sure if you could tell the difference."

Crick stopped short in the act of wrapping tape around Deacon's ankle to hold the plastic bag in place. "That's not true," he said quietly. "That's not—"

"Afraid of crowds, afraid of the people I *can* stand leaving me alone, afraid of losing you in Iraq, afraid of losing our home—Jesus, I don't know when you *haven't* seen me afraid."

"Which just makes you one of the fucking bravest men I've ever known," Crick snapped, "because you deal with all of that, and now we all look to *you!*"

Deacon was sitting sideways on the toilet seat, one arm propped up on the back of the toilet. He leaned his head against his palm and smiled, one of those tired, still-fighting smiles Crick could remember almost from the beginning, when Deacon was recovering from mono and still working out the horses every day.

"Don't be dramatic," he murmured. "Can I strip now and shower?"

Crick shook his head. The stitches were extensive, and he knew Deacon's whole body would be sensitive to things like hugs until the pain meds kicked in.

"Promise me you'll... I don't know. You won't just keep all this shit to yourself again? Didn't we promise that? Something like that? Wasn't it in our wedding vows or something?"

"Nope," Deacon said, holding back a smirk. "I would have rewritten that bullshit—if you all had given me a chance."

Crick found a grin creeping out at the memory of their surprise wedding. "Could you promise anyway?" he asked nakedly, and Deacon reached out and grabbed his hand.

"Crick?"

"Yeah?"

"I promise that we can feed that baby. I promise that we can change it, we can clothe it, we can keep it clean. I've done that part before—it's a challenge, don't mistake me, but I promise it can be done. I cannot promise nothing bad will happen. You've heard Collin's story—his dad passed away in an instant. His mom—you've met her. Sweetest goddamned woman in history. And Collin? He is the first person to confess that he was a class-A fuckup right up until he tested positive. All we can do is love this kid. It is *literally* all we have. That, and the hope that the people around us will keep us from fucking up when things get hairy. We've got people around us who will do that. And we've got each other. If, God forbid, I go tits up before this little fish is fully grown, you will *still* have me, because you've *had* me since you were a little kid. I won't go away in your head or your heart. I'll still be there, just like Collin's dad was in half the stuff Natalie did to try to keep that idiot alive until he came to his senses. Just like my mom haunted this goddamned house when Parrish couldn't remember to talk more than once a goddamned day. It's the only promise I can give you, okay? You and me, we can love this baby."

Crick felt the smile stretching his cheeks for no good goddamned reason. "So you just *had* all that fucking wisdom and you kept it to yourself? What an asshole!"

Deacon laughed, but his eyes were closing and the pain meds were obviously kicking in.

"C'mon, let's get you in the shower." They'd kept the shower chair from Crick's worst days back home after he'd been wounded, and Crick had moved it in so Deacon could just sit and get pounded by the warm water.

He came back with a dry towel and some briefs and sweats and a shirt, and Deacon generally let himself be attended to—although Crick could tell by the long-suffering expression on his face that it was mostly for Crick's benefit, not his own.

By the time Crick was done with his own shower, Deacon was mostly asleep, and Crick took a moment to look at him before he turned off the light.

"Deacon?" he asked quietly as he hit the switch.

"Mmm?"

"Why didn't you at least tell me you were going to the doctor?"

"'Cause you were finally painting the nursery. Didn't wanna fuck that up. Looks real nice, Carrick—go to sleep."

Crick sighed. Not perfect. He was *not* perfect. He was an irritating, close-to-the-vest, insecure martyr. Crick was damned sure the one thing that had made him survive Iraq was the thought of Deacon in this world without Crick to take care of him.

Their kid? *That* was going to be an interesting person right there.

Crick couldn't wait to meet it.

And here Benny was, whispering to him in the middle of the night to look at her stomach. He pulled himself mostly awake and felt it first.

He felt it, and the movement was familiar by now, the smooth glide of muscle and bone, making itself comfortable inside her body. "So. Fucking. Cool. Turn on the light, Benny, I wanna see."

Benny did, and Crick stared at his sister's larger body with interest.

She was wearing drawstring pants tied under her stomach and one of Drew's old T-shirts over it. She stood up and hauled the shirt above her stomach and tucked it under her boobs.

"Classy, Benny," he muttered, and she smacked his head.

"Yeah, I'm classy. Now feel me up before I have to pee."

Crick put his hand on her stomach again, and sure enough, the thing inside pushed back. Hard.

"It's fighting me!" he said, startled.

Benny giggled. "He doesn't do that for Deacon—"

"He?"

"She, it, whatever. *It* doesn't do that for Deacon."

"Well, why is it fighting me?" he asked, pushing back at the little demon spawn.

His sister's giggle yanked him right back to their childhood, when he would come home and tell her jokes he'd heard in the fourth grade, and Benny, at barely four, understood them. "Because it knows you," she said, still giggling. "C'mon, Crick—you don't think this baby's going to get into fights with Deacon, do you?"

Crick looked at her belly then, saw the skin move like the surface of a flesh lake while a big predator pushed up inside.

He stared at it, enthralled. "Jesus, Benny, that *can't* be comfortable!" he said, and she shrugged.

"It's actually...." Her piquant little face scrunched up, and her chipmunk cheeks popped, and she smiled so tightly her eyes got squished between her cheeks and her brows. "It's sort of magical," she confided, her voice hushed, like a little girl telling a parent about fairies.

Crick found himself smiling too. He looked up at his little sister in the dim light of the bedside lamp and suddenly saw her all the ways he'd ever seen her. As a smart little kid. As a precocious and angry adolescent. As the pregnant teenager who had helped save Deacon when he hadn't been there. As the competent housemate who had balanced the raging emotions when he'd returned.

As a brilliant young woman with a mind of her own.

He stood up then and hugged her, smooshing her big pregnant belly between them.

"Thanks," he said into her hair. "This thing you're doing... this thing you're *giving*. Deacon tried to warn me how hard it was going to be on you. He did. It was one of his big reasons for not doing it. I don't know what you said to convince him, but thank you."

Benny turned her body a little sideways so her belly swung outward and she could hug him back harder. "You're welcome. Thanks yourself. I know this thing with Missy hurts, but you... I mean, you'll always be my big stupid useless brother"—she was sniffling, and he smiled because that was Benny—"but you were a *really great* mom."

She went back to sleep on the couch a few minutes after that, still sniffling, and he crawled back in next to Deacon. Deacon was warm and safe, and he grasped Crick's hand automatically as Crick circled his waist.

"Did you finally see it?" Deacon mumbled.

"Magic? Life? Redemption?" Crick said into the back of his neck, and he was reassured when Deacon breathed out a sleepy laugh.

"Yeah, sure. All of it."

"Yeah."

"What's it like?"

"Like the first time I saw you," Crick murmured. "Like proof that God exists."

"Oh Jesus—"

"Shut up and go to sleep. I love you."

"Love you too. Night."

A good moment. A happy, glowy moment. The next morning Shane called them and told them that if they wished, they would have an excuse to see Missy again after all.

Chapter 23

Shane: Closure

MIKHAIL'S face was white and tautly drawn, and his hand in Shane's was icy, the grip so hard and so bony Shane was pretty sure he'd be bruised the next day.

Shane's grip back was much the same, and he wasn't sure what his face looked like.

He was too busy looking at the girl in the morgue.

"She...." Mikhail struggled with the words. "She was coming back to us."

"Yes."

She'd called them the night before, her voice sounding slurry and high, with the shrill pitch of desperation in it. She'd seen the fliers, she said. They were everywhere. Were they true? Could she come home?

"God, yes, sweetheart. We'll come get you—just tell us where you are."

"Downtown. By the shelter. But I'll come to you. I don't wanna be here no more, Shane. Just wanna come home."

The thought of her out there in the rain had spurred Shane and Mikhail out. They went to Loaves and Fishes first, and asked, and were told a girl matching the picture—only much thinner, much more strung out, much less healthy—had been hanging around for the past month or two. She'd been selling herself and using, and they'd been worried for her.

Mikhail literally grabbed Shane's hand and dragged him from the place, back into the car, to wander the streets until they saw her.

They saw the flashing lights of the ambulance pulling away first.

Shane had been told the victim of the hit-and-run would be taken to the morgue at Mercy San Juan—but to give them a few minutes to clean her up first. It wasn't pretty.

And here they were. And here she was.

Her face was thinner. Her teeth were yellow. Her lips were cracked. She had sores on her cheeks, and her fingers were blistered from whatever she'd used to inhale.

But all of that, and Shane thought Mickey might have reclaimed her, made her whole, from force of will alone, just like his mother had done for him.

The shyness, the sweet hope that had looked out from her dark eyes was hidden. Forever.

"She was coming back to us?" Mikhail said again, his voice a child's voice, a pleading voice. One Shane had never heard before. This girl had reduced him to the child he'd sworn he'd left behind, the lost one, the angry one, and Shane could only hope he'd be enough to reclaim Mickey from the storm detritus when the wave of grief had passed.

When they'd asked to see the body, the doctor asked them who they were to the victim. When Shane told him, the doctor bent his head and then left and came back.

He had one of the fliers with him. Mikhail had taken the picture—she'd been brushing one of the horses at The Pulpit, and when he'd called her name, her thin, dark face had relaxed into a rare, whole smile. Her eyes had held hope that day. They'd held animation, and humor, and all of the things Shane and Mikhail had loved.

The flier was crumpled, and the stains around the edges were still bright red but turning brown from the air.

"She had this in her hand when the car hit," the doctor told him. The doctor, a middle-aged man with eyes sunk into a nicotine addict's wrinkles, didn't show any animation, but then, he didn't have to. The fact he'd brought the flier said more than it needed to about compassion in silence.

Shane nodded now and brought Mikhail's hand up to his mouth and kissed it.

"Yeah," he said softly. "She was coming home."

Mikhail swallowed audibly.

Gulp it down all you want, Mickey. It's going to come up and eat you whole if you don't let it out.

"Then we shall have to bring her home," Mikhail said, and the look he turned to Shane was absolutely naked with implicit faith. "Can you do that? Can you make it so she comes home?"

Shane nodded. It was four in the morning, and his eyes burned with tired and his heart burned with grief, but he knew who to turn to. "I'll call Deacon," he said softly. "I think we can bury her ashes at Promise Rock."

"Not...." Mikhail swallowed again, because his voice was breaking. "Not the place where the weddings are," he said, his breathing ragged. "The outside of the rock, where it's all fields, wherever you look."

"Yeah," Shane said. "We'll take her home and set her free."

Mikhail made a sound like a hurt kitten, and Shane decided that dignity could fuck itself. "C'mere," he demanded. "I need you."

Mostly Shane needed him to break so Shane could pick up his pieces, because that's all Shane could do right now, pick up the pieces, be there for him. Otherwise, Shane was fucking useless, fucking useless and impotent, and if he couldn't comfort Mikhail, then he had nothing to shore him up, nothing at all—

Mickey threw himself into Shane's arms and Shane crushed him, and they broke together and mourned. Their sobs echoed in the cold room with the still and silent girl and the smell and metal tang of death.

IT TOOK a couple of hours for Shane to get the information and make the arrangements for cremation and a marker. At seven in the morning, he called Deacon and asked him the favor.

Deacon said yes, yes of course, and shouldered his part of the funeral arrangements like a student shoulders a backpack.

There was nothing to do after that but go back to Promise House and tell the children.

Halfway home, Mikhail spoke up, surprising him badly.

"I would like to tell Missy," he said quietly, and for a moment, Shane's mind reeled with all of the very bad things that could happen. "You may be there," Mikhail told him, interrupting all sorts of worst-case scenarios. "But do not worry." In the stillness of the car, Shane could hear him breathe through his nose. "I think I will make you proud of me."

They were on the freeway, so Shane could grab his hand. "Every day," he said hoarsely. "Every moment. Everything you do. I'm proud of you."

Mickey squeezed back. "You are very foolish," he said simply. "But I think I shall not tell you that very often. My soul could not bear it if you didn't believe the things you say."

Shane had to blink very fast to keep from crying again, and they were calm and collected when they made their way into Promise House fifteen minutes later.

"PATIENCE, children," Mikhail said as they walked in. All twelve of the kids, the other three counselors, Kimmy, and Lucas—*everybody* was gathered in the living room when they came in. All those expectant faces looked up, and Shane could see Mikhail's performance cloak bearing him up with presence and acceptance as he spoke. "We will give you all the details eventually, and Shane and I must speak to Melissa alone. Before we do that...." His composure slipped. "Shane?"

Shane stepped up and put his hand on Mickey's shoulder.

"I'm sorry," he said simply. "Sweetie—LeLauna—was killed in a car accident last night. We...." The flier, covered in blood and crumpled, still rested in the pocket of his big black waterproof jacket. "We have reason to believe that she was coming home to us. When she called last night, she wanted to come home."

He looked out at the people in his house, the eight boys and four girls in his charge, and watched as various stages of grief and disbelief spread through them all. He was responsible for this, he thought wretchedly. He had to help them through this. How as he supposed to do that? What was he to them?

His sister caught his eye before he could spiral into that sort of self-doubt, and he remembered himself.

"Mr. Winters at The Pulpit says we can bury her ashes at Promise Rock. We're putting together a date and a time for that. Everybody is required to go, people. There's no dodging out on this one. All those things your counselors tell you about dealing with the pain—this is what it's all about." He realized that might sound a bit harsh, so he dropped the power speech and went for the real. "It's going to hurt," he told them honestly. "It's going to hurt for a while, in unexpected ways. This isn't a big high school where we know someone by name and nothing else. Sweetie was a friend here, she was a sister. She wasn't outgoing—I know that. But everyone in here, at some moment, said something to her, looked kindly at her, *was* something to her that was important. She was coming home, people. This place was her home."

That was all he had. He was done. He looked out and saw kids holding kids and rocking, counselors with hands on shoulders and on defiantly turned heads. They would be grief-stricken and mourning for a long, painful time, and he allowed himself one bitter thought: would Sweetie have done this to them if she'd known the wreckage she'd leave behind?

Then he saw Missy whirl on her heel and Mikhail go stalking after her, and he strapped on his mental greaves and his titanium loincloth for whatever was coming next.

Missy didn't even bother to slam the door shut, and Mikhail made no pretense of not following her into her room. The place was a dump. Missy had been looking more and more despondent in the past month, and the room was filled with dirty clothes and dusty bottles of beauty products she had ceased to use. He didn't have time to dwell on those things (or on the smell of mustiness that meant they really *had* to help the girl clean up her act), because Mikhail dove right into action here, and he was not taking a breath before a furious deep-end swim.

"Where are you going?" Mikhail demanded. Missy had one of the reusable shopping bags and was shoving dirty clothes into it, as well as some personal trinkets of her own.

"Where do you think?" she asked bitterly, turning a pinched, angry red face to him. She hadn't worn makeup in months, and her complexion was spotty, and right now her nose was swollen and her eyes were puffy. She looked nothing like the self-assured little vamp who had stomped past three runners on a miserable August morning. "It's not like anyone here liked me anyway, but look! Look what I did! I killed her! The girl's name was *Sweetie*, for sweet fuck's sake, and I'm the bitch that killed her. My life is fucking over. No one can love me after this. *No one!*"

"You'd like that to be true, wouldn't you?" Mikhail snapped. "That would be wonderful. You have blown it, you are sixteen, your life is over, and you don't need to try anymore. Mission accomplished, life over, you can go and waste it now, and nobody will expect anything different, isn't that right?"

"That's right—look at me now! I'm a fuckup! I'm a bitch and a whore and now the world can just get off my back and—"

"And what? And watch you walk into the sunset and sell yourself for filth? You think that's what we will do? You think it will be heroic?"

Mikhail's voice cracked. "Because I tell you this—I tried it. Yes, you think you are the inventor of self-hatred, but I *tried* this plan! I got high, and I got fucked in alleyways, and you know what? You will love this. This will make everything right in your small world. Yes, I *too* was responsible for someone's death. How does that make you feel? Do you want to go out and kill yourself now? Because I did!"

"Yeah, what stopped you?" Her lips pulled back from her teeth in a snarl, and Mikhail stood right there in her face, on his tiptoes, because she was taller than he was, chest to chest.

"My mother tied me to a bed while I detoxed, and then, when we found my friend dead with a needle in his fucking arm because he got selfish and shot everything we had, she held me while I cried. And I had to *live* with that. I had to *live* with what I did. And what was I to do? I could not get high. I could not hit my mother—*again*. What was I to do?"

"I don't know, Mikhail!" she shouted. "What am I supposed to do? You won't look at me anymore. *Nobody* will look at me anymore! I fucked up! I was a fucking cunt and I fucked up! But I didn't want her to die! I didn't want her to run away! I just wanted everyone to stop looking at her and see *me*!" Her voice broke then, shattered messily into a thousand blood-spattered pieces, and Shane found he was rocking back on his heels, in awe at what Mickey had just accomplished.

"Well, I am looking at you," Mikhail shouted back. "*I* am looking at you! And I see a young woman who fucked up. But *I* fucked up. *I* hurt someone I didn't mean to. And you know what I did?"

"No," Missy said on a sob. "No. I have no idea. I'm stupid. I've always been stupid and ugly—how am I supposed to know how you fix something like this?" Her shoulders shook, and her head was drooped, and for the first time in sixth months, Shane saw, really saw, the hurt child in the body of the bitter, angry woman.

Mickey saw it too. Maybe Mickey had always seen it, but he wasn't going to let that child hide one more time.

"You cannot fix it," he said softly, and to Shane's surprise, Mikhail moved his hands up to the girl's arms and stroked in comfort. "You cannot fix this, Melissa. But you can live with it. You can look yourself in the face and say, 'I have done this. But it is not all I will do.' Can you do that? Do you have the strength to do that?"

"Noooooooo…," she wailed. But she collapsed into Mikhail's arms as she said it, and he held her, rocking her like the child she'd never been allowed to be.

A FEW days later, Martin drove through the rain to Promise House, specifically to talk to Shane. Shane was expecting him—Jeff and Collin had bought the boy a plane ticket and flown him to California expressly for the funeral service. Shane didn't even want to think about the strings they had to pull or the people they had to beg to get that done, but here the boy was, looking nothing like the defiant, pissed-off asshole who had spent less than a month here three and a half years ago.

In fact, he looked very, very much like a young man.

Shane had an office of sorts—it was also the library, lined with eight of those cheap plywood shelves that were stuffed full of paperbacks (many of them with questionable sexual content, but Shane wasn't picky)—and it held file cabinets full of the independent study packets the kids used to make up units at the continuation school. It also held a desk, and office supplies, and a computer, and a little schoolwork table, as well as big comfy chairs, because sometimes the kids wandered in and pulled a book off the shelf and just settled in to read in the quiet while he was working.

Martin knocked once and then came in, probably because he remembered his own days there, and there wasn't anything going on in the office that couldn't be interrupted for a kid in need.

Shane stood up to offer the boy a hand and found himself pulled into a solid hug instead. He gave some back and squeezed Martin's ribs until they cracked, and then released him, laughing a little from the enthusiasm.

"Wasn't my fault," Shane said mildly. "You started it."

Martin smiled, and Shane hadn't forgotten how that big white smile on his square black face could literally light up a room. "No, Shane. You started it. You think I don't remember, but I do. I was a stupid kid and I did a stupid thing, and you and Mikhail made it better when I could have made it so much worse."

Shane swallowed past a sudden lump in his throat. "It was our pleasure," he said honestly, and Martin's smile faded.

"She was coming home," he said softly, and Shane closed his eyes and saw her, still, shrunken, wasted, the damage to her body so extensive that the plastic sheet that covered her sat unevenly.

"What?" he said, and his voice sounded tinny in his own ears, like it was coming from that cold room.

"I said she was coming home. Jeff told me that." His voice wobbled, broke a little, and Shane wondered how much time Jeff and Collin had spent consoling him so he could come back here and be a grown-up about his broken heart.

Shane nodded and tried to pull out of it. He was the grown-up. This kid needed him. "Yeah. Actually, that reminds me." He went to his desk and opened the bottom drawer. There was a small box of personal possessions—at least the ones worth keeping. Her drug paraphernalia he'd thrown away, of course, and most of the clothes she'd carried in the same reusable shopping bag had been worn to tatters, even the new brown coat Mikhail had bought her, that she'd been so proud of.

But still, tucked in the pocket of her jeans and in the larger pocket of her coat there had been two treasures, both of them wrapped tight in plastic bags, pristine and perfect, and Shane pulled them both out now.

Martin's face softened in recognition of the small gold heart-shaped locket Shane pulled out, and he held out his hand. Shane dropped it into his palm carefully, making sure the chain fell in like liquid.

"I thought you might have given these to her," Shane said, and Martin looked at him, perplexed.

"Well, the necklace, yes." His full lower lip quivered, but he pulled it together. "We weren't... going steady or anything, you know? But I sent her a real letter over Thanksgiving, and... you know, I kept sending her stupid YouTube videos."

"What'd you send her?"

Martin shrugged, breathing through his nose. "The Temptations. Marvin Gaye. Jackson Five."

"Motown," Shane said simply, and Martin nodded. "So not official, but...."

"Yeah." Martin took a deep breath and his hand clenched on the sparkly gold. "The necklace was mine. Pretty thing for a pretty girl, right?"

They both grimaced, and the silence was laden like a storm cloud. Martin shook himself then, and Shane bet he was probably as wrung dry as Shane felt.

"The little stuffed animal," Martin said, his voice stoic. "That one wasn't."

Shane frowned. "I wonder where she got—"

"Mikhail gave it to her—I thought you'd know that. She...." Martin smiled in memory. "She said he just came back from shopping one day and threw it at her. When she asked him about it, he said, 'I know very little about girls, but they seem to like these things. You should have one.'" Martin did a passable version of Mikhail, even secondhand, and Shane was torn between laughter and tears. He tucked the cat in the pocket of his hooded sweatshirt and nodded.

"I'll make sure he gets it," he said quietly. "I wanted to talk to you about one more thing. It's about her service."

Martin nodded, and Shane made his request. By the time he was done, the boy's eyes were red, but oddly enough, he looked happier, and—as he should, at eighteen—young.

THEY held the funeral three days after the rains stopped, so that the mud wasn't too bad, and the sky was scrubbed clean and bright. There was a granite grave marker set against the sun side of the swimming-hole boulder. It was the side that got too hot in the summer, the side where Shane and Mickey had stood, dancing, the day of Deacon and Crick's wedding, and Mikhail Vasilyovich Bayul had told Shane Perkins that he was *never* giving him back.

Shane looked out at the group of people and wondered if Sweetie knew how many people would miss her now that she was gone.

The kids from Promise House were there, dressed in their very best and covered in their coats, because a bitter wind blew from the river across the fields. Missy stood a little apart from the other residents. She'd washed and french braided her reddish hair—Shane recognized Kimmy's work—and had even put on a new dress. Kimmy hadn't let her get black, and it was a rich spring brown. She'd put on makeup, but not with a trowel—and Shane actually thought she looked a little like Crick. Kimmy and Lucas stood closer to her than to the other kids. Kimmy tucked herself against Lucas's chest: Shane's "little" sister was crying.

All of Shane's friends stood in the cold sun—Deacon and Crick, Drew, Benny and Parry, and Jeff and Collin and Martin, of course. Jon and Amy hadn't been able to make it out, but Amy had sent a *glorious* flower arrangement, yellow- and peach-colored roses, an entire spill of them, that Shane had set over the headstone. They looked exotic, rich and out of place in the field of mustard flowers and foxglove and poppies, but Shane liked them. Sweetie deserved roses.

Mikhail stood next to him, both of them wearing dark suits and their shiniest shoes. "I hope you are happy. I did not even buy a suit for my mother's funeral."

"I would have let you dance for this one too," Shane told him, thinking he looked very handsome, and very… upright and Russian. Shane had given him the stuffed kitten, and Mikhail had taken it. His jaw had been tight, and his eyes pinched, but he hadn't said anything at the time. The beanbag was drooping from the pocket of his suit right now, shiny brown eyes taking in a mournful view of a funeral in the spring.

"She did not care about my dancing," Mikhail said, a study of indifference. "I was a parent, nothing more."

Shane reached down and squeezed his hand. "Haven't you learned yet? That's everything."

"Perhaps," Mikhail grudged. "It certainly hurts that way."

Shane pulled in his breath and realized that if he didn't start now, he'd sit here forever, under the blue sky, pretending he was out for no other reason than the sun on his face.

He took a few steps to the small two-by-two hole in front of the headstone and surveyed the crowd with a gentle smile.

"It's a pretty day," he said randomly, and everyone he loved nodded, like that was the most natural thing in the world to say. "I have no idea if LeLauna Saunders liked spring or not. I think she might have—she said continuously that the sun in August was trying to kill us dead, so I think a pretty day without that might have tickled her."

He smiled faintly and looked inside the grave. The small box he had hand sanded, hand beveled, hinged, and latched was sitting quietly, seemingly so far removed from what he had to say here that it might as well have been a cloud, or a kitten, or a star. If it did not remind him so very much of Mikhail's box of treasures, he might have been able to pretend it *was* one of those things, but he wasn't great at lying to himself. Never had been. Or to other people either.

"The fact is, there are volumes of things I didn't know about LeLauna. There was not enough time, and LeLauna was not... forthcoming. But the few things I know—that any of us know—make me wish with all of my heart that she had given us more time.

"I know that LeLauna liked horses and cats and pretty much any animal that came her way. She felt safe with them, and she didn't mind if they made extra work, they were her friends. I know that anything we asked of her, she did. She didn't always do it cheerfully—doing dishes, for example, she wasn't a fan—but she always did it competently and with quiet grace. I know that she liked to read love stories but that she didn't like anyone else in the house to see. I know that she treasured any gifts that came her way, and she was proud of the things she did here in Promise House, proud of the fact that she was trusted. I know that her grandmother taught her how to make shrimp and grits and yarn dolls. The shrimp and grits, I'm afraid, she didn't give to the rest of us, but the yarn dolls she passed on to another little girl, and that knowledge will not go away. I know that in spite of what she said before she left, she absolutely loved that we called her Sweetie. She told me so herself. She said that was special—no one had ever given her a nickname before."

He saw Mikhail's gaze, wide and stricken, searching his face as he said this. It was something he hadn't remembered until Martin had come to see him in his office, and something Shane hoped would be a comfort.

"So, see, there's a lot I didn't know about her—but the things I do know hurt. There was so much potential for there to be more. That's the kind of world we live in. Everyone here has cause to know that the universe doesn't always forgive our mistakes. For every person here who has made a mistake and recovered, there is someone who wasn't so lucky." He breathed hard through his nose, swallowed down his grief, and finished.

"Sweetie, we wish you were one of the lucky ones. But we can't hate you for failing. Everyone fails. We still love you. Wherever you are, whoever caught you when you fell, we just want you to know that."

He was done.

He looked up and caught Martin's eye, and Martin nodded, stepping forward to stand next to Shane.

Shane knew, because Martin told him three years ago, that Martin sang in church. Well, Martin was fully aware that Promise Rock was church to Shane's people, and Shane expected nothing less than reverence.

Martin caught his eye and smiled bravely, then closed his eyes, centered himself, and began to sing.

"I got sunshine, on a cloudy day…."

The entire crowd brightened for a moment, and when Martin sang next, more than one voice chimed in.

"When it's cold outside, I've got the month of May…."

Martin kept a steady snapping, and Shane felt the entire collective take a breath and join in for the chorus. As the song died out, Shane knew that mistakes or no, he and the people he loved the most had taken a frightened, guarded runaway and made her their girl.

Chapter 24

Benny and Deacon: Convergence

BENNY'S stomach stuck out of her coat on the day of the funeral. She was wearing a dark-lavender dress, because she refused to wear black for the sweet kid she remembered making yarn dolls on the porch, and she had to resist the temptation to keep trying to pull the flaps of her leaf-green coat over the seven-month baby bump. She'd finally forgotten about it as Shane started to speak, but Missy's first words to her, after the song had faded and people started moving across the creek bridge and the cattle guard to their cars, were, "Jesus, you're really doing this shit again?"

Benny was going to snap something irritated and mean, but then it occurred to her: those were the first words she'd heard from her little sister in five years.

"Yup. The first one turned out okay. I figured I'd work on a second one and give it away."

Missy let out a breath of something that might have been a laugh. "Well, congratulations. You're a better fucking person than I am."

Benny shrugged and decided to make light of it. "Why yes, yes I am."

And again, Missy laughed. "Seriously," she said, and her voice was whiskey rough, deeper than you'd expect from a girl with such a pretty face. "I'm... I'm glad you and Crick seem to be okay. I'm...." And this next word *really* seemed to hurt. "I'm *sorry* that I haven't wanted to see you."

Benny pulled in a breath and tried to find Crick in the crowd. He was looking with concern at Deacon, who had spent a lot of time out with the horses since Sweetie's death and who had his "stoic" face on now. It was the expression he wore when he was the most devastated, and Benny wondered if he was thinking of all the ways Crick and Benny could have ended up dead from all of the stupid decisions *they'd* made. It had certainly been on *her* mind a lot, so she couldn't blame him. Beyond Crick and Deacon, Martin was hugging Jeff like a drowning man, his shoulders shaking with sobs. Collin was steering them to the shady side of the rock, but looking at them hurt like a shock of cold to an open wound. Looking at Mikhail and Shane keeping their game faces on hurt too. Okay, well, the men were occupied, for better or worse. It was her turn.

"Mommy, who's that?"

Oh thank God. Saved by Parry Angel.

"Hey," Benny said brightly. "You two have never met! Missy, this is Parry Angel, my daughter, and Parry, this is Missy, your aunt."

Parry smiled at her brightly. "Are you like Auntie Kimmy or Auntie Amy? Are you going to sneak me cookies and take me shopping?"

Benny's face heated. "How often has Kimmy taken you shopping?" she asked, totally surprised.

"She and Crick and Mickey took me last week. I got lots of clothes for Easter, but you aren't supposed to know that." Benny's daughter said this with a knowing smirk, the kind that showed off her dimples on her chubby little cheeks, and Benny flailed for an answer. Next to her, Missy made a choke-snort sort of sound, and Benny shot her a glare.

"Little shit is just like me," Missy said only a little apologetically, and Benny blinked.

"Yeah, I wondered where she got that," she said. Somehow it was less irritating in her kid than it had been in her know-it-all kid sister. She sighed, and some of her attitude leached out. "Parry, honey," she said, bending down enough to kiss her daughter on the top of her fuzzy little head, "do you want to go help Drew cover the casket?"

"What's a casket?"

"It's that wooden box that has Sweetie's ashes in it." Oh hells. *This* was the worst part of parenting. Benny would rather change a thousand diapers than have one conversation about death.

"'Cause Sweetie isn't here anymore," Parry said soberly, and they'd talked about this.

"No, honey, she's not. If we bury her ashes here, we can hope that the part of her that lives forever will be free and happy here."

"'Cause we love this place, and she was nice," Parry filled in. She was good at lessons, and Benny hoped wretchedly that she and Drew and Deacon and Crick had taught this one right.

"Exactly."

"Do you think there will be worms?" Parry asked hopefully. "Because that would be *gross*! Maybe I could touch one!"

"Yeah, sure, kid. Go find worms!"

Parry loped off across the green grass and mustard flowers, shouting, "Drew! Mama says I can touch worms!" and Benny clapped her hand across her mouth to mask the laughter. She looked up and met Missy's eyes and caught that little closed-mouth smirk, complete with dimples, and she felt an entirely new ache in a morning that already ached enough.

"I was hurt," she said quietly. "Crick and I busted our asses trying to see you and Crystal, and you didn't want to see us. I mean, I get it—Step-Bob and Melanie would put anyone off of parents, but—"

"You called him Step-Bob?"

"Well… *yeah*. Did *you* want to be related to him?"

Missy's face went through an odd series of contortions—expressions as wide and as varied as laughter to despair. Finally she just clapped a hand over her mouth and said, *"No!* Oh my *God*, no! Who *would* want to be related to him! *Or* Melanie? Are you shitting me?"

Benny laughed and watched her daughter help Drew with the big pile of dirt. "Nope," she said seriously. "See? So, you know. Step-Bob. And I just pretend you *can* pick your family."

Missy looked at them too. "So, uhm…."

Benny felt her heart melt. She knew where this question was going. "Do you want me to pick you?"

"We… we don't know each other that well. Maybe… you know."

Benny tucked her hand under Missy's arm and started walking toward the shade of the oak trees. "Here, walk me to my car while we talk, 'kay? My back is *killing* me."

"Okay. Yeah. Okay. So, why are you pregnant again?"

"So Crick could say his sister's having his husband's baby," Benny replied with a straight face. If this didn't make her little sister break up, they'd have nothing to base a relationship on.

Missy did a spit-take and started to laugh. Not a giggle but a chortle, down from the depths of her slender body. "That *asshole*—does he really?"

"Wouldn't you?" Because, seriously—who *wouldn't* want to tell people that?

Missy laughed some more, and Benny had the feeling that maybe Missy would want to visit the next time Crick tried.

SHOOTING STAR was going to end up as glue. Not only had the fucker practically maimed him while Deacon was feeding her carrots, but the goddamned horse kept nipping at Even Star's flanks when they were out in the field. His best stallion *ever*, and the horse was starting to look like hamburger. The stables were full, the fields were full, and Shooting Star was angling for her own goddamned pen and her own goddamned stall. Deacon had about *had it* with a horse that tried to throw him, crush him, or kill him dead with every breath that fucker took.

About the only human being on earth that horse had liked had been Sweetie.

Deacon and Sweetie had rarely spoken to each other, but then, they hadn't needed to. Brushing, feeding, picking feet—it was all quiet, instinctive, most of the work talking to the horses. Drew liked to keep a running monologue to Deacon, and Deacon didn't mind—he sometimes chatted back.

Sweetie just wanted to be with the horses, and her presence in the barn had been… quiet. Compassionate—for the horses, at least. Powerful.

He'd missed her when she'd run away. Her death almost undid him.

And the fucking horse was never going to be the same.

Deacon pulled on the halter to try to get the horse to the field next door. It would mean tripling up with three of the yearling mares, but they were all sweethearts—Even's foals usually were—so he thought they might manage better together than Even would spending one more day with Shooting Star.

Shooter yanked back against the halter *hard*, and Deacon had about enough.

"You wanna get *shot*, ya fucker?" Deacon shouted, thumping the horse on the side of the neck. "I'm the only asshole on the planet who wants you alive *maybe*, and you're gonna go and pull that shit with me?"

He gave the halter an unfriendly yank, and the horse snorted but *did* haul her slow fat ass in through the gate. Deacon closed it behind him and tried to release the halter so Shooter could run to her heart's content and not be accountable to another soul for a couple of days. The horse tried to kick him—twice—and one of those times she succeeded in grazing Deacon's bandage, and Deacon swore again, seeing stars. Fuck it. Horse was keeping the halter on for a day. Deacon would spend tomorrow working the damned thing out until she whinnied for mercy, and maybe after that, she'd show the guy who gave her carrots some fucking respect.

He turned around to the gate and was surprised to see a tall girl with messy red hair bundled up on her head leaning against the gate to the pasture.

She wore worn jeans with flared legs and a T-shirt—tight around the boobs but not overly so—in a bright, neon green, and a surprisingly patient expression.

It took him a minute to remember that the girl was Crick and Benny's sister. "Missy?"

"Hi," she said quietly, and she smiled against the sun and wrinkled her nose. "That horse is a real motherfucker, ain't he?"

Deacon nodded, feeling the ache in his shin all the way to the pit of his groin. "It's a she, but yeah. Motherfucker is right. You have no idea. Here, let me through. I don't put it past her not to charge the gate."

"Why do you put up with her?" she asked earnestly.

He looked at her, remembering how Benny said they'd talked at the funeral, and she'd been tolerable. The softness in Benny's eyes, though, said a little more about hope.

"Because sometimes she's not such a vicious bitch, and she's worth saving."

Missy colored and looked down. "I'm cleaning houses now. They don't hate me."

Deacon nodded. "That's good to hear."

"I, uhm. I mean, I don't age out of Promise House for a couple of years, but, well. You know. If I have family, they think it's better if I can stay there." She looked up at him, the hope naked on her face. "I really loved this place when I was a kid," she confessed.

"We loved having you," he told her soberly. It was true. He, Parrish, Crick—they'd all gone out of their way to make sure Crick's little sisters were safe, were fed, had fun. Seeing Missy so hostile—that had hurt.

"Well, Shane says you have a tack room—you used to let kids stay there when they needed to."

Deacon nodded. "If they did their share," he said carefully. "Usually, they had to prove themselves first."

Missy smiled hopefully. "I don't run... well, not as fast, anyway... I try not to dodge out on hard work. I'd...." She let out a breath, like she was trying to remember how to do this without being needy. "I know you've got kids working here from Promise House already. I'd like a chance to join them and prove myself."

Deacon nodded, thinking Crick hadn't gotten around to painting the guest bedroom yet. He wouldn't scare her with that, he thought painfully. Too much hope was a scary thing.

"I think we can do that," he said. The sun was neatly dissected by the horizon, and even this close to April, that meant it got a little chilly. A breeze picked up across the fields, still smelling like wildflowers and a little like water at twilight. "You want to come in for dinner and discuss it? What time is Shane coming to pick you up?"

Missy's cheeks colored. "It's sort of my day off. I told Kimmy I was coming and I walked here."

Deacon nodded. "Fair enough. Well, come in for dinner and we'll take you back when it's time. Crick would love to have you."

She smiled, looking embarrassed, and said, "Thank you. Thank you a lot. That's... I... I'm not that nice a person, and—"

"Melissa?"

"Yeah?"

"Second chances, sweetheart. We all believe in second chances."

She nodded, and her brows drew together, and her lower lip quivered. "I really did love this place when I was a kid. I don't know how I could have forgotten...."

She was going to cry, and he wasn't up to that, not now, not so soon after the funeral.

"Really? What part did you like best?" he asked, starting a stride back to the house.

"You used to let us ride the gentle ones," she said. "Remember? And you or Crick or Parrish would be behind us, but you'd let us pretend we got to steer—I loved that. I haven't ridden a horse since, but it was am*a*zing!"

Deacon looked at her, horrified. "Haven't ridden since? That's criminal," he said, and he meant it.

She laughed, and yeah. She had the shape of Crick and Benny's eyes, and Crick's narrow face, and Benny's pointed chin.

"Can I ask you a question?" he asked after watching her do that.

"Yeah, sure."

"What's your favorite color?"

"Oh, Jesus—green, brown, anything but pink!"

Awesome. Whether they were having a girl or a boy, they could *finally* paint over the flower barf in Benny's old room.

KIMMY was a wise woman. She used the shower as a shameless excuse to engage Missy in almost everything: from the decorations (daisies everywhere) to the games (the one with the diapers full of chocolate bars was really gross) to keeping track of who gave what in a little notebook while the guys (looking embarrassed and uncomfortable) opened the gifts—Missy had a hand in it.

It was even better when Kimmy came by and confided to Crick and Benny that she hadn't been bitchy once about the family at The Pulpit since the funeral. She walked away looking pleased with herself, and Crick looked at Benny, both of them thinking the same thing.

"Did Kimmy shake the gifts for snakes or spiders?" Crick asked, only half kidding.

Benny shrugged. "You know, maybe she's just growing up, you ever think of that?"

Crick's smirk (and Benny was only just now noticing that it was a family trait) started to fade. "Well, it happens to the best of us," he said softly.

Benny watched Parry make one more trip around the room, offering tiny ham sandwiches on a plate.

"And it happens *really* fast," she said wistfully. The baby moved, and she put her hand over the squirming thing in her stomach. She wanted another one, wanted another one for *herself*, but she wasn't out of school yet, and even if she was, she and Drew might want to spend a couple of years without one, just for kicks.

Crick ruffled her hair—in spite of the goop she'd put in it to make it look like that flyaway thing was on purpose. "Jesus, Benny, what are you? Twenty-two? You know, you could wait five years and *still* have time to pop out six of the little goobers. I mean... *look* at everything you've done with your life so far!"

Benny did the math in her head and then grinned at her brother. "Six? Hell. I'm going for ten! But I'll tell you this." She rubbed her tummy then, thought of the eight and a half months she'd spent with this little person inside. She knew its moods, she knew that it got extra spazzy at the sound of Crick's voice, and she knew that it calmed down and rocked softly at the sound of Deacon's. "*This*," she said passionately, trying hard not to think of saying good-bye, "is the *last* time I'll share."

Deacon came up behind her then and put his hands on her shoulders. "No one expects you to, Shorty. I'm pretty sure you've done your duty, times about a thousand."

Oh, he smelled so good, like oak and long grass and horses and even a little bit of aftershave. And he'd worn new jeans and sneakers and a new green henley shirt, and he'd water-combed his freshly cut hair. He still made her heart beat a little faster, and his voice was still the gentlest she'd ever heard.

But....

But his touch on her shoulders was like Crick's, or Shane's or Jeff's or Mikhail's—it was neutral, and warm and male, and it wasn't for her.

Deacon moved the hand on her shoulder and put it on Crick's, squeezing very differently, she'd wager. He bent then and kissed Crick's cheek, and Crick looked up at him shyly.

"Did you have fun opening all those presents, Carrick James?"

Crick's smile was almost girlish in complete glee. "Oh *hell* yes! Like the best birthday ever!"

"Good. I'll flip you for jobs—which one of us gets thank-you cards, which one of us gets cleanup?"

Crick looked at him in horror. "Oh hell. Cleanup, no question!"

"Too bad. While you've been eating cake with the lady of honor, Mikhail and I already cleaned up."

Benny looked up and realized that most of the trappings—the diapers loaded with chocolate bars, the wrapping paper and the ribbon, the empty plates with daisies on them and the empty drink cups—had all been thrown away. She was sitting in the recliner, and after shifting her weight against the pillow at her back and checking her fluid levels (she predicted a preemptive pee would be needed in twenty minutes), she thought she might take the pregnant woman's prerogative and catch a fifteen-minute sleep. (She'd need five minutes to maneuver her amazingly swollen waddly body off the damned recliner when she *did* have to pee.)

Crick was giving Deacon shit about the thank-you notes, which was funny, because everyone knew that while Deacon's notes would be warm and gracious, Crick's would be frickin' hilarious. While warm and gracious were *great* qualities in a hug, a thank-you note that read "Thanks for the plastic things that makes diapers into little white bag-covered turds. Best goddamned toy *ever!*" was something the people in *this* house would treasure for *always*.

The boys were fine, Benny thought, contentment filling her chest. The boys were fine, Drew had promised her a foot rub tonight, and Parry Angel was currently impressing everybody by making a little bonnet out of package bows.

Benny put her hands on her stomach and cocooned herself with the little person inside her. *Don't worry, little fish. I'll have to leave you when you come out, but I think you're in good hands.*

ALL of the people were gone, all of the trash thrown in the recycler, and Crick managed to finish the thank-you notes while they were nibbling on the last of the lunch spread for dinner. Deacon was impressed.

Drew had taken Benny home, which was probably a relief to *her*. Crick, much to Deacon's disgust, had wanted her to stay. In the middle of the shower, she'd dozed off and started snoring. Crick had taken footage on his camera, and Deacon had been in the middle of telling him to knock that shit off when she'd farted, choked on a snore, and rolled out of the recliner and onto all fours, screaming, "I'm *up*, Parry, I'm on my way!"

Deacon had been the first one to her side to make sure she was okay, and she was, but Crick had to be beaten over the head with a pillow before he'd get off the floor and stop laughing. Collin had done the beating. After Benny got up and Drew helped her to the bathroom, choking on his own snickers, Deacon snatched the pillow from Collin's hands and said, "Collin—*wiener!*" just to watch him fall apart. By the time Benny got back from the bathroom, everybody could pretend they hadn't seen *her* little gaffe, because Collin was in a fetal ball of his own.

So there had been a lot of laughter, and some awkwardness (Deacon's least-favorite moment had been smelling the candy bars in the diapers. Benny too. Both of them had looked at each other and wrinkled their noses. They remembered the real thing—hadn't been that funny then, wasn't that funny now). There had been small moments of grace—watching Missy help Parry put on her ribbon bonnet had been one of those. Watching Jeff and Collin take turns cuddling the baby doll in the crook of their arms and talk about how best to pick up the real thing had been another.

All things considered, it was nice to have the house back to their own, with the exhausted donkey/dog crashed out in the front room and the frightening pile of presents resting in the newly painted mint-green and earth-brown guest room.

"We didn't get any clothes," Crick said thoughtfully. He was exaggerating—they got a packet of unisex T-shirts and a packet of unisex onesies, but in general, no. Most babies were up to Mama's eyeballs in outfits by now. Parry had been, and Deacon and Benny had put the little tiny pink things away in the drawers with awe and a terrible fear there wasn't enough, there could never be enough, and that the baby would spend her first six months wearing a diaper and nothing else.

"We will," Deacon said, taking a bite of the chocolate pudding cake while Crick wasn't looking. His health was great—the pacemaker and the laser surgery seemed to have cleaned him right up, and he was careful, most times, without Crick's nagging. But everyone had their secret vices, and cake was cake. And those little shortbread cookies with the fudge in the middle were all gone, so Deacon was eating cake, with little daisy frosting things on top, and not regretting it in the least.

Crick looked up and scowled, and Deacon grinned through a mouthful of chocolate and frosting. He swallowed and washed it down with the milk at his elbow and said, "It's Benny's secret plot. Everyone *knows* what sex the baby is, and when she has the baby, they'll all bring clothes."

Crick put down his pen, stole Deacon's fork, and scooped himself a bite of chocolate cake. He didn't wait to swallow after he put it in his mouth. "How in d'hell d'you know dith?"

"Gimme that!" Deacon swiped the fork and got another bite—there was really only a largish piece left. They should clean that up, right?

Crick swallowed. "Answer my question!" He was so damned cute! Lean little mouth pushed out in a pout, big limpid eyes narrowed with playfulness. They were sitting kitty-corner, and Deacon reached over and scooped a last blob of green icing off Crick's cheek with his thumb. He popped his thumb into his mouth and sucked off the frosting, regarding the love of his life with dancing eyes.

Crick's mouth worked as he struggled to keep his pout, but the smile won out in the end. "Yeah, you're sexy as hell. Now tell me how you knew that!"

Deacon's laugh snuck past his thumb, and he pulled it out and shoved in the next bite of cake, just to make Crick wait until he was done.

"You think you're clever, don't you?" Crick asked, his eyes narrowed.

Deacon nodded, his mouth sealed shut as he savored the chocolate cake.

"You think I can't *make* you tell me?"

Ooh... there was a wicked arch to his eyebrows, and Deacon smirked, then swallowed half the bite in a definite challenge.

"I can make you tell me!" Crick growled. He stood up carefully and grabbed the cushion he'd been sitting on—it was one of Benny's hemorrhoid pillows, but Deacon's mouth was still full, so he didn't have much room to smirk. He concentrated on swallowing that last bite instead so he'd be ready when....

Oh yeah.

Crick threw the cushion on the ground and knelt gingerly, careful of his leg, and then lowered his head to Deacon's crotch. He grabbed the corner of the button fly with his teeth and tugged gently while kneading Deacon's groin with his good hand.

Deacon sighed and slouched down, thrusting his pelvis out to give Crick better access. He'd wanted this so bad.

The first button gave, and then the second, and then Crick gave it up and used his good hand to pull and his game hand to anchor. Deacon shifted and Crick fumbled down the front of Deacon's briefs, gasping when he pulled Deacon out, more than partially erect.

"The cake made you hard, huh?" he asked, still miffed.

"You made me hard, dumba—" Crick engulfed him completely in his mouth. "—sssss...."

Hot, wet, hard. Crick was good at this. Deacon lifted his hips again and shoved his jeans and briefs down past his knees and spread his thighs, giving Crick an all-access pass to his body. Crick took the e-ticket ride, starting out with his crooked hand giving a soft, uneven stroke up Deacon's cock and his good hand going for the skill work, fondling Deacon's balls and stroking back in the recesses to tease the crease of Deacon's ass.

"See?" Deacon hissed as Crick sucked the crown of his cock to the back of his gulping throat. "All you!"

Crick was going to try to argue, but it was hard to do when your mouth was full of erection, and Deacon puffed out a laughing breath as he bucked deeper. Crick made a noise of protest, then grabbed Deacon's shaft with his good hand and squeezed deliberately.

Oh yeah, they were doing this in earnest, weren't they! Deacon thrust up into Crick's wet fist and then pulled back. His crown was constricted by the "o" of Crick's fingers, and every thrust ramped him higher, and higher, and—

"You're gonna get hard again, right, Deacon?" Crick actually *pulled back* to ask him that.

Deacon growled, grabbed his hair, and shoved him back down. "You think I'd leave you hurting?" Deacon panted. "Don't you know by now that I'll *always* take care of you?"

Crick sighed then, and took him deep, and pulled back, and again, and again and....

"Augh!" Deacon came inside Crick's mouth, spilling over Crick's tightened fist, and Crick swallowed as quick as he could.

It didn't mean his mouth wasn't still glazed with spit and come when Deacon's breathing stilled. Deacon's hand still clenched in his hair, and he tugged gently, giving Crick a hand to grab and help himself up. Deacon let go of his hair and stood with him, then grabbed it again and hauled Crick down, tasting his spend on Crick's mouth, around his lips, tasting Crick's laughter and his love, and only, just a little bit, tasting the last of the chocolate cake.

They left the cake on the table, and the rest of the buffet, and called it a real holiday and went to bed.

And yes, Deacon got hard again, because no, as long as Deacon could move and breathe, he'd *never* leave Crick hurting.

When they were done, Crick was facedown on the bed, spread out, with Deacon tucked under his arm, facing him.

"You never told me," Crick mumbled. "How did you know about Benny's plan?"

"I gave her the idea," Deacon said back, almost falling asleep. "She's telling Mikhail first." He didn't mention that he'd told her to do that at Christmas, when Mikhail's heart had been weeping loud enough to hear it across all of Levee Oaks.

"You are just a scary, scary general in the war for our souls, aren't you?" He didn't even open his eyes to say it.

Deacon laughed softly. "Yeah, well, I won yours. Made me greedy."

Crick leaned close enough to give him a kiss good night in the dark. "How long, do you think?" he asked. "The waiting is killing me."

Deacon smiled as he said it, so happy he could have waited a whole other year just to hold on to this moment here, when they were two. "When it's ready, Crick. You know that. Babies come when they're ready."

A WEEK after the shower, well into the heat of May, Benny couldn't sleep.

Drew rubbed her feet, and she complained because his touch was too hard. She took a shower, and the water was too hot. She *would* have taken a bath except her back hurt too much. The salad dressing was too salty, Parry's cartoon was too loud, and why couldn't everybody leave her alone and let her knit, thank you very much? She'd finished the blanket—it was wrapped and ready with the bag she'd packed for the hospital—but she was still trying to knit Parry a sweater for next year. She'd gone up a size, and it was taking forever, and the squishy pink yarn with the little fuzzy things sticking out wasn't a picnic.

Drew looked at her, eyebrows raised, half-fearful, like a quizzical hound dog, then just put in *How to Train Your Dragon* and did what all men did anywhere when their mates were pregnant: shut the hell up and stayed out of the way.

Good thing too, because she was getting Braxton Hicks again. Damned practice contractions. They'd been plaguing her all week. Oh fuck. There was another one, and this one she needed to breathe through. Fuck. Fuck. Fuck— that one *hurt*. Fuckers.

She scowled and worked another three rows of the sweater, and then... oh no. This one was gonna crack the motherfuckin' world. Oh fuck. Oh fuck. Oh fuck. One more....

Okay. Thank God. That one was over. And yeah. Great movie. Great score. Loved the movie. The dragon was *great*. Except... there it went.... Oh fuck. Oh damn. Oh hell. Fuck, fuck, fuck, fuck....

She set the knitting down and breathed through the next one, and looked up, aware Drew was on the phone, and *dammit*, what was he doing on the phone when she was trying to watch the goddamned....

Oh fuck. Oh *fuck*. *Oh hell* to the *fuck no*!

And was there a knocking at the door? Really? Who was visiting her *now*?

She put her knitting down again and looked up at Drew, suddenly too tired to even yell at him for being on the phone.

"Drew, I don't think these are practice contractions," she said, feeling suddenly vulnerable, like her body was going out of control without her. Had it felt this way the last time? Had it always been like being pushed off the top of a downhill ski jump?

"No shit, Bernice," Drew snapped. He bent down and shoved his shoulder under her arm. "You've been contracting every seven minutes for most of the damned movie." He grunted and stood, and she allowed him to haul her to her feet. "Kimmy should be here in about thirty seconds for Parry. Crick and Deacon are waiting outside. Now let's move it, okay? All stations are a go!"

"No," she murmured, suddenly stricken. "Drew, I don't think it's time yet. It can't be. It's not ready to leave me yet. It *needs* me. I'm the mama, and it's not time, and—*oh hell!*"

She couldn't walk through this one. Couldn't talk either. Parry had been a quick labor, she remembered that, but this one looked like it was going to jump the gate and run.

When she was done, Drew was on one side of her and Deacon was on the other, and they half walked, half carried her between them. Parry gave her a quick hug and a kiss, which was good because she did *not* want to be touched right now. Kimmy kissed her cheek, and when did Kimmy get there? And suddenly she was being belted in Crick's car while it was moving down the driveway, and her entire body screamed with the indignity of moving *right the hell now.*

Everything was inward.

Her body was contracting, the baby was putting up a fuss, she suddenly had to take a poop like no woman in history—it was all happening *inside her body.*

The trip to Kaiser was interminable—it was a good thing she was all inside her head when it was happening. She wasn't all there for admissions, although she *did* focus when the doctor shoved a hand up her cooter.

"Miss Coats?" the doctor asked, shucking off his gloves.

She glared at him. He smelled like cigarettes and too much coffee, and she resented the hell out of being pulled away from… well, *everybody* at this point. "What?"

"You're dilated to eight and a half centimeters. What made you finally decide to come in?"

"My boyfriend picked me up off the couch and shoved me in the car."

"Smart man. He'll make a good father."

"This isn't his kid," she said. "It's my brother's husband's baby."

The doctor blinked like he was trying to put that together in a puzzle, and she was assaulted by another contraction. *"Holy mother of fuck!"*

"And it's time to get you to labor and delivery!" And wasn't he just too fucking chipper about that! Probably still trying to figure out whose baby it was.

"Deacon!" she snapped when they had her in the wheelchair. Someone was pushing her toward another room.

"I'm here, Shorty," Deacon said behind the wheelchair. "Wouldn't pass up seeing this show again, right?"

"You gotta tell Drew how it works," she said, suddenly tearful. Yeah, they'd talked about this and laid out duties and everything, but Deacon had *been* there for it. Deacon had *held* her first baby. Deacon could teach Drew everything he needed to know.

"I'll tell him how it works," Deacon said.

"You gotta tell him it's fast, okay?"

"Like I didn't know *that*!" Drew muttered, and she looked next to her, and there he was.

"You're gonna hold my hand, right, Drew? You're not going to care that it's not yours, right? You didn't care with Parry. You're not gonna care, right?"

They were helping her onto a gurney now, and she *hated* this part.

"Right on my back. Could you smack them, Deacon? Right on my fucking back!"

"I'm rolling her to her side," Deacon said in a tone that brooked no argument. The doctor tried to give him one, but Deacon ignored the man and reached over to grab both her hands, his own hands crossed for leverage.

"Drew, get behind her and pull the bottom toward you and push on the top. Everyone ready? One, two, three, and…."

"Oh, thank God, thank God, thank God," Benny mumbled. The contractions were still there, one on top of the other, but she could breathe again, and Drew was here with her, and he wasn't leaving, and Deacon was here, and she was so damned grateful.

The gush of water between her legs was a surprise, even though the doctor had been fiddling down there with something small and sharp. And suddenly, oh God, there it was, the whole world crashing down on her cervix!

"*Drew!* Drew, it fucking hurts! Kill one of those motherfuckers for me, would you?"

Crick's laughter just pissed her off more. "Oh my *God*, Benny, could you be any fucking louder?"

"Miss Coats, you need to be ready to push, okay?"

Benny waved at the nurse. "Go away! Go away! They'll help me—they've done it before!" She remembered—she'd been so proud of both of them when they were EMTs. And she trusted them right now, trusted her guys, trusted Drew, when she didn't trust random people in white, didn't trust anyone with this baby but them—

"Oh, *fuck!*"

"Benny, for fuck's sake, stop swearing and push!"

"Crick, you"—grunt, groan, bear down—"stupid motherfucker, if you think this is easy, *you* do it!"

"If anything came out of my ass besides crap, I would! It doesn't! Now stop yelling at me and push!"

Oh God, there was an image.

"I'll never—" Pant, pant, pant. "—sleep again!"

"The hell you won't—you're sleeping for a week after this, Bernice."

"*Augh!* Sure! You just come in and violate my body and pump my boobs while that happens!" Because seriously, dignity? When all these men were watching her be naked, fat, and pushing something out her privates?

Deacon's low laugh told her she wasn't the only one thinking that way.

"I wouldn't pass up on that invite if I were you," he chuckled. "Don't think Crick or me are qualified. Now, Bernice, stop yelling at us and push!"

"Deacon—"

"Stop it! Shut up and bear down and squish this little fucker out!"

"*Deacon!*"

Oh God. It was like being ripped in half. She knew it. She remembered it. It felt the same way this time, she'd just blocked it out. Ripped in half, ripped in half… *squoosh!*

And then there was a roaring in her ear, her own panting breaths, and that faint, precious sound that was never as loud as it seemed like it should be.

THE baby nurse grabbed the baby as soon as the cord was cut, and Drew and Crick hovered over Benny, telling her she'd done a good job, telling her they were pulling the afterbirth now. Deacon watched the pediatric nurse and listened to the blessed, blessed sound. He watched the pink little arms and pink little legs flail around, and reveled in that precious, mad-as-hell, scared-to-death, someone-fucking-explain-this-to-me *sound*!

Boy, was that kid pissed off.

Crick didn't deal with pissed off well. "Jesus, kid, would you give it a fucking break!"

There was a sudden hiccup, and a puzzled silence from the direction of the baby.

Deacon met Crick's eyes over the gurney and grinned. Oh my God, fatherhood sat well on him.

"Quiet now," Crick muttered. He leaned forward and kissed Benny's sweaty forehead. "It's okay," he said softly. "You did good. Our little fish is swimming, okay? No worries. Deacon!" Crick called, his voice as bright and shiny as the baby's.

"What?"

"The damned thing's born—what'd we have?"

Deacon laughed a little. Benny was still gripping Drew and Crick's hands while her bottom half was being tugged on and pushed at and wiped down, so Deacon didn't bother to ask her, even though she knew.

"Nurse?" he asked, and the woman didn't even bother to look over her shoulder.

"It's a boy!" she sang, and Deacon grinned at Crick, tired, and happy, and only half-panicked on the inside.

"It's a boy, Carrick."

"Great!" Crick said, looking very relieved—and very pointedly *not* at his sister's private parts. "*Those* parts I know something about!"

Deacon watched then as they bathed the baby, weighed the baby, put drops in his eyes, measured him. He squalled a lot, but not the whole time. There were a couple of moments when he seemed to say, "Well shit, this isn't getting me anywhere," and Deacon was glad. A little bit of Deacon, a little bit of Crick—that's all he wanted.

The short, round, comfortably middle-aged nurse walked up to the three men looking very confused—and Deacon didn't blame her. "Who wants to hold him first?"

"Too weak," Benny mumbled, and since they were moving her to another bed now that she was all cleaned up, that wasn't going to happen anyway.

It was Drew who poked him in the back. "Step up, Chief. I'm support team on this one. My job's all done."

Deacon bit his lip to hide his smile. "Yeah?" he asked no one in particular.

"Yeah," the nurse murmured.

Deacon took him, supported his head, and tucked their little fish into the crook of his arm like a football. His entire body shuddered, and he felt time slow to a halt, right... right now... and he leaned forward and kissed his son's head.

Time resumed, and he knew firsthand how fast it could go.

"Carrick?" he said, and the love of his life walked around the bed to be at his side.

"Oh my God," Crick said. Then: "Jesus, Deacon, do these things *ever* look right when they come out? I mean, you'd think our own kid wouldn't look like a skinned rabbit, but—"

Deacon hushed him with a kiss over their son's tiny body. "Carrick James? Meet James Deacon Winters. He's fucking beautiful, so shut up about it, okay?"

He looked at the baby again and gave up fighting the swelling chest and the burning eyes. Crick shut up and reached out a long artistic finger to stroke JD's fat, pink little cheek.

"He's gorgeous, Deacon. He looks just like us."

Deacon looked up to thank Benny, to weep at her feet like the goddess she was, but she was being hefted to the other gurney, and it was time to give the baby back for more fun and baby games.

Drew followed her, and Deacon and Crick were left hugging in the room while the staff hustled around them, cleaning up the worst part of the best part of being human.

Chapter 25

Deacon and Benny: Twain

BENNY was *so* impressed with Deacon. He hadn't told her about the Princess Plan at all!

Drew must have known—he *must* have, because he'd repacked her overnight bag with the basics: big girl underwear, toothbrush, and shampoo. At first she'd been indignant—she'd had an *entire gym bag* packed with stuff that only she wanted. But then Drew had produced a new iPod, via Deacon, loaded with some of her favorite television shows—via Drew—and told her that before she left the next day, she'd have everything she needed.

She looked at the iPod with shining eyes. "Ooooh... *pretty!*"

Drew laughed and grabbed her hand, twining their fingers together. "We're going to take *very* good care of you, Bernice."

She got a little wobbly then. "Everyone's going to be taking care of the baby. Have you seen him?"

Drew's smile into her eyes was tender. "He's gorgeous. But he looks mostly like Deacon."

She felt a moment of being completely herself. "Our babies will look mostly like you," she told him, because, well, no shit!

Drew winked. "They might be a little paler," he laughed, and she nodded, still grinning.

"Just a little."

"Are you ready?" he asked then, and she was nonplussed. Hadn't she done the thing? All she had left to do now was bleed and bitch.

"Ready for what?"

"Your admirers, baby. You think you did this alone?" And with that he went to the door and let in her first round of people. And that should have been her first clue.

Her first people were actually Jeff and Collin, and she should have been a little suspicious when they arrived with sausage McMuffins, *no* egg, and a new set of yoga pants and summer-weight hoodie for her to wear home. They also brought flowers, a teddy bear, and a video collection of *The Hangover* movies.

And her laptop on which to watch them.

Drew kissed her on the cheek then and told her he'd be back in the evening, and her day never stopped. The nurse came in with JD so they could hold the baby. She watched them, thinking about how this was the last time he'd get to room with her—but that she was lucky he did, since she was going to be Auntie Benny anyway. Jeff and Collin finished mooning over him and then told her how well she'd done—and although Jeff got a little misty and Collin's arms tightened, the baby, the star of the show, was still *not* the star of *her* show.

She began to realize that *she* was.

She thought maybe that was just Jeff and Collin, because, well, they were awesome, but before they left, Jeff gave her one last gift.

A white cardigan, lace weight, as delicate as a butterfly's wing and as finely crafted as a Fabergé egg.

"Jeffy," Benny breathed, fingering the down-soft wool. "You must have been making this for—"

"Since we heard your grand plan," Jeff said, patting her hand. "It's for your wedding dress, sweets, which means you and me on the same diet so you can go strapless in the fall."

Benny swallowed. Her grand plan. Marriage to the man she loved. Her own career as an accountant. Their children. Their home with the daughter they already loved. Something to look forward to when she didn't have a crib or a nursery or a baby to call her own this time round.

"That's awesome," she said. "Stupid fucking hormones, ignore them."

Jeff handed her a tissue, then wrapped the sweater up again and put it in a neat little pile with the teddy bear and the basket of movies. She cried on both of them as they hugged her to leave. She couldn't help it.

Next was Patrick.

Deacon's father's old hired man was in his seventies. Since he moved out of The Pulpit, he'd been living with his sister and her husband, helping them with their animals, and generally enjoying the more relaxed pace of not getting stepped on, bitten, rolled on, or kicked, which happened on a horse ranch all the goddamned time.

But he sat down with Benny for a good half an hour, grizzled gray hair—what was left of it—sticking out in tufts, rheumy blue eyes still sharp—and he held the baby, smiling so serenely into that scrunchy little face that JD stopped wiggling and just stared back.

"Lookie that," Patrick murmured. "Lookie. See, Deacon was only two when I first saw him. He used to do that for his daddy. Get all restless and squirmy and sure as shit just calmed down as soon as you looked at him. See? See him? Just like Deacon."

Patrick reached over and grabbed some Kleenex for himself, wiped his eyes, honked his nose, and smiled at Benny with a sort of worship.

"I remember when he took you in. I was so worried about him—he was so broken up back then. And I thought, 'Oh God. These two—they could totally wreck each other.' But not you and Deacon. You're his sister and his daughter all rolled into one. And look what you gave him." Patrick smiled down into JD's face. "Look? The one thing Parrish ever worried about, did you know that?"

"No," Benny said, too tired for tears. "I didn't."

"Yeah. Deacon's daddy, he didn't mind Deacon liking boys. But he knew Deacon always wanted children. When he was a little kid, Jon would come over, and when he left, Deacon would say, 'If I had a little boy like Jon, I'd be home.' See, even then. He wanted to be raising someone. It's like horses. It's what he was born to do."

Benny fell asleep then, with the old man rocking Deacon's baby in his arms. She woke up a little later, and Deacon was picking the baby up, shushing her back to sleep. He had the bracelet on, she realized. The one that said that he was the daddy. She didn't have that bracelet on. She wasn't the mommy. Not really.

She felt young. Young and disoriented and sad for things she couldn't put a voice to. "Deacon, sing for Parry'n'me, 'kay?"

"Yeah, Shorty. Yeah. 'I heard there was a secret chord that David played and it pleased the Lord....'"

"Hallelujah" was a good choice, she thought as she fell asleep. It went on forever.

There was the nurse, sometime after that, but the baby wasn't in the room with her, so after her blood pressure, and the pad change, and the painkiller, she was out again. When she woke up this time, it was late afternoon, and JD breathed softly in the basinet. Kimmy and Mikhail were in the room, and when she narrowed her eyes, she saw Shane was asleep on the bed next to her.

"What in the—"

"Sh," Kimmy murmured. "We got a new recruit in last night. I had Parry, so he dealt with her the whole time. He's sort of wiped."

Mikhail was standing next to Shane, and he leaned over for a moment and kissed his forehead while he slept. Shane was wearing sweats and a hooded sweatshirt, and his dark hair was mussed over his forehead, erupting into curls where normally it would be slicked back. Benny thought about his quiet confidence the day of the funeral, and how one Thanksgiving, they'd all been mostly thankful that Shane survived.

Mikhail looked up and caught her eye.

"Those children are *our* babies," he said proudly, his hand absurdly tender on Shane's cheek. "My cop here, he is the best parent."

"I think he's part of a team," Benny said, remembering Mikhail's heartbreak over the sound of her own right now.

Mikhail shrugged. "I can cook," he dismissed and then cut in front of Kimmy to sit primly in the little visitor's chair.

Kimmy didn't notice. She was hovering over the basinet, her hands half in and half out, and Benny spared a moment of grogginess to realize Kimmy must be terrified of that sort of pain.

"Pick him up," Benny said quietly. "We're going to be aunties together; the least you can do is learn what he feels like."

Kimmy did, JD going so gracefully into her arms that a part of Benny mourned for what Kimmy couldn't have.

But that wasn't what Kimmy was thinking. Kimmy's eyes were closed, and her body was swaying to silent music.

Benny looked at Mikhail, and he was staring at his sister-in-law with bright eyes. Together, they watched Kimmy dance until the song was done, while JD simply made gurgling vowels, his first attempts at sound.

"Here," Mikhail said, holding out his arms. Kimmy gave him the baby reluctantly, and Mikhail sighed, cuddling the child like a Prussian general, but protective just the same. He looked back up at Kimmy and said, "Kimmy, darling, Benny must be starving. We brought food in a cooler we left in the car. Would you want to go get it?"

Kimmy grimaced. "You couldn't remember that when we brought the gifts, you little Russian bastard?"

"No, cow woman, I was too busy avoiding your great and powerful ass. It was in my way. Now make up for it and go fetch like the peasant you are."

"Bitch."

"Heifer."

Kimmy bent and kissed his cheek and danced away.

Mikhail was left holding the baby that was not Benny's.

"Benny, little one," he said softly, "you and I must have a talk."

"Don't I get a day's grace? I just pushed that critter out of my cooter, Mikhail! No big scary talks, right?"

Mikhail shook his head. "No, my dear. This talk must be held now. You look at this baby with such sorrow. I cannot help but think you need to hear this."

Benny swallowed. "I'm going to need a tissue," she decided and grabbed the entire box.

"You are very wise," Mikhail said, smiling a little. JD was asleep in his arms, and for a moment, Benny wanted to ask for him back. But there would be no baby for Kimmy, no nephew for Shane and Mikhail. This baby was theirs as well.

"Babies are wonderful things," Mikhail murmured. "Can you not see? All of the possibilities he has? All of the sunny days and the rainy days, all of the things we have to give him? We try to give to the children at Promise House, you know." Sadness etched his face like acid etched glass. "Shane and I, we try to give them love, to give them parenting. It is difficult. They do not know how to take anymore. They don't know how to accept gifts. You do." Mikhail looked up. "We have brought you lengths and lengths of crinoline and taffeta and tulle. Kimmy and I, we have made our costumes for years. We will make you such a dress. Let us make you a dress for your prince, so that we may see you married."

The light went on then. "All of you?" she asked, feeling a little overwhelmed.

"But of course," Mikhail said. "Do you not see? You have given to all of us—not just Deacon and Crick. You have given hope to Jeff and Collin—they plan to have their own. You have given solace to Kimmy, who can't. You have given...." His voice clogged, and his triangular face with that strong, no-compromise chin grew even tighter in expression. "You have given Shane and I comfort. All of the broken children, Bernice, yourself included, and we are all here at your feet, grateful, blessedly, blessedly grateful, for the gift you have given us. This baby, he is unbroken. We will keep him that way for as long as we can. You and me, we have seen children discarded, we have seen them beaten and hurt. This baby has no scars, no strikes against him. He will be cared for. We can erase the past with him, we can make a future that none of us had. Do you not see? We cannot thank you enough. Look at what you have done."

Benny was crying almost too hard to see by then, but Mikhail was gentle with her. He stood up and dropped the rail of her bed and settled JD in her arms. She held him then, and for the first time, he didn't feel like hers.

And that was okay.

When Drew came back that evening, he brought the iPod speaker from home. He played soft music and said blessedly very little. And then "Crazy in Love" by Beyoncé came on, and she smiled shyly. When she looked up at Drew, he was smiling back and holding a shiny, sparkly, baubly confection of an engagement ring.

It fit perfectly.

BENNY looked beautiful on her wedding day—even if she wore sequined, beruffled white high-tops with her sleeveless princess dress.

August had been a brutal motherfucker of a month, so she and Drew had agreed to have the wedding in September, when the weather had gotten a little more sane, and Benny stood in the shade near the rock, looking amazing and regal and glorious in a dress that had been as lovingly stitched as Gabriel's wings.

Drew? Drew was wearing a full tuxedo, courtesy of Jeff, who had taken care of every detail. No faux simplicity for Benny's wedding, no scraps of burlap on glass bottles—Benny's favors were tiny handbags emblazoned with the date and filled with lip balm and key chains and pens and paper, all with the graceful, simple curve from their wedding invitations, and their names, and the wedding date.

The flowers were all roses.

Benny's sister stood there next to Kimmy and Amy, all of them wearing bridesmaid's dresses in various shades of lavender and pink. It had taken a couple of months of careful, neutral acquaintanceship, but Missy had eventually been ready to move into their spare room and was working now as part of the family. She was more acerbic than Benny, and sometimes she could still be a flaming bitch. But she and Crick were a lot alike, and Deacon was coming to enjoy her company and her help. The week before, as Deacon had been leading Shooter around the ring in more penance, she'd shouted over the practice ring.

"Deacon, stop rehearsing your lines or that fucking horse is going to *kill* you!"

Deacon had looked up from an admittedly distracted state of practicing for the ceremony, and sure enough, Shooter was flattening her ears and looking to go apeshit. Deacon put the big horse in her place and then grinned at Missy.

"Thanks, darlin'—needed the reminder!"

She'd preened for the rest of the day. It hadn't been until that evening that Crick had told him, "You think an adult *ever* thanked that kid for knowing best?" that he realized what he meant to her.

She looked grown-up and beautiful standing next to her tiny sister (pink dress and redhead complexion notwithstanding), and Deacon was proud to call her family.

In front of the women, Lila and Parry were holding hands, wearing flower girl dresses in the same colors. They were so thrilled to be together again, it was as though they'd never been separated, and Deacon was, as always, amazed to see how much Jon's daughter had grown.

Shane and Mikhail helped to seat people with the aid of the children from Promise House. Watching Mikhail interact with a painfully underfed teenage girl made Deacon's heart hurt. The two of them had more courage than anyone Deacon had ever known, because they knew what heartache was, and they threw themselves at it again and again and again.

Jeff and Collin ran water to anyone who asked. They were almost like a tag-team stand-up delivery service—Jeff would say the funny thing, Collin would be the straight man. Jeff told Crick that he and Collin were looking into adoption. Children. Hope. They all had it. Thinking about his son and his lover, Deacon could finally concede hope wasn't the enemy anymore. Hope could do glorious things if you let it—and if you gave it a big hand and some painfully crafted faith.

The men—*his* men—all wore matching black suits like the one Deacon had, with brightly colored shirts that matched the girls' dresses. Not everybody's usual or casual, no, but not one person had complained about it—not once. It was Benny's wedding. They would have worn leather and chains, but they were just as glad it was a simple suit.

And there, leaning against the rock itself, was Carrick James Francis, in a tuxedo too, and their son, James Deacon, suspended from one of those little baby front-pack things, his chubby bare legs sticking out and his pert little face peeping over the barrier that kept him still.

Deacon smiled at the two of them, and waved, and JD ignored Deacon (who, apparently, was just going to be Deacon, since he and Crick hadn't gotten a handle on the two dads thing) while Daddy (that would be Crick) waved happily back like a little kid.

Deacon laughed and turned his attention back to his job, as uncomfortable as it was, and that was welcoming people to Promise Rock.

When he saw the cab, he almost blacked out.

And *then* he saw red. He strode across the stream to the gate and swung it wide open.

"*You* were supposed to have some big bad day in court, asshole!" he snapped, and Jon smirked, looking rumpled and sleepy in his best suit.

"*I* wasn't able to get out of it until yesterday morning," Jon said, but he looked entirely too proud of himself.

"Great—does this mean you're presiding?" Because *fuck* had Deacon tried to get out of it.

Jon shook his head. "And deprive Crick of being able to say 'My husband married my sister after she had his baby'?"

Deacon snickered, because Crick had said *just* exactly that.

"No, brother," Jon told him when they could talk, "you've got this bit handled."

Deacon tried to stay irritated, but it wasn't easy when Jon was hugging him hard, and he was hugging back. "I'm so glad you could come," he said, nakedly grateful. Amy and the kids had been able to, but it had hurt—bad—when Jon thought he couldn't.

"I threatened to quit," Jon said, his blond hair falling in his face, unkempt and unstyled, and then he shrugged, and Deacon knew he wasn't kidding.

"Well, hell. For that, I'll just have to officiate the damned wedding."

Jon nodded, his eyes searching Benny out in the crowd. His smile was a little ruined by proud-uncle tears. "You know, sort of the least you can do."

Benny's wedding wasn't small.

The kids from Promise House were there, as attendees and not attendants. Half the parents from Parry's soccer team made it, and Collin's entire family, as well as Patrick and his sister and some of Amy's family as well. They'd needed to rent chairs for everyone, and not just for the reception. When Deacon stood at the rock itself, and Benny and Drew stood in front of him, he was looking at a crowd of eighty or so people who were all expecting him to know what in the fuck he was doing.

Carrick James and their son stood back by the reception book and looked at him that way too.

Of course, Crick had been looking at him that way since he was nine years old, a little boy standing on the outside of the practice ring, watching Deacon put a horse through its paces, and for a breath Deacon was there, in that moment, seeing the liquid brown eyes of the boy he would grow to love.

In another breath, he was in that moment under this very tree, when he and Crick had first loved each other.

In another breath, he was in a hotel room in Georgia, when Crick left.

One more heartbeat, and he was here on a spring day, praying Crick would live.

One more, and he and Crick were here, saying vows like the ones he was about to recite.

And again, and again. Breath after heartbeat, summer, fall, winter, spring—and it all came back to this, this place, this moment. It came to beginnings and endings, of promises you made and promises you kept and promises that got broken in spite of your best intentions. It came to fixing what shattered, making do with what wouldn't fix, and building again and hoping, hoping for this moment, when everything was as shiny and perfect as a baby's first cry.

It's why they all gathered here, weddings, funerals, the introduction of their son—it was the promise and the heartbreak of the place Deacon's family called home. It was the legacy of a community, a simple swimming hole, a place made sacred by love.

Promise Rock.

A fear of crowds was nothing to a promise made here. Deacon, of all people, should know that.

Without hesitation, he stepped forward and nodded to the gathering, catching the eye of people he knew and loved.

"I promised," he started, and his throat clogged. He looked at Crick's little sister, her heart-shaped face shining with joy, and had to start again. "I promised Benny a traditional wedding," he said. "Because nothing about the lot of us has anything to do with tradition. So we're going to start with the old words, and then we're going to throw in the new, and then we're going to end where all things begin: with a kiss. Is everybody ready?"

He heard some laughter, and a gentle murmur from his friends and from his family. Jon gave him the thumbs-up from his seat, where his wife and son were trying to crawl in his lap, and Parry reached out and grabbed his hand from her place by her mother.

"You ready, Parry Angel?"

"Say the words, Deacon."

"Dearly beloved, we are gathered here together...."

AMY LANE is a mother of four and a compulsive knitter who writes because she can't silence the voices in her head. She adores cats, Chi-who-whats, knitting socks, and hawt menz, and she dislikes moths, cat boxes, and knuckle-headed macspazzmatrons. She is rarely found cooking, cleaning, or doing domestic chores, but she has been known to knit up an emergency hat/blanket/pair of socks for any occasion whatsoever, or sometimes for no reason at all. She writes in the shower, while at the gym, while taxiing children to soccer/dance/gymnastics/ band oh my! and has learned from necessity to type like the wind. She lives in a spider-infested, crumbling house in a shoddy suburb and counts on her beloved Mate to keep her tethered to reality—which he does, while keeping her cell phone charged as a bonus. She's been married for twenty-plus years and still believes in Twu Wuv, with a capital Twu and a capital Wuv, and she doesn't see any reason at all for that to change.

Website: www.greenshill.com

Blog: www.writerslane.blogspot.com

E-mail: amylane@greenshill.com

Facebook: www.facebook.com/amy.lane.167

Twitter: @amymaclane

The PROMISE ROCK SERIES from AMY LANE

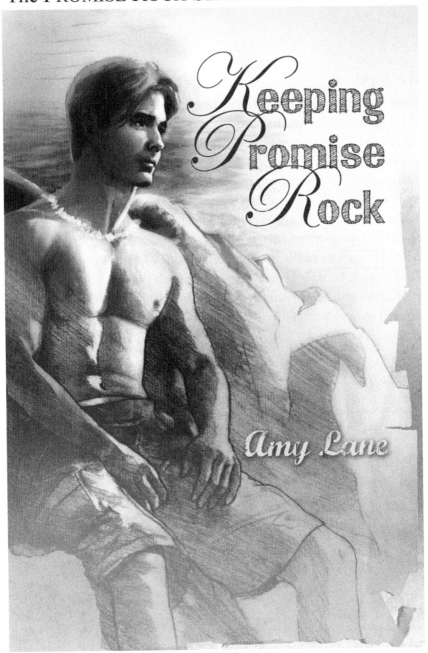

Keeping
Promise
Rock

Amy Lane

http://www.dreamspinnerpress.com

The PROMISE ROCK SERIES from AMY LANE

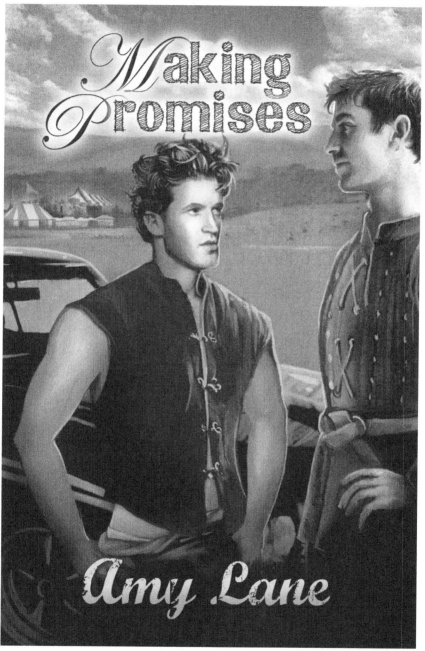

http://www.dreamspinnerpress.com

The PROMISE ROCK SERIES from AMY LANE

Living Promises

Amy Lane

Also from AMY LANE

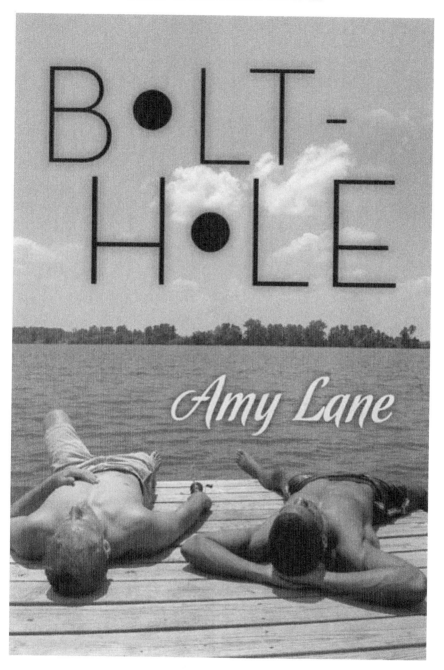

http://www.dreamspinnerpress.com

Contemporary Romance from AMY LANE

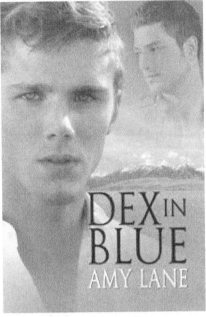

Foreign Language Titles Available

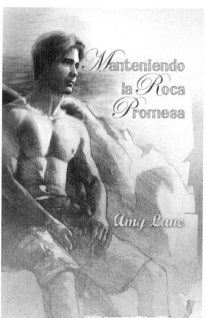

The Knitting Series from AMY LANE

http://www.dreamspinnerpress.com

Fantasy Romance from AMY LANE

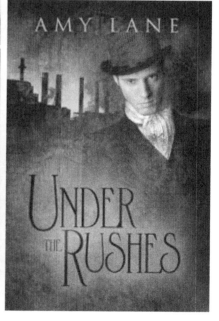

The Talker Series from AMY LANE

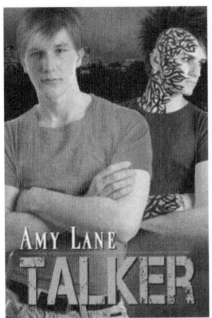

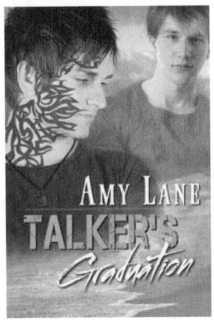

http://www.dreamspinnerpress.com

Also from AMY LANE

http://www.dreamspinnerpress.com

CPSIA information can be obtained at www.ICGtesting.com
Printed in the USA
BVOW11s1352221213

339795BV00007B/256/P